Assignment: Sunrise

By
I. Christie

ISBN 10: 1-933113-55-3
ISBN 13: 978-1-933113-55-5

First Printing: August 2006

This Trade Paperback Is Published By
Intaglio Publications
Melbourne, FL USA
WWW.INTAGLIOPUB.COM

CREDITS
EXECUTIVE EDITOR: TARA YOUNG
COVER DESIGN BY VALERIE HAYKEN (PHOTOGRAPHY@VALERIEHAYKEN.COM)

DEDICATION

I would like to dedicate this book in memory of my parents.

ACKNOWLEDGMENTS

Thank you so much, Martha Elser, for your tireless editing when you have a very busy life of your own and for your steadfast encouragement. It really means a lot to me.

Thank you, Ken Kimura, for your help in picking out spy toys and for telling me what will work and what won't. I just hope I got it right.

Thank you, April Bradley, for being ever encouraging and enthusiastic about my writing. You're a good friend.

Chapter One

A night guard shined his lamp along the uneven ground and sang tunelessly to a song bleeding through his earphones as his feet crunched across the gritty asphalt.

Eyes hidden behind night vision goggles watched until the guard had treaded on to the next set of buildings before moving back behind the warehouse.

The noise of flying sand against the backside of the building covered the sound of the small window being unlatched. After making short work to disengage the alarm, the veiled figure dropped into the dark warehouse. Landing in a crouched position on the concrete floor, the figure paused to readjust her goggles. Her covered head moved slowly, scanning the area for any hot objects, then she pulled out a TD-53 radio frequency transmitter detector to scan for bugs.

No change in the pattern.

But someone else's sloppiness didn't give the intruder comfort. If the gang being monitored was not so insistent on taping its own meetings with various business associates, the intruder knew this visit would have been a lot more difficult. Warily, she sniffed the air in the warehouse. Smells from the stacked goods and stale odors from sweaty laborers mixed with the distinct scent of marsh and ocean air, blowing in from the opened window. There was no sound from the air conditioner that had been running throughout the day to keep the heat at bay. Not sensing anything that posed a threat, the figure's attention moved back to the window to close it and re-engage the alarm.

A faint whirling noise came from the thin stealth rope as it snaked out and wrapped around a steel ceiling crossbeam. After securing and testing the rope, the figure scaled onto the beam. Once comfortably seated, the interior of the warehouse was inspected. Confident the equipment monitoring the ceiling was disabled, she moved above the office and dropped another rope down. She slid down, stopping just above the office window. A pinhole video camera was installed above the warehouse surveillance equipment. Having completed that job, the figure moved back up the rope.

Not wanting to rely on one exit, her next job was to secure a second in the roof. The rusted hinges on the ceiling window required special attention without the distinctive odor of WD40.

Finished with that chore, the intruder pulled back a black strap covering a wristwatch.

Still have lots of time.

The figure dropped to the warehouse floor, leaving the rope dangling, perhaps overconfident the rope wouldn't be seen even if the lights were turned on or perhaps not willing to get rid of a backup exit. With bug detector in a gloved hand, she moved around the pallets and bulky stacks of goods, using them to hide from any monitoring devices. Just inside the double delivery doors, a stack of empty pallets inconveniently placed gave the figure pause.

She turned around, looking for monitoring devices. Satisfied the area was clear, she walked around the pallets. A pale object lay inside the stack. Leaning in for a closer look, she saw a folded envelope was pinned between the concrete floor and stacked pallets. Reaching through a small opening, she pulled at the discovery, but it held firmly in place. With a knife, the envelope was cut away, placed into a plastic bag, and tucked into one of the vest's pouches. Another plastic bag came out, and with the blade, the dark spot on the concrete was scraped. The curled black substance ended up on a swab, placed in a plastic bag, and added to the pouch that contained the envelope.

Lights flashed through the front door window, illuminating the interior as far in as the stairs to the office. From the sounds, more than one vehicle had arrived at the building. Two angry voices argued, followed by two doors slamming shut. The insertion of a key in the lock caused the intruder to scan for a place to hide. Behind the empty pallets was not a secure option.

The sound of a click and the sudden blinding light sent the intruder dropping flat to the cement ground.

"No lights!" Danny Brucker's voice barked.

"What are we going to do, wait for them in the dark?" Amos Anders, owner of the warehouse, demanded sarcastically.

"Turn the lights on in the office where someone passing can't see it."

"What's the big deal? I own this place."

Visually, the two men were polar opposites. Danny's muscle-building pastime filled his clothes impressively. He had no need to add gold or color to attract attention, while Amos, thin as a rail, wore flashy clothes and expensive jewelry.

The clanging of footsteps on the metal stairway was muted in the packed warehouse. The office hung above the cement floor with the machinery, lockers, and break area tucked underneath it. Another light came on, the main light in the warehouse went off, and a door slammed shut, rattling everything attached from the windows down to the metal stairway.

Quickly, the prowler was up and moving into the shadows, confident there were no traps or security beams along the way to her dangling rope.

Click!

Moving hastily backward and behind a stack of marked boxes, she clipped her calf on the corner of a carton. Collapsing onto the floor in pain, she dragged and rolled until safely hidden behind some crates. While kneading the injured leg and hoping not to have made too much noise, her ears strained to hear any further sounds from the direction of the window. A cold breeze heavy with salt spray brought the distinct smell of a newcomer. The strain to hear anything other than the arguing voices in the office was rewarded with another click. Through the stacked pallets, her night vision goggles picked up a glow moving away from the window.

Awkwardly, the dark figure rose and limped to the rope. Instead of removing it, she climbed up. Less than a minute later, she was stretched flat on one of the dirty steel ceiling beams looking down at the office. Eyes behind the goggles opened wide at the sight of a man suspended outside of the office wall. Minutes later, the man dropped down and moved away, disappearing behind fluorescent green shapes of machinery.

The ebb and flow of sound from the angry voices in the office nearly covered the now familiar sound of someone opening a window. She studied the two visitors as they struggled to fit through the small window that was already more popular than the much larger and convenient opening commonly referred to as the front door. Just as the window was closed, the front door opened and three figures moved up the stairs into the office as if they were familiar with the route.

With a gloved hand, she pressed the earpiece more firmly into place, annoyed that with the added watchers, there was more of a chance that something would go awry.

"Well, it's about time," Danny's sarcastic voice greeted the newcomers.

"Y'all got somewhere else ya need to be, don't let me keep ya," a deep Southern voice drawled. The voice sent chills skittering down her spine. Suddenly a jammer cut the rest of the conversation off. She strained to hear the conversation coming through the thin walls.

"Just hand over the money. You keep changing the time and place like you don't trust us," Danny continued.

"Trust...now that is somethin' interestin' coming from y'all," the voice drawled slowly. "Bo."

There was a moment of silence.

A voice said something she could not make out.

"That's crap. You owe us the full price," Danny objected hotly.

"Let me remind y'all," the Southern voice rose, then paused as he was about to make an important point. She couldn't make out his words.

"That's full of..." Danny's objection was cut off suddenly. Furniture moved noisily accompanied by a heavy thump.

"Ah do think we need ta get a clear understandin' here," the cold Southern voice rose. Again the voice dropped to where it could not be heard outside of the office. There was a pause and more murmuring. Something heavy was dropped with more furniture being noisily moved about.

The next few minutes was filled with murmuring and a few expletives for emphasis, escaping through the thin walls. Then Danny's voice rose again in argument.

"That's just an excuse not to pay us the full price!"

"Ah won't argue with y'all," the Southern voice rose also. "It's already been agreed 'pon by yer boss. Bo."

A loud grab for the doorknob announced the end of the meeting, and two sets of boot steps clattered down the stairs. The outer door to the warehouse closed, and after a pause, an engine started and moved away.

Something slammed onto a table with enough force to make the listener cringe from the amplified sound through the now clear earpiece.

"Two days before this was going down and you didn't tell me that Mike was out?" Amos Anders exploded. "Where do you get off running your own game?"

"Everything was well under control!" Danny contested hotly.

"Control is following the plan unless an unforeseen event occurs. You were to call for new instructions if you couldn't follow the original plan. Everyone in this organization works together and has no problem following those instructions—except you."

"I adapted to the situation."

"You stupid, kochon." Anders sounded incredulous. "The merchandise belongs to Bobby. You were the drone, nothing more. You are out of this operation," Anders stated flatly.

"*They* are thieves…and liars! That's how they make their money. How do you think Bobby got to be second? The buyer picked her up and on time. I'm not some amateur." There was a pause. "The Feds won't find any trace of her," he continued in a calmer and more confident tone. "With the recent rains, there's no evidence left around the cabin."

"You hid her up in the Crest cabins?" Anders asked in disbelief. "Imbecile. Fou? That will be the first place the law will look. Does Mike know this? If Mark Scripts looks into this woman's disappearance…" Amos Anders didn't finish, but instead continued on another troublesome thought. "It's bad enough that those idiots kidnapped another FBI protected witness, but it's worse that they did it in our backyard again. Their private vendetta with the FBI will be a cunja on us." A safe door slammed shut, then another. "Scripts's worse than a hound dog on a scent," he muttered disgustedly.

"Harper's Pet? Mr. Shinny Badge Cop? He's not going to find a thing, and if he even gets close, I'll take care of it."

"You'll do nothing! Didn't I just say you're out? We don't knock off the local police. Then we'll have Judge Parker calling in favors. Jesus H. Christ. That's all we need is to have the Feds and every other law enforcement group here. You're not to do a thing. Do you hear me?"

There were a few moments of absolute silence, then the sound of a doorknob grabbed violently was heard without the aid of the microphone. The office door slammed shut, and after the noisy decent down the metal stairs, another door banged shut. A heavy-duty eight-cylinder Ford truck engine roared to life, and big thick tires skidded on the sandy surface before gripping.

Faint tapping came from the office.

"This is Amos...Yes, they delivered, but short...Chill out. I just blacklisted your buddy. Pass it around to the others to do nothing until we get word...No, nothing...You talk to the imbecile...I don't care! He threatened to take out Scripts if it looks like he's onto us...Yes...All right, you do that...I don't know, but when the Boss says this is going to be home base, that's what it's going to be come hell or high water." The phone receiver dropped loudly into its cradle.

The lights went out, and a few moments later, the front door was closed and locked. She peered down at the floor, spotting two glows as they detached from behind some boxes next to the office and moved in an erratic pattern to avoid the monitoring devices and back to the window. After two figures clambered out, the window shut with a slight bang, followed by faint cursing from outside. She waited for the other visitor to leave, who instead landed quietly on the stair platform and disappeared into the office.

The earpiece picked up little movement. After about ten minutes, the sound of a click from the safe was heard.

The second dark figure moved out of the office, using the front door to exit. The light above the outside of the door was out, so without night vision goggles, not even a silhouette of his figure would be seen.

She glanced at her RT device. There was nothing reading at first, then the alarm light flickered on. Whoever it was knew how to disable the system and get out before the backup came on. Now more concerned about getting out undetected, she dangled above the office where she had inserted her camera, pausing a moment when hearing a sound. The veiled head turned, surveying the area slowly.

Nothing.

The small camera was secured into a vest pocket, then she climbed back up the rope. Once the rope was detached and packed, she headed for the other rope. Dangling for a moment, she wondered if escaping through the ceiling exit would be the better choice. A faint whirling noise came from the right. Twisting toward the noise, she could see the overhead warehouse crane approaching and almost silently on well-greased wheels. She quickly released the rope, but not before the solid bulky machine clipped her shoulder, sending her crashing into a stack of goods. The overhead crane kept moving on its track into a dark corner. She bounced off the plastic wrapped toilet paper boxes and dropped onto the hard concrete.

Pulling herself up, her knees were wobbly, and the goggles dangled around her neck. With both hands, the visor was readjusted and tightened. The tops of the nearby stacks were scanned. A sound from above made her move quickly, reaching up and wrapping strong fingers around an ankle and pulling the other figure down. They grappled until she drove her uninjured shoulder into the midsection of the new visitor, who then slid to the ground limp. Something rattled on the concrete floor. Not wanting to risk too much time and be discovered, she kicked it away and darted behind another stack.

Loud slamming of doors and deep male voices from outside the warehouse announced the start of the monthly militia gathering. The one squeak that had not been eliminated from the ceiling exit sounded loud in the warehouse. The dark head cocked to one side straining to see who was using her exit.

Whoever that was knew I cleaned the joints to that exit. With the militia around, the front door's out and the back window's out. I guess I'm going to have to go out the top and hope there aren't any surprises left behind.

Retracing her steps back to the dangling rope, her boot kicked something she was sure had not been there earlier. With a small light, the object was located, and she secured it in a pocket. Retracing her steps to the rope, a short curse was hissed when the rope was found missing. Touching the knob on the night vision viewer, the missing rope was shown curled on the beam with part of it looped down for anyone to see in broad daylight.

The second rope shot up and was quickly secured, tested, and scaled. Once back on the beam, the stolen rope was reclaimed. A careful inspection was made of the beam. Pulling a brush out, she brushed away any evidence of someone being there. That completed, she opened the skylight exit and with equal caution, extended her body through the roof window. Sensing nothing, she rolled onto the roof and quietly closed the window. Hugging the roof, she moved to the side stairs, studying it for a few moments before climbing to the sandy ground.

Glancing around for company and finding none, she scaled the neighboring building to see where everyone was gathering. The wind buffeted against her as her Kevlar-gloved fingers clung onto the roof and she hoped not to be spotted. The men were gathered at the edge of the marsh.

Sliding down the side of the building, a hidden recorder was collected and tucked into a stashed backpack along with the rope coils. Pressing against the warehouse wall, she peered around the corner. A black and white cruiser with a canine hanging out the window approached. The dog barked and growled as the handheld spotlight swept across the area, revealing the SUVs, trucks, and one or two plain vehicles parked around two of the warehouses. The vehicle then moved off into the night.

At the sound of movement in the area, the dark figure took refuge behind a trash bin. It was the sudden intake of breath that was warning enough. Instinctively dropping to one knee, a rifle butt whizzed overhead and crashed into the Dumpster. Before the camouflaged attacker could recover from missing his target, she elbowed her assailant into his Kevlar-padded chest. The assailant recovered with a rifle butt to her shoulder, but a spin kick was made to the militia member's midsection in anticipation. He went backward into the trash bin, breaking the silence with a crash and a flood of curses. Scooping up the dropped rifle, she hobbled out of sight.

Once behind the trees that marked the beginning of the marsh, she slowed down. Moving through the tall grasses and breathing heavy from the adrenaline rush, ammunition was removed from the chamber of the stolen rifle. Her eyes kept scanning around her, looking for specific hot objects nearby. Pausing for the length of time it took to shove the rifle barrel deep into the soft mud, she moved farther into the grasses.

A voice from her right had her dropping to the mud, hoping the grasses would be enough cover. Something apart from the natural decomposing marsh life settled heavy in the air.

Smells like a dead body.

A deep male voice from over a handheld communicator penetrated the night. The voice was cursing the find of a mud-encrusted rifle and attributed it to the other team.

The smell of the salty ocean foam gusted by. Reversing direction, she headed toward the rocky beach, stopping long enough behind a dune to pull out a dark elastic band and wrap her injured leg. It took forty-five minutes to get to the beach.

The pre-dawn sky lit the beach area, revealing colors where there was once dark gray outlines. Agent Adison had napped on a protected ledge on a cliff overlooking the ocean until dawn, not wanting to arouse curiosity if she were noticed limping back into town at such an odd hour. Her dark attire was exchanged for a long-sleeved green sweatshirt that deepened the green color of her eyes. The matching sweatpants hid the calf muscle comfortably wrapped with an Ace bandage. From her backpack, she pulled out flat-soled canvas shoes, devoid of marsh mud and dry. Studying herself in a small mirror, she wiped sand off her chin, brushed her shoulder-length blonde hair, then tied it into a ponytail. She tucked the mirror back into the side pocket of her fanny pack and adjusted her water bottle. Her dark clothing and tools were hidden to be picked up later.

The one-hour jog back into town allowed her to warm her cold limbs and work out some of the soreness in her leg and other body parts. Relieved at reaching her destination, Adison climbed the steps to Crimson Rose Bed and Breakfast, halting when a voice hailed her from the street. Turning, she brushed a stray strand of hair out of her face.

A tall dark-haired man, dressed as a jogger, was standing outside the gate with a gawky Irish wolfhound prancing around his legs. The dog's tongue lolled over the side of a long jaw lined with sharp teeth, panting. Her master's sweat-stained shirt attested they had been on a long run. He looked military or ex. It was not just because he wore his hair short, but more of the presence about him.

Probably a cop now, she guessed. There was no nervousness about him, nor wariness. Just self-assurance. She picked up something familiar about him and knew this was a person she needed to be careful around.

"Ma'am, out a bit early."

"On the East Coast, this isn't that early. Are early morning walks discouraged?" She gave an innocent smile.

The man shook his head, still smiling. "No, ma'am, just unusual. Most people like to sleep in on their vacation."

"Ah. Well, I do this out of self-preservation. I like to eat good food, and this place certainly has some tempting menu selections," she responded, keeping in tune with her cover, and being careful not to be condescending.

"Yes. They have a good chef. Try *Mollie's Creations*. A local favorite. Have a nice day."

"You too, and thanks for the tip." She didn't wait to watch the two move off, not wanting to show any interest in the runner.

Back in her room, a routine inspection was made to assure no one had come in while she was gone. She had requested no maid service. Satisfied, she moved to her next task—a review of her cover. She stood before the full-length mirror behind the bathroom door, looking for what could have led the runner to pick her out. The only thing that stuck out was her canvas shoes. They had no arch or heel support for even a walker. She snorted to herself in disgust. No tourist would forget to pack tennis shoes with an arch for walking, even it was from a hotel to a shop or two. The shoes she wore were from another wardrobe—another face.

Not able to do anything about the mistake at the moment, she pulled on surgical gloves. Taking the envelope from her pocket, she removed the sheet within. The paper looked like it had been folded and refolded many times. The outside of the paper had ink marks on it, reminding Adison of a note carried in a woman's purse. Unfolding the paper, she held it up to the light. She picked off some lint and a few hairs and put them in another plastic bag.

Carefully, she unfolded the rest of the page, lying it flat under a thin sheet of plastic. It was a list of names, some she recognized.

1. Mike Learner ✓
2. Johnny Redfield *
3. Amos Anders ✓
4. Bob Mayhew ✓

5. John Melville *
6. Henry James *
7. Marvin Larimey *
8. Gene Blackmond * ☠
9. George Matthews *
10. Mike Housten *
11. Thomas Meadows *
12. Jinks Wilde *
13. Al Brentwith *
14. Bill Prost ♌
15. BJ Headers *
16. Sam Henry Adams ♌
17. Carl Gates *
18. Richard Mack *
19. Ed Carson ✓

Mentally, she marked off the names she knew—Mike Learner and Amos Anders. No Mark Scripts, Harper, or Judge Parker. Thirteen asterisks, four check marks, and two astrological signs for Leo. One skull and crossbone with an asterisk.

Putting the names to memory, she focused on her next search. The Crest cabins. She remembered a brochure downstairs advertising camping there.

Adison took a shower, and while under the warm water, planned her next move. Out of the shower and dried, she packed her fanny pack with a camera, first aid kit, and a granola bar. For hiking, she pulled out what she needed and dressed quickly. Finished, she stood before the room mirror, checking for anything out of character. She lifted her arms to make sure her P7K3, about seven by four inches snuggly tucked under armpit, didn't show and turned around to check for any lines that gave away the harness. Satisfied that only what appeared as a bra line could be seen, she headed downstairs for breakfast and a brochure on the Crest.

"Hey, boss, I sent you a draft for the travel story. Expect a package of knickknacks that I thought would be good examples of the local talent. I'm checking out the surrounding landscape to see what else the town has to offer. I'll keep in touch," she reported to the voice mail.

Adison hung up the battered receiver. She pulled her sunglasses down the bridge of her nose, looking around her. The pay phone was outside of the ranger's office at the bottom of the rock steps to the left. She avoided the use of a scrambler on her conversation because it would alert Ranger Mayhew that she was more than a travel reporter, just in case he had the phone tapped.

7. Christie

According to the brochure and Ranger Mayhew, the U.S. Forestry Services oversaw a group of two dozen cabins along the Crest, which the government rented out or leased long term. There were a few privately owned cabins intermixed, which Mayhew had not mentioned. While she was speaking with Mayhew about the possibility of renting or leasing, another ranger entered and mentioned one of the cabins was for sale, which seemed to give Mayhew a bit of a start. That piqued her interest, so she said she would like to look at it, giving the excuse that owning was better than leasing. Ranger Gray Horse retrieved the key while Mayhew gave her directions.

Back in the rental car, Adison pointed the vehicle up the winding mountain road. Twenty minutes later, she was still slowly climbing, scanning the unpaved side roads for any recent passage by a heavy vehicle and making a recorded list of license plates of cars leaving the area. Adison pulled her car to the side when her rearview mirror showed a dark blue Toyota coming up fast behind her. Instead of passing and moving on up the winding road, it pulled in front of her and slowed to a halt. She slid the tape recorder into the leg pocket of her khaki pants as she pulled to a stop at the side of the road.

The tall runner from the morning now had a badge looped over his waistband in clear view, with a leather belt holding a holster and a semiautomatic. He wore a plain blue baseball cap and walked slowly toward her car. She knew it was not because he was studying her vehicle; he would have already had it checked out before he stopped her.

He leaned in front of her window, motioning her to roll it down.

"Good morning. Are you following me?" Adison asked politely.

"Nope. A woman traveling alone up here, though, can be dangerous. Heading anywhere special?"

"I was looking into buying a cabin up this way."

He nodded. "That would be up along the Crest."

Adison continued to smile while reading the cop's body language.

"I'm Mark Scripts, detective with the Sunrise PD, and you might be…?"

She held out a hand. "Kay Smith."

"So," he continued when she contributed nothing more, "the cabin you're looking for is straight up this road. The dirt road you want is marked with a bright yellow flag. I'll follow you to make sure you find it. Sometimes the flag isn't up and sightseers get lost."

"That's kind of you. I hope it's not interfering with something else you have to do."

He smiled. "Not at all."

Just great, Adison thought disgustedly.

At the road where she was to turn off, she could see why he followed her. The rental car's carriage wouldn't have cleared the first part of the entrance nor do well over the heavily rutted road. The entrance either was intentionally kept that way or not maintained regularly. Both could see a vehicle had passed over the road during or after the rain from two nights previous, leaving deep tire marks now filled with mud.

"Want a ride?" he offered.

"I would, thanks." *Bet that surprised you. I think I'd like to check you out, Mr. Shiny Badge Cop.*

Adison locked up the rental car and climbed into the lifted truck's cab, grateful she was agile. "You come up here often?" she asked casually, as the truck cleared the obstruction and moved through the mud.

"Often enough."

Adison's eyes scanned three scattered cabins for any signs of life and found none. The truck bounced off in another direction, moving farther into the wooded area.

"That's the Quintons' cabin that's for sale, Ms. Smith."

Adison turned her attention back to her driver and to where he gestured. "Oh. Looks…rustic."

Scripts smiled, pulling up near the cabin. "The Quintons split up. Ed kept it out of spite, but the rules are you have to keep it up and he's been living in Europe to get away from child support payments. You're lucky. Besides not wanting his wife to have it, he doesn't want the government to buy it. It's one of the few cabins that are privately owned and those that do own are vehemently against government buyouts." He gave her a quirky grin before opening his door and sliding out.

That's more than what I need to know. Something push his button?

Adison climbed down from the cab. Before following the detective, she studied the terrain that could hide snipers, snakes, and bugs. At the door, she produced the key the ranger had given her but paused to look around before opening it.

It felt as if she was being watched…through the crosshairs of a rifle. Hearing nothing besides birds and squirrels, she returned her attention to the door. Before stepping in, Adison swung the door open and peered in. The interior odor wafted out and settled on them, smelling of unclean bodies.

Adison heard a snap as the leather secure strap on the detective's holster was released. Scripts firmly pulled her back with one hand, and with the other, he pulled out his weapon. Moving forward, he wrapped his hands around a 45 Springfield 1911A that fit comfortably in his large hands, extended before him in the classic cop pose.

Adison waited near the door, simultaneously listening to noises from inside and outside the cabin, ready to come to his aid if needed and ready to duck inside the cabin if the goose bumps on her arms got worse.

Scripts came back looking grim. "This place is not open for viewing."

Adison stifled her look of dissention. For a brief moment, she entertained the idea of using her magazine credentials to get a look, then realized it was not in keeping with her cover's profile.

She followed the detective toward the cabin with smoke coming from its chimney. Adison could feel the hairs on the back of her neck rise. As she made a grab for the detective's arm to pull him down, he was reaching back for her. With greater strength, he gave her a firm push in the opposite direction toward a big tree trunk while he rolled behind another. It all happened so fast as each of them reacted instinctively to danger. Both could hear a pop, as if someone was using a silencer.

Adison hit the ground and flattened herself behind a tree. Her insides were shaking from the narrow escape. She watched the detective move toward where the sniper had been, knowing by now he was gone. They could both hear branches snapping as if someone was running away in a hurry.

"Wait here," he commanded and took off down a faint trail in the direction of the sniper. Within the forest, the echo of a motorcycle engine roaring to life told Adison they wouldn't be catching the shooter unless he ran into a tree. Adison stood, letting her eyes search for movement. A faint sound behind her had her turning quickly and dropping to one knee.

A white-haired man stood before her. His eyes flickered to where the detective was, then back to Adison. "Danny left four nights ago," he informed her softly. "Delivered a sick woman to a dozen men dressed in camo he met along the fire road. Heavy on the armament side. Someone returned this morning. Just about tore the place up looking for something. Not part of either group, though. He returned about an hour ago with someone else."

The old man looked past her at the approaching detective.

Adison busied herself with looking at her torn blazer.

"Morning, Mark."

"Good morning, Sam. Back from vacation early, I see." He nodded toward the cabin where they had just come from. "Would have been here sooner, but I got an early morning call for a body on the beach."

"Murder?"

"A couple of teens sleeping off whatever they had the night before. Ms. Smith, why don't you go on and wait for me in my truck? I'll be but a minute."

Along the beach? Adison replayed any unusual activity along the beach early in the morning and could not recall any. *I'll take a drive to the cliff and see just how secure my hiding place is.*

Adison's attention moved back to the men. She nodded and started to walk back to the truck, carefully placing her feet on the uneven ground while she looked around. She spotted a reflection from within the woods. Turning to look at the men, she decided the conversation was going to last longer than a minute. Stepping into the shady part of the forest, her eyes attempted to see beyond the darkness of the shadows. A dozen steps farther and the shadows disappeared, revealing a cabin all by itself in the center of the late morning light. From where she stood, there was nothing around to show it was presently habited, though it was well cared for.

Moving in for a closer look, she approached from the porch side. The curtains pulled across most of the windows kept the interior dark from any peering eyes. Walking around the square building, she found a small storage shed thirty yards away. A solar collector was on top of the shed roof and the shed door was secured.

"Four rooms. One of the few with a basement. It's got a toilet, stall shower, new jacuzzi, small kitchen, and just was equipped with solar power. There's a wind generator four of us share. Battery stores inside the shed. Great for one or two people, but only if you don't intend on staying indoors much. Gets cold in winter."

Sam and Scripts had caught up with her.

"Who owns it?" She turned to look at Sam.

"A writer. Used to do his writing up here, but he's getting on in years. He's a widower with no kids. Chances are he'll be selling it soon, and if he doesn't, his estate will. You interested?"

"Yes." Aside from her cover of coming up here to look at cabins, she really was interested, though she had not the slightest idea what she would do with a cabin. When she did get vacations, it was usually to let off steam at some resort where strangers only shared the carnal side of each other, provided safe sex was practiced. It was the type of short-term relationships that her job worked well with.

"I'll mention it. Got a card?"

Adison pulled out her card holder with her business cards and handed the old man one. Sam didn't look at the card but put it in his breast pocket. Adison knew the detective would have liked to look at it but would probably wait until she left to ask Sam. Or would he?

The ride back to her rental car was bumpy and thankfully short. Scripts was deep in his own thoughts. He dropped her off at her rental, and she drove back to the ranger station to return the keys. The detective was close behind her and remained to speak with Ranger Gray Horse. The other ranger was gone and so was one of the two U.S. Forestry SUVs.

As Adison left the detective and ranger talking, she wondered how she was going to go back without the detective on her tail. Ten minutes down the winding hill, the dark blue truck caught up with her and followed her at a respectable distance. She made sure she was driving the speed limit, which was intended to drive him crazy. About five minutes outside the Sunrise town markers, he finally pulled ahead of her and sped off.

"It's about time," she muttered.

Once the truck disappeared from view, she made a sharp U-turn from one of the turn-offs and headed back up the mountain with the gas pedal to the floor. The rental made a gallant effort climbing close to the speed its occupant was pushing for, knocking and gurgling from the thin air and steep terrain.

Once headed in the right direction, Adison pulled out her cell phone. By habit, the conversation scrambler was on. She had faith in the GPS attached to her cell that she would get a clear signal on her first try.

"Hi, Mel, Adison here….Ah, Sam filled you in, eh?...Yes, that pretty much sums it up. Did you get the list of names I faxed you?...I found it in the warehouse. Three names I've identified…Okay. So, what's the plan now?…Okay. Got a resume ready?.. I can't wait to see what you have me down for this time…What?" She gave a short embarrassed laugh. "Yes, I told Sam I was interested in the cabin…I've stayed in a cabin before," she returned huffily. "Well, yes, it has an indoor toilet and running water." Adison chuckled, "Yes, it's got a real jacuzzi. You know I wouldn't be interested in it if it didn't have some hedonistic amenities." Her expression became serious when the conversation switched to business. She listened for the next few minutes nodding to herself and making uh-huh noises where appropriate.

"Roger that. Bye." She folded up the thin phone and slipped it inside her pocket, making sure it was buttoned in.

Instead of driving up the road that would take her past the ranger station, she took another that led behind the cabins. Her topographical map of the area showed a way to the back near a popular hiking path. Mel instructed her to have a chat with Sam. So far, she had no need to contact her backup; generally, she preferred working alone.

At the bottom of one hiking trail, she pulled into an available spot on a scenic turnout. Tourists were taking pictures and hikers were returning from their hikes. No one looked particularly interesting. Exchanging her coat for a sweatshirt, Adison pulled out her fanny pack and two bottles of water to Velcro to her pack. As she snapped her pack around her waist, she scanned the area for a motorcycle or anyone looking out of place. She approached a hiker putting away his heavy equipment.

"Hi there," she greeted the young man. She sized him up for a college student with money. He had an expensive camera, drove a BMW sportster with the dealer advertisement in the license plate holder, and a parking sticker for UC Berkley.

The youth nodded to her and slammed his trunk shut. "Hi," he replied, taking his time to check her out.

By the aroma that clung to his clothes, Adison figured he was determining whether she was a narc.

"Is the trail up this way moderate or for a more seasoned hiker?"

"It's easy enough. You look like you can make it up to the top in about three hours, but it would be too dark by the time you were halfway down unless you have a light."

She nodded. "How far can I get if I didn't have a flashlight?"

"The first ridge in about an hour. Nice view of the Crest. Best time to start is early morning just as the sun is rising. Not many people on the trail then."

Adison looked around. "Doesn't look like many people are up there now."

"There's another turnout around the bend. As you're beginning your ascent, there's going to be a lot of people coming down."

Adison nodded. "Is there a less crowded trail?"

"Yes, but not a good idea to take it. Some of our group got roughed up last weekend by some military types. Said we were disturbing their games."

"They dress up with war paint and all?" she asked mockingly.

"I didn't see them personally. I was farther up the trail. I came back when I heard blowing whistles. The creeps were gone by the time I got to the main group."

"Was it reported?"

"The professor spoke to a ranger. She was one of the people they roughed up. Those good ol' boys from the South don't seem to like dyke types," he grinned.

Adison lifted her eyebrows. "Did you see any of those characters today?"

He shook his head. "No, but we stuck to the busier paths. None of us wanted any trouble." His smile grew wider. "It didn't sit too well with the professor. She doesn't want us to take the busy trails."

"Did you get anything?"

He shrugged his shoulders. "The usual—squirrels, birds, a deer, and hikers. You better get moving if you want to at least make the first ridge."

"Yes. Thanks for the information and warning." Adison moved off.

At the first chance, she left the winding trail and moved straight up in the direction of the cabins. The climb was steep, and she had to dig her toes into the rich soil in some places to prevent herself from sliding back down. Before she reached the top, she paused to catch her breath and drink some water. She leaned against the trunk of a pine tree, enjoying the feel of the bark at her back and the noise of the forest around her. Without closing her eyes, she focused on the sounds of the wind roaring through the treetops. It brought to mind memories of her summer vacations with her twin aunties. Adison sighed. She missed them.

Awkwardly, she dropped to her stomach and inched her way to the top for the last yard. She paused to pull one particularly annoying pine needle out of her waistband. Moving the binoculars around, she studied the area, then shifted her sight to the cabin below. A black pickup truck was pulled up near the Quinton cabin. She counted three men dumping things from the cabin into the truck bed.

A sound from behind her had her rolling to her left and bringing her leg up to kick.

"Hey! You could have gotten hurt," she hissed, dropping her leg and catching herself as she started to roll down the slope.

"You need to be more careful," Sam told her quietly as he held onto her arm to steady her. He nodded to the men below. "They started to clear the place out right after you two left. They're stripping it of everything, not trusting anything to be gone over by Mark." He chuckled. "The man has them spooked into believing he's a super detective. We need to go. They have spotters around here."

"Who?"

"The Jaded Amulet, the local gang. Too bad Mark had to return to town for his evidence kit. I think after today he'll be making sure he has one in his truck."

Sam led her to her vehicle.

"Did you get a chance to look the place over before the evidence was destroyed?"

"Yep. Danny and a woman were staying there for two days. The woman was sick. I found a needle in a corner behind the trashcan. Sent it on up to your headman, Mel. Looks like the same MO as the others."

Adison nodded. "The chemist said Ketamine is what they used to keep the first group manageable, but they may be using a cocktail these days."

Sam grunted.

"Just how legit is the local PD?"

"The only two not to trust are Danny and Mike."

"You said someone came back looking for something?"

"He had a different feel than the others. The second time he came up, he brought someone."

"Were they here before you had a chance to check out the cabin?"

"I slipped in after Danny left with the woman. Caught up with Danny midway down the mountain. It pays to know the territory," he told her.

By his tone, she got the impression he was giving her a piece of advice. She readily agreed. Since her job was to provide recon information to SID—Sensitive Issues Division—she knew how important it was to get details right.

Adison was silent for a moment, sorting through what she heard and knew.

"So you had a big audience last night?" Sam asked.

Adison glanced at him, surprised.

He shrugged his shoulders. "People tell me things."

"Your detective friend was there. Two guys from the White Knights came in before the party began, and a woman came in after everyone but me left."

"Mark couldn't peg you, but he spotted the two guys from the White Knights."

"He saw me?" She was surprised and disappointed. Her skills were obviously slipping.

"He said he felt someone was already there but wasn't able to figure out who or where. He used his backup plan when it was time for him to leave."

"Shutting off the main power so there was a slight delay before the backup system kicked in," she guessed.

Sam nodded.

"About the detective…it's a bit unusual that a small town cop knows so much about the spy business."

"Ex-SEAL. He's one of the good guys and so is his boss, Chief Eugene Harper. Harper used to head the FBI Bureau in Cincinnati. That's where he met Mark, newly promoted to detective." Sam gave a little smirk at something he recalled.

"Something I should know about?"

"Mark was assigned to find a missing person who witnessed a murder. He found out the FBI was interested in the missing person, too. He got the runaround from the local agents, and instead of waiting for them to get back to him, he went directly to the director, Harper. Harper was impressed with his questions and non-belligerent tone, considering how Harper's agents were treating him."

"So Detective Scripts isn't afraid to be bold when necessary. His visit to the warehouse proves that."

"Harper learned about the local players about a year ago and has been trying to put associations together since. They don't know the gang's name or their Southern business associates, the White Knights. They've only recently found a local connection to the kidnapped FBI protected witnesses and are trying to collect information on its implications. What makes it difficult is it's on federal property."

"And they are possessive about their property," Adison murmured.

"Yep. Especially when one of them is part of the loss, eh?"

Adison glanced at him startled, then nodded.

Mel, her boss from SID, had told her that Sam Bear was a retired operative for the CIA and did favors for the local law enforcement in exchange for them alerting him if they had something going on in his area. Sam may have retired, but he was keeping his finger on the pulse of things in his neck of the woods. Adison guessed he had enemies he liked to keep track of. She was to treat him as part of her team if she should need him. From that remark, Adison guessed he was more than a retired agent.

"According to last night's conversation, someone they call the *Boss* intends on setting up a base camp here, and Mr. Detective heard that. So I would say Chief Harper and Detective Scripts will have their hands full."

"I heard you're staying a while."

Adison stifled a sigh. "Yes. Hopefully, this doesn't take too long to where it feels like I'm setting down roots," she muttered, instinctively feeling this operation was going to call for more detail than normal.

"That's not good?"

"I like to keep moving."

"Still interested in the cabin?"

Adison smiled, "Yes. Mel thinks if his agents have a permanent address other than a P.O. box somewhere, it'll make them more stable." Adison glanced toward Sam and for a few moments had a disconcerting feeling he understood more than she intended to reveal.

Adison stopped where Sam indicated he wanted to get out.

"Try Katie's Rentals. She operates out of her house, so if you're not too late, like after nine p.m., she'll help you out today. Tell her I sent you." Sam noticed Adison's hesitation. "She's honest, discreet, doesn't ask unnecessary questions, and doesn't have ties with anyone law enforcement is interested in."

Adison nodded. "All right."

Adison knocked on the door to what was posted as the oldest and best apartment hunter in Sunrise. The door was flung open by a young boy dressed in a swimsuit with his damp hair standing up. The door would have bounced back on him if an elderly woman had not grabbed it.

"Matthew, dear, go on into the TV room. Your movie is starting," she directed firmly, then turned her attention to Adison. "Yes, dear, what can I do…You're the travel writer."

"Yes. Sam mentioned you were the person to go to if I was interested in renting an apartment in Sunrise."

"Well, come on in." She escorted her into her office.

Bookcases on two walls were stuffed with books. There was one out-of-place bookcase near a window that overlooked the backyard. It held just children's stories written by Libby and Kathy Mathews for the physically disabled. Libby was her physically disabled sister who died in her early thirties. It was one of the many tidbits of information she learned while trolling the town for other information.

"What size do you want?" Katie offered her a seat in a reading chair.

Adison made sure her elbow didn't nudge the table piled high with books as she sat down. "Not big. One room. I never was good with cleaning."

Katie's brow was wrinkled as she studied Adison.

"Sunrise is a nice town," Adison offered.

"It is," Katie agreed brightly. "So besides one room, would you prefer living in an apartment complex, a four-plex, or something over a garage?"

After listening to what Adison wanted in an apartment, she printed out a list of a dozen potentials and produced keys to five.

"The ones with the picture of a car means the apartment comes with parking, the ones with the dollar sign next to the car means parking is extra," she explained. "On Monday, you can see the owner/managers for the keys for these other apartments. They're out of town this weekend. They fish together."

Adison's Sunday itinerary jingled in her pocket as she left Katie's.

7. Christie

Chapter Two

On Sunday morning, with the list of what was to be found in the bachelor pad, her fourth apartment, Adison felt she found the right place.

Single pad above a store. Good location. No shared walls. The living room is the size of a bedroom and living room combined. Nice big window with a view of the sky.

The only set of windows in the living room were opened, airing out the paint smell and letting in the cool ocean breeze. She took a deep breath of the ocean's scent and peered out the window, letting the breeze sweep her hair back. Her views were of rooftops for two blocks, a busy street below, a coffee/donut shop, and small artsy stores across the street.

A different breeze whiffed by, carrying the scent of doughnuts and fresh roasted coffee, tempting her nose and sweet tooth.

Closing the windows carefully, she studied the latch. *A novice can open this with a card.*

She pushed the windows back open. Turning around, she inspected the walk-in closet with the built-in dresser and mirror, grateful she didn't accumulate things. The bathroom had an old iron-clawed bathtub, deep and roomy. It had a new shower stall, toilet, and sink. The floor was also new with a roll of cushy soft green vinyl. The bathroom was a combination of pale and dark green, with a colorful underwater scene on a strip of foil that ran around the walls just below the ceiling.

"I don't think I've ever had a bathroom this nice," Adison said aloud.

And now last and least I'm interested in…the kitchen. Turning back into the front room, she walked past the stairwell and stood for a moment looking over the kitchen.

Everything's new here. But this lock to the back stairs into the alley is interesting. A new deadbolt in a new door… I wonder how many people have a key to this? I'll have it retumbled.

Her RF scanner gave the apartment a clean bill of health: no hidden cameras or monitoring devices in the smoke alarm, wall sockets, mirrors, lights, air conditioner, vents, or walls. *That's going to change.*

She nodded, pleased. Though it was over two busy streets, the walls were soundproofed, and it had two entrances and exits. According to Katie, in its previous life, it had been used by the landlord's nephew for his band to practice in. The back stairs led to the alley where the store downstairs received supplies.

Adison mentally stored the measurements of the place and took pictures to pass onto SID. They would put together some belongings for her, making it look like she was a real person. Hopefully, Alice, who was into the frilly home decorating thing, was not going to shop for her again. Adison had no permanent address to keep anything personal and refrained from renting a storage facility. She had no wish to have anything that reminded her of the cases she worked on when she was ready to settle down.

Monday she would shop for her immediate needs and get to know more of the town from a different perspective while waiting for Mel to cook up a deeper identity to fit with the job he had in mind for her. It would also give her a chance to flash around credit cards that had the name she would be living with here and explain why she wrote under a different name.

Adison had been waiting for a short time and was expecting it to be even longer, but footsteps on the porch had her looking toward the doorway. The door swung open without a knock and Chief Eugene Harper of the Sunrise PD stepped inside quickly, closing the door behind him. For a few moments, they studied each other, each wondering how to make this collaboration work for their benefit.

Adison rose from the chair. "Chief Harper," she greeted.

"Agent Adison," he returned. "Would you like some coffee while we wait for Sam?"

"Wouldn't mind it at all," she replied.

The meeting place was one room with no windows. It contained a chair, couch, two fold-up chairs, and a card table folded against the wall. Against another wall was a small table that had a water cistern and propane stove. Three milk crates stacked beside the table had food staples that could keep for months at a time. She had looked.

The room had also been recently cleaned because it smelled as if it was aired out and everything was dusted. It was a safe place for a few people at one time.

Adison didn't sit down again, expecting the chief to say something about a federal agency strong-arming him into sticking an undercover agent amongst his rank and file.

When the coffee was ready, Chief Harper pulled out three Styrofoam cups from the top crate and filled them with strong black coffee.

The front door opened soundlessly, and Sam slipped into the room.

"I'll have a cup of that," he said.

The two men sat on the couch, and Adison took the one reading chair.

"I heard through the Sunrise telegraph that you've got yourself an apartment above Ed's Tinker Shop."

Adison gave him a nod, thinking how much information he gave her in that one sentence: He let her know that she was of interest to Sunrise residents, her name change was acknowledged, and that he was aware she had the apartment before he had agreed to Mel's arrangement. The investigation would have gone forward, with or without his participation. He knew the game, having once been a player.

"Sunrise is an interesting town," she offered.

"Sunrise is a town of diversity. Tolerance is a dirty word to most folks here. It implies that someone is better than another. We have our troublemakers and people who find it hard to fit, but Sunrise believes community is important and inclusion of its residents. Even the ones who disagree with our mandate. It's what makes a healthy and successful community."

Chief Harper watched her a moment. Adison was not certain if he expected her to say something, of which she had nothing to offer beyond what she had said.

"This gang that's settling in our town, I want them out of here, and I lack the resources to see that happen. I won't put you in harm's way, but my town comes first."

Adison nodded her understanding.

"Do you have a problem with reporting to me instead of your headman?"

"My orders from Mel are that I report to you first." *Unless I feel your orders are detrimental to Mel's plan and or my well-being.*

"You have any questions?"

"Who knows about me besides you two?"

"Just us. As I'm sure you noticed, there are few secrets in Sunrise, and information passes quickly. If you were ever seen with a stranger, talk would reach the gang you're here to investigate. That's the real purpose of you reporting directly to me."

"Okay." *You mean, not because you want to stay in the loop with a federal investigation that might find someone in the White House involved in the slave trade and your town sacrificed to keep it under wraps?*

"Anything else?"

"Not right now. Once I'm settled in my role, we'll go from there."

"Good enough. That's the plan then. Sam, do you have anything to say?" Harper asked.

"How long have you ever been undercover in one place?"

"Six months," Adison replied, returning his grin.

"You'll be at this job longer than that and will need a safe place of your own. I'll see about getting you a place."

"Okay," Adison agreed, all the while wondering why it felt like she was being sold to a new owner.

"I'll start working on bringing you into the PD fold then. Sam, you want to make sure she's out safely?"

Sam returned twenty minutes later and sat on the couch while Chief Harper poured them a second cup of coffee.

"Well, what do you think of her?" Harper asked.

"She's a survivor. Likes to work alone with her support team tending the perimeter, but I'd say her trust in her support team is earned." He sipped his drink for a few moments, staring at the tips of his feet that were stretched out before him. "I don't think Mel understands just how difficult it will be for her to get ensconced into a small town to appease the gang as just another hire. They'll be keeping their eyes on her and testing her."

"According to Mel, this is what she does. So, you think she'll be here longer than six months?"

Sam nodded. "How many undercover ops have you been involved in that took less?"

"For the hard ones, years." He rubbed his chin, smiling ruefully. "This will be a long haul. I have little on this gang, and I know Mel has drawers full of information. He's only agreed to let me know what his agent digs up."

Sam grunted his comment.

"For the first few months, I want to see just what type of person she is. I take it you're going to be running her through weekend games."

"Just going to make sure she knows the difference between a bear and a skunk." Sam grinned.

"Knowing Mark, he's going to give her a mini-boot camp drill to test her out."

"Yep. She's going to be needing a few months to adjust to her change in life."

"I hope she copes with the pressures because from here on out, day and night with no weekends or vacations off, she's Detective Alex Adison of Sunrise Police Department."

Wednesday, Adison set up a bank account, made sure she would have the proper bills coming to her new address, and purchased a few more items, namely civilian wear that fit Sunrise, underwear, and a few more sweat suits that didn't clash with her new running shoes. Running in the morning or in the early evening was a good way to get a view of Sunrise landscape and who was about at those hours.

By now, the residents knew she was starting a new job as a detective and stopped her to talk about how she felt going from travel writer to a detective, trusting Chief Harper to have made a good evaluation of her qualifications.

Thursday at seven in the morning, Adison was sitting in the squad room in a new dark brown uniform of the Sunrise PD, being introduced to her co-workers. Detectives didn't have to wear uniforms except maybe at funerals or official get-togethers, so she was looking forward to the end of her probation or the end of this assignment. Adison disliked uniforms, seeing them as a bull's-eye to a sniper or crazed citizen.

"All right, everyone, listen up. This is Detective Alex Adison, new addition to our SPD staff." The chief looked over the group. "Alex, over in the corner holding up the walls and looking like one tired alley cat is our full-time night shift officer, Gary Krieger. Full-time dayshift for weekday staff consists of yourself and Lieutenant Harriet Sams, who is in charge of new hires. Then there's Officer Eric Burns—our very own computer geek, and Detective Mark Scripts, who's out for the day but will be your immediate supervisor. Our two street patrol officers for weekdays and whom we move around as needed are Mike Learner, who is on medical leave, and Danny Brucker, the big guy there.

"Harriet will introduce you to our part-time staffers who work the weekends, Seda and Rajpal Arellano, Stender Hall, and Robert Gronlund. Harriet, you get Detective Adison first. Show her the ropes. When you're finished, shuffle her over to Eric. Eric, unlike some of our other co-workers, she has computer skills, which I'm sure you're happy to hear. All right, troop, dismissed. Danny, stay."

Adison studied Officer Danny Brucker as he sat alone in his own space at the oval table, indifferent to those around him. His arms and legs were crossed, but his gray eyes studied her with intensity that could be read a variety of ways. His unnaturally black hair was combed straight back, and bruised knuckles were tucked under his crossed arms. His starched uniform, pulled taut over his muscular shoulders, had sharp creases on the arms that went through the arm patch identifying him as a Sunrise police officer. His dark brown pants with the golden stripe down the legs also had sharp creases. His badge pinned over his right pocket shined as much as his black shoes. She didn't get the same feel off Brucker as she had with Scripts. Scripts had a professionalism and command presence, whereas Brucker was just another soldier who kept his uniform spotless and creased.

They filed out into the main office with the exception of Brucker, who sat heavily into the chair across from the chief's desk. Lieutenant Sams closed the chief's office door behind her. Adison's new co-workers shook her hand and introduced themselves with more vigor. They seemed to be pleased she was on board.

Lieutenant Sams' first stop was to show her the six cells they had in the basement.

"Each cell has a camera monitoring it. Anyone with a password can check the cells from his or her computer. The chief determines who will be the monitor. If we keep anyone overnight, we have people who've been trained to watch them. There are motion detectors for the surrounding area. Keys to the cells are in a lockbox near my desk. Come on, I'll show you where. Only three of us have the authority to access these keys," she explained as they clomped up from the basement. "Mark, myself, and the chief."

Harriet, as she liked to be called by friends, was the person people called when they had a beef with a neighbor and wanted a third party opinion. That was the impression Adison received after listening to two hours of calls. Adison relayed that observation to Harriet to see if that was the intended impression.

"Oh, yes," Harriet easily laughed, waving a hand in casual dismissal, "the chief calls me the department's arbitrator. Looks nice on a résumé. These adults squabble like kids sometimes, but all in all, we're a nice community that's close regardless of differing politics. In the fifteen years I've been part of this department, I've been called out for attempted suicides all of five times, family squabbles a dozen times...but that was before the counseling staff for the House got established."

"The House?"

"It's the women's shelter in that beautiful restored Victorian house on the other side of Town Square. They have a twenty-four-hour hot line with trained counselors to handle domestic situations."

"Most women's shelters like to have their exact location unknown."

"In this town, there are few secrets. That's very important to remember when you talk to anyone or hear anything. The House is for out-of-state women who are fleeing their abusers. We don't feel it's right for them to have to hide inside when they aren't breaking the laws."

They were interrupted by a call, which Adison was given to handle. Her typing skills came in handy as she listened and typed in what the caller was reporting. Without a goodbye, the caller hung up when he felt his complaint was taken.

"So how do you code male underwear disappearing from the rest home's laundry room? Is it under the umbrella of the disappearing sock phenomena or probable misplacement?" Adison asked as she typed in the last part of the caller's comments.

"Well, first off...you don't want to call Ocean View Retirement Community a rest home. The residents are very vocal and have a lot of pride. They may hang you in effigy. Though, they do save that kinda stuff for once a year." Lieutenant Sams rested a hand on Adison's arm to take out the sting in her correction. "This phenomena of underwear disappearing has been occurring for about two years, so it goes to the detective queue, which I see Eric hasn't added your name to yet, so it'll go to Mark's queue. See how the Sherlock Holmes hat there—that's the detective icon—pops up telling you what it will do with the call? Normally, it would beep Mark since his name's the only one under page Sherlock right now, but he has this coded as miscellaneous. It's so old and not an emergency."

"So if it were an emergency or a new case…?"

"Mark's beeper and his PC will get a message that he has a new case. If it's an update, depending on the code, it will beep him or just flash him when he signs on. See these boxes? Those are what the automated voice will tell him the call is about when he checks in. You have to get the right code, so the software labels it correctly and will tell him what he needs to know. Then he can decide what action to take: return to the office, go to follow up a new lead, or ignore it for the moment. You don't have a pager yet, but it will be a text pager where you can type in a response, send in an email, or text page someone else. The detectives, myself, Eric, and the chief are the only ones who get these fancy things. Lots of do-dads."

"I've never seen a program like this before."

"Eric and Angie Burns wrote the Sherlock program with the help of some of the high school kids." She laughed at the surprised look on Adison's face. "Projects like this keep the smart kids out of mischief and give them some money for their participation."

"Just how secure is this?"

"We use Secure ID, an outside vendor. We found out the hard way that sometimes people just aren't to be trusted. There was a rape case about a year and a half back concerning a wealthy socialite. Some freelance writer got a computer hacker to hack into the PD server. It just about turned everyone's life upside down. It wasn't pretty. That was before we got Eric Burns."

"Rape even in a small town, huh?"

"I see you have that misconception about small towns not having the same sins as the city," she smiled ruefully. "Actually, this was up at the campgrounds we cover for the forestry service. Getting the FBI involved is too cumbersome, and they have an unwritten agreement to let Chief Harper take it unless it's some real public eye opener. You know, something that will bring in the news cameras, then the FBI jumps in. Except this one, no one wanted to handle. The case was rather interesting and would give you a good idea of how things can go topsy-turvy around here. It would be a good idea to read about it."

"Okay," Adison nodded. "So, just what does everyone do around here?"

"Well, you know pretty much my part: training people and keeping our department business in order. Sometimes I feel like a glorified secretary, but I make arrests and give out tickets, too, so don't forget to give me a card on secretary's day," she joked. "Chief Harper and Mark Scripts do the investigative jobs in four counties, and when not busy with that, Mark handles police work. Eric Burns manages processing the evidence, gets updated equipment necessary for investigations, and handles all the computer stuff for this department and for Sunrise City Hall, with the exception of the Web page for our town. The Sparks' handle that from the tourist bureau. They also run the local tattoo shop. Tourist office is the one upstairs above our workout room. The workout room is right there, through that door.

"Mike and Danny do patrol work. They walk through the business parts of town, keeping an eye out for thieves during the weekdays, direct traffic, and answer tourists' questions. If they think an arrest needs to be made, they have to clear it with Mark, the chief, or me."

Adison grimaced at picturing Danny making nice with tourists.

"Yes. You haven't met Mike yet, but they have it harder than any of us. It doesn't come natural to those two to be tourist friendly." Harriet chuckled and moved on without giving any further information. Adison guessed she would get the inside story soon enough.

"They also secure an area after a crime until Mark or the chief arrive. Seda and Rajpal Arellano, the twins, they only work the weekends doing daytime patrol work. Now, those two are our tourist faces. Not only are they nice and friendly, but they always know where and what is going on any given day. Tourists love them and drop off notes on how grateful they were for their assistance. Stender Hall works the second shift on weekends and Robert Gronlund works the nights on weekends." She smiled impishly. "You'll also be working the weekends. As detective, you'll be on call. My suggestion is walk the beat in your uniform to get a feel for what's going on, and for the residents to get to know you, that way when you're called out, you'll have some idea of who and what the call is about."

Adison nodded.

"I've learned to never take a call at face value," Harriet continued. "I'm sure you know never to relax on the scene, like a firefighter, thinking a fire you worked so hard at containing is a done deal. It doesn't take much to reignite if there's kindle nearby, so I'll just repeat it for safety sake."

Adison nodded while her mind was running with the worry of what would happen if she were called out at midnight and the person didn't recognize her as a new hire. As if reading her mind, Harriet laid her hand on Adison's arm.

"When you go out this weekend, I'll be assisting you, just so no drunken fool forgets you work for SPD. The chief and Mark will be out of town on court business this weekend, otherwise one of them would be backing you up. They got some sensational murder trial going on and they've been working with the DA on getting it nailed down," she explained.

Harriet returned a wave to one of the people who walked by the glass doors to the SPD office, then continued, "We used to have twenty-three full-time officers and now it's eight full time, four part-timers working the weekends and six reserve officers when we need assistance."

"Twenty-three officers to eight? That's quite a reduction."

"Money and politics. Those on the counsel who were voting for a big police force were voted off, and the new order is 'use part-time and reserve officers when necessary.' Insurance and the like make it expensive to keep a large number of full-time staff," she explained. "We do get investigation calls from the court in Bales that covers Bales, Brisbane, Antioch, and Sunrise. Because of Chief Harper and Mark's backgrounds, they are used for serious cases that the surrounding towns and forestry service don't have the depth to cover. Chief Harper is the court's official investigator. We prefer not to call in big guns from the city. Small town pride, you can say. Getting real talent in the detective field for a small town can be difficult with the reward not being in the pay.

"Come on and I'll show you around our workout room. Best time to use the gym is in the mid-morning hours when Mike and Danny are just starting their foot patrol. The volunteer fire department and city employees, including the Sparks, are authorized to use it but only during weekdays. Insurance doesn't cover them for the weekends, but the chief made sure it does cover the PD."

Lieutenant Sams pushed opened the door to the exercise room. It was a comfortable-sized gym. It had two different types of treadmills, three lifecycles, and a nice collection of weights with three workbenches. There was one new weight pulley center, where every muscle could be worked on. The floor was padded in some areas, concrete around the weights and under the two punching bags. One was a boxer bag and the other a long one that was ideal for kickboxing.

"Rules of use are up on all four walls and in the locker area. If you don't follow them, the chief bans you from the place for six months. Insurance," she said.

There was one shower room with enough room to change clothes and a door that could be locked for privacy. Lockers with names on them lined the small room adjacent to the shower room.

For lunch, Harriet took Adison to Mollie's Creations. Their time waiting for their meal was filled with townsfolk stopping and introducing themselves. If they meant to impress Adison, they did with their genuine warmth for a stranger who now worked for their city.

After returning to the station, she tapped on the PD's server's secure room for her next set of lessons with Eric Burns. Angie Burns, his wife, taught computers, science, and math at the local high school during the day, and at night, the two gave computer classes to local geeks and wanna-bes. Burns encouraged her to take some additional classes if she wanted to pep up her skills. While he chatted, he took her fingerprints and iris scan for her to gain access into the server room.

Adison spent Friday walking the beat with Harriet.

"Now it's important to talk to all the shopkeepers. Take your time. If a tourist asks directions or some question like you were a sales clerk, it's no big deal. It's important to know the people you're hired to protect."

Harriet shaded her eyes and waved. "There's the twins now. They have lunch with a few other teachers about this time," Harriet said as they headed to the benches that circled the center garden.

Se brushed crumbs off her dress and nodded to Adison. Raj stuck out his hand to Adison.

"Welcome, Detective Adison. I'm sure you will find everyone..."

His sister cleared her throat and gave him a pitying expression. "He was going to say everyone is friendly, but they aren't. Welcome, Detective Adison." She wiped her fingers on a napkin and shook Adison's hand.

"Nice meeting you two."

"This is Alyson, Jay, Carson, and Halley. They teach at the high school," she introduced the others sitting at their lunch table.

Harriet had been pulled aside by a young boy who looked happy to see her.

"Okay, Grandma!" he said, then took off to join his friends.

"Grandma?" Adison asked.

"He calls all women that are older than his mother, grandma. We'll see you two later," Harriet waved at the group and headed toward the shops.

Harriet was taking her to meet Stender Hall next. He was a graphics designer with his small office over Grandma's Tools hardware store.

"Alex, this is Stenie. Stenie, this is our new detective, Alex. Don't you think he looks like he should be a police officer?" Harriet teased.

"I thought I was a police officer who moonlights as a designer," Stender returned. "Nice meeting you, Alex. I'm glad to say that it's nice the chief finally filled the detective slot. I think Mark was going to out on a recruitment jaunt if Harper didn't hire by the end of this month."

Harriet laughed. "He's kidding. Linda, Mark's wife, would have gone out and done it herself."

Robert was their next stop, and he was trying his hand at building a model car out of toothpicks.

"Robert, this is Alex, our new detective, and, Alex, this is Robert. He's a transfer from New Jersey."

"Hi, Robert. Nice meeting you."

"Likewise. So, you're the newbie. I hear you took a sabbatical from police work for a while. Welcome back into the fold."

"It was nice to travel around and get paid for it, but you're right, it was just a sabbatical. There are some jobs that are difficult to get out of your blood."

Robert laughed. "Have you met the other part-timers? Then you know how true that statement is."

7. Christie

That night, Adison felt exhausted. She had been firming up her character and her face felt tired from smiling. To fit in with Sunrise, she was outgoing and pleasant, yet discreet about herself, giving just enough truth to not feel entirely made up. After all, Alexandra Kay Adison was her real name, and she grew up in Washington state not that far from Northern California. Though young Kay was timid and moved around a lot due to her mother's personal problems, SID had done enough extensive background research on her before she was hired to know that Kay Adison in her youth was not a memorable person, and therefore they didn't need to worry about her past getting in the way of her covert assignments.

On Saturday and Sunday, Adison met the twins in the office and got a briefing on what to look out for and what time to take lunch to beat the crowd. Harriet stopped by periodically to make sure she was okay.

Adison was watching some kids who kept glancing around as if they were up to no good. They moved along the table of one street vendor who was occupied with a customer. They had not seen her yet as she was standing next to a pillar. However, Harriet's sudden appearance had them moving on. Harriet watched them, then turned to Adison.

"Found me again," Adison remarked. "It's got to be this uniform and the crowd it attracts."

"I think it's because you're an attractive woman dressed in a uniform, with just enough leather that they'll keep their distance," Harriet teased.

Adison was speechless for a few minutes.

Harriet laughed at her expression. "Those kids' parents run the bicycle shop on Atherton. They're all adopted. They're city kids having a problem adapting to a small town."

"Something wrong with their home?"

Harriet smiled at her. "My exact question. Carl and Allie are into work and believe the kids should be, too. They aren't into repeating things twice and demand more than what the boys can give right now."

"Counseling," Adison replied.

"They need something more immediate. How's your walk?"

"More than what I usually do. In my other job, I drove or flew to my interviews," she laughed.

"Well, you're going to have to build up on your walking muscles. Even Mark does foot patrols."

Monday morning, Detective Adison sat in the small meeting room off the chief's office with Chief Harper and her new partner/supervisor, Detective Mark Scripts. Feeling better in a less starched uniform and warmed up with three intensive days of inquisitiveness, she thought she could face the detective with more ease. Her character was nearly finished with the unsuspecting assistance of Sunrise's residents.

"Alex Adison, Mark Scripts. I understand you two have met," Chief Harper said.

Adison nodded and smiled at the detective whose dark eyes were openly appraising her. She wondered what he was thinking.

Chief Harper clicked on an audio jammer.

"Mark will show you the ropes and see where your strengths and weaknesses are. His job as your supervisor will be to build on what you know and add to your repertoire of skills." The chief gave Adison an amused look.

"We have ten open investigations that you can read up on," he continued. "Two are a priority. The first—ten undocumented Mexican nationals were found buried in a mass grave in an open field between here and Brisbane about a year ago. The second is that we've had five women disappear around the area Judge Parker calls his territory. These disappearances have occurred over a one-year span. Three were supposed to have been in the FBI's protective care with new identities, which the FBI has not officially admitted to, so the investigation is technically ours. This other problem..." he indicated the audio jammer, "Mark will fill you in.

"Every second Saturday of the month, five of us meet for a three-hour meeting on what's new in law enforcement and review cases that we're not making much progress on. Don't forget to keep each other briefed on whatever cases you're working on since I'm sure neither of you will want to be bothered on your days off.

"Alex, you'll be taking Wednesdays and Thursdays off, our two slow days. Weekends, as you found, are pretty hectic with the tourists and keep our part-timers busy. Having you working the weekend means we can get to theft reports faster and cover areas the twins can't, like the warehouse and shelter area. Mark gets weekends off with no calls, unless you need him." He glanced at Mark who grinned at the news.

"I don't like surprises, and I don't like having to go before the town committee about objectionable police tactics or behavior. Don't forget you work for these people."

He studied her for a moment. "I expect you to familiarize yourself with the town by attending these meetings. However, I don't expect you to sit through them all the time." He smiled a little. "One of the disadvantages or advantages of living in a small town is that there's not too much that is a secret here, so be careful about what you say to anyone. However, though gossip flows easily, there is little in the way of malice. If you should hear of it, bring it up to Harriet, Mark, or me. It's usually a problem that if we get to the source we can prevent a small dispute from becoming more serious."

Adison nodded.

"Do you have a vehicle?"

"No. In my previous job, it wasn't practical," she said. "It's on my shopping list."

"Purchase a vehicle that's going to do well over bad roads like a four-wheel drive that has an oil pan with good ground clearance. Since there's no long-term parking over at Ed's shop, you can park in the police lot. Max, our mechanic, has enough alarms and cameras there to frustrate a car thief. Mark, get her settled in. Have a fine day, detectives."

"Will do, Chief," Mark responded.

"Likewise, Chief," Adison replied as she gathered her cup of coffee and rose to follow her new partner out.

"That will be your desk," Scripts gestured. "You've already been cleared to look through the closed and open cases, so like the chief said, they're a good example of what happens in Sunrise and the other three counties we cover. You're set you up with a Secure ID," he handed her the key fob, the thumb-size device that changed numbers every 60 seconds. "You're the second new hire I know who got access to our database before probation was over. You have some pretty impressive references," he said. "So you a Smith or Adison?" he finally asked.

Adison's lips curled into a smile. "Both. I write under Kay Smith."

He smiled, too. "Write any romance?"

"Nope," she said, nearly shuddering at the thought. "Just travel stuff."

"We have two resident romance novelists who give workshops should you ever get the inclination to try it," Scripts offered, not missing her quick dismissal of the topic and wanting to see what she would do with his dig.

"Not even in my dreams."

He picked up a flyer and handed it to her. "Our first job for the morning. We'll be visiting the women's shelter. We give talks on self-protection, how to recognize a stalker, and how to search for surveillance equipment. You have any experience on those subjects?"

"Yes," she murmured, studying the list of discussions the SPD would be giving at the shelter and on what days for the month.

"Good. Before we go there, you're going to have to change out of that uniform into civvies. Some of the residents get nervous about uniforms in their safe space. Then we'll head over to the coroner in Bales. They have the remains of a hand found in the marsh a couple nights ago. Dr. Fishbach, the head coroner, doesn't have the PMI yet, but he has something of interest. Think your stomach can handle it?"

"I'll bring a barf bag just in case." As glib as she was, she didn't do well with looking at or smelling corpses or body parts.

The three-level Victorian house had a curving driveway that opened to a parking area to the left of the house. As Scripts parked the car, Adison studied the front yard that had more garden space than lawn. Along the base of the building, the plants had one thing in common—they all had needles or thorns. Stairs led to the second story, which had a covered porch crowded with flowerpots and no space for a chair. In a quick glance, Adison spotted two surveillance cameras with a sign that warned anyone that the place was wired for security.

Detective Scripts gave a tug on the bell that sent an echoing ring within the house.

"This place used to be a Catholic nun retreat for over fifty years. A little over two acres were donated by a family to the Daughters of Charity," Scripts explained. "The church sold the property. The developer who purchased it went bust before he could do anything with it. Claire, the manager and owner of the shelter, bought the convent and half an acre around it at an auction. The city and another developer bought off the rest of the plots the land was divided into. Their small chapel," he nodded to the building on the next lot, "is now used for town functions."

The door opened to reveal a medium-height woman with the roundedness of someone who had reached her midlife. Her faded orange hair was pulled back in a ponytail with a bandana wrapped around her neck. The tails of her shirt hung out over faded blue jeans. Her tennis shoes were all that showed as new. She faced them brandishing a broom and looked like she was ready to use it more as a club than for sweeping.

"What are you doing, Claire? Giving housekeeping lessons or transportation?" Scripts quipped.

"I'm working on how to scare the living daylights out of that blasted mouse that insists on chewing up my *Home and Garden* magazines! I plan on transporting *it*. You must be the new detective. How are you?"

"Claire, meet Detective Alex Adison. Detective, meet Claire, manager of the shelter."

"Fine thanks. And you?"

"Just fine and dandy. Come on in."

"Are the gals ready for us?" Scripts asked as they followed her into the long entrance way.

"Yep."

Claire led them past two closed doors on either side of the entranceway. On the left was a stairway and immediately across was a large sitting room. On the other side of the stairs was a dining room with a large table and the last doorway down the hall was the kitchen. The baking smell of cake brought memories from Adison's childhood into her consciousness—happy memories of baking with her aunties.

Claire opened a door across from the dining room and waved Scripts and her down a staircase. They entered a large room where a dozen chairs were set up with women gathered in small groups chatting amiably. Three PCs lined the wall with a posted class schedule. Conversations became louder as hellos greeted Scripts.

Introductions were given, and everyone welcomed Adison to Sunrise. By Scripts' relaxed manner, there was no hurry to get this meeting started. Some of the women Adison recognized from stores she had visited when she was playing magazine writer and later in an official SPD uniform. It reminded her of a phrase her aunties used—"Remember to be nice because you may be back."

"These classes on abuse are open to any of the women in town," Claire said for Adison's benefit. "If the men are interested, we give a few next door in the meeting hall. The last time the men asked to participate, it was to be a talk on defense, so we dressed some of the men who volunteered in these padded outfits…they wanted action rather than listen to a lecture."

Adison got the distinct impression that these women thought the classes should only be for women.

Scripts pulled out boxes with different types of cameras, all small and difficult to look for if hidden correctly. Pinhole camera, smoke detector camera, radio camera, a few clock cameras, clothes camera, a fern in a pot camera, and a lamp camera.

When the class ended, Adison met Genie, Claire's partner. She rolled in with refreshments from the elevator on the other side of the room.

"So you're the new detective they're talking about at the coffee shop. Nice to meet you." Genie gave her a firm handshake, sizing her up as she did. "Looks like you need some time with a good cook. You're too skinny, Detective."

"She means that, too," Scripts told her between bites of his cake. "She hates anyone who doesn't look like she spends time eating."

"I've been eating *too* much good food around here," Adison disagreed.

"Ah, now we have the truth. The reason she decided to stay was the food. Hi, is it Adison, detective or Alex? My name's Cindy. I work in Grandmother's Gift Shop. You bought a set of wind chimes the other day. You know, that's the mark of a true cop," Cindy told her.

"You're getting food confused with the doughnut shop theory, Cin. She doesn't look the chowing down or doughnut type. Hi, I'm Ellen, I own Grandmother's Gift Shop."

"Any of the names will do. Just what type do I look like?" Adison was hoping she was not stepping into something too deep, but she needed to know what impression she was giving.

"Greasy foods," another woman nodded confidently. "Cops like greasy foods. Hi, Alex, I'm Leslie Hill. I'm a real estate agent if you're looking, and artist and the local gadfly for the *Sunrise Daily*."

"That would be Harry's Sandwich Shop, where if it doesn't drip, it isn't a good sandwich," Claire added.

The women laughed.

"So what do you think?" Claire turned to Genie. "Have you sized up Detective Adison yet?"

"Given the chance and opportunity...she would eat out every day. Hates to cook. Her method is to buy large quantities of take-out and nuke leftovers for the rest of the week. For desserts, chocolate is her first choice."

Adison felt slightly uncomfortable. "Well, you got the part about not being the cooking type right, but for dessert, anything sweet with coffee to help cut it is fine by me." Staying with her cover as a travel writer, she had sampled all sorts of menus, including desserts, so she wondered how Genie came to that conclusion.

"Genie can read anyone's gastro desires and habits. She's like a diviner. She's doing about ninety-nine percent, with only one error this year," Scripts said.

"I don't want to bother arguing with you on that point, but I got that right, too," Genie informed him.

The ride to the morgue in Bales was silent, and Adison was fine with that. She studied the landscape around them. There were a lot of official turnoffs and possible places a car would pull off for a picturesque view, leaving people vulnerable to predators...the human kind. Weeks earlier, she had been over the sites and others numerous times in a rental car looking for clues.

When trees began to give way to a few farms, then into a suburb, Adison memorized the terrain, streets, and landmarks, should she have to come here on her own. Scripts parked at the back of a hospital where a sign identified the morgue in the basement and had a parking space reserved for police and two for the coroners.

She had to just about trot to keep up with long and quick steps of her partner. "Hey, Detective Scripts, the body part isn't going to walk away. Can you slow down a bit?" she called from behind.

He stopped suddenly, surprised. "Sorry, I was thinking." When she was even with him, he continued at a slower pace. "This body part was found by John Malstron's dog, Salvatore. He lets the hound run loose around the marsh because he's sure Sal won't bother anyone. What I retrieved was pretty hard to recognize as a hand."

A dog? So none of the militia members mentioned it. If I could smell it, I'm sure they did. Is John Malstron a member of the militia?

Scripts didn't stop at the guard station but pulled out his ID from his waistband, flashed it, and continued past the guard who had been eyeing them since they came into view.

"Hold on there, Dee-tect-ive. Ah don't know who ya got there with ya."

Scripts muttered something under his breath but turned back to the slightly overweight guard.

His uniform had two patches, one for the company he worked for and the other with the hospital's name. Adison watched his eyes as he squinted at her, moving his mouth in a disagreeable expression. His cap was askew which he adjusted, as he did his belt that had a holster for his flashlight, a noisy collection of keys, and two small black pouches.

"I'm Detective Adison of the Sunrise Police Department. And you are?"

"North-side guard Pearlie, *Ms.* Adison. And Ah got ta see yer credentials before Ah letcha in. Yer not dressed like a po-lice officer."

Adison pulled her new badge with ID from her waistband to give him a better view. Just then the door to the morgue swung open.

"Good day to you, Mark." A tall ebony-skinned woman with her hair pulled back showing off a nice facial profile, dressed in slacks and a pullover sweater came strolling out. Her ID was clipped to her shoulder. She had a thick folder of notes that she shifted to her other arm.

"Morning, Doc. Dr. Fishbach asked if we could stop by..."

"Yes. He said you would probably stop by when he's at a meeting so he asked me to brief you. Come on over to my office. I just picked up his notes for what we've done so far. It's been busy lately. Full moon."

The three turned away from the door and walked back up the ramp.

"Hey there! Dr. Sher-wood! I can't let you leave the premises with official papers!" Pearlie hollered out and moved to follow them.

"Mr. Pearlie..." the doctor enunciated as she turned back to the man who came to an abrupt stop before her. He took a few steps back to put more space between them. "I have the authority to walk in or out of that building with whatever I chose, as do all the morgue doctors." She turned around and continued back up the ramp with the two detectives following.

She looked back at Adison. "I suggest you don't use this entrance if you're alone. Try the longer route through the hospital. Better he be employed than unemployed."

They passed through an office reception area to a collection of offices. Dr. Sherwood pushed her office door open and gestured the two to precede her. The detectives found seats in front of her desk. The doctor opened the file and pulled out two sheets. She handed one to Scripts and another to Adison. "A severed right hand. There's markings of a tattoo design on the wrist. Also something circular burned in the palm. The two pictures you're looking at are different types of photos to pick up the designs on the skin."

"It's not quite like the other four we found." Mark moved to pull out his notepad.

"I'm Dr. Mandy Sherwood, by the way. Mandy to my friends."

"Detective Alex Adison. Alex."

"Sorry," Scripts apologized, looking up startled.

The two women nodded.

"So you know about the severed hands from a year ago?" she asked Adison.

Adison nodded. "A dozen documented Mexican workers in a mass grave, all with their right hand missing."

"That's right. This hand was in a freezer for a while before it was dumped," Mandy said. "It also differs from the others with a tattoo on the wrist and the circular mark burned in the palm."

"Retaliation? Usually if one gang attacks another, the other evens the score quickly and you get more bodies," Adison offered. "This is only one."

The two nodded.

"All that is the same is that it's the right hand cut off at the wrist. This one has burned into the palm what could be a coin, whereas the other four hands we recovered had a coin wrapped in the hand," Mandy said.

Adison noted in her pad that the right hand usually was the one used to strike or represented "doing." So were the coins meant to be something like the Greeks with their coin stuffed in an orifice of the corpse to pay his or her way across the river Styx? If so, the person was robbed before he reached his destination.

When they left Dr. Sherwood's office, Scripts took a different route back to Sunrise, giving Adison another perspective of the area they covered.

"So what's with the jamming equipment in Chief Harper's office?" she asked.

Scripts glanced at her, then moved his eyes back to the winding road. "We think a local gang is listening in on the conversations. We also scan the office regularly for bugs and do a visual. We don't find them like we used to."

"Do they know you're spying on them?"

"It's hard to say. It's not often the chief turns on the voice scrambler. We know when they're listening in, and we tell them what we want them to hear. That way, they aren't really sure if we know."

Scripts pulled into a camp turnout, and they bumped along a rough road until they reached a small parking area where three SUVs were parked. One was marked with the U.S. Park Ranger sticker.

"The ranger station had a call this morning. I want to see if they need any backup from us."

Gray Horse was surrounded by young girls and a few adults. He waved at them and excused himself from the group.

"Detective Alex Adison, Ranger Gray Horse," Scripts introduced. "Gray Horse, Alex Adison."

"How are you? I hear you're interested in the Mitchell cabin," Gray Horse remarked.

"Fine, thanks. Yes, the Mitchell cabin looks well cared for."

"It is. It's also a nice area for someone who likes solitude."

"Gray Horse knows this area like the back of his hand. If you get lost, just bang on a tree and he'll find you."

45

Gray Horse nodded and added, "Remove the concrete roads, people lose their way."

Adison chuckled, identifying herself as one of those people.

"Any cautionary bulletins we need to know about?" Scripts asked.

"We had a report that there was a man exposing himself. He could have been relieving himself, or he could have been getting off with so many young females in one place," Gray Horse answered. "I followed his trail to an abandoned camp. It looks like he left in a hurry."

Scripts grinned. "He must have realized you were on his trail."

Back in the car, Scripts described the type of calls they received from the U.S. Forestry and what SPD assisted in. At the office, Scripts went over cases with Adison, asking her opinion. She appreciated that because if the roles where reversed, she would be curious to find out about her partner who she suspected was more than what she claimed to be.

Upon reaching her apartment, Adison changed into an oversized T-shirt and shorts and rolled into her sleeping bag exhausted. Each evening, she reviewed her cover; however, this night, she fell asleep in the middle of rehashing a conversation she had in the women's shelter with...

Chapter Three

While Adison was doing early morning stretches the next day and imagining how nice it would be to have a real bed and coffee maker, she heard a knock on her back door. The only reason she was up this early was that she could only sleep for short periods on the hard floor.

Taking her semi-automatic with her, she peeked out the bathroom side window that had a mirror she placed to show her who was on her stairway without exposing her in front of a window. She sighed. Padding into the kitchen, she turned on the outside light, unlocked the door, and pulled it opened. With pursed lips, she studied the dog and her master. It was easy to figure out what Scripts had in mind.

"You want me to run this early?"

"Best time. You're up, so you're halfway ready." He sniffed the air, "And you don't have coffee. By the time we get back, all the places that serve early morning coffee will have it brewing." He grinned at her expression. "As your supervisor, I need to know about your physical limitations."

She waved them both in while eyeing his outfit, thinking how lucky she was to have had the foresight to buy new workout sweats and at least had two days to break in her running shoes.

While Angel wandered around the apartment sniffing it out, it took ten minutes for Adison to dress in her new sweats and shoes.

Once on the streets, it didn't take long for her to find that his long strides were going to kill her. He gave her a break when they reached the beach, but then the only break was that she walked to catch up with him as he sat waiting on a rock. He was tossing a ball for the still energetic Angel to chase down.

After she caught her breath, she began, "If you run me ragged before we start work, I'll be slumped in my chair for the rest of the shift...and no telling how I'm going to be walking the next day."

"Well, you do have tomorrow and Thursday off. Consider it boot camp. Which means there will be training in the gym downstairs and some night training, too." His grin at this hour was not contagious.

"Oh, gods," she moaned softly.

"Not a morning person?" he surmised. "How about a carrot? You don't have to wear the uniform you spent your first paycheck on during weekdays."

"Geez! You just comprised me with a bribe!" she said in mock horror.

She didn't have time to discuss it further because he was up and started an easy lope for him and Angel back toward town.

Adison found her way back to her apartment alone and grumbled through her shower. Seldom did she work directly with a partner, and this was one good reason why she should continue with that. This was probably his way of getting back at her for suspecting she was not who her job application made her out to be.

She pawed through the few clothes she had to choose from, ignoring the three uniforms hanging with her one business suit. She found a pair of loafers, brown slacks, one unwrinkled not too casual top and a sweater to wear over it.

She walked quickly to the PD station. There were a lot of early morning risers, mostly shop owners preparing for the day. Those who spotted her smiled and nodded as if they knew her well. She would have stopped at the Donut Shop for coffee and a bagel, but the line was long and she felt she was late. She forgot to put on a watch and had not spared a glance at her travel clock.

"Good morning, Lieutenant Sams."

"Morning, Alex. It's Harriet. Remember we're not big city formal here. Coffee's fresh and the doughnuts are still warm." She smiled too brightly for the early hour.

"Okay, Harriet. Coffee...and a sugar fix." Adison sprinted up the stairs and hung her coat on the rack near her desk and glanced around to see who else was present.

"Morning, Scripts."

He looked up at her and waved. He was sending sheets of paper to the printer they shared. She glanced at Gary Krieger from the night shift who was leaning back in a chair nearly asleep.

"Chief, we about ready for the meeting?" Harriet called as she walked into the office.

"Yes. Gather your mugs and doughnuts and lets start," he said.

Krieger, Harriet, Burns, Scripts, and Adison sat around a table in chairs that had a lumpy appearance as if they were castoffs from someone's office. Officer Brucker, whose new start time was ten, was absent.

"Eric, the mayor asked if you can stop by and look at his computer. He thinks he has another virus. Harriet, do you have anything to remind us of?"

"Yep. The town meeting for this Friday is at five pm...we all need to be there. The mayor will be reading gripes and compliments about our handling of calls."

"And I don't want to hear any noise from any of you when Mrs. Edna gets her list out," the chief warned, then nodded to Harriet to continue.

"We need donations in the kitty to buy more coffee and to keep the doughnut supply coming. If you don't give...I'll bring in veggies and..."

Boos followed and Harriet grinned. "I see I got your full support."

"Gary, anything you need to update us on?"

"Nope. Quiet as a church mouse."

"Mark, have you planned your day out?" the chief continued.

"Yep. Something to add?"

"Fit in a visit to the retirement community. Mr. Grady wants to speak with the detective working on his case."

"Well, that won't be me, Chief. That's one of the cases I've reassigned to my partner here. I thought a fresh look at the case may help." He nudged the papers he brought with him over to her.

Adison caught the muffled laughs in the room. "The case of the missing underwear," she remembered aloud.

"It's good to see you keeping up with your cases, Detective," the chief said. "We're facing a three-day holiday, so don't forget to remind your loved ones you'll be on call and wearing your uniforms. Alex, on your two days off, get a lot of rest. You'll need it. You'll be on call for the second shifts except your days off, and Mark will be doing the late shift except on his days off. We'll test that schedule out and see how that works.

"Okay, troops, start practicing those smiles for this weekend. Get your uniforms freshly pressed and shoes shined. Everyone wears a uniform for the tourists so they can find us easily in a crowd," he explained to Adison. "I'm sure you've already discovered that on your weekend shift. Everyone, have a great day."

As the group rose from their chairs, Scripts leaned over and dramatically whispered. "Don't forget to take a pen and notebook. Mr. Grady expects you to take notes. You don't want him to complain to Mrs. Edna that the detective assigned to his case was unprepared and inattentive."

"Now, Mr. Grady, you said the last time you saw your shorts was when you put them in the washer at one a.m.?"

"That's what I said!" He tapped his cane tip on the floor, nodding and moving his mouth as if he were playing with his false teeth. Adison noticed the end of his cane was leaving marks on the linoleum floor.

"And you didn't see anyone in the laundry room because you didn't wear your glasses."

"That's what I said."

By the look of his glasses, she doubted he would be able to distinguish much without them, and by his loud voice, he wouldn't hear anything short of a boom.

7. Christie

Adison took a deep breath as she figured how she was going to word the next suggestion. Her eyes caught sight of a small Chinese woman who pushed a finger against her lips. Adison thought about it.

There was Mrs. Edna's list to consider. If the old man did take offense and he mentioned her to Mrs. Edna, keeper of the list, and her name appeared at the next town meeting...that wouldn't be good. This was her first official case. What could possibly be going on for about a year with this case of missing underwear? What had Harriet said? She had only half listened to Harriet's sketchy but amusing tale of a year of men's undershorts going missing at the retirement home.

"Do you do your laundry on a schedule, like the same time, same day, Mr. Grady?" she continued.

"Time? What's time when you're retired?" He raised his skinny wrists and turned them around for her to see that he didn't wear a timepiece. He resumed tapping the cane on the floor waiting for another question.

"But you remembered this particular time. Why, sir?"

"The Mystery Readers Group got together and determined the time. Mrs. Kingsmen said she heard me close my door two times around one a.m." He leaned forward. "She's always complaining I'm closing my door too loudly. Can't take her too seriously 'cause she's hard of hearing."

"So, uh," she looked at her notes to think what else to ask, "why did you call for a detective to visit, Mr. Grady, when all this information had already been taken by Officer..."

"Gary," he said. "Mrs. Kingsman was wandering around in that see-through nightgown, getting the lad nervous. She's gonna give someone a heart attack looking like that. And at her age!"

"Mr. Grady, about your underwear disappearing...have you thought about setting a trap for this thief?"

"Eh?" His head came up and his eyes widened.

"Well, you said you have a group of mystery fans that get together...maybe y'all can think up something to catch this thief in the act."

The cane rapped a few times as the old man appeared to be somewhere else.

"What if it's one of us?" he demanded.

"Go by elimination. Who would wear men's shorts? Who does laundry when you do yours? You might consider when you purchase your next pair, buy something no one else here would buy or write your name on the tab. Then you can stake out the laundry room to see who is washing your shorts. With enough of you...you can rotate shifts."

The old man appeared to be thinking about the suggestions. He was moving his mouth and twitching his eyebrows. Adison wondered if it was from medication or just him.

"I never saw a label on my shorts, so there's nowhere to write. Now for getting shorts nobody wants...what are you suggesting? That I get pink hearts or something on them?"

"Uh," Adison gulped back her giggle. "That's....good, Mr. Grady. You're getting the idea." Her mind came up with something to change the direction of the conversation. "How many residents in this...apartment complex?"

"Don't know."

"How many people in your mystery group?"

"Enough for four tables of bridge. We play bridge to keep our minds sharp for our detective skills."

Adison asked if he had anything more to bring up, then left him to his cronies who wanted to know how it went with the new blood. Adison went in search of the Chinese woman. She spotted her getting a class ready for exercise. Before Adison could exit unseen, the woman gestured to her to come in.

"Hi, I'm Mai Oberman. I hear you're the new detective."

"Hello, Alex Adison. Yes."

"Would you like to join us for Tai Chi? We do some Chi Gung before practice."

"It'll keep you healthy," one of the residents piped up as she noisily shucked her shoes into the corner and shuffled onto the floor.

"Edna swears by it!" another added in an equally loud voice, "but it's more than that!" the quivery voice continued. "Gotta do some walking. Get in some golf!"

"There aren't any golf courses around here, Able, and there isn't going to be anytime soon. So drop the hints," another said. The old man turned to her and added, "He's been pestering the city council to put in a golf course to draw in more business. He's a retired real estate agent. Still thinks like one."

"Come on, Detective. Surely, you don't think you're going to look any more ridiculous than us," another old woman taunted.

"I haven't done Tai Chi for a long time, but I'll give it a try."

If she was going to get background on this underwear thief, she was going to have to bond with the group.

Adison shucked her shoes and socks, laid her coat over a chair, and joined the group. Her holstered gun was shifted so it was snug against the small of her back. She then not so gracefully moved along with the others into slow-moving poses that were centered on breath and balance. She was tired by the time they finished the Chi Gung exercises, just warm-ups, she was told. By the end of the class, she was grateful she was surrounded by people familiar with the routine and moved slow enough for her to follow. She had forgotten a lot.

"What is nice about Tai Chi is that you learn by observing, much like we do in our ordinary lives about most things," Mai told her as the two walked through the parking lot.

Adison read the door to a van marked "Clinic" that Mai was climbing into. Words circled the name indicating it was a holistic clinic. "I like how you explain the purpose of each Chi Gung exercise. Have they been doing it long?"

Mai smiled. "No. A month now. They've been doing the Tai Chi longer. They had another teacher who was let go due to budget cuts. He taught just Tai Chi. I do it for nothing, so I'm within their budget. I teach Tai Chi every other day at the hall, next door to the women's shelter, if you wish to continue, or you can join your new friends every day at this time. The one at the center is thirty dollars a month and more intense. It lasts about two and a half hours."

"I don't think Chief Harper would think it too professional for me to take more than an hour off for personal relaxation during work hours, so I would probably continue with the practice at the hall. It's nice to get back into it."

Mai smiled. "I don't think Eugene is worried too much about how you go about gathering information on a year-old case that has the town amused and the men whose underwear goes missing, befuddled. Besides, the way Mark and Eugene work, they never are off duty, and I'm sure, Detective, your life will be similar."

"What makes you think I'm gathering information?"

Instead of answering, Mai smiled and drove off.

Friday was just a warm-up to Saturday and Sunday of the Labor Day weekend. As tired as Adison felt, she attended the infamous Friday night town meeting and found it was not so bad. Maybe because she was new. Danny Brucker was not getting good marks, though there were some grumpy men who put in a word for him. It was his militia buddies. Adison found the meeting unusual and surprised that the children were obligated to participate. By their expressions, they would have preferred not to.

For Saturday and Sunday, Harper, Scripts, and Eric put in an appearance during the afternoon hours when the twins and Adison took a lunch break so there were always more than two visible officers available. Adison noticed Danny was not required to put in the extra time.

The stores that were open were busy during the three days, and there were no available parking spaces in front of any of the stores. A lot of illegal parking in red marked zones or yellow loading zones was occurring, bringing in revenue as tickets fluttered under windshield wipers. Saturday mid-morning was when the moving van arrived with Adison's furniture and whatever else her handler felt was necessary to complete her cover. Harriet and the twins waved her off to take care of moving in.

"Just park it in the alley," she told the driver.

The back of the van door slid opened and Adison hopped in to see what was in the back.

"I can get this." She nearly dropped the medium-sized box that turned out to be heavy.

"Computer stuff," John laughed. "Here, this is kitchen stuff...the lightweight kind."

She delivered the box marked kitchen in the front room and began to unpack until she found a coffee maker. "I found it!" It was promptly plugged in, and coffee poured into the filter.

"You guys hungry?"

"Yes!" they said in unison.

"While the coffee's getting ready, I'll get us some sandwiches. I know a place that makes them really good."

For the guys, she purchased the largest size they had, and for herself, half that, expecting to save some for later.

Running back up the stairs, she found the two SID techs engrossed in the setting up of her PC.

"Figures you two would do the techie stuff first," she teased.

"What do you have there?" Eric asked.

"Meatball sandwich. Two big ones."

They ate in silence. Once the edge of her hunger was appeased, Adison settled in front of another box marked kitchen and investigated its contents. It seemed there were more than enough boxes marked kitchen.

"Oh eech! Pink and yellow flowers on cups and plates? Does she think I'm giving tea parties at a church function?"

John chuckled and left for another load of belongings.

Adison looked up at the sound of grunting and John shuffling backward into the room. The angle was wrong when they first tried to get the frame in, so they lifted it up at one end and took tiny steps to maneuver it into the front room. Adison was nearly dancing with joy. Her bed!

They then went back downstairs for the pad while Adison hummed to herself and rearranged the bed so it was against the wall but in the center of the room. That way, if she should be sitting up at night, she could see right out the window.

The men moved over to the futon couch frame and dropped the brand new, five-inch thick cotton stuffed pad on top.

"Oh, yes," she warbled.

John laughed. "Not into the sleeping bag thing, huh?"

"The appeal disappears after a week on a hard floor."

While she sipped her coffee and dug through the boxes, the men laughed over the knickknacks she presented to them before rewrapping them.

"Come on, John. Let's get to the more fun stuff. Time to wire this place for sight and sound." Eric nudged John who was peering out the window.

Adison returned to the two remaining boxes marked clothes. "Now this is where Alice is good," she muttered.

Keeping with her character, not much was packed. There was one silk pantsuit, winter vests, four skirts, a dozen blouses with warm shirts, and T-shirts. No shoes. With the camping equipment and gear she had recently purchased, she was quickly filling up her small closet.

Adison's beeper went off as she was storing her T-shirts in the built-in bureau.

"Your new phone's already connected. You can go ahead and use it," Eric informed her. The secure phone had its own countermeasure circuitry hidden inside to prevent bugging or tapping attempts, and Eric wanted to test it. He waited with his own bugging equipment to see if he could tap into her conversation.

Before she could pick up the handset, it rang. Adison put it on speaker. "Hello?"

There was heavy breathing, then panting, followed by the sounds of someone getting off.

Adison snorted in disgust, "Get a life!" then hung up.

"Your first call is from a public pay phone," Eric read off the caller ID.

"Looks like you got someone interested in asking you out already," John teased.

"Not how I wanted to initiate my phone." She picked up the phone and called into the office. The recorded message stated a tourist reported that her purse was stolen. The woman was waiting inside Toys for Adults.

"If you have a pencil sharpener camera, I want one," she hinted. "No one thinks of the pencil sharpener being more than a sharpener. I better pick up some pencils to make it look right," she said.

"We'll leave a list of what and where we set up the stuff on your PC," John said.

"Perfect. Have a fun day, guys." She hurried down the stairwell. Before pulling open the front door, she brushed off her uniform pants, adjusted her gun belt, made sure her shirttails were not hanging out, and did a quick toe shoe shine using her trousers.

"I hope I'm not leaving a black smudge at the back of my pants."

Martin McBride, the owner of the shop was ringing up a sale, engrossed in conversation so he only could give her a wrist flick toward a group of women.

"Hi, I'm Detective Adison. I heard one of you had your purse stolen."

"Hello. I'm Angie Wells. Actually, I found it. Nothing stolen. I called back, but the line was busy so we thought we would wait until you arrived."

The speaker wore expensive clothes, all the way down to the dark brown leather shoes. Angie's smile was nice and the attraction the woman felt for her was just at the surface to be recognized as a polite inquiry if she was interested. She was. However, the chief had said no flirting or picking up on tourists…while on duty. And as a detective, she was on duty 24/7.

By the time she left the group, Adison was counting the days until she could take a trip to San Francisco. The bar one of the women mentioned was Girls Night Out.

When she returned to her apartment late that night, Adison spent time getting settled in her new residence. Eric and John had left a cleaned and secured apartment for her.

Pleased with what she saw, she went to an important item in her new place—the PC. She powered it up, and while it booted, she unfolded the futon bed frame and fell onto it for a few moments, her arms splayed out in bliss.

"Wonderful," she moaned. Sighing regrettably, she rolled off the cushion before she fell asleep and went into the kitchen to boil water for tea. While she waited, she opened a box of crackers. With tea and crackers she settled in front of her PC, intent on finding out just what her team left behind to make her apartment secure.

Pinhole cameras gave her views all around her apartment, down the alley, and under the stairs in the back.

"Nice," she hummed. She clicked on the icon to bring the stairs into better view. Satisfied, she reviewed the interior cameras and monitors, then checked her software of spyware, shadowware, and counterware for anyone who thought it would be nice to come unbidden into her PC. SID had their fingers in her system, but it was embedded with enough alarms and whistles to fool anyone who was smart enough to get this far.

Adison was awakened Sunday at four a.m. by another heavy breathing phone call. Since she was too irritated to go back to bed, she sat in the comfort of her reading chair, sipping coffee and mentally organizing her SID duties and SPD duties. Until she was further embedded in Sunrise life, her energies would be devoted to establishing her character.

"Character?" Adison muttered startled. "Gods, but that's funny. Who is Alexandra Kay Adison anyway? I didn't even know her as a child." She snorted and took another sip of coffee. "As an adult, I've put on more faces than a multiple personality can handle. The last time I was Adison, the assignment didn't have a good ending." She sighed and thoughtfully plodded on. *So who is* this *Adison going to be? According to Agent Sinclair, when you create a character for a long haul, don't create one that is too different from who you really are. What if I don't really know who I am?*

By the time Scripts's tapping on the back door sounded, she was dressed and had completed her warm-up stretches. Angel naturally was excited by the new smells in her apartment and promptly sniffed around as did her master, though not in the same obvious manner.

"Nice setup...I noticed your PC is old stuff. Officer Burns can help you put some pizzazz into that and save you a lot of money."

"Okay, I'll look into it, though, it was mostly for my writing job. Is it common to get obscene phone calls in this town?"

"Who reported it to you?" By her expression, he gathered it was her who received one. "They have your phone number already? That's interesting."

She nodded. "Started yesterday about twenty minutes after I plugged my land phone in, then again early this morning."

"The calls started about a month ago. We think its teenagers. Panting?"

"Yes."

"As of yet, we haven't been able to get a recording of the voice."

"I'll see if I can oblige you."

She wondered how much Scripts saw as he looked around the room. She handed a cookie to Angel as they prepared to leave. She never had a dog and had no idea what to do with one, but on her foot patrol, she had visited a pet shop. In a conversation with the clerk, who was cute and flirting with her, she wound up buying dog biscuits. She was glad Angel liked them. As they were leaving, Scripts studied the doorsill.

"A security alarm. You worried about something?"

Adison snorted in mock disbelief. "Let's just say, what goes on at the station, I don't want to bring any of it with me here."

As they began their run, she went over in her mind whether it was too heavy-handed to have so much security in her apartment. It didn't take her long to decide it was not.

There has to be one place I can feel safe. Besides, all he can see is the alarm in the door frame and that's supposed to be obvious.

The next weekend, Saturday morning, was Adison's first attendance at a monthly departmental meeting. Never in her entire law enforcement career was she aware of such meetings. As she pushed open the door, she could smell coffee, which led her to the break room where Scripts and Chief Harper were filling their mugs and picking out doughnuts.

"Morning, Alex," Chief Harper nodded.

Scripts smiled. "How's your calf muscle?"

"It'll survive. I'll carry a first aid kit from now on."

"You take her over some rough terrain?" the chief asked as they headed to the meeting room.

"Nope. All flat land. Agility is not her strong point...we'll work on that next week."

Adison glowered at the back of Scripts's head. "I would have been fine if that rabbit hadn't decided to double back to avoid Angel."

"Rabbit?" Harriet asked, stirring her coffee, already settled at the table with Burns.

Scripts started to laugh, hastily setting his mug on the table to keep from spilling it. Harriet and Burns looked toward Scripts for explanation.

Adison groaned to herself. She adjusted her gun belt to fit in the chair and sat down to her doughnuts and coffee.

"We were about twenty minutes into the run when Angel takes off after something. I called her back, then there's this rabbit hopping between Angel and us. It wisely decides not to go toward Angel, so it bounces past me, and when I turned around, there goes my partner running the other way with the rabbit chasing her."

The group hooted.

"I was trying to get out of the way. That's a big dog. With her hot on the trail of that rabbit, she would easily run me over."

That only caused them to laugh harder.

"Okay..." The chief took a deep breath, chuckled some more, then opened a folder in front of him. "Let's start with previous evidence the coroner has on severed hands and work our way to the more recent, bringing Alex up to date...and refreshing our memories."

The pictures that were spread on the table were from the coroner's office. The shots were of different hands, then the most recent, with dates at the bottom of each picture. For the next hour, they went over old photographs of the slain Salvadorians who were identified as Mexican field workers and how it could tie in with the recent hand. Then another set of pictures were spread out on the table.

"Who's this?" Adison pointed to one picture of a person she tailed for SID, wondering if they had more information on him.

"We don't have a name. Meets once a month with a member of *our* local gang," Scripts explained.

"And him?" She held up a photo of another man she didn't recognize, but he met on occasion with her White Knight targets.

"Officer Mike Learner. He was knifed in a bar outside of San Francisco some weeks ago. He's a lieutenant in the gang we're investigating," Scripts informed her.

So that's Mike Learner. "When did you get the idea that something was worth investigating?"

"When we found Judge Parker's chambers bugged. It was during closed doors discussions for charging a local character for abetting the kidnapping of an FBI protected witness," Chief Harper explained.

"It led us to check our own office, and we found we were bugged, too," Scripts added. "From there, we've been slowly making connections and trying to figure out what's going on."

"That would give me a healthy dose of paranoia," Adison said. She continued through the folder, recognizing some and memorizing those she didn't. "This guy…" She held up one photo. "I saw him at the airport in San Francisco," she told Chief Harper. It was the White Knight messenger she had been tailing and that led her to Sunrise.

"How long ago?" Scripts asked interested.

"A month. He stuck out because he was so big and his briefcase small. He reminded me of someone on steroids." She slid the picture back into the file and pulled out another. "Ranger Mayhew and Officer Brucker?" *An unlikely pair.*

"That's from two days ago. They were at a sleaze bar in Bales," Scripts said. "They're not the type to be conversational buddies, even at a drinking fest."

"You tailing Officer Brucker for a reason?" she asked curiously. She wondered if Chief Harper would reveal too many departmental secrets so soon, thus creating more suspicion with Scripts.

"He does odd jobs for the local gang. We believe he has ties with another gang that does business with our local group. The two groups are involved in kidnapping and transportation of stolen goods, we just haven't been able to catch them with anything…yet."

And by these pictures, it's not because you haven't tried. Adison continued going through the folder. Maybe this was why Mel loaned her out to Harper. Through her own tailing, she knew the two groups on the whole were meticulous about covering their tracks so the photos from the file had to have been taken from a powerful camera. She was relived she was not in any of them.

Chapter Four

S unday, Adison was looking through the crowd of people at Mollie's hoping to spot at least one seat available at the bar. Mollie's was her favorite eating place due in large part to the atmosphere. She could not explain what it was, just that it felt right. The coffee shop was divided into three sections—the main dining area where families gathered; the patio area; and the center area that had one wall with bookshelves and plenty of books where you could curl up and read, sip your favorite beverage, and munch on baked goods or share a cozy conversation surrounded by friends.

"Alex, come and join us," a voice from the din offered. Adison was going to automatically say no when she remembered her role in Sunrise was to blend in, be warm, and friendly. Her eyes sought out who it was addressing her when Genie from the shelter stood and beckoned to her. Genie resettled next to Claire on the bench seat.

"If you don't mind me intruding," Adison said.

A waitress appeared at her elbow. "Can I get you something, Alex?"

"Number four on your menu and..."

"Vanilla nut coffee, two creams, two syrups, two butters...will that be all for you?" she asked smugly.

"Add an orange juice," she added, just to be unpredictable. However, coffee, orange juice, and crème were immediately placed before her.

When the waitress left, Adison let out a puff of air. "How does she do that?"

"You're predictable. Whenever you order number four, you ask for the same," Claire said. "Even we know that."

Adison looked at them annoyed. She didn't know what their likes and dislikes were; however, she would if they were her targets. Then all the details of their life would be important. "Well, next time I'll ask for three syrups or three butters." She really had to be more careful in all levels of her cover. Predictability was not good.

"You sure don't like being figured out, do ya?" Claire teased. "Why do you want her to work so hard for her tip?"

The first question took Adison off guard. Under the pretext of sipping her coffee, she thought about it. Being predictable was deadly, but this was not something vital or even serious. In fact, most people were predictable because repeating things gave comfort. But this was not a major point. In the seconds it took to take two sips, she determined the best way to handle this observation. To cover for her lapse, she started a story that occurred to her.

"I heard of this guy who always ordered the same thing because someone anticipating what he wanted gave him a sense of importance..." Adison grinned over her cup of coffee.

"Certainly, that's not your failing," Claire mocked with a grin.

"Eating the same thing every day is boring," Genie commented.

"He went to a dozen different restaurants. At El Piqué, he always had salmon with rice pilaf, white wine, no dessert. At Leonard's, it was steak and lobster, red wine, and ice cream; Cordon Bleu was chef's salad, white wine, chocolate mousse, and so on. His control was never going to the same place on the same day the following week. Lunches, much the same habit...but breakfasts—now, that was his downfall. Every day...same place, same time, same meal."

"Downfall?" both women asked.

Adison nodded.

"Was he a mob boss or something?"

"Just a guy that hated to cook, clean, and be alone."

"Your father," Genie guessed.

Adison blinked at that, then smiled. "Nope."

"A relative of yours?" Claire asked.

"No," Adison laughed.

"If one of us guesses it, what will you give?" Genie asked.

"What are you willing to sacrifice if you don't win?" Adison countered.

The two women glanced at each other, then at Adison, grinning as if they had a prize.

"Here's the wager, we lose, you get three lunches per week, dessert included, for a month," Genie offered.

Adison's eyes opened wide. "If you're cooking, I'll take that bet."

Claire smirked.

"What happens if I lose?" Adison asked suspicious.

"Now that's not a sacrifice on our part," Claire huffed, looking offended. "A month of you disturbing our peaceful kitchen with all that noise of purring and humming when you bite into one of Genie's cakes...sounding like a woman in the throes of passion."

Adison nearly choked on her laughter. "Hey! There isn't one person in that weekly class SPD gives at your place who doesn't make noises over Genie's snacks. So what's my loss, should I lose this wager?"

"It won't embarrass the bejebees out of you," Genie assured her, but the snicker and smug look on their faces left Adison unsettled.

"I like to know just what it is I'm giving away," Adison insisted.

The discussion was halted when their meals arrived. For the next thirty minutes, they ate and made small talk.

"Well, are you going to take it?" Claire asked after they had their dishes cleared and coffees refreshed.

"All right. You have my curiosity piqued. But you have only two guesses."

"All right."

Genie looked at Claire. "You go first, hon."

"Is it a fictional character?" Claire asked with a grin.

"Yes," Adison sighed, resigned to her losing the wager.

"Albert Hindson in *Crimes Against the Innocents,* by H. Clark. The movie star fell in love with the waitress at the diner who was twenty years his senior," Claire rattled off quickly. Genie excused herself and went to pull a book from one of the shelves. She came back and dropped said book on the table.

"You knew," Adison said.

"Of course. I prefer to make sure bets. Paybacks are sweet," Claire said.

"And she does love her sweets," Genie assured the crestfallen detective.

"I've been suckered," Adison moaned.

"Doing anything Monday night?"

"No," she admitted, wanting to get her loss paid off as quickly as possible.

"Come on over for dinner. At five," Genie smiled.

"Why?"

"So we can collect on our bet. We need one more person for canasta after dinner. You don't have to know how to play."

"I hate card games," she whined.

"Good. The loser has to suffer a little bit. That's what makes winning worthwhile," Claire chuckled. "We have to go. The counseling staff should be finishing up with the residents about now."

The two women slid out of the booth and left.

Adison shook her head, grinning at the exchange, finished her coffee, and followed in their wake. She was halfway to the cash register when she realized she left her bill. Turning back, she was stopped by a waitress. Connie.

"Genie paid. She said she didn't want you to feel too bad about losing to Claire. You know, you shouldn't bet with her," Connie confided. "She's got this twitchy thing. You know what I mean?"

Adison looked startled. If someone was referring to her late aunties, it would mean they were clairvoyant. That didn't bode well. Adison needed to rethink her strategy in Sunrise if she were dealing with psychics.

Every town had its odd psychic community as it did its nuts and obsessive habits. It was her job for SID to find these things out and assess whether it had anything to do with SID's interest in that community. She allowed herself some leeway in criticism in her forgetfulness because this was only her second job that required over a six-month stay. But after this reminder, she was going to root out all the oddities this community of gossips had. It helped that Sunrise residents loved to talk.

To Adison's amazement, though she was terrible at card games, she had fun on Monday night and accepted an invitation to come back the next week. Mondays were game nights, Tuesdays were for Mai's class in self-defense, Wednesdays were for baking, Thursdays were for discussing books, and Fridays were movie nights. The shelter had other activities, but those were what stood out in Adison's memory.

She never heard of a women's shelter being run like a social club, though it was members only with a cop thrown in for good measure. It also filled in her evening time since she dared not do any skulking about until she understood the rhythm of the town. Between soaking up the gossip in one local coffee shop and listening to the shelter's residents banter, she began to get a picture of the town and its residents' peculiar hobbies and pastimes.

.

Chapter Five

After two months of learning the internal workings of the SPD, adapting to Scripts's morning workouts, going snipe hunting with Sam, experiencing the quirks of Sunrise's citizenry, and assuring herself she was not being followed or watched by any villainous nosers, Adison was ready to begin her covert duties.

Adison rapped her knuckles on the chief's office door. By the grumbling all day, she gathered he was working with the office budget. When he thought he had it, Harriet was given it to review and shot it down for some deleted necessity.

"Come in," Harper barked. On seeing who it was, he let his face relax into a grin. "Has Harriet gone?"

"Yes, said she had too much fun for the day and was going to stop at the salon," Adison teased.

"Every two months, she has me run an audit on the department, so by the end of the year, I don't have nightmares. Remember, when you ask for help, be ready to do the unpleasant—change."

"I'll keep that in mind." She gave Harper a nod, which had him pulling out his jammer and Adison keeping the door open to see if anyone came into the office.

"I'll be busy Wednesday night," she told him.

He nodded his understanding.

She walked to his wall map and pointed to a bar in Bales.

He nodded again.

"Good night, Adison."

"Good night, Chief."

Adison's target for surveillance was a bar in Bales that she had identified as a meeting place for Jaded Amulet and White Knight visitors and was confirmed by Chief Harper as the militia's favorite hangout. If fights didn't break out in the parking lot on a busy night, it was unusual.

Wednesday was chosen because Jaded Amulet met with their customers then, a normally slow night for bars. Running into Detective Scripts was not a worry, Harper assured her, since he was on call and would be sticking close to Sunrise.

7. Christie

One street over from the bar and separated by a vacant lot was a two-story parking structure that marked the beginning of the newer business section of town. On the second level, with a field scope attached to her camera, she would have a good view of the entrance and parking lot of the bar through the metal lattice work that encircled the structure. Besides keeping out taggers and homeless, the lattice prevented anyone from seeing her should someone glance that way; however, on her first visit, she discovered that the night guard did periodic rounds through the structure. For that reason, she left a remote-controlled camera that gave her a panoramic view of the bar area.

Dressed in genderless clothes that were unclean and smelled like it, Adison moved in the gait of a person who was tired and wary of his or her surroundings. At the base of the parking structure was a vacant lot that had a chain-link fence closing it off to vagrants, as well as drug dealers and other low life. She cautiously slid through the cut in the fence, nearly losing her precious bundle. Regripping the small bulk under her oversized jacket, she moved toward a spot close to the opening but away from the others. A dirtied hand with broken nails and reddened fingers from the cold clasped the bottle of beer, letting out a small noise of glee at getting a chance to settle and enjoy what was in the plastic bag. The other homeless caught the sounds of the plastic bag and quickly gathered around her.

"What do you have there?" a gruff voice demanded, followed by a dozen pairs of hands pulling her away from what she was clutching.

"Nothing. Get your filthy thieving hands off me," a muffled voice gurgled. She kicked out and head butted, but her adversaries found the bag of partially eaten fries, a hamburger, and half a quart-sized bottle of beer.

"Hey," she yipped as she was pushed aside when her bag was fought over. Peace was returned when one of them decided everyone there but her could have a sip from the bottle. She lay on her side, panting and waiting for the men to move back to their places, hoping some of them would also eat the fries. There were plenty. After an hour, she looked around her, pleased the muscle relaxant had done its job. Righting herself, she faced the bar, watching the customers come and go.

From the films of the place, she knew the bartender left a bottle or two outside after he closed up to award the homeless for not pestering his customers. After the bartender locked up, the group in the lot descended on what was left behind, including going through the trash for leftover food, then retreated to the lot to find a space to squat and enjoy the treasures.

Adison noted the patrons paid little attention to the homeless and viewed them as nothing more than a nuisance. Her eyes focused on two cars she recognized as out of state; but her angle prevented her from seeing the license plates clearly. Unconcerned, she knew the camera on the building would get that view.

By two thirty a.m. when the bartender left, there was one car still parked in the lot, and she was sure there was more than one person inside the building.

Adison lifted herself stiffly from the ground and, along with two others who managed to come out of their stupor, trudged to the bar parking lot for the booze and leftover food.

While one man searched the trash for food, the other looked in the usual place for the alcohol. Adison limped toward the back door, flopping down with a partial burger. Her listening device picked up voices from inside. Someone was yelling.

"...John, and it's not up for discussion!" a woman yelled.

"Mari, it..."

"Shut up and do it!" the voice ordered.

Adison could hear someone angrily heading to the door she was sitting in front of. Restraining her impulse to jump out of the way, she forced herself to remain sitting. If she should suddenly get up, it wouldn't fit her cover. The locks being pulled back were her signal to get up, and clutching her sandwich, she fell against the trash bin. The man grabbed her by the coat and shook her, dislodging the sandwich.

"Hey," she objected, and moved to grab the meat and bread that scattered on the ground. She could feel she was being watched as she gathered up her meal and shook out the dirt. The man shoved her to the ground and stepped on her hands and food. He kicked her a few times before getting into his truck and driving off.

Adison moved slowly to get up, holding her hand to her chest and looking over the remains of the burger. Whoever had been at the backdoor slammed it shut but not before she heard another name.

"Listen, Margo," the voice started and was cut off with the closing of the door. Adison thought it wise to move off and did. She stumbled across the corner, not faking the limp where she was kicked, glancing to where the guard to the parking structure sat in his shack. He was dancing to music on his headset. She melted into the darkness.

Blocks away, she paused, listening to what could be footsteps, more than one person heading her way at a fast pace. She ducked behind a trash bin. Two women passed by, then stopped in front of her car, staring at it for a few moments. She could not hear what they were saying and didn't have her listening device handy. Instead she took pictures of them. They moved on. After a few moments, lights from a car came on farther up the block. As it approached the car, it slowed down. The sound of smashing glass reached her, then the car sped off with no squealing tires.

Now what was that about?

Adison squeezed off a few pictures of the Toyota truck. The light above the license was out. She pulled out her cell phone.

"I need a car replacement…Roger that," she murmured, then hung up. Harper and her had agreed that there were some things SID support would be needed for, and this was one of them. She argued with Harper that her backup team was discreet and had been with her for a long time. Expecting Sam or him to back her up was not practical. To her relief, he allowed her that point.

She drove the Volkswagen to a turnout where she met her contact, Agent Adam, and picked up another nondescript vehicle.

"Hey, this doesn't have any bad karma like the VW, does it?" she asked.

"This one was bought off a used car lot in Oregon."

"Where was the VW last?"

"Well," he drawled, "seems I recall when it was delivered, the gent said it was used for surveillance in Southern California on a branch of the Jaded Amulet."

She took a deep breath, then expelled it, "Jaded Amulet."

"Guess HQ was testing a theory bringing it up here. I hope it doesn't mark you or you'll soon be dancing over a hot plate."

"No kidding," she snorted.

On her drive home, she thought about the coincidence. She shook her head. *Dog gone, Mel! When you set me up, tell me.* She rubbed her forehead tiredly. "Well, he got what he wanted, if that's the case. We ID'd them," she murmured. "Another collection of potential members to the Jaded Amulet." That gave her a good feeling. She now had twenty-four members identified to SPD's six. Harper should be happy. These women, she didn't recognized from Sunrise.

Just before dawn Thursday on her second day off, Adison received a wakeup call from Linda Scripts. Scripts was down with the flu and Adison was to fill in for him. There was no way she was going to go running that morning if she didn't have to.

"At my time, when the body is strong and the will isn't weak," she muttered, falling back into bed with a sigh.

Two hours later, her watch alarm woke her; she was due to breakfast in fifteen minutes. No matter how late she stayed up the previous night, she made sure she was always up by nine. Sunrise coffee shops were buzzing with information by then.

Her morning consisted of breakfast at Mollie's, hearing all the latest gossip, which ranged from social issues to who is going to get cited if they didn't clean their septic tank, then walking the shops to "make nice and chatty" with the businesses. Those stores she knew Danny wouldn't do a patrol around since the owners were predominantly gay, lesbian, transvestites, and transsexuals. It was nicknamed rainbow row, though not all the stores were gay owned and operated. It was the most decorative of the streets and difficult to miss.

After she had walked off her breakfast, she returned to her apartment to do some paperwork. An advantage of working on her day off was not having to go into the station. Dialing into the SPD server on her PC and working on the paper side of her cases was her first priority. While waiting for the connection with the SPD server, Adison glanced around her apartment, giving herself a few moments to enjoy the coziness and the familiarity. It certainly was a nice life, until the midnight calls came in, she thought wryly. Taking a sip of her tea, she began her report on the shop thief. Finished with that, she turned to the photos from the previous night.

Darn. The pictures aren't very clear. John isn't a familiar face, even as a blur. Mari and Margo are new names and faces. I'll see if Harper recognizes them. They have to be important to the bar because the bartender let them close up.

Under each photo, she added date/time/location and attached it to her notes on the incident. SID had the technology to sharpen up the photos, but they would have to go through Harper first. If this was the only thing she did, the delay would be annoying, but her day job kept her busy enough.

When the photos are returned, I'll see if I can recognize either of the women. A Toyota truck. How common is that up here? I can eliminate two-thirds of the truck population in the surrounding towns. Harper may recognize it. Too bad they had the license masked.

Adison glanced at her clock.

Time for another spin around town, then dinner with Genie and Claire. Let's see, tonight is a discussion on...darn. Which book was I supposed to have read? Oh, here it is. I already read it. One book ahead of their reading list. How funny is that?

Speed reading was something she found to be an advantage in her line of work. Adison smiled wryly. Sunrise had strange customs. At this point, she didn't think about a tomorrow where a new assignment would take up her time and attention, and those she met on this job would be put away just like the clothes in a theatrical closet.

Friday morning, she was up at the usual time Scripts and Angel would come over, but Scripts was still too sick. Instead of running his strength and agility type of course, she started out at an easy jog with the intention of going for an hour before turning around. During this time, she could think without structure and let whatever case was bothersome work itself out. Like the incident with the VW bug. Shadows were turning into recognizable objects by the time she was out of Sunrise and running up the road toward the forest, farmland, and cliff homes.

Adison waved at the white pickup containing Marsha Haley and her family packed in and the pickup bed filled with supplies for their pet shop. She made a turn onto the old dirt road that wound around a knoll, taking her back to town, or so she guessed by the topographical map of the town she had purchased. However, the map didn't show the fence that ran along the property that had a "Do not trespass" sign posted every twenty-five yards with a picture of a shotgun.

Unconcerned, Adison doubled back along the same path, grateful it was sloped downward. A rustling in the bushes to her right caught her attention. She lost her footing over the uneven ground and skidded on her side, falling in a rut. Panting, she lay still, letting the blood and pounding heart calm so she could concentrate on the rustling. A pitiful whine came from the bush.

Pulling herself to her knees, she crawled to the heavy underbrush trying to see what was causing the shaking and whine.

"Hey, what's going on?" she asked softly. She pulled the brush back, nearly releasing it when she was stabbed by the rough branches. Tiny little eyes stared back at her. "Hey, little one."

Reaching in, she found the small dog held in place by a twisted collar that was caught on a thick branch. The dog whimpered again.

Adison reached under the dog's throat to unbuckle the collar. "You are lucky this is a buckle and not a choke chain. I would have had to hack this bush down with my bare hands," she mocked as she wiggled for a better angle to use one hand to undo the clasp. Her other hand was holding the branches away. She could feel a cramp beginning in her back from the awkward position.

The small dog started to wiggle out of the brush and into her face as she held the brush wide enough for the puppy to get loose. It tucked itself against her throat and curled up.

"How did you manage to get in there?" she asked.

"Probably chased by a bigger dog," a voice behind her answered.

Adison rolled on to her back and sat up startled. She looked up into the palest pair of eyes she had ever seen.

"I was driving along and couldn't help but wonder what a grown woman was doing in the dirt."

Adison cleared her throat. "Well, I heard this dog whine and stopped to see what it was."

"I thought you had tripped."

Adison burst into laugher. She was intrigued.

The tall women knelt to look at the dog. "Hello, puppy." She gently ran her hands over the dog, brushing her hand against Adison's skin. The woman lifted the skin as if pinching it, then let it drop. Obviously, she had done this before. "Dehydrated. Looks like she's been here for a while. Not a Sunrise dog."

Adison raised her eyebrows.

"Good morning. I'm Dr. Sandra Rogers. Local veterinarian."

"Ooh. Timely arrival." Adison extended her hand. "Good morning, I'm…"

"Detective Alex Adison. You're the newest Sunrise resident, therefore one of the most discussed these days."

"Oh." Adison noticed her hands were dirty, and wiping them on her sweaty and equally dirty T-shirt would still not have made them presentable to a very attractive Dr. Sandra Rogers. She would shake her hand another day, but the thought was dropped as her eyes spotted the wedding band.

"Don't worry. I'll leave off how I found you and just embellish the rescue," the observant doctor told her wryly. "Would you like a ride back to town?"

"Yes. If you don't mind. What are we going to do with the dog?"

"We?" she teased. "Well, you rescued her and delivered her to a vet. We'll post her picture on the lost and found column in a few newspapers and offer her up for adoption if no one claims her."

"Sounds like a good plan. If you need money up front, until you find the owners..."

"We have a rescue fund we could use donations for. This is a purebred puppy. A Basenji, to be exact. There's a breeder about an hour outside of Antioch. I'll contact her and see if she sold a pup recently. Would you like to pick her up?"

"Yes." Embarrassed at getting caught staring at the woman, Adison picked up the animal.

Dr. Rodgers dropped Adison off in front of her apartment, insisting she could handle the sleeping puppy for the next three minutes, the length of time it would take her to get to her clinic.

Adison shook her head at the images her mind was conjuring up about the woman. She ran up the stairs to take a shower.

"Adison," Chief Harper waved her in his office. "Close the door."

Adison balanced her coffee and bagel in one hand and closed the door quietly behind her, noticing who was in the office.

Harper's listening devices were pulled out along with a jamming device. "You have a report?"

Adison smoothly pulled out the encrypted CD she had burned her report on. She had thought it would be easy to pass her information to Harper, but it did bother her. She reminded herself she was on loan and needed to focus on the mission.

"Detective Scripts will be out for two weeks. Once he's over this flu, he'll be working in Bales with Judge Parker. We have a big case coming up."

Adison nodded.

"He wants to know if you have any problem with that puppy you found being adopted by Martin."

Adison looked startled at the question. "His son's friend. No. Why would he think I would be?"

"You've been over at the animal hospital every day."

"I did find it, so I'm partly responsible for it until it finds a good home."

"And probably also heard that Dr. Jane McLaughlin, Dr. Rodgers business partner and spouse, is taking a class in the city, learning to use laser surgery."

Adison's lips curled into a smile. "I learned that at breakfast. Seems a lot of people just wanted me to know that bit of information. However, the ring around her finger was a dead giveaway." She pointed at the disk, "New faces and names to add to your group."

"Like I need more," he grunted. "You still looking for a vehicle? Check with Burns. His brother works for the San Francisco Police Department. They just had a big drug bust and seized the assets of a man claiming to be a courier to a drug business. He had twelve brand new vehicles, some with only enough mileage to cover from the car lot to his garage. Just don't come back with a Humvee or BMW sports coupe. Oh, and don't forget to check Mark's files, too, will you?"

Adison snorted in disbelief. "He assigns me the cases he wants to hand over to me before the beginning of the day. Rain or shine, vacation or out of town, he checks his work queue. The guy is too perfect."

Adison tapped on Burns's computer room and let herself in. "Morning."

He looked up from a book he was reading, pushing up the thick glasses before grinning at her. "Boy, have we found the right SUV for you. How does a Discover II, loaded with everything money can buy sound?"

"Sounds beyond my budget, but tell me about it anyway."

"I'll give you the phone number. Don't bid everything in your piggy bank," he hinted. "They owe us."

"Okay."

It was a good deal, so on September 30, she became the proud owner of a nearly new Discovery II. It would have emptied her savings if two favors were not called in. One with SID and one between two PDs.

The first Friday of the month was militia night. Adison sat high up in a tall tree hidden within its leaves. Through long-distance night vision goggles, she was viewing a group of men practice hunting, using three of their buddies as targets. Officer Brucker was one of them. As obnoxious as he was, Adison readily admitted he was very good at these games.

Shifting, she moved her binoculars to the periphery of the games.

Gotcha! Only two. Blast. The tree's in the way. Well, they aren't together.

Boosting her depth vision, she tried again to study the two figures, losing one but quickly recognizing Scripts as the other. *I think Harper and I will have to come to an understanding here. Too much overkill in surveillance, and they'll know they're being watched.*

Wednesday, Adison followed Officer Mike Learner to a nearby airport. Her nondescript car was left in the small parking lot, close to the exit.

"This guy is not what I would call the sharpest knife in the drawer," she muttered. She would give him some slack that he was slow due to his injuries, but his sloppiness in looking for a tail was not commendable. *I thought this Jade Amulet group was slick.*

Nervously, she looked around her, alert for being set up. Maybe he was a decoy. Adison caught sight of someone hiding behind a pole, too intent on Learner handing an overnight case to someone else to spot her.

Now who is that character? She laid her newspaper down and picked up the last of her stale sandwich. The camera in her ring was angled to catch everyone in the airport lounge.

A copy of her photos and notes were burned to a CD and a copy emailed to Harper. Scanning her own email, she found a reply to her inquiry on the list of names she found in Amos Anders's warehouse. Since this was evidence she gathered before she was put under Chief Harper, she was surprised Mel had a notation to pass on the results.

Okay, Mike Learner, presently employed with the Sunrise PD as a patrol officer, spent five years in the army, discharged as permanent inactive. He had been charged with child endangerment, but the charges were dropped. His commandant's daughter? Sixteen!

If that happened on my watch, you would have been busted and served time with a record so you would have to register in every state you live in.

From the military, he bummed around for some years, got involved in the Jaded Amulet in the L.A. area, and eventually came here. He's risen in the ranks from soldier to lieutenant. He must have some value to be in that position. I personally can't see why. The guy's a slob.

Johnny Redfield, she moved on. *Went to a private school during his adolescent years. His father's money seemed to have gotten him out of a lot of trouble. Likes...liked rough sex. He was found dead in a ditch. Heart attack. All tied up and with whip marks on his body. He was out of town on a business meeting.*

I would think if someone is going to play like that, he would do it with someone he trusts. He died a couple of days ago. Let's see...that would be October 4 Heart attack. I wonder if Chief Harper can get a copy of the autopsy.

Next. Amos Anders is from New Orleans. Joined the Army to get away from home. Served his time and got out. Moved to California. Joined the Jaded Amulet seven years ago. Bought the warehouse and has been busy since trafficking in stolen goods. ATF and FBI have a file on him. So far, they've not been able to find evidence linking him to anything illegal. He knows how to stay clean or he has someone on the inside letting him know when he's going to get raided. Connections.

Bob Mayhew. U.S. Forestry Ranger. Following in his father's footsteps. Moved to California from Oregon. Does not have any gang ties...interesting. Is believed to have given false information to the FBI in a case involving a woman who disappeared about eight months ago. Nothing definite...just a notation in a field agent's notes...but his supervisor didn't seem to think it was important enough to follow up on. I'd like to know if that agent has been transferred. Okay. He's a family man, has two sons who go to school in Bales, divorced, but lives in the same house as his ex-wife, new husband, and his kids. That's an odd affair.

John Melville. White Knight. Messenger. No kidding. You are the fella who led me to some very nice pots at the end of the rainbow. You get gold stars from me. Bet you'd get fired in the real sense if they knew how helpful you've been to me, she chuckled.

He was initiated into the White Knights at eighteen. Should I ask what that entailed? Spent two years in the Army. Hmm. Just what was his specialty? Armaments. So he's their bomb maker.

She footnoted the document for some questions to discuss with Chief Harper.

Henry James. Truck driver. He's served time for moving stolen goods. Has a long record for brawls outside of bars. Has problems with alcohol and uppers. Bad mix. Doesn't mention what his route is.

Marvin Larimey also drives a truck. Doesn't work much but seems to have a lot of money. Not inherited. Has been charged with driving with stolen goods, but the charges were dropped. They couldn't prove he knew what he was carrying. Has a wife and a kid, but he left them five years back. She's looking for him.

Next. Gene Blackmond, an MD. Worked for an Alabama prison, got busted for selling drugs to the inmates. Probably got busted because he was charging too much. Whereabouts unknown since he was released after serving a few months of his time. He's the one with the skull and crossbones. I wonder if that's a symbol for MD. Why would they use that symbol? Must mean something else. Deceased maybe. Could also be because he's a drug addict.

George Mathews. Another member of the White Knights. Someone important. Attached to one of the next generation leadership hopefuls. Served in the Army. I'm sure SID has already noted this coincidence. Looks like quite a few have been going into the Army for training in things one doesn't get from civilian schools.

Mike Housten owns the topless bar and was a trucker before that. Has five kids and had been married three times. Present wife manages the bar with him. I guess she wants to keep an eye on him. Another trucker.

Thomas Meadows. Been in and out of prison for petty crimes since he was a kid. Very tough guy. Profile says he's not one to play with. He'll more than likely cut your throat than argue with you. And he's only been jailed for petty crimes?

Jinks Wilde. Nothing.

Al Brentwith and his family run a Web site that sells survival gear, legal and illegal weapons on the side. Nice family. Fourth cousin to our favorite gang, the White Knights, and we all know it's family only.

Bill Prost, bought a liquor store in Sunrise. He's moved around the U.S. without having any real job until four years ago. Became an official member of the Jaded Amulet about three years ago. Kind of old to be recruited. Wonder what talents he brings to the club.

BJ Headers is an unknown.

Sam Henry Adams is the manager of a lab at Bales Hospital and the local lab. He has a wife and one kid on the way. He works part time because he has a girlfriend in Sunrise, who's also pregnant. I don't think lab techs make that much money. I'll have to check up on the girlfriend and wife and see what they do.

Okay, next. Carl Gates is a warden in Alabama. Deceased. That's it?

Richard Mack is the chief guard at the same prison. Deceased. What's up with that? Not much more information.

Sighing, Adison made another notation of questions she would send to Chief Harper.

Ed Carson last worked in Vegas as a lab tech. Took a vacation and didn't return. Divorced and skipped out on child support payments. Has a detective looking for him.

So, what have all these men in common besides being on someone's list?

Adison tiredly stretched, then sent off a note to Chief Harper. Unless it had direct effect on her assignment, she knew getting updated information on the list was nil from SID, but working with Chief Harper may be different. Mel liked his agents focused on their assignment and not getting sidetracked with issues not pertaining to their job. Of course, she was not playing a waitress or auto parts dealer here. She was a cop who may need the information to prevent her demise. Adison laughed to herself. *Don't get melodramatic on me, Adison.*

She began to prepare her PC for shut down: backing up to her zip, removing the drive, erasing evidence of it.

That night, her dreams were busy reviewing everyone and chasing one of many dark-clad figures only too late realizing she was chasing herself and the real crook got away. However, there was a clue left behind. She just could not remember where she put it.

Thursday night, Adison was back at the bar, taking pictures of the same clientele, with Learner and Brucker amongst them. They came with a group of men that Adison identified as members of the militia. This was more like it. Personalities and names she could now add to pictures.

Chapter Six

Alex." The chief gestured to her to meet him in his office. His tone indicated something was up.

Adison hung up her coat and shifted her gun belt. On a Monday morning, just about anything could happen. Since she worked Sunday, she knew it wasn't from her shift, and Scripts was due back from Bales late in the afternoon, so that meant something came up that morning that called for a detective.

"Chief," she nodded as she stepped into his office.

Chief Harper handed her a piece of paper. "This was just called in. It's in the forest. This will be an overnighter, and it looks to be raining later this afternoon or tonight. Gray Horse will meet you at the turnoff near Piles Trail with all the equipment you'll need for camping. Ever ride a mule?"

"No."

"It's going to be a two-hour ride in. It gets real cold up there," he warned. "Garrett's always in his store this early and will open up for you if you need anything. Call him before you head over."

"Okay. I'll get on it."

After picking up a crime scene investigation kit from Burns, Adison happily headed for Murphy's Sports Outfitter for rain gear. She loved visiting that place.

Adison could not miss Gray Horse. He was surrounded by people with cameras who appeared to be fascinated with the three mules.

Gray Horse raised his hand that held a radio, acknowledging her arrival.

"Good morning, Gray Horse. Lovely day for camping," she said as she held her hand out in greeting.

"Good morning, Alex. It's going to be a good day for travel. Genie said she fixed our dinner for tonight—and breakfast," he grinned.

"I have to get used to this town and its telegraph service," Adison told him ruefully. She began to remove her equipment from the back of the police vehicle, handing it to Gray Horse to secure on the back of the pack mule. He fastened her backpack that had a camera and lenses onto her saddle. She made sure they were accessible should she suddenly need them.

"This is Angie," he gave a pat on the mule's dark brown neck, thick with her winter coat. "She's a veteran of these trails and old enough to not be spooked by squirrels or bad footing."

"Angie," she acknowledged, tickling the nose of the beast.

Adison pulled out her skullcap, remembering how chilly it got this high in the forest. Her boots were too big to fit through the stirrups, so Gray Horse gave her a leg up and showed her where she could slip her feet, just above the stirrups in the leather.

"Who found the body?"

"A hiker."

"Anyone from the coroner's office going to meet us?"

"Mandy. They're already on site. Her team is composed of three trainees they're hoping can be transitioned into the CSI department that the next budget is financing. They won't be staying for dinner unless you mention it's Genie's stew."

"Not a word from me," she promised. The thermos didn't look like it had enough for that many people, and Genie's stew was always good for second helpings.

Adison spent the first hour admiring the trail, nearly falling asleep from the rocking motion. She ended up getting off her ride periodically and walking to stay alert.

"Hold up." Gray Horse held up his hand. Angie stopped immediately behind the pack mule. "Got a camera with a telephoto lens?"

Adison pulled out the camera from her pack, removed the close-up lens, and put on another with practiced speed. "What is it?"

"Point it in that direction. Tell me what you see."

"A line...from a parachute." Adison clicked pictures of what she was seeing.

"How about you stay here with the mules and I'll go see what we have?" Gray Horse slid off his ride, nicknamed Chief because he always wanted to lead.

Adison quickly exchanged the distance lens for a close-up and handed it to him. She pulled out a set of binoculars and studied the area while he made his way through the brush. Her best view was on top of Angie, so she balanced in the saddle with her leg wrapped around the pommel, looking for anything out of place.

Gray Horse returned after a while.

"Find anything?"

"Equipment for setting up a camp. Looks like either someone lost it or the intended recipients never made it back."

"Why would someone parachute equipment down? Why not pack it in?"

Gray Horse smiled. "You're the detective. I'm just the guide."

"Right. Gotta remember the pecking order," she said wryly. "So what do you suggest we do with the equipment?"

"Leave it for now. We'll pick it up on our way back." He held up an item.

Adison stared at the .223-caliber bullet, then took it from him to look closer. "Just what kind of camping gear is it?"

"Whatever it is, it's illegal. There's no hunting up here. Three rifles. Dakota Magnums with lots of ammunition like that. The tent equipment was used to protect it from the drop. It also has canteens, two packs for hiking, food and cooking gear that were packed on top...well-used gear." He handed her camera back to her, and she repacked it. "I took lots of pictures. I hope they come out."

He waited until she had her camera put away before he handed her a second item he retrieved—a detonator.

"Jesus H. Christ!" she yelled. "You could have gotten hurt!"

"Nope. I know better. The parachute line was a bungee cord. It's used when someone is jumping from a plane with equipment he doesn't want to be separated from. He pushes the package out of the plane and jumps behind it. The bungee cord is attached to his harness. When almost to his target, he cuts the cord to the package and drops himself nearby."

"Then why this? It has compound on it, so I know it was armed."

"It fizzled. The wire came loose from the C-4 plastique...maybe due to the drop."

Adison looked back at where the package was. "How long has it been there?"

"I don't know exactly but not over a month."

"That means whoever dropped it off was not able to return, and the tamper button was left to clean up the evidence." She looked around her.

"There's too much animal life around for anyone to be watching it," Gray Horse assured her.

Adison put both items in plastic evidence bags, labeled them, tucked them safely in the saddle bag, and climbed back up on Angie. To make up for the detour, Gray Horse had the mules pick up their pace. It was bumpy for the rest of the ride.

The sound of mules braying shortly ahead let Adison know the crime scene was near. That was a relief. Mules came into view. Their backs empty of gear. Dismounting, Adison was pleased she was not feeling as stiff as she might have.

Adison spotted Mandy up in a tree, dangling nose to nose with a corpse. On the ground were three interns collecting and tagging. One of the interns looked up at their approach, laid aside a light with a magnifying glass and came over to them.

"Can I get a look?" Adison asked.

He clicked on a radio and called up to the dangling coroner.

"Come in, Doc."

"Go ahead."

"The detective wants to know if she can approach the site."

"Not unless you're finished up with the area. Hey, Alex! Great to see you again. How's your bottom?"

"Fine," she called up at the dangling coroner.

"Max, give them the scoop, then finish up. We want to be out of here by noon."

"Roger. Out." Max turned to Adison. "We found body parts, bones, and bits of clothing around the ground under the body." He gestured to the inside of the taped area. "From here, you can see dangling parachute lines," he pointed to another tree farther off. "Our corpse is not wearing a parachute, and Doc said to leave you something to look for, so we've only been working around here. Anything else?"

Adison shook her head and Max returned to his work. Adison noted that Gray Horse had disappeared. She turned around slowly to get a feeling for the place. Except for the soft mutterings of the three on the ground, an occasional bird call, and squirrel chatter, it was peaceful.

Adison turned to face Gray Horse who reappeared. "Find anything?"

"Yes. Near the parachute lines. You can carry the camera and I'll carry the crime case."

"What are we looking at?" she asked, noting that the entangled lines had been cut pretty high up in the tree and there were no remains of a chute.

"Spent bullet casings and some not used. Like the one I showed you."

"Pretty careless."

"Not if you're panicking and loading as fast as you were firing. Place your feet where I place mine and watch out for the branches, some have thorns."

The two made their way into the forest with Adison mirroring the moves of her guide. She stopped when he motioned.

"Here is where the panicked shooter was."

"How can you tell?" Adison laughed embarrassed. The fallen tree trunk was riddled with bullet holes.

Both dug for bullet casings, dropping them into bags Adison supplied.

A bit of cloth was dangling from a thorn nearby, which Adison collected.

Gray Horse squatted in one area and gestured her over. "Someone fell here. Caught his boot in the undergrowth."

Adison tweezed from the tip of a broken branch what could have been gouged leather from a boot. The person had to be moving fast to make that much of an impact.

For the next thirty minutes, they worked around the area, with Gray Horse finding things and Adison recording, taking samples, and labeling.

"We'll need Mandy to look over this place. She's done so many body retrievals up here she's getting almost as good as me."

"I doubt that."

Both looked up.

"That perch in the tree has a good view of this entire area," she explained. "We're going to lower the body, so if either of you want to get a look before we do, you might want to get over there. The kids don't want to spend the night here," she grinned, "and neither do I. So what do you want me to look at, Gray Horse?"

"Alex, why don't you skinny up the tree and do your detective thing? Mandy and I will look over this place. We'll use Mandy's camera."

Adison nodded, though not really wanting to dangle within reach of a corpse, but there was no reason for the ranger to inspect it.

With guidelines fastened to the harness around her, she moved slowly up the tree as awkward as it was. Finally, she leaned back against the trunk and eyed what was left of the body. Not much. She took pictures of the surrounding area, getting a good shot of where Mandy and Gray Horse were in relation to the corpse.

The deceased had a good view of the area around the tree, so no possibility of a surprise visit. It had to have been from sniper fire.

The angle of the body suggested it died from the puncture of the tree limb right into the chest or maybe the damage to the back of the skull did it. Adison looked farther up the tree, then searched the surrounding trees. She took more pictures, and then checked the camera's memory stick.

Back on the ground, the trainees began the process of bringing the corpse down. The head was the only part that was not held together in the camouflage jumpsuit, and it was collected separate when the body was lowered. The bones to the hands were probably what Mandy's crew found under the corpse.

Adison photographed the process until they secured it into a body bag. That done, she walked around to inspect the surrounding trees. She found a rifle partially buried, perhaps dropped. She lifted it and checked its chamber. It was empty. She returned it to its resting place, wanting Gray Horse to give his input. She moved around the tree, looking up through the branches. It looked easy to climb. Broken branches on the trunk were noted and photographed. She moved to the other trees, keeping an eye on the twitching ears of the mules to give her an anchor of where the crime scene was.

Adison shined her SureFire light on a tree trunk that looked like it had taken shots. Gently, she stuck the thin dowel into the hole and followed the line of shot, marked it on a pad, then did the same with the other bullet holes. Gray Horse's appearance reminded her that she wanted him to look at something before it got too dark. She tucked her notepad, pencil, and light in her pocket.

"We need to set up camp," he said.

"Okay. Do we have time to look at another place first?"

"Briefly. Tomorrow, we'll look at it closer."

Gray Horse squatted by the partially covered rifle. "Not like the others in the package. This is a sniper rifle. We used it in the Army." He lifted the weapon and checked the chamber and exterior, then moved around the tree, looking up and glancing to where the body was, with Adison pointing her light, so they both could see the trajectory. He nodded. "Good find."

They set up camp five minutes from the crime scene. Adison was sure the mules liked the idea of being away from the place. Their ears were still twitching but not as nervously as they had been, or so her imagination said.

"Well, at least it didn't start to rain like the chief thought it would."

"Tomorrow. Hopefully, we'll be headed back by then."

"I bought some rain gear at the Outfitter. Be nice to test it out."

The stove was boiling water and warming Adison's cold hands. Contents of one of the thermoses was dumped into a pot and heated. Gray Horse had French bread and hot tea along with the stew.

She rubbed her hands in anticipation as Gray Horse poured a generous portion of the stew into a bowl and handed it to her. It smelled stomach-rumbling good. Adison chewed contently on a chunk of lamb with one hand wrapped around the bowl for warmth. Though the air was near freezing cold, she relished the clean air that filled her lungs. All she needed to make it complete was a nice warm cabin with a roaring fire to return to instead of the hard ground and sleeping bag. She sighed, still content.

Adison crawled out of her sleeping bag into the cold morning. She flashed her light in the direction of Gray Horse's bag. Empty, and it was cold to her touch. She stretched her way out of the tent to find the spot Gray Horse designated as their waste dump.

By the time she had the water boiling for morning coffee, her hands were beginning to thaw. Instead of rummaging in Gray Horse's supplies, she went over to hers. She had her coffee in small packs so all she needed to do was pour hot water over it.

It was not the noise that caused her to look up, it was the sensation of being watched. A dark figure headed toward her. By the way he carried himself, she knew it was Gray Horse.

"Morning. How are the mules?"

"Good and hungry. Coffee. Hmm. You don't want to try mine?"

Adison tipped her head at him and tried to see what the smile in his voice indicated. "Sure. I didn't want to go into your stuff."

Adison returned to the inside of the tent to grab some gloves and roll up her bedding. By the sounds outside, Gray Horse was getting breakfast ready.

"I hope you don't mind if I do the cooking," he said when she returned.

She took her place on the handy log they had pulled over the previous night. She sniffed the air appreciatively. "Nope. I thought maybe you heard the rumor that nuking food was as far as my cooking talents went."

Gray Horse handed her a cup of steaming coffee. She added cold water to cool it down, desperate for a sip.

"Arggh!" Her eyes opened wide and she tried not to spit it back out. "What...grmmph...what did you make this with?"

"Nuts, grains...all natural stuff without the side effects of coffee."

"Wow! It will turn my peach fuzz into coarse hairs." She held up her hand. "However, a strong hot cup of...something to counter a cold morning in the wilderness is a good thing. How's the food?" She didn't think too much harm could be done to a breakfast of...she sniffed again. "Pancakes?"

"Yep. Syrup is right there. Butter pecan is in the mix. Genie's special."

"That's what was in the other thermos," she guessed. "If I knew my campouts were to be supplied with a cook and smart guide, I'd go on more," she smirked. "But then, a cabin would have to be part of it. This sleeping in a tent is for the more hearty."

Gray Horse nodded, flipping a pancake on a plate that he handed to Adison. She breathed in the scent of fresh pancakes that provided warmth in its smell.

Both ate quickly, not exchanging any more conversation. Camp was efficiently broken down and packed, with Adison showing she was not entirely without skills.

Light was just streaking the early morning sky when they returned to the crime scene.

"I was thinking that there had to be at least three people here for the shootout. The person in the tree, the person who was running, and the person who lived long enough to chase the second person and maybe kill him or her."

Gray Horse agreed. "The person in the tree may have been shot with the rifle you found. The angle is right. Mandy thinks the victim was wearing some kind of hard hat, most likely a motorcycle helmet, so most of the impact was absorbed by the helmet, like grazing the hat but with enough impact to stun the wearer."

"So if where the rifle was found was where the shooter was, he or she may have had their aim interfered with because it was a good clean shot to the person in the tree and should have gone right through whatever head covering the victim was wearing. Instead it grazed the head covering, knocking the person forward. And there's no evidence of a helmet yet.

"The area Mandy and I were studying around the tree trunk had what could have been fabric. She took samples. Probably won't show much due to the exposure and time, but we can make an assumption we can't prove. Mandy said she would send over the pics and her findings to your department as soon as she can."

"How nice and tidy if we can connect the cache of equipment to the body in the forest. It would make sense why no one returned for it," Adison said.

"FBI or ATF will be asking that, too."

"Yes," she agreed. *Parkland is federal territory. This is something they'll send agents over to collect evidence. Wonder if Chief Harper and Mel have influence to slow down their arrival. You can't have more than one gang operating in a territory. So which gang is this? If someone in the FBI is tipping off the White Knights or Jaded Amulet, evidence will disappear if either is involved, and Harper's team will be blamed. The bright side is, then we know one of those groups is connected to this drop. So just what was going on here?*

For the next two hours, Adison watched Gray Horse work the area, pointing out things she needed to note or take pictures of. By ten, they were ready to start their way back. They still had to pick up the abandoned gear along the trail.

"Hey, I felt a drop," Adison called to Gray Horse. Once said, the sky opened up and poured on the two riders and mules.

Adison kept her face down, her hands tucked in her coat pocket and hummed an off-key tune. Suddenly, they came to a halt.

Adison peered through the rain at a dark figure who walked toward her.

"It's through there," Gray Horse pointed.

Adison slid off the mule and stumbled to keep her balance on the slippery ground.

If it was a trail Gary Horse was following, Adison didn't see it. From behind a decaying log, he dragged a locker to where Adison could assist.

"Oh, boy," Adison grunted with the weight, but gamely carried her share of the load back to the mules. By the time they returned, the downpour lessened to a steady rain.

"I hope we get a chance to look this over before the Feds claim it," Adison said as she steadied the load while he secured it on the mule.

"I can delay my report until tomorrow, but no later. You can also take custody of it and deliver it over to the lab first chance you get."

"Sounds workable."

"Think it has something to do with Chief Harper's gang?" Gray Horse asked.

"Only one gang per neighborhood. Unless this is neutral space," she added. "I gather all the rangers will know about this."

He nodded.

When they reached the turnoff where the horse trailer and her vehicle were parked, Scripts was waiting in his truck.

"Hey, Detective. Do you like sitting out in bad weather?" Adison yelled above the noise of braying donkeys and rain pounding his rooftop.

"Go take a look at your patrol car," he hollered back, grabbing the lead rope of her mule.

Adison peered through the rain and went for a closer look, shining her SureFire at the tires. She drew her finger across the slice.

That took a big knife to make that slit.

Adison returned to Scripts's side as he latched the trailer hitch.

He looked over his shoulder at her. "I drove by on my way home yesterday to make sure you didn't drive your SUV. It's too vulnerable to vandals and car thieves."

"As if I wouldn't think of that," she sputtered, more from the rain in her face than disbelief that he would actually think she would put her pride and joy in jeopardy.

"What's this?" Scripts asked.

"Someone's camping and hunting gear," Gray Horse responded. "The kind of gear that's illegal to have up here. Detective Adison is taking custody of it for safe storage until the FBI or ATF collect it."

"I see," Scripts drawled. "Is it part of the crime scene?" he asked, glancing at Adison.

"Don't know. But it has promise," Adison told him.

"I'll drop it off with Mandy tomorrow," Scripts offered.

The gear was dumped into Scripts covered truck bed, and everyone moved into their respective vehicles, cranking up the heat.

"So what did you find?" Scripts asked, after he and Adison were settled in his warm cab and heading home.

"At the crime scene: a corpse, decomposed badly, lying face down on a limb too high for some predators to reach. Trauma to the occipital bone. The blow left a nice crack back there. Also trauma to the chest. It could have been as a result from the blow to the back of the head with the victim falling on the branch. The hands were all that were missing. Mandy doesn't think they were cut off but rather fell off from natural decomposition of tissue. The jumpsuit held most of the torso together. The coroner's team found bone fragments, plastic, and some other stuff beneath the body in the tree and will let us know if they belong to the corpse. A M14 was found within sniper view of the corpse, and we found evidence of a shootout.

"The load you have in your pickup bed Gray Horse spotted on our way to the site off the trail. It was attached to a bungee cord. Gray Horse found three Dakota Magnum rifles, .223 caliber, camping gear, and a tamper button with C-4. The detonator pulled loose so it was a fizzle."

Scripts whistled.

"I'm curious why the bungee cord wasn't spotted sooner," Adison said.

"We'll check out the pictures." He gave her a quick glance and raised his eyebrows in question. She nodded back that she did take pictures. "Off hand, it could be that the wind blew the cord into sight or it was hanging where people normally don't look. It's not a popular trail because it's rough going and it takes nearly a day to get to a space where a camp can be set up."

"So why would anyone go up there?"

"Survivalists were the last group five months ago. Drove Gray Horse nuts because they were starting campfires within the forest where they aren't safe to be. How did your new gear hold up?"

"The rain gear is tops. In this downpour, having dry pants and head is very important to me. As for the sleeping bag, I'm going to have to get one for polar environments. So what made you stop by, and don't give me that 'just making sure you didn't drive your SUV'?"

Scripts shrugged. "Just thought I would."

"Well, for whatever the reason, I'm glad you did. Thanks."

The next day was Wednesday, Adison's day off. It took a lot of focused determination to get up for her run with Scripts. She rewarded herself with breakfast at Mollies and headed up to the forest for her meeting with Sam and Chief Harper.

So, how does this fit in with WK or JA? It doesn't. No one returned to clean up the evidence. Definitely does not fit the MO of either. Does this mean there's another gang moving in? Or does it mean neither WK or JA know about it yet? Maybe I'm jumping to conclusions. It's a big forest and anybody can have his own private party.

She parked in a turnout and pulled out her backpack and added two water bottles to the side pockets. Ten minutes on the path, she heard a loose rock.

"Not real subtle," she muttered.

Sam dropped on the path next to her and grinned. "I just wanted to know how noisy I had to be before you heard me. Ten to one, ten being the best, you got a seven."

"You watched me from the boulder that was sitting at the curve of the road, so you can see the traffic from both directions. It has a great view about ten miles up and down the road. You then gave me a walking start five minutes up the trail and followed me along the tree line. The loose rock was just a confirmation that you were going to join me," she informed him with a smug smile.

"Humph. You're just guessing," he accused.

"Maybe. So where's our meeting going to be this time?"

"Around," he answered shortly. "What are you carrying in your pack?"

"A laptop. I have pictures to show."

"Then I'll have to get some popcorn," Sam answered. He pointed to a tree off the trail. "Wait there. You got binoculars?"

Adison nodded. She climbed the slope, trying not to leave too much of her passage visible. From her pack, she pulled out her binocs and studied the area. Five minutes later, Sam gestured for her to continue up the trail. He joined her at the fork where she waited.

There was the remains of a shack about ten yards off the path. Vines overlapped the worm-eaten wood, but Sam wasn't concerned about bugs and lifted a corner of a board that revealed a cellar cover.

While Adison clambered down, Sam checked the area again and followed her.

"Aren't you worried someone will see you in the daylight?" Adison asked.

"The whole place is peppered with surveillance equipment," Chief Harper said, "because of Sam's paranoia."

Sam snorted and went to unfold a table in the small cellar space.

"Who owns this property?" Adison asked, to keep up on who all was involved with her undercover operation.

"Me," Sam said. "It's where I had my first cabin. Had a past acquaintance pay me a visit while I was out. He left his calling card."

Adison unpacked the laptop and powered it up. She pulled out three CDs.

"You're not paranoid. You're damn dangerous, Sam," Adison said.

"So what have we here?" Harper asked.

"Pictures of Officer Mike paying off someone, and I got a good shot of someone following him. No one I recognized."

For the next forty minutes, they studied the pictures of Mike, his contact, and his tail, discussing various points.

"I recognize the guy he's delivering to," Harper said. "He's a clerk at the court, but not assigned to any of the judges. He's in the pool where a judge's office will request assistance and the manager will pull a name from the pool. Usually, law students working on their degrees or clerks work the pool."

"We're assuming there was money or something unlawful going on," Adison pointed out. "So if you want this to be evidence, it won't work."

Harper snorted in disgust. "If you noticed in the files you looked at, that's all we've got. So what else?"

"Well, I was hoping one of you had ideas about the body in the forest." She pushed in the next CD to show pictures she and Gray Horse took of the site.

"You know of any sharpshooters with contracts for this area?" Harper asked Sam.

"I know of five who Interpol lost track of. With Homeland Security hamstrung with lack of leadership, I don't think the FBI who normally tracks domestic shooters will be able to give an accurate accounting. Especially with their own who have gone rogue. They aren't about to admit to that."

Adison nodded in understanding. "Any that you have to worry about?"

Sam looked at her surprised.

"Not that I'm not concerned about your welfare, but I don't want to get caught in crossfire." Sam didn't volunteer anything further. Adison turned to Harper. "How many gangs does a small town average anyway?"

"If there's more than one in Sunrise, it's not showing in our crime rate. We have better stats than our neighbors. Sunrise residents are a lot more active in reporting anything unusual, which is to say they are more aware of what goes on in their neighborhoods."

"Chief, did you get a chance to study the list of names I sent you?" Adison asked.

"I got a glance. Gave a copy of the list to Sam. You said you found the list, but you failed to mention where."

Adison hesitated, then grinned. "It was before our time."

"Does it put you in a sticky situation to give me a hint?"

Adison glanced at Sam, then back at Harper. "I found it in Amos Anders's warehouse. It was under a stack of pallets."

"Amos, huh?" Harper was quiet for a few moments. "I'm going to introduce your list in our next monthly meeting. I want Burns to have a go at it. He's amazing when it comes to ferreting out information from Internet sources."

"Okay by me. I thought the information was too sketchy." Adison looked at Sam.

"I can't say I have anything to add to the list. You figure out what it's a list of besides men's names?"

Adison shook her head. "Since I sent the original to Mel, I was hoping he would have identified fingerprints by now or had information on the hairs I picked from the folds in the paper."

Harper indicated that he had not received any information. "I'll give him a call."

Friday, Adison was back at the usual mundane work, wondering if Mandy would get upset with her if she called for information on the corpse and crate Scripts dropped off. When the Feds step in, everything would be seized and there would be a lot of unanswered questions bothering her.

"Hi, Mandy, this is Adison..." she laughed at Mandy calling out to someone in the background. "I guess I don't have to ask because Detective Scripts is there...I won't bother you...Sure, you too."

Adison sighed after hanging up. Now she would have to wait until Monday unless Mark sent what Mandy found in an email to Harper and her.

Saturday, dressed in her neatly creased uniform, Adison headed out for her ritual breakfast at Mollie's. There she joined Jane and Sandra, the two veterinarians, rather than wait for a table. They were midway through their meal when Adison's pager vibrated against her stomach. She muttered in exasperation as she pulled it out to see who was paging her.

"Gotta go?" Jane asked as she speared her pancake heavy with butter and syrup.

"No. It can wait," Adison said, as she tucked the pager back in her belt pouch.

"Girlfriend?" Sandra asked, knowing like everyone else in Sunrise that she didn't date anyone in town.

"No. It's from the retirement home. They're all too old...err, I mean too mature, for me."

"Ah. The disappearing underwear thief! She's struck again," Jane whispered dramatically.

"You didn't hear that from me," Adison told them, not wanting to leak any departmental information.

"Mum's the word. Right, Jane?"

"Oh, yes. I hear the boys are training Lady Holmes to find things. Maybe you can let her nose around and look for the missing items."

"The dog's still a puppy. Besides, that's bloodhound work." Suddenly, she gurgled, realizing what she just said. "Oh, please don't mention using bloodhounds to find missing underwear. I would never live that down."

"You're passing up a good idea."

Adison laughed with the two women. It occurred to her in a brief flash that this assignment had some really fun moments.

"I hear you have the dog field trials in March outside of Bales," Adison said, drawing her coffee toward her when her emptied plate was removed.

"Yep. A working class dog show. The land between the farms and Bales is ideal. There's a lake that's clean enough for the dogs to jump in, and the best part is there's enough space for parking."

"We already have fourteen veterinarians signed up to be there."

Chapter Seven

It was the first Friday of the month, the militia's monthly gathering. The location and type of activity was posted on its Web site for anyone who wanted to join though the boys kept it men only. It was bring your own toys or you couldn't play. That night, they met above the cliffs on a sandy plane, an ideal place for setting a trap. According to the Jaded Amulet's MO, they threw periodic parties just to close a trap around any unwanted guests. Adison had watched a few unfortunate teenagers get rounded up. And giving credit where credit was due, the militia boys didn't rough them up, merely scared the bejeebees out of them. The militia fronted well for the gang and its meetings with customers.

Adison was using the ROV, or remote observation vehicle. The beach was perfect to provide the plane with a takeoff where the breeze would help lift it. Her ROV was one of the many test planes NGA, National Geospatial-Intelligence Agency, was using for domestic surveillance.

She set up her new telescope to use stargazing as her cover. Glancing longingly at the hot thermos of coffee, she sighed.

Okay, my pretty spy, get on up there. Mel, you have more connections than a Washington madam for all the toys I get to play with. I feel so special. Ooh. Nice baby, up.

Grinning at the ease of its use, Adison sent the silent craft over the militia's meeting site. Forty hot spots were busy with field maneuvers. Gently, she moved the joy stick to begin a bank around the area to set its inspection parameters. Once they were keyed in and locked, Adison set it on autopilot and watched the plane began its inspection.

A flash of light through the tinted SUV windows had her looking up. A glow of lights slowly passed by. She watched the brake lights come on, then the truck swung around.

I remember that truck. It's got those silly balls hanging from the tow bar. Cruising me?

It passed the parking lot entrance again. She slid out of the SUV and walked to the edge of the parking lot, waiting for the next drive-by. As the big white truck came abreast of her, she surprised the group by shining her SureFire light at the passenger, then the driver.

"Is there a reason why you're cruising here?"

"Ah, sorry, Detective. We didn't know it was you. We thought it was someone else with a chick or something," Alan Watts apologized. His father was one of the members of the militia group on the cliffs. Adison guessed that their initiation into the group was to run checks on people nearby to make sure they were not being spied on. But this was below the cliffs. She was sure they were just curious what she was up to. By the expressions on the faces of four boys in the vehicle, they were all trying not to snicker at Alan's reply.

"I'm the only one in town with a dark green Land Rover. You thinking you're going to see some action, like peeping Toms? Not likely. I scared all the neckers and backseaters away."

"Hey, Detective, we aren't like that," Johnnie Hoehl's deep voice objected. Johnnie's father was also on the militia and one of the leaders in setting up the monthly mock battles.

She shined her light on the other two boys. Both from Brisbane. Brisbane Panthers was the high school logo on their all-star jacket sleeves.

"Good to know. Good night." Adison just stared at them with her hands on her hips and waited for them to leave. The nose of her telescope was protruding out the back of the SUV, so she knew they were aware what she was pretending to be doing. The truck sped off, sending some sand and bits of rock onto her clothes.

"Right," Adison muttered and returned to her vehicle.

By her screen, the militia was spread out with a smaller group of four stationary. She knew there were thirty regular militia boys, plus Brucker and Learner. As far away as she was and the angle of her view, she wouldn't be able to recognize anyone immediately. Her attention refocused on the four on the outer parameter. They were moving, widening their circle. Another person alone to the left of them didn't move. It wasn't Scripts since he was out of town.

A car was moving along the road adjacent to the games. Maybe it was the boys.

The small plane moved out of the area, and Adison began to bank the craft, making a wide turn over the ocean. A handful of cars were parked along the cliffs with hot spots in them. She interpreted the occupants as couples, probably on a date. They were far enough away from the militia not to be overrun by their games. However, one figure from farther up the road was moving toward the militia's position, using the road, then started to cut over, now fully off the main road along the cliff.

Adison looked up when her movement detector beeped. She moved to the telescope and peered out at the stars, her attention on what was closer to her.

I wish I had a nice big dog right now. I wonder if I borrowed Angel if she would tell her master what we were up to.

Her left hand reflexively wrapped around her Taser gun. She moved her eye from the telescope and turned the red light, pretending to write something. Out of the corner of her eye, she watched her ROV locate her as it passed overhead and a body ten yards away.

Whoever was out there was content to just sit and watch her. She pulled out her binoculars and peered through the tinted side windows to study the figure. The lights from a car on the road swept by, missing the figure huddled behind the brush. Worried, she checked on the plane.

Well, let's keep this all up and up. She pulled out her police radio. "Krieger, come in."

"Gary here. What's up, Alex?"

"I'm out at the beach, the East First entrance with my telescope, and I have someone hiding out in the bushes watching me. Do you think you can swing by and help me check the area out?"

"Sure. I'm on the other side of town. It will be about ten minutes. That okay?"

"Yes. Thanks, Gary. Out."

"Don't mention it. Out."

Adison glanced back at the figure behind the bushes. Still there. She checked the plane. It was back over the militia area. The moving hot spots were encircling one other hot spot. It must be their prey. Four figures were moving toward a fifth spot. A meeting? No, the fifth suddenly turned away and moved back toward the road. The four were quickly moving after it. She looked up to check the figure in the bushes and found him or her gone. She scanned around the SUV first and moved her binoculars farther out. Nothing.

She glanced back at the screen. The ROV was circling over the ocean and coming back toward her. She covered the screen with a blanket and grabbed her Taser. Cautiously, she slid out of the back of the SUV, shining the red light around her. A movement caused her to move her light and Taser to the left just as a hand came down on her arm.

Through the training sessions with Scripts, where he had her repeat this very attack over and over so even in her dreams she reacted without thought, she moved with the blow and spread her arms out and brought them back to hit the figure between the head with the base of the Taser and light. It was enough to surprise him, but even as she was moving to hit him, he was moving away, so she only got a grazing hit to both sides of his head.

The figure didn't give up. Using his head as a battering ram, he aimed toward her midriff. Adison grabbed his body and twisted, dropping to one knee. Her hand grabbed for clothing and got more than she intended. His quick action to protect himself had Adison twisted around. A back kick knocked her to her knees. As she moved, she was able to grab a coat flap, pulling her assailant off his feet. She punched him in the gut and could tell she had the upper hand now.

Suddenly, a searchlight came on, blinding her. A push sent her off balance into the side of the SUV. Krieger's dog was already barking with excitement. When Adison picked herself up off the ground, locating her SureFire and Taser, she was alone. Krieger came running toward her with Gus on the end of a leash straining to run after something only he could see.

"Hold up, Gus. Sit. What happened?"

"I had a scuffle with an assailant." Adison took a deep breath to give her adrenaline-hyped body time to slow down. "I'm all right. Good dog, Gus. You earned a biscuit." She brushed her legs off and glanced around in the darkness. Whoever it was, was gone. She was grateful Gary didn't let Gus loose to chase after the assailant. Then both would hang around.

"I'll take a look around the beach farther up. That's usually where the transients like to sleep. If he's there, Gus will nose him out. Are you all right here?"

"Yes, I'm fine. Don't bother with the check along the beach. I wouldn't be able to pick out whoever it was in a lineup. It's too dark to have gotten a look."

After Krieger left, Adison located her plane and had to land it before she had any more visitors. It came coasting to a stop a yard from her. She grabbed it up and slid it in the back of her SUV and tossed a cover over it. Now more than ever, she could not risk taking it back to her apartment. The shack she kept her surveillance vehicle in would have to do. As she drove, she kept looking behind her to be sure she was not being tailed. Just to be sure, she stopped her SUV and used her binoculars to spy the black sky above her, hoping not to find a plane watching her.

She kept reminding herself that paranoia was healthy in her line of work.

After storing the plane and her equipment, not satisfied with her nearly being caught, she drove up the coast to the parked lovers. She glanced at her watch. Over an hour had passed. She wondered if the lone figure had been caught.

It was pitch dark and her lights were not welcomed. Voices shouted unkindly at her arrival. By memory, she found a turnout, parked, then pulled out her night vision goggles. She was above the flat land with not much view of the militia area, but it was where the five figures were headed. She located one, then two more hot spots. She removed the goggles. They were too close to her position for her to be wearing them. She pulled out her binoculars and studied the area closest to her. She spotted a familiar figure, tired, limping along the gully. It was the chief.

She panned her binoculars and located only two of the players. They must be encircling him. She got back into the SUV, and without turning the lights on, she relied on her goggles to move her to an intercept point for the chief. Finding a place to pull over and appear to be legitimately interested in stargazing was not that easy to find. She picked a narrow shoulder, leaving little room between the road and her SUV. The chance of being struck was slim, she hoped.

A small neon cone was placed a few yards from her vehicle. She was sure she had passed the gully the chief was in but not exactly. Trusting in luck this time, she pulled out her bright white telescope and pointed it to the sky. She sat in a three-legged camel seat, which was easy to store and break out. She held the book on stars in one hand and with her flashlight verified the location of the stars above her. She found it. Staring through the lens, she wanted to be sure she was right.

Through years of practice, she was able to quiet her heart and concentrate on what she was doing. She let the person she was rescuing do his part and rustle up some of his own luck to find her. She heard the movement of sand and heavy breathing and felt her SUV shift through her elbow. She continued to look through her telescope, turned her red light on for directions in her book, and acted startled when lights suddenly flashed in her face, blinding her.

"You about scared the crap out of me! Get that light out of my eyes!" she yelled.

"Who are you and what are you doing here?" one of the figures demanded, not moving the bright light from her eyes.

"Henry, you know who I am. I'm the one who gave you the speeding ticket two days ago, and if you don't shut the lamp off, you're going to be spending some time in jail for harassment of an officer of the law."

There was an uncomfortable standoff. Adison didn't move out from behind her telescope, but her hand was wrapped around the butt of her off-duty pistol, a P7, under her coat, pointed in the direction of the light. They knew what her hand was wrapped around and they knew she knew.

"Kill that light," she said in a low voice.

The silence continued until they all could see car lights swinging down the winding road. If they were going to do something against her, they would have to do it now.

"Sorry, Detective. We thought you were part of the games," Joey leered.

"Yes, right, Joey," she responded. *You creep.* The group melted back into the darkness, and the car that was winding down the road passed her without slowing down. She could hear one of the voices in the dark imitating the panting she had been hearing on her phone.

"Remind me to point Scripts in their direction to finding the breather," she muttered as she waited for her eyes to adjust back to the darkness, then she repacked her telescope and headed home.

As she turned into the police parking lot, she glanced back at the chief who was lying on his side and munching one of her sandwiches.

"Chief, I wish you had told me you were going to be out there. I told you I was going to use the drone."

"If I didn't go out there and have something to report, Mark would be feeling bad that he wasn't here tonight, then he would be wondering why I let him take a few days off on this night of nights."

"Can I ask why you just don't make it official that I monitor them?"

"Mark is your supervisor. He thinks you need more work before he moves you to night sleuthing."

Adison could hear the smile in his voice.

"Right," she replied sarcastically. "Well, have a nice walk home. I would drop you off, but rumors would get around that we spent the night together."

"Humph," he grunted as he slid out of the SUV.

Adison put her backpack on, hoisted the telescope on her shoulder, and carried her camel seat back to her apartment. Just for grins, she set it up in front of the bay window and for a while, yawning now and again, scanned the skies for something interesting. She left it pointing at Venus.

The next day at first light, she needed to be back at the beach to see if there was anything to be found of her attacker. She was grateful Scripts and his family would be out of town, so no early morning running.

Back bent and slowly moving from one bush to another, Adison could smell old urine. She clipped a leaf that had captured some liquid and slipped it into a glass bottle and bagged it. She snipped another and bagged that, too. She moved to study the scuffed ground and broken branches but didn't find any fabric or dropped articles. She covered the entire area looking for a salvageable footprint and found none.

Whoever it was ran in pitch darkness...So someone is watching the watcher.

After dropping her evidence at the station, she met Claire and Genie at Mollie's. Following breakfast, Adison spent time in various shops, listening more than talking, and walking as far as the shops spread. It would bring her close to the retirement apartments, where she wanted to visit.

The old folks had a lot of information, and they were nonstop talkers who needed little prodding. They were not bound by the usual sleep cycle of the younger crowd and took golf carts out at night for the thrill of it. Even with fading eyes and ears, they did see a lot of after-hours business.

Who said small towns were boring?

Monday morning, Chief Harper was walking with a slight limp but said nothing about Friday night. "Alex, I'd like a moment of your time," Harper mentioned as the others moved out of the morning meeting.

"Sure."

"Mark and I read Gary's report about your attack Friday night. We also read your report and looked over your evidence collected. We don't get many transients in town, so I'm not inclined to believe Gary's assumptions. We also don't get criminal attacks at night either." He hesitated for a moment and asked, "Think you would have been able to disarm your attacker if Gary hadn't arrived?"

"I had him before Gary's light shined in my eyes. He didn't show any special skills."

"Male for sure?"

"Oh, yes. I got a handful of male while we wrestled. If he was a transient, the dark clothing and smell were not typical. I just hope that liquid in the leaf is urine from a person, so I didn't waste my time collecting. For someone to run away that fast in pitch dark and avoid tripping, he had to be wearing night vision goggles. Which makes it rather interesting because the person I was wrestling with wasn't wearing any and I only heard one person running."

"So either he had great natural night vision or two people were there with one person acting as decoy, except Gary's dog would have sensed the other person. It takes a week for the lab results to come back." The chief rubbed his chin. "I think I'll stop by today at Shayne Bell Labs and review their security and see who is handling the test."

"Who works there?"

"Mike King, Thomas Haynes, Linda Ames, Sherry Carroll, and..." he hesitated, "Sam Adams is the manager." The chief rolled his eyes.

"One of the names on the list."

"He goes by Mac and doesn't really interact with our department. His assistant, Linda, does most of the PR work and gets us results faster than the civilian population. By the way, Mark decided you're less dangerous if you were working those nights you go out. So from now on, you're on the rotation roster to monitor the militia. When he gets back, he'll brief you. I also spoke to Mel about the ROV. If we keep it quiet that we're using a NGA domestic surveillance drone, I'll be able to drop it on Mark that he has a new surveillance toy."

"Okay. I'll hand it over to you before Mark gets back. Tonight?"

"At the forest turnoff. Eight tonight. It's pitch dark by then."

Harriet Sams, Eric Burns, Mark Scripts, Chief Harper, and Adison had different methods on approaching stalled investigations, as well as views of what they were all seeing. Gender, culture, and age differences, to say nothing of experience, were used in their brainstorming sessions. It was something Adison didn't experience with SID, who handed down orders and information on a need-to-know basis. But it was a totally different working environment. With SID, she was a covert operator who was sent to gather information, turn it in, and move on to the next assignment. Adison viewed the Saturday meetings as ongoing classes and was able to put aside her dislike for that day because she was the only one wearing a uniform.

The scent of freshly brewed coffee greeted her as she pushed the office door open. Breathing deeply, she took the steps two at a time. The aroma was stronger in the foyer. The SPD door was open and the lights in the office were on. She could hear Burns whistling a tune from *Phantom of the Opera.*

"Morning, Burns. Do I smell my favorite flavored coffee?"

"Hey, Alex. Any flavored coffee would be your favorite," he teased. "You have an email marked urgent in your inbox."

"Urgent? I'll be right back."

A few minutes later, she was back to help Burns set up the meeting room. Her grin was difficult to hide.

"So, you got a date for your next round of days off?" he taunted.

"Better. The Miller cabin at the Crest that I was looking at buying—it's now a done deal. I own my own cabin. No phones, no pagers, and no neighbors who speak my language."

"Hey, that's great. That should make your SUV a lot happier. When you learn bear language, let me know how to say 'get out of my car.'"

They both laughed, remembering the family who kept their food in an unlocked car and the bear opened the door and feasted. Unfortunately, the door closed behind the bear, and until the park ranger arrived, the animal trashed the interior, trying to get back out.

"Good morning," Harper greeted. "How did your practice night out with Mark and Genie go?" he asked Adison.

"Basic," she waved her hand.

Scripts nodded, sipping his coffee. "She shows potential, Chief. She and Genie are going to become the next GI Janes."

"Not in this lifetime," Adison said. "This soldier keeps her hair and does not slosh around in mud. I don't care how chic some people think mud baths are."

The others laughed.

"We're starting with the body found in the forest," Chief Harper began. "It has been identified as Henrich Reiner, a German national. Worked as a sniper for hire internationally. Used disguises to escape detection."

On the overhead screen appeared a plain face with thin off-white hair. Other pictures of him in disguise appeared on the screen. If his picture was not circled in some of the photos, Adison wouldn't have recognized him.

"He didn't travel to a continent without having thirteen contract hits," Harper continued.

"Sounds like he had some strong convictions," Harriet drawled.

"Did the FBI give you this information?" Mark asked.

"Interpol. The FBI officially took over the case October 29. They removed all evidence we had at the coroner's. Mandy just returned from vacation and picked that information up on her voice mail from Fishbach last night." Harper looked over at Adison. She was wondering why he had not told her sooner.

"Why didn't he tell me when I was there two weeks ago?" Scripts asked irritated.

"That was my question to Mandy. She pointed out that Al is doing her work, and his regular secretary who would handle this is out on maternity leave. The reason why I brought up the sniper information is in case it has anything to do with our gang-related cases. Keep your eyes and ears open if you hear of any club members missing."

Harper waved a paper to get his staff's attention. "Let's get to our local group. We have a list of names I've been provided with from one of my inside contacts. It was found near one of the meeting places of our gang...Amos's warehouse. The list may or may not be connected to them, but it does have a few of their names on it, plus one we're all familiar with but not associated to them."

Soft whistles could be heard from some of the staff when they recognized who he was speaking of—Sam Adams.

"What does that say about sending lab tests to our local lab?" Harriet asked.

"Let's not jump to conclusions," Scripts cautioned. "We don't know what this list is about."

"Eric, I'd like you to start a background inquiry on all of them. All the way down to their DNA, if you can. Let's build a deeper file on them."

"John Melville...I remember checking a driver's license on him. I can't recall exactly why," Scripts said.

"Well, it'll come to you eventually," Harriet encouraged.

"Do you remember what he looks like?" Mark nodded. "Then get over to the artist and get a drawing made sometime today. Anyone else? Okay, next case, the attack on Alex while she was stargazing." The chief pulled out a disk and some papers from a laboratory test. "I have the DNA results back. Only one person from the samples on the leaf. Eric..." he handed him the disk, "this is what we received back from the lab. See what you can come up with. How are you coming with the program on crosschecking our clues from various cases?"

"Just about done."

"Can we trust the results?" Harriet asked doubtfully. "I think until we know just what this list is about, anything we send to the lab is going to be in question."

Chief Harper nodded. "I'm having a second run done. I agree with you, Harriet. But we're going to have to find a darn good reason why we don't send them any more tests without raising a red flag with the gang we're trying to appear slow on the uptake."

"Why not use two labs? Then when they do mess up, we have cause," Adison suggested. *This is getting to be too time-consuming. Maybe Harper can twist Mel's arm to give him a secure lab to send stuff to. That way, we'll be looking at the same results.*

"We only have two labs and he works in them both," Scripts said.

"How coincidental," three voices returned.

It was Thanksgiving Day and Adison spent her time wandering by stores that had the football game blaring and smells from apartments reminding her of Hallmark card versions of a happy family life. She switched days off with Scripts so he could be home with his family, doing his own celebrating.

Chapter Eight

Monday morning, the daily departmental meeting had been rescheduled for later in the morning since the chief had an early budget meeting with the mayor. Adison and Scripts went out to a store that was burglarized the night before to take pictures and a report from the angry owner. They drove back to the office in silence, wondering why someone would steal baby apparel.

Scripts held the door open for Adison, who was carrying one of the crime scene cases, when both heard boisterous men's voices in the workout room.

"What's going on?" Adison asked Harriet, who didn't look happy.

"Good morning, Harriet," Scripts greeted, his voice becoming solemn.

"Mark. We'll be combining our meeting with the patrol officers," she said tersely.

"Okay. Is the chief back?"

"In fifteen minutes. Just enough time to grab a fresh cup of coffee and a bagel," she suggested. She exchanged eye signals with Scripts, which neither explained to Adison. Scripts didn't give Adison a chance to see who was in the gym, instead he tugged her sleeve to follow him upstairs. She all but had to run to keep up with him.

Adison read the bulletins from the FBI and other law enforcement departments and sipped her coffee, She glanced up suddenly when someone noisily enter the room.

"Mike," Scripts greeted shortly. "This is Detective Adison, she was hired…"

"I heard," the tall blond forty-seven-year-old interrupted. He chose a chair nearest the door with Brucker taking a seat next to him. The two, ignoring everyone else, continued a loud conversation on Rose Bowl prospects in January. They were the two voices from the gym.

Adison studied the two men, interested in the nonverbal communication going on. This was a different Mike Learner than the one she had been tailing. His persona was of indifference to the point of rudeness. The only thing he seemed to care for was the expensive wristwatch she had not seen before. She wondered if it was an early Christmas present to himself. His arms and legs were crossed away from Danny and toward the door. His displeasure of being in the room caused Adison to go down a mental list of reasons. Claustrophobia was crossed off as not likely. This was his workplace for ten years.

Brucker's demeanor took a complete reversal. Where he had been blending in with the office background when Learner was gone, he now had a swagger and a lip curl that was directed at her, that is until Harriet entered the room. Harriet's usual bubbly personality was toned down. She merely looked at Leaner and Brucker, who pointedly ignored her. She took a seat next to Burns, wishing the group a good morning. Now Adison understood what was bothering Harriet and Scripts that morning.

Chief Harper walked into the room and both men became quiet.

"Good morning, everyone. As you can see, Officer Mike Learner is back on duty. Detective Adison, meet Officer Mike Learner. Officer Learner, Detective Adison." The chief held a sheet. "I want you all to fill out the form that looks like this on your PC for supplies. It's in your email basket. The expense committee wants to prepare for next year, and they need to know what supplies you've been using and what you haven't. Make sure your mileage, clothing upkeep, medical expenses, and whatever you put down under miscellaneous is precise. Remember you are not paid for anything miscellaneous unless you specify exactly what it is and have the receipt. I do hope you all have been keeping up with this stuff over the year. If not, we all lose. Mark, do you have the assignments ready? Go ahead."

"Danny, you're working the stores on Main Street up to Pine this morning until noon, then move to take the west side. Mike, you have desk duty for a month, which will be working the switchboard. Start at your usual time, ten…"

"Now wait just a minute here, Harper." Mike jumped from his seat. He suddenly sat back down when he caught the chief's glare. "I don't want to do some simpleton's job that minimum wage earners can do. I can drive a patrol car!"

"In case you hadn't noticed, gas is expensive and Sunrise isn't that big a town to warrant a patrol car for your entire duty. Your doctor ordered light work for a month or until he clears you for something more strenuous. That's all the light duty we have, unless Mark can think of something else." He glanced at Scripts.

"That's it."

"The alternative is I can release you without pay for a month, if you so desire," Harper offered.

"Well?" he prodded when Mike didn't respond.

"I'll stay on the job," he muttered.

"Mark, you have anything to add to his duties?"

"Same requirements as everyone else who sits on the switchboard. At the end of a month, if you can handle taking calls without making Mrs. Edna's list, put the calls in the right queues accompanied with a report with the pertinent details, and the department doctor clears you for heavier work, I'll move you to a few hours of light street duty," Scripts continued.

"You're giving me rookie work!" At that comment, he threw a dirty look toward Adison.

"Light duty is what your doctor ordered, Mike. If that's what you call rookie work, then you should be able to ace it. I expect you also to be courteous to your fellow officers." The chief returned to the others, "Mark and Alex, you have five investigations that I want status on. Sorry, Mark. Continue with your duty roster."

Mark nodded. "Alex, Claire wants one of us over to be introduced to a new resident," he continued. "I'm giving that to you. Harriet, you have the foot beat on the north side since Mike will be handling the phones."

"Before you hit the beat, Harriet" the chief said, "can you go over to the council chambers and show Janey how to work that new program she has on her computer? She keeps crashing her system every time she tries to print something. Eric, you're back at the mayor's office. He has a virus again. Anything else, Mark? Everyone, have a good day. Dismissed."

Brucker and Learner were out the door first. Adison waited as Scripts put a restraining hand on her arm.

"You need to watch yourself around Mike. His MO is to make rude and crude comments when there are no witnesses around, except Danny, who backs up what he says. I'm warning you because of the way he reacted to you."

"Isn't that harassment?"

"Yes. But his lawyer has put a slant on it that we are the ones who are harassing him and Danny. Those two make sure if there are any witnesses that they're their friends."

Adison smiled. "I can handle it."

Scripts took a deep breath. "Listen to me. It does no good to swap nastiness with him. It just feeds his…"

"Who said I plan on fighting rudeness with crudeness? When does Frank's Electronics open?" *My aunties taught me well. No fighting fire with fire. Cold is what is needed. A cold dose of reality.*

"Nine. Why?"

"Just give you the answer without you even trying to figure it out? No way, Detective."

As she walked by Harriet, she glanced at her and stopped by her desk.

"Harriet, why the smirk? First time I've ever seen you with a sour look this morning and now you're smirking. What's up with that?" she teased.

She gestured Adison to come closer and whispered in her ear, "Found listening devices around my desk and the office this morning. Since we don't know if it's Mike and Danny, Eric moved the lumpiest chairs to *their* corner."

Adison leaned back astonished. "No! Why on earth would either of them put listening devices around the department after all this time of it being clean?"

"Who knows? Can't say my conversations are all that interesting. Since Mike's sitting here for the day, I want to make sure my stuff is secured."

Saturday, at the monthly meeting, everyone was quietly reading notes while sipping or munching on snacks. Burns had ID'd all but three of the names on the warehouse list. His results were similar to her source with the exception of those they knew to be working around Sunrise.

"Looks almost like a death list, even if the majority are still alive," Adison offered, wondering if the others felt the same way.

"It has that smell. Maybe it's a prison connection," Harriet suggested.

"Eric, can you find out if any of these other guys were ever in prison, which one and for how long, and those in the military, find out what troop they were in?" The chief made a notation.

"How about finding out what college these other guys went to?" Adison marked off three of the men.

"Maybe they all went to the same prostitute," Harriet broached, "and she's got a grudge she's taking care of, or maybe her kids are doing it for her," she added, thinking of how difficult it would be to arrange a hit list of this magnitude alone, if it were a hit list.

The men looked at her startled.

"That's a thought," Adison murmured. "A trucker and a man in uniform could possibly share the same brothel or stop and maybe near a prison or detention center." Adison looked over at Burns, grinning at the impossible challenge, but he could find bits of information where few could.

Burns nodded. "It's going to take a while. Let me work on it."

"Let's move on to three recent burglaries." Chief Harper motioned to Burns to turn the overhead on.

For the next hour, they discussed evidence and commonalities and possible suspects to a rash of night burglaries in the Rainbow shopping area.

"All right, we'll work on those new angles. Okay, everyone, let's end this meeting on a good note. We're making progress on the burglaries and we have more information to digest."

"Yes," Harriet grinned wryly, "and the next part is where do we put the new stuff?"

Burns grinned back. "Well, we got plenty of hard drive space for new folders."

"Not in my brain you haven't," Harriet returned.

They all laughed.

Scripts prodded Adison's elbow as they exited the office. "Wanna meet for lunch at Mollie's? The kids are planning you a surprise birthday party."

Adison's face turned bright red. "Okay."

"You're a good sport, Alex," Scripts said.

"Thanks for the warning."

"I noticed you don't take some surprises too well," he teased.

Harriet leaned over and pinched her cheek. "You better be there and no taking calls during your party," she warned.

Burns grinned. "Yes, the chief or Mark volunteered to take the detective calls."

"Did anyone tell the twins they'll be on their own?" Adison asked.

"They'll be there, too," Scripts said.

"Oh, gods," Adison groaned. "How do I page myself again?"

After two weeks of being subjected to Learner and Brucker's insults and listening to their opinions of women in uniform in general, Adison presented her recordings to a local lawyer Claire recommended on December 20, who filed for her the next day. Adison had made sure she reported the incidents to Scripts, her supervisor and Chief Harper, and they were documented. The pair had been spoken to, which was marked by increased hostility and by their remarks she caught on her body recorder and button-hole camera. They made the mistake of voicing their contempt of her complaining to Harper and Scripts. Her lawyer talked to Philip, Mike Learner and Danny Brucker's legal counsel. Until a hearing by the judge was convened, the two were ordered to desist. What Adison's lawyer held in reserve were camera recordings of what the two were placing in her belongings ... body parts of rodents. Adison could not believe those two didn't think to look at the clock that faced her desk which had a recording device in it.

As the holiday neared, Adison found herself besieged with invitations to spend time with not just friends, but different families for Christmas Eve and Christmas Day, Thursday and Friday. However, she was determined to leave for her cabin Tuesday, the 21st, after her shift ended to spend five days off surrounded in snow and probably drinking with Sam, if he was there.

Adison unpacked her food for the next five days, then made her rounds through the cabin, still finding it difficult to believe it was hers. Sam no doubt would have snow maneuvers to keep her from getting bored or lonely, but she already made up her mind he had two days of her time, then she was going to sleep and read.

A tapping on her door had her pulling her weapon from her back holster and approaching from the side.

"Hey, Alex! It's Sam. Open up, it's cold out here!"

Alex still peered out a peep hole before opening the door.

"What is that?" she asked, taking one of the bags from his hand.

"Dinner. I can hear your stomach growling all the way over at my place."

"That's not true. I ate on the way up. But I left you some. Half a loaf of bread from the French bakery." She sniffed the air, then poked her nose in the bag.

"Yum."

"Get your nose out of there and set the table," Sam ordered.

Adison complied. "So what do you have in that pot?"

"Lamb stew. I taught Genie how to make it. Then we're going to talk about this list of yours."

Adison's eyes opened wide.

After they feasted on Sam's half of the bread and his stew, they settled around the table with a cup of tea.

"I want you to pass this information to Harper. I have a good idea on what happened in the forest. Henrich Reiner, the sniper, was given a list of names, thirteen from that list you found in the warehouse." Sam paused to take a sip of his tea.

"Right...thirteen," Adison muttered. "There were fourteen, but one of them was a drug addict and died of an overdose. The medical doctor. His was the only one with a skull and crossbones. Maybe that means suicide."

"Here's a photo of Reiner with a woman. He was training her. I couldn't find anything about her, not even from what country she's from.

"Reiner, Thomas Meadows, John Melville, one other person, and the trainee were out in the woods. Five people. Reiner and his trainee intended to take either two or three of them out. Reiner was shot and killed. His MO for hits is he has his trainee herd their intended target to within Reiner's sights and he picks them off."

"Looks like this one shot back," Adison said.

"Right. From the evidence the FBI has, Meadows and Melville are dead. Meadows's remains were found in Sacramento with a wound that he couldn't have lived longer than a few minutes with. Melville was a victim of a hit and run in San Francisco. He was mistaken for a transient at first because of his dress and was nameless for a while. DNA ID'd him. Before Reiner and his trainee hit the West Coast, he knocked off three others on the list. Johnny Redfield, Richard Mack, and Carl Gates. Their bodies were found within a day's drive of one another but killed about the same time. Mack and Gates were at a conference for equipment and training of guard personnel and Redfield was on a business trip in the same area. Either it was a planned rendezvous among the three or it was engineered. Redfield's death was most probably the doing of the trainee since it does not fit Reiner's profile."

"Was Reiner a serious cross-dresser?"

"A transvestite? Yes. It was one of his methods of avoiding detection."

"Maybe his trainee is, too," she mused. "A woman who can pass as a man. I don't think he would do well with competition if it were the other way around."

Sam chuckled. "That would be an interesting twist."

"Well, the next department meeting is going to be really interesting," Adison said. "We can now call this someone's death list."

Chapter Nine

Adison unlocked her back door and laughed at the bundled person standing on her balcony. "Is that you all wrapped up in there, Scripts? Hey, Angel. You're looking sharp with your festive bow, girl."

Sunday morning was cold and snow was everywhere. Scripts took off his overcoat and tossed it on a kitchen chair. He obviously was not interested in running.

"Wow. Nice jogging outfit. Looks very warm. Christmas present?" she asked.

"Yes, my parents are in town. They overdosed us on presents. Even Angel is overwhelmed. They missed last Christmas because Dad was sick overseas, so we have last year's presents, too. Good thing I didn't grow much."

"Want some coffee or do you want to run?"

"I'll give you a break and take some coffee." He sniffed air that was scented with fresh-roasted beans. "It's too cold out there," he said. Scripts moved into the front room with his coffee and studied her mandella pattern of index cards she was going over with her new information from Sam. She had made sure before she answered the knock on her door that she didn't have anything out that Sunrise PD didn't know about.

"I couldn't find a military connection. Maybe it's like Harriet mentioned and it's a prostitute out for revenge," Scripts said.

"A jilted prostitute? Sounds as good a connection as we have going. Now all Burns has to do is figure out where they met her, then who...or maybe it's a he." Adison laughed. *With the information I'm going to give Harper...we're going to be shifting theories around.*

"The thing I'm puzzled about is what it has to do with our investigations." Mark picked up one card.

"You mean besides that a few of these guys are connected with our neighborhood gang and the list was found in one of their meeting places?" Adison asked.

"Yes. I'm curious why Mike was only attacked once. So far, no one's finished the job, and as far as I know, no one has attacked Amos."

"Well, if it's a hit list with different people hired to knock them off, that would leave a lot of people around knowing too much. Didn't Harper say Heinrich came out for thirteen hits? Let's see…"

"A superstitious person doesn't change his pattern even if there's a gun pointed at his head."

"Exactly. So he came out for only thirteen and someone is hired for the remaining," she suggested. She was about to add the information about the asterisk when she remembered Harper didn't have the symbols alongside the names. She was going to have to change that. It was her mistake.

Adison handed one of the cards to Scripts.

"Jinks Wilde?" he asked.

"It reminds me of a high school nickname."

"You going to look through every high school alumni book? Good luck."

"I've already checked and came back with one hit. Car salesman who said his father was called "Jinks," too, when he was in high school. He died in Vietnam. But there's no military record of anyone by the name of Jinkins Howard Wilde Jr. or Sr. that I could find. Think you can do better?"

"I'll give it a whirl," Scripts said.

Monday, the group meeting was scheduled for later in the morning Because Chief Harper was on the phone for a teleconference. By ten, Harriet, Burns, Scripts, and Adison were called in for a staff meeting.

"I just got off the phone with the judge, council, and mayor. Mike and Danny are on a year's probation. If any of you have a complaint about them, see me or Mark. They're on suspension for two weeks, so we'll all be stretched for foot duty. I'm going to work on our duty schedule, then I'll get back to you. Dismissed."

After they had filed out of his office, Harriet pumped her fist. "Two weeks of peace and quiet. You've done a mighty fine job, Detective," Harriet nodded to Adison. "That Philip has been getting away with his sly talk about this being a very understanding town and how those two are just a product of the old customs of this country that helped it become the great nation it is today."

"Why not fire them?"

"Judge Parker's wife is a counselor. She believes that if you just punish people, you'll just have the same criminal back on the street, meaner and smarter," Scripts said.

"That may work for some, but not everyone wants to change. It's like with addicts. You can't make them *get* better."

"Well, I'm going have to make a girl detective doll with blonde hair and a cute little badge hanging from her belt."

"Why?" Adison's eyes opened wide, remembering that in her gathering of information on her fellow officers that Harriet and her husband made

porcelain dolls for a hobby, sometimes using the likeness of Sunrise residents.

"I like to reinforce the good energy people give by making dolls of them."

"Uh, Harriet, I don't think that's necessary," Adison started, not knowing what to say. What if someone recognized her from a previous job? "A 'thank you' will suffice, and I'm sure you would have thought of doing that yourself."

Mark Scripts sat in his chair, leaned back, and grinned at her discomfort.

"If Mark and Claire don't mind being made up as the town's matchmakers, I can't see why you would get so embarrassed as a detective." Harriet's face broke into a wide grin as she added, "I'll be giving your dollie a silver bullet on her gun belt and a superwoman T-shirt under her..."

"Harriet!" Adison squeaked. She turned to glare at Scripts, who was bent over in laughter. "Matchmaker?"

He suddenly sobered up. "Yes, yes." His grin turned to a good-natured scowl.

"How come I didn't hear this in any of the town scuttlebutt? So that's your...uh...hobby?"

The others had laughed at her question. She looked around at the faces of her fellow officers.

"Nope. I'm a weekend handyman."

"So what about this matchmaking thing? You advertise on the Internet, too?" she asked.

The three laughed uproariously.

Am I missing something here?

"That stuff is like a gift that when it's ready, it happens," Harriet explained, being the first to be able to speak. "It's poof and bang."

"Poof and bang? What happened to the arrows and the little guy with the wings?" Adison asked, still dubious.

"That's old stuff," Harriet said.

"Uh-huh. Well, nice to be warned," she said. "I'll make sure I wear something to ward off any such influence. What is it, garlic or something?"

"Alex, Mark?" The chief peered out of his office. "I'd like to see you two. Harriet and Eric, the duty schedule is posted on the department bulletin board. I'm putting you both on foot patrol for the busy hours. Gladys will fill in on the switchboard."

"Can I just put up cameras and monitor the streets that way, Chief?" Eric joked.

"Well, that's no fun," Harriet said as the two slipped on their coats. "Can't get much conversation..." her voice faded when Adison shut the door to the chief's office. Scripts and she took the couch while the chief turned his desk chair to face them.

7. Christie

"Alex, since you're getting familiar with faces here and settling into your workload, I'd like to bring you in on some of our night surveillance work. As you know, we monitor our local crime group. Mark thinks you're doing well with the night drills, so you'll be taking my place." He pushed a file toward her. "Study these faces and their gang affiliation. First Friday of each month, the local militia meets. Under the cover of this meeting, our local gang meets up with some out-of-town characters shown in that file. They all have long and violent histories."

Adison nodded, understanding the implicit warning and grateful he didn't go into detail as if she were wet behind the ears. She shuffled through the pictures, realizing that SID would have to share more of their findings with Harper's group to save time and resources. Many of these people were not on her list. She would let Harper know he could do some information swapping with Mel.

Chapter Ten

Alex, by this information I just received from Mel," Chief Harper spoke softly, "we're dealing with an organization that covers *all* of California. How come I haven't heard of them before? I wish Mel let me in on that bit of information when I agreed to bring you on board," he complained.

"You suspected it was a large organization. How else do the members we do know of have so much money to spend and crime isn't all that high here?" she asked. "You just didn't know their name. Jaded Amulet. The man I identified at the airport, the muscle guy John Henry, belongs to the White Knights, one of Jaded Amulet's customers. WK can provide JA with high-end weapons, sometimes prototypes, still in development. WK deals in everything, and JA moves it along the California coast to their customers. Some of these customers fly in from other countries and some sail in. Judging the type of people who have been coming up here during militia nights, weapons are a heavy commodity."

"Very big. Interpol big," he said reproachfully. Adison bit back her reply, which would be that he was the one in direct contact with Mel, not her.

"So this Jaded Amulet…do you happen to know who their boss is?" The chief had a hopeful look on his face.

Adison shook her head, looking regretful. "You've been looking into JA longer than I have. My focus was on WK before I started working with you. Got any ideas?"

"No."

Adison thought about it for a moment. "I personally believe it's more than one person who runs the operation. It's too big for one, even with lieutenants. As for why they want to set up here, there are a lot of places to dump bodies. You have an ocean with a nice little harbor that isn't patrolled by the Coast Guard and a small police force. It could also be that the boss or bosses have an invested interest up here."

"Thanks. I needed to hear that."

"The additional information Sam came up with on the sniper should add meat to our suspicions that JA and WK are involved in the list of names from Amos's warehouse," Adison offered.

109

Harper nodded, looking thoughtful. "With the symbols showing clearer, we can get another fresh look at it. I'll get with Mark later and we'll go over it and organize it for our next meeting. I heard Mark got you a nice gizmo for night viewing."

Adison smiled broadly. It was better than what SID had given her. Scripts wouldn't tell her where he had managed to get it, just that he had friends with connections.

"Something better than I've ever used."

"How are you holding up?"

"I'm fine, Chief," Adison said. Mel's occasional concern about her mental and physical state was difficult enough to handle without having another person to fight off. *Maybe it has to do with men at a certain age.*

He shook his head. "Adison," he started.

Adison felt her face turning bright red and would have said something, but she was tongue tied. With Mel, she had her reply well practiced.

"You're human and you aren't some young teenager with hormones giving you all that excess energy to sustain your sleepless nights. Maybe we need to use your time better on your days off. Sam isn't running you ragged when you go to visit, is he?"

"Chief, I'm fine. Really. And January is going to be a good month because there isn't going to be any militia meetings in the cold weather, so we'll get a break."

The militia meet was not canceled. Adison suspected it had a lot to do with the men wanting to show off their new equipment they received for Christmas. Moving carefully across the dirt road, she paused behind a truck to take another look around. It was near freezing and she was worried her vapored breath would be spotted, even though it was pitch dark. There was a guard who was always posted around the vehicles. She finally caught a soft murmur to her left. Jimmie Henderson from Bales was the guard who was left behind. He moved side to side to keep warm, then hunkered down again in his coat and answered a question. Adison thought she heard him say "honey," so he was probably talking to his girlfriend on his cell phone.

Satisfied he was preoccupied, Adison moved toward the three new vehicles to write down their license plate numbers. If she used an IR to photograph it, it would no doubt set off someone's IR detect. Sometimes the old-fashioned way was the only way to get something done. The new cars didn't look like rentals.

Finished, she repocketed her notebook, readjusted her night vision goggles, and focused on locating Mike Learner, suspecting that where he was so were the three new guys. Danny Brucker was in the field stomping in the mud. She scanned the rickety outhouse that was used by the field day laborers during the season. Slowly, she made her way around the shed, hearing Learner in a one-way conversation. Her listening device picked up his voice but not whomever he was speaking with. She paused for a moment realizing that someone else was nearby listening and would spot her.

She was out in the open, and there was no tree, shrub, trash can, or shed to give her protection should the camo dressed figure turn her way. She straightened up and walked as tall as she could, like one of the guys, pulling at her crotch as if she had an itch while tucking away her listening equipment in pouches, getting ready for anything. She moved away from the area heading back toward the vehicles. Lights from an approaching car that neared the parking area would soon shine on her. Still she walked at an even and unhurried pace, hoping the guys were focused on other things.

She had a few more feet to go before she reached the parked cars, but the headlights would cover her in one second. She turned her back toward the light, knowing that anyone who was watching her through binoculars or night vision goggles would need a second to register what they were seeing. She dropped to the ground and crawled as fast as she could under the nearest vehicle, then under another one, moving out to sprint between them, looking for a way to the field.

Shouts and yells from the guard told her that she was seen. Whistles were blown. Each tweet and hoot meant something. She had been to enough of their meetings to know that she was going to be herded. As she moved behind one of the cars, she caught the movement of another figure, also dressed in dark clothing with no weapons belt.

The men were in full adrenaline mode. They were a hound dog with a scent, and from the sounds of radio signals being quashed, they were going up and down the car aisles.

"I got him! Arrgh! Oufff." It sounded like someone hit the car hard.

"Get him. Get him," deep voices shouted. Banging, like feet dropping into truck beds, and scrambling across them rang loud in the dark. Adison's heart pounded in her ears.

Then she heard the sounds of something sliding to a stop and wheels sliding in the mud as an engine roared. Dozens of vehicles turned over, and yells of who would pull out first. By the sound of the horns, that part was not well organized.

When Adison first heard the "I got him," she was out of the parking area, using the bushes and muddy trenches along the field to hide. By the time the cars had peeled off after their interloper, she was inside the line of trees that separated the farms. Leaning against one of the trees, she took a moment to breathe and to evaluate her situation.

Peering behind her, her head moved slowly as she deciphered what her night vision goggles revealed. *Someone's out there. I can feel it.*

Breathing shallow to hear anything, the beating of her heart was all she heard. But the feeling remained. She trusted those feelings for too long to ignore them now. Cautiously squatting to make herself a smaller target, she felt like she was in the crosshairs of someone's rifle. A recurring fear. Her stomach was in a cold knot.

There! That sounded like a foot stepping too heavily into mud. It was difficult to judge where the sound came from in the dark. She peered from behind her tree and was able to see the person clearly, kneeling and aiming a rifle her way. Rifle fire sounded the moment she stuck her head back behind the tree. She almost stumbled as she ran to the next tree. From there, she looked around frantically for somewhere to hide. The rifle fire was sure to gain attention. The militia swore they didn't use real bullets. A second shot missed her, but the bark from the tree hit her raised hand. Now she started to zigzag and stop and start to make herself a hard target to hit. She could hear a siren in the distance.

He expects me to run. All right! Let's turn this around.

Spinning around in ankle deep cold mud, Adison dropped to her stomach. Pulling off her gloves, she stored them in a zipped pouch and reached behind her to pull her small P7 off-duty pistol out from her back holster tucked under her coat. Awareness only of her target was all she knew as she waited for her pounding heart to quiet. Ignoring the approaching sirens and mud she was lying in, she concentrated on the figure trotting toward her.

This was someone who obviously felt he had plenty of time to escape. She fired at the person's leg, hearing a curse above the ringing in her ears from her pistol. She rolled to her feet and sprinted toward the road. She found a tree to climb and hurriedly scaled it, grateful it still had leaves to hide her. Adison quickly pulled out her night vision binoculars. A limping figure made his way to a motorcycle hidden from her earlier angle. A rifle was slung over his shoulder. He took off and headed toward the approaching police car. Five minutes later, a black and white came roaring by with Mark's dark blue Toyota hot on his tail. They headed to the Zielinskys' farmhouse. The Zielinskys no doubt put the call out.

Adison sighed heavily. She had been lucky so far.

Angel found her jogging back to her mountain bike.

"Angel, what are you doing out here? I could have shot you," she told the prancing dog.

Angel whined, then headed toward the road, turned around to look at her, and sat down.

"Angel, that's not a good place for me to be at the moment."

But Angel was persistent. So Adison followed her back to the outskirts of the militia meet. Scripts and Krieger were searching a small area with lights. Gus was locked in his vehicle due to Angel's presence. The two cavorted about with too much disregard to a crime scene for both to be let out. Angel obviously had seniority due to her master.

Since Adison was not dressed in casual clothes and had more mud on her than not, joining them was out of the question. Adison pulled Angel next to her. She took off her watch and gave it to Angel. Scripts would recognize it. His daughter had wanted one just like it because it had Mickey Mouse on the face.

"Take to Daddy, take to Mark," she instructed as she heard Linda tell Angel on occasion, handing her a soggy ball or sock stuffed with rags.

Angel galloped to her master in a playful manner and pranced around him until he finally paid attention. Scripts turned to Gary whose focus was the field, shining his light in a slow sweep across the trampled area.

"Gary, why don't you take off? I don't think we're going to find anything in the dark. Tomorrow I'll be by and check the place out."

"All right," his vapored breath puffed in the light the two vehicles provided. "I'm going to stop by my place and pick up a warm meal. Call me at home if you need me for the next hour."

"Will do. Come on, Angel." Scripts moved to his own vehicle. He turned on his engine and turned his truck around. Adison came running out of the dark and hopped into the partially opened door on the passenger side. She took the space on the floorboard, grateful she was flexible. Angel made it difficult by sticking her nose in Adison's ear. She pulled off the muddied sniper veil while pushing Angel's face away.

"Are you hurt?" Scripts demanded.

"No, but someone tried. I left my bike at Stanton's gas station. Could you swing by?"

"Yes. What happened?"

"I went looking for Learner after I copied down three new car licenses. The guard spotted me before I could find a safe place to hide. Instead of finding me, they chased someone else who was snooping around. She had a getaway car that served as a fox to the hounds. However, someone stayed behind and took shots at me. I returned one shot. I aimed for the leg and I think I got him. He took off on a motorcycle."

"Sniper and a motorcycle. That sounds familiar. You're okay? I mean you wouldn't say yes and be hurt?"

"Of course not! Who else would I go to for a battlefield dressing?" Her shaking hands were gripping her equally shaking knees. Fortunately, it was not often that someone aimed to kill her. In the back of her mind, she thought about Reiner's partner who got away. Was this the trainee? Was it male or female? Her guess was it was female.

Adison slept past her alarm and didn't wake until Script's pounding on her back door woke her. Groaning, she stumbled to open the door.

"Hold on, I'm awake," she growled. A bark greeted her. She unlocked the door and flung it open, looking with disgust at a happy dog and a wide-awake partner.

"You look terrible. A run along the beach will do you a world of good," he smiled.

"Why? It's still dark. I won't see a thing unless I wear night goggles. Give me a minute," she mumbled. She paused to give Angel her cookie.

She dressed quickly for someone not very awake, out of habit. As they ran, Adison thought about the previous night and the woman she saw. When they stopped for a breather, she turned to Scripts. "That guy who took a shot at me last night..."

"Yes?"

"I know I got him in the leg, so there has to be blood along the road until he had a chance to stop and wrap it."

"DNA. Maybe we can get a match to someone on file." He looked up at the lightening sky. "Meet you in the office. I'll call Harper to let him know we may be late for the Saturday meeting." Scripts took off in a long-legged ground-eating pace, followed by his dog. Adison was not too far behind since she was getting faster.

"Scripts! Over here!" Adison shouted. Someone had visited the site where she thought the sniper had taken a shot at her. They had driven a tractor with a rake over the entire muddy area.

Scripts looked over the area disgustedly. "Someone is trying to hide something. Same thing where I was looking. Let's take a walk up the road. Where it hasn't been raked the field is trampled beyond identifiable clues and the parking area is mush for tracks."

For the next hour and a half, they carefully walked the road, looking for blood or a track showing the motorcycle had left the road.

"Alex!"

Adison quickly joined him.

"Wow!"

There was one bloody handprint on the tree trunk and one dark splotch in the mud below. Two footprints planted in the mud made it appear that this may have been where the sniper took the time to wrap his wound, bracing himself against the tree. It was at the split in the road where you can either go into town or to the beach.

"Score a point for our team," she said softly. "He must have stopped here and waited for you and Krieger to pass."

Scripts took charge of collecting evidence from the scene while Adison followed the road to where it branched off to the beach to the left and another set of farms to the right. It was about ten minutes up the road that she found what she was looking for. More raking. Since it was done in the dark, not all evidence was wiped away. She was sure the rider fell here. Copious photos were taken, leaving nothing of the scene and the surrounding area unrecorded.

She walked back to Scripts, letting her eyes wander along the road and over the fields on the other side of the trees. She sniffed the chilly air. Damp earth and the crisp scent of eucalyptus trees warmed by the sun. Nice. She stopped and closed her eyes.

"Hey! You meditating?" Scripts's amused voice called out to her.

She kept her eyes closed and smiled. "Yes. I thought I would take time out to smell the roses only all I smell are eucalyptus."

"Find anything?"

"Yes." Reluctantly, she opened her eyes and gestured behind her. "Another raked area. But what wasn't raked looks like he fell. Someone had to be watching for him because getting shot hurts like the dickens," she remembered with no wish to revisit that feeling.

"What direction did the militia take when they took off after the other figure?"

"I don't know. I was too busy fleeing the scene. With all the mud tracks, it's hard to tell which way they did go. A group of them may have returned just to mess up the scene."

"They succeeded. Let's look on the other side of the road, and maybe we'll get luckier."

After spending an hour finding nothing, Adison stood in the middle of the road, trying to figure out where the three men could have met without her seeing them. Slowly, she walked up the road to the small turnoff. Behind her, she could hear Frank's voice hailing them. In a whiny voice, he informed Scripts that when he let those military boys use the field for the night, they didn't say anything about using real bullets and he could not be held accountable for what happened. Then he asked what happened.

Adison crouched in the middle of the turnoff where the rake missed a four-foot area. Something shined in the morning sun. First she photographed it, then studied the deep heel prints that gave her the impression there was a scuffle. Either the mop-up crew was running out of time to be as thorough as it normally was or this person was not as careful. Or maybe it was meant to be found. Between two gloved fingertips, she pulled the gold medallion free from wet leaves. It had a sword with flowers twined around the blade. Turning it over, there was nothing on the back.

White Knights. They were here. This is the same design as the one Mandy found on the severed hand.

"Hey there. Did you find anything? If it's worth something, it's on my property." Frank walked over with Scripts beside him.

"For whatever it's worth, it belongs to the city. This is a public turnout," Scripts said as he pulled a plastic bag out of his coat pocket. "And if it were your property, we would still have to take it as evidence. Frank, step back. We need to take some castings of boot prints. My partner here needs the practice."

115

Adison dropped the medallion into his bag, trying not to glare at Scripts for the remark. Turning to her crime scene case, she began the mix for a mold. Finished with that, she pulled off her gloves and glanced at her watch. "Well?"

"It's a wrap."

"Well, can I claim it?" Frank demanded.

"No," the two detectives responded. Frank moved back to his farm in a huff.

The two were quiet until they pulled into the PD parking lot.

"You know, the bottom of that sword on the medallion reminds me of the tattoo outline that was on the wrist of the hand you collected from the marsh," Adison said.

"Yes, I noticed."

Scripts and Adison found Burns waiting for them. The two unloaded their evidence and carefully packaged what was going to be sent to Mandy's team to analyze.

Monday, Harriet, Adison, Burns, Mark, and the chief huddled in the cold meeting room. The heater was trying to warm up the room, with its fan noisily spinning out warm air.

"Okay, we've got plenty of new information to sift through," the chief began the meeting. "We now have a name for our local group. The Jaded Amulet. We also have the name of one of their customers from out of town called the White Knights. The White Knights belong to the tattoo and the medallion Alex found. They hail from Alabama. Sounding any alarms for the rest of you?" He looked around the table.

"Alabama seems to come up a lot," Scripts said.

"Uh-huh," Adison and Harriet agreed.

"Add this to your Alabama list," Burns told the others. "There was a small science college called Rotterman College of the Sciences that worked with a hospital a block away and had a contract with a pharmaceutical company in the same town. Four of our names were at the college either as employees or students."

"Got anything more on what they studied or worked as?"

"It's not Rotterman anymore. A religious organization took it over and turned it into a Bible college about two years ago. No records of the previous students or employees. That's all I have on that for now."

"The forest case," the chief held up a sheet of paper they all had copies of. "We have some new evidence on that, too. So far, we have Reiner, the professional sniper who does jobs on each continent in groups of thirteen, an apprentice we have no name for, John Melville, whose bloody fingerprints were on the rifle along with another set of Thomas Meadows. Thomas Meadows's body, badly decomposed, was found half-buried along the freeway outside of Sacramento. According to the coroner's reports, he died from a gaping chest wound that broke his sternum and spine. John Melville was killed by a hit and run in San Francisco last month. Add to that Redfield, who died of a heart attack back in October; Carl Gates, who died of a self-inflicted head wound the same week; and Richard Mack who also died of a self-inflicted head wound."

"Five down," Harriet mentioned. "Any information on why the locals think they died of a self-inflicted wound?...I mean, it's kind of suspicious since they both work at the same prison."

"Six. The one with the skull and crossbones died of an overdose of heroin," Adison reminded them. She held up a sheet Eric had included in their notes. "My guess is the skull and crossbones means suicide. That would mean there are thirteen asterisks and Reiner contracts for thirteen hits."

"Seven, if you think about the attack on Mike," Eric pointed out. "He nearly died."

"If it is a hit list, Amos Anders and Sam Adams are on it, and I haven't heard of anything happening to them," reasoned Harper, taking the devil's advocate role. "We need information on what the investigation turned up on their deaths, Eric. And do some checking on what those marks on the side could mean."

Eric nodded. "I'll check on these other guys with the asterisks to see if they're still alive. Maybe the trainee will fulfill the contract."

Chapter Eleven

Mark, you left this here for me?" Eric asked, waving an envelope at them. Both detectives were typing in their case notes, hoping to not be caught with the end-of the-month blues, where all their information was still in their notebooks, not copied over to their computer files. They had one more week to get caught up.

"Yes. The clinic asked if you could do a background check on her. That's our Gary's girlfriend, Margaret Hamilton."

Eric nodded. "I'll get on it."

Adison looked surprised. "We do background checks on other business's employees?"

"The clinic's insurance rates are lower if its employees are bonded. It's a service we offer for a small fee. Separate from police work. It pays for some of the things we get, and everyone knows we aren't going to be blabbing whatever is found."

"I've never met Gary's girlfriend."

"I think I've only seen her once or twice. At the grocery store or shopping in a store. She travels a lot between here and Orange County, just outside of Los Angeles. Gary said her mother's been ill for the past year. Sometimes she spends weeks or a month with her."

"That must be hard on a relationship," Adison said. *Margaret. Why does that sound familiar? I don't know any. But I do know a Margo and Mari.*

The next four months were spent gathering information on the local gang, solving criminal investigations, and training with the new CSI department the four counties budgeted for. Dr. Mandy Sherwood was given the department to manage, and she was starting with only three assistants. She and Harper went over a training class that the chief and Scripts would give to the three counties' local PDs, so when they were on site first, they could protect the site better until Scripts and Sherwood's team arrived.

June was spent cleaning up cases that Judge Parker wanted well documented and cleared off his docket for his retirement at the end of the month. Adison was given some of the cases that were follow-up phone calls, while Harper and Scripts spent the majority of time in the other counties doing the foot work. All she had time for was to spend a few nights at the House reading or watching movies with the residents and Genie and Claire who insisted she take time out to relax. She received lessons on stargazing from one woman at the shelter who knew what she was looking at. Adison was pleased her gift of the telescope was appreciated.

July brought in Judge Mead, who originally came from Southern California. She worked as a lawyer for the Antioch children's home and was an advocate for families but hardnosed on issues of abusive spouses or siblings. She had a three-part plan on how to handle abusive cases to end the cycle of violence in homes, and it was that platform that won her the election.

Judge Mead had been a police officer for five years while working her way through law school, giving her a view of both sides of the arrest and trial process. Once voted in, she did her homework and knew about the problems Judge Parker had with the FBI and of the Jaded Amulet and White Knights. It was up to Chief Harper, the court's lead investigator, to continue in that capacity and to educate the new judge in the art of gang warfare with an international flavor. The departmental monthly meeting on the eighth was going to be a meeting with Judge Mead attending. She insisted on being there to see what was going on in her territory and, Adison shrewdly guessed, to make a decision of whether to keep Chief Harper on as her lead investigator or hire someone from the outside who she knew personally, like her husband.

What Chief Harper and the mayors of the four towns knew was that hiring an outsider was not in the budget, so everyone had to get along. Besides, Harper and his detectives were the most experienced that their combined and separate budgets could ever hope for, and they worked well with their new CSI crime lab, headed by Mandy.

Adison pushed opened the doughnut shop door and stood in the long line. By the time she reached the office, she was in the second stage of awakening, where she could contribute to a conversation.

"Morning, Officer Burns. I got the coffee and doughnuts. Boy, do I need a pickup."

"Morning, Detective Adison," he returned in mock seriousness. "Hey, I got a hit on Mike's site. He sent out a handful of emails, and I've got the who's who on them all."

Eric helped Adison set up coffee, hot water, napkins, and doughnuts before the two returned to the server room where Eric gave her four sheets of information on the fifty-five names and addresses of them.

"This is hot, Eric. But how do you know that these are them?"

"I got my ways, Detective. Do you give away all your secrets?"

Adison snorted. "Of course not. I want some mystery behind how I leap tall buildings in a single bound and run faster than a speeding bullet."

"Well, when you get to the tights and cape part, let me know. I know a lot of people who would pay to see you dressed in tights," Eric chuckled.

Adison grinned and leaned on the table to continue her reading while Eric went to set up the laptop and room for the meeting. The names were mostly members of the local militia. There were three who bore further investigating. They were sent from three different coffeehouses in Southern California—Laguna Beach, Long Beach, and Newport Beach.

When she heard voices from the stairs, Adison gathered her papers and joined the others as they sat for the meeting. When everyone was ready, Judge Mead was introduced. She wore a dress, modest amount of jewelry, high heels, and a hat. Adison had gotten used to the relaxed dress of everyone in Sunrise. Judge Mead was overdressed by Sunrise standards, even for church.

"Judge Mead has only an hour, then she has a speech and breakfast brunch at the Women's Club, so let's give her a rundown on just the local group. Officer Burns, since you're the closest, get the lights, will you?"

Judge Mead's expression didn't give away her thoughts and she offered none. When she left, she only said she would think on the subject and get back to Chief Harper.

"Why do we have such a bad feeling here?" Adison asked.

"I sure wish we had some idea of just what she thinks of this. Chief, didn't you and Judge Parker go over with her about this business?"

"The way Judge Parker explained it, it sounded like a conspiracy was going on and the FBI was part of it. She hasn't been in a large city courtroom since her early years of practice. The last five years that she's lived up here has been in family litigations and such. Let's call it quits today. I'll let you all know as soon as I hear something. Alex, you're not dressed in your uniform, forget to pick up your laundry?"

"No, Chief. I woke up late. I'll change before I hit the streets."

He nodded and left.

Adison looked at Mark and pointed at the sheets Eric had given her. "What do you think? It looks like it's an invitation to a party, but where?"

Mark shook his head. "I don't know, nor can I even guess. He refers to the *alley* which doesn't mean a thing. It's the first time they've used it."

"Think Judge Mead will continue to give us the same authority to investigate?" Eric asked worried.

"We gave her a lot of solid proof. It was smart of the chief to leave off the leads that weren't solid. Well, I have to get changed. Have a nice weekend y'all." Adison rose to get ready for weekend duty. She noticed one of the twins left a note on her desk to stop by the Willow Tree, a stationery and card shop.

As she walked the five blocks, Adison mulled over why she liked this assignment, even if it was working two jobs. Maybe it was the friendly greetings she received from residents and tourists or maybe it was working at the same job for more than a month and not feeling like every time she opened her eyes, it would be to a gun muzzle staring back at her.

You're ruining the mood, Adison.

A week later, Adison received an email from Mel letting her know that Chief Harper had asked SID to profile Judge Mead to see if he could trust her. Adison shook her head regrettably. The favor was going to cost Chief Harper. Nothing came for free. Mel knew Judge Mead. Her ex-husband was an FBI agent.

"Well, Mel, this is one bit of news we knew before you. You should visit a Sunrise coffee shop sometime."

Monday, Adison was balancing a bagel and coffee in one hand while tossing her jacket onto the chair when the chief poked his head out of his office. He was not wearing his usual friendly expression.

"Detective, I'd like to see you before you get settled. Bring your coffee and bagel."

"Yes, sir."

She closed the door behind her and sat in the chair she usually took when visiting.

"What's up?"

"After Judge Mead left Saturday, she asked in addition for our files, in detail, with our personal notes attached, on what we have on the Jaded Amulet. I gave them to her on the tenth. Her remarks at that time were that we were to desist from monitoring anyone having to do with this group for the sole purpose of their membership until she finished reviewing the legal boundaries to this type of investigation."

Whoa. "Does she know how sensitive this is or that there could be a mole in her staff, as well as the FBI? Jeez. Homeland Security is the most incompetent organization with the authority to fail," she ranted. What she feared was her cover was blown.

"She acknowledged all those points and that she doesn't know if we can do all this monitoring without a legal leg to stand on. The federal government with its Homeland Security rules can investigate anyone without letting anyone know, but it seems she has qualms about our local PD being so invasive. She sees what we have as loose ends to various cases and only hunches attaching them to one another. She believes it should be left to the FBI, who has shown interest in it and has stated in papers to Judge Parker to that effect. She also pointed out that we could be better serving the townships she represents by concentrating on actual crimes.

"She also believes that my acting as chief investigator is no longer warranted now that we have a budding CSI. She believes each town should handle its own investigations to build on the strength of their people." Chief Harper's face was grim as his voice sounded exasperated and near anger.

"She'll have to do some politicking on that point, and I know each mayor. They won't go along with developing their own detective staff because of the costs involved, though some of the police chiefs would like to add maybe one detective to their crew. It took a lot of budget squeezing and sacrifice from all the counties to make Mandy's CSI department a reality, staffed with competent personal, equipped with state-of-the-art hardware and hire some decent guards to keep the area secured from unauthorized visits."

Adison shook her head at the chief's nightmare. "I'm not comfortable with her having the files, to tell you the truth. What does she know about safeguarding it from Jaded Amulet?"

"I made certain she knew how to secure them, though that is not to say she will." The chief scrubbed his face. "Her husband is ex-FBI, and I don't like the idea of him having access to those files."

Adison raised an eyebrow.

"You don't think I would give her everything, do you?"

"Just what did you give her?"

"Enough to show local residents meeting up with known gang members. She didn't seem impressed, which is disturbing."

"She didn't ask for anything else?"

He shook his head. "She only wanted to know who we knew as belonging to the Jaded Amulet. If she had not read about the documentation you had on Mike and Danny's behavior, I think she would have had me on the carpet for harassment. Your other boss says she's clean."

"What does her husband do now?"

"He owns a consulting firm dealing with security over the Internet."

"Now *that* is suspect. I'll bet she shares our notes with him. Has Burns had any recent hits?"

"Seventeen for the month. Not unusual. But Burns noticed some of them aren't like the normal attempts at seeing if we're vulnerable. It's using a specific string of words." The chief leaned forward as if something dawned on him. "Like in our reports on the Jaded Amulet." The chief picked up his phone. "Eric, get in here as soon as you can."

A knock on the door was followed by Eric sticking his head in the office, then coming in at the chief's nod.

"Have you found the source of the recent taps to our server?"

"No. They're good, but I got the sniffer poised and ready for the next hit. I'll get them."

"Do you know Mead's Security Consulting for Internet Businesses?"

"Yes. They offered me a job before I even had my bags packed for here. They're pretty aggressive in their recruitment."

"They may have our files on the Jaded Amulet case, which is confidential and wouldn't be legal."

Eric nodded with understanding. "No worry, Chief."

"We do have warnings that they are entering a restricted site and will warrant arrest and guaranteed jail time?"

"A lot of good that does to deter them," Eric snorted and turned to leave.

"And, Eric?"

"Yes, Chief?"

"If they have our stuff, wipe it out."

"Right, Chief." The door closed firmly behind him.

"Alex, you're going to be on your own until we get this problem cleared up. I suggest you not share anything with me, just so that I don't have to lie to her. When we do start working together, I don't want secrets that will be embarrassing for us."

Adison nodded. "All right."

Chapter Twelve

Alex held a clutch of cards. Her partner, Elaine, was slow and deliberate in her card selections, just as bad a player as Alex. Alex looked around the table at Claire, Rhonda, and Elaine. Claire's green eyes were sparkling in the room's light, her eyes settling on each woman at the table, joking about Alex's card skills, which Alex didn't mind. She hated playing and was cajoled to play by Claire with the promise of pumpkin cookies fresh out of the oven.

Alex had been in Sunrise for a year, comfortably settled into the rhythm of friendships and a normal life, or close to normal. She visited the House on a regular basis to avoid being alone in her apartment that reminded her of work she needed to be looking at. A year was the longest she had ever been on a covert assignment. She glanced at her watch and realized it was late. The next day was Saturday and the monthly departmental meeting, which had not been as interesting since Judge Mead's decision to get involved in SPD's investigations.

"My, how times flies," Claire said as she laid her cards on the table.

Elaine peered at the cards Alex laid down. "I don't think card games are something that keep your attention for long."

"You're right," Alex stretched to get her blood flowing. "All the waiting makes me want to take up smoking or eating."

Elaine nodded. "Idle time is the road to the devil, or that's what I used to be told." She looked up shyly before going on, as if gauging her audience, "but I can see now that it all depends on if these leisure moments get in the way of other responsibilities."

"Elaine, that is the most you've said since you've gotten here. I think that warrants a warm glass of milk and pumpkin cookies that I can smell are done. It'll help you sleep better, too," Claire said.

"We won't pick you next time for an extra hand, Alex. But a good card or chess player keeps your detective skills honed," Claire reasoned, tapping the card in Alex's discarded hand that was supposed to mean something.

Alex looked at her disbelievingly. "You've got to be kidding. I have enough work on my desk to keep me in practice."

The women rose from their chairs, putting cards away and collecting snack dishes to take to the kitchen where they would pick up still-warm cookies. Claire rubbed Alex's back soothingly as she accompanied her down the stairs.

"It's just a joke, Alex. You do need to take a break from this police work and Mark's workouts. Before you came, it was just Genie and Mark, with Genie doing it because she missed her combat games when she was in the Army. Now with the three of you, he's been making these games of his harder. Genie told me she thinks she's getting too old for it. That tells me he's working you too hard. I worry about you. Genie has me, and Mark has his wife and kids, but you only have work. You don't even have a hobby since you gave us your telescope. Don't you get two weeks off soon? You've been here long enough."

"You don't have to worry about me, Claire. I need to be in good shape and not bored with my job. I do have a two-weeker coming up. I'm going to spend it in my cabin, with a friend, if that makes you feel better. I sure know it does me." She grinned. "My friend is a contractor. She's going to look over the walls and insulate the place so when the snow hits this year, I won't shiver so much."

"Alex, you leaving without your cookies? That's a first," Genie said. She handed Adison her goodies wrapped in tin foil. "I burnt the first batch. I'm still getting used to this new oven."

Adison gave her a hug. "Genie, you are so good for my sweet tooth. By the time I get home, there won't be any left."

Saturday morning, Alex thumped up the stairs to the office, taking them two at a time. Against the desire of Judge Mead, Harper and his team were still the chief investigators for the court. There were seventeen murders that occurred in rapid succession outside of the forest since she took office. The way Judge Mead expressed it to Chief Harper was that she held him responsible because it was in her jurisdiction, making it his to investigate. She would have launched an investigation of her own on Harper had Dr. Sherwood and the mayors of all the towns not voted her down with adamant refusals to pay the cost. Her threat of bringing in the FBI was withdrawn for some undisclosed reason. Claire and Angela, from the child welfare office, volunteered to help mend the fences, to encourage team building. So far, the two main characters were not sitting at the same table.

Alex looked up from the coffeepot to see Mark and Chief Harper walk in with bags of doughnuts, bagels, and grins.

"Did we all just get a pay raise?" Alex asked.

"Better than that. I'll tell you in the meeting."

The four settled in their chairs, with Eric, Harriet, and Adison squirming with impatience.

125

"Judge Mead has given us the okay to continue our investigation into the Jaded Amulet. She hasn't told me just what made her change her mind, but I do know she attended a judge's conference in Los Angeles. I had a cryptic message on my voice mail when I returned from vacation that she wanted to see me as soon as I got back," Harper said.

"She also authorized my request to seize her husband's hard drives that had attempted to access our servers to make sure they had not copied information they shouldn't have."

"The only reason she said that is because I wiped out all traces of our files!" Eric hooted.

They all laughed, and those nearest Eric pounded him on the back.

"The point is, she admitted that she didn't authorize the hits. That puts her in a compromised position of sharing confidential information with a civilian not authorized by me to review our documentation, and it's her husband. So we have an agreement to work together, not against each other."

Everyone gave hoots of victory.

"Now let's get back to what has become my priority. Back to the Jaded Amulet. Mark has printed out what we put aside for a while. I've added some information I've received recently from my contact. As you can see, our group is still doing some kind of business with out-of-town arms dealers and drug groups, in Sacramento, Los Angeles, San Francisco, and San Diego. I want to get back to finding the leader of this gang. We left off with…"

There were four sheets of paper that represented four separate lists and focus. One was the over a hundred possible suspects for the leader of the Jaded Amulet. Another was the names of known members who lived in and around Sunrise and those who visited from out of town. The third was a list of suspicious people they had identified as doing business with the Jaded Amulet. And the fourth was the list Adison had found in the warehouse a year before. For about five minutes, everyone reread the information, then Chief Harper began the discussion on Emma, the next suspect.

The clock on the desk let out a muted ding as it marked the hour.

"All right, our three hours are up. I think we just about flogged to death the possibility that Emma could be the boss. In our next meeting, we'll move to Mrs. Dodd. Remember, she has a very touchy lawyer and doesn't like the law asking about her business."

"Our list is getting smaller," Eric sighed, "but the likelihood of some of these people on our potential list is crazy, like Mrs. Dodd. She wouldn't be on it if she didn't keep disappearing for days at a time. I can't see her old legs taking her very far or her muddled brain coming up with strategies for running a statewide business."

"Maybe her lawyer is her partner," Harriet joked.

"But she manages to elude the staff, Eric. I don't think she is all that muddled. I think she does that to keep away those she doesn't want to talk to. I overheard her once carry on a lively debate with her lawyer, Edmond, on stocks. She didn't sound muddled to me. All we need to do is find out where she disappears to," Alex insisted. "The only reason we haven't looked into her disappearances is because Edmond says she has the right to leave when she pleases." Alex looked at her list. "But I'm sure curious where and why she takes off. Is it medical, chemical, or just a need to get away?"

Everyone moved out of the room with their belongings.

From Chief Harper's glance her way, Alex knew he wanted to talk with her. Mark received the same nod. The two moved to sit in the chief's office. When the office was quiet again, Harper started. "Judge Mead has requested you two escort a prisoner to Chicago." The chief watched his detectives. "Between us and the Chicago district attorney, you'll deliver Mr. Smith to a pair of bounty hunters he has hired. Due to Mr. Smith's connection to misdoings in the PD there, the Chicago judge wishes to make sure he gets to court safe and alive." Chief Harper leaned over his desk, pushing a picture toward them. "Just so you know who to turn him over to. They'll make contact with you before you reach San Francisco."

Alex looked at her partner. "So they'll trail us and the prisoner to see if we are being followed, then take over when they're satisfied things look okay."

"Just as long as this is not putting us out as sitting ducks." Mark handed the photos back to the chief.

"It's a legitimate reason why the two of you are out of town. This will be moving up our plan for the visit to the bar by three days. But I can't see it hurting anything."

The two detectives sat up straighter. This bit of news was more to their interest.

"Our target bartender Haggert is in the Alaskan wilderness, not in as deep as we had originally planned, but enough. The cousin you'll be posing as, Alex, is occupied elsewhere and won't be turning up suddenly. If either situation changes, I'll let you two know."

"What happens if Amy's cousin calls her when he returns and wants to know what the message is?" Alex asked, knowing the purpose was to avoid having any evidence pointing to official involvement.

"That'll be taken care of. Two days is all you have. I'm sure you both understand why this will have to move along quickly. If it looks like they're not buying your story, get out of there with as much low-profile finesse as you can. It's better they be suspicious than to know for sure where you're from." He studied the two who gave a nod of understanding. "Good luck."

Mark and Alex clattered downstairs thinking about their assignment. The sound of clanking metal came from the workout room.

"Hey, Dad!" Johnnie piped up while Katie, his daughter, ran up to him to be lifted and tossed for a brief thrill.

"Hi, kids. Linda." Alex waved.

"Hi, Detective Alex!" Two small voices greeted her enthusiastically.

"Hi, Alex." Linda smiled. "Hi, hon. I thought you might have forgotten that we're going out to the movies this afternoon," Linda said as she rose from the weight bench.

Mark looked abashed. "I did." He kissed her on the cheek. "Thanks for reminding me."

"No problem. You can take us out to lunch before the show starts. We would invite you, Alex, but you can't sit still long enough to even finish your popcorn. Someone would think you don't like movies," Linda teased.

"Well, I just don't like sitting still for that long," Alex said, grateful they didn't ask her along. This was the third time they were going to see *The Lion King* on the big screen. She barely made it through the first showing. How Linda and Mark could do it had to be something in the parenting gene.

Once out in the fresh air, Alex set out at a brisk walk, determined to work off her tension. Lately, her guilty feelings about lying to some of the people in town who let her share in their private lives so easily was coming up more often. Mark was the hardest because she knew he knew she was not all who she presented herself to be, yet he continued to train her and bring her into his family life. Glimpses into real lives with real relationships she was used to, but to be invited in without reservation…this was where having a good friend to talk to would be nice. Only she didn't have one. Another job handicap. She forced herself to think about Mrs. Dodd.

What if she's not spiriting off somewhere, but rather hiding in a closet or somewhere still on the premises? If so, who's visiting her prior to her disappearances? The visitors' log doesn't have anyone down. Something has to be happening in her life that is triggering her to want to be left alone or hide.

She grinned to herself.

Maybe she had a doctor's appointment and she didn't want to be there when he or she got there. I'll have to check and see who her doctor is…probably Dr. Moser from Bales. The old grouch.

Nodding to herself, Adison's thoughts moved on to something more exciting, like infiltrating a private biker bar. She recalled a conversation where Amos alluded to Danny that the boss knew of his visits to "a so-called biker bar," but the boss didn't know what he did there. Meaning the boss didn't have membership or contacts there. Mel also admitted that one of his teams failed to get inside the bar where White Knight locals met. She wondered if he and Harper had arranged for this visit.

Well, that should give me some comfort. They think Mark and I can get in. This is the same bar where Mike was stabbed and nearly died. Was it a hit because he was on that list or because he was at a bar that has closed membership?

She frowned. *I don't see Danny as an assassin.* Mike had the same mark after his name as Amos Anders, which to Alex meant that the same person was assigned to get rid of them. As much as Danny and Amos knocked heads and egos, she could not see him knocking Amos off, either. So was it someone at the bar and Danny was enlisted to bring him?

Chapter Thirteen

Adison swung her leather-covered leg over her bike, a bit more stiffly than she would have wanted, but it was in keeping with her cover that she had been riding for days and not several hours. She leaned the bike sideways, casually pulling off her helmet and stuffing her leather gloves inside. She stretched her back and glanced at Mark, not missing what was around her. They had ridden for hours to get Adison's bike skills back up to par while Mark was just having fun. She liked the feel of the leather against her skin as she moved to stand beside Mark.

"Amy, you sure this is the place Billy's at?" Mark sounded dubious.

She nodded, running her fingers through her short, obviously dyed, raven black hair. Her dark red nails looked like blood spots moving through tangled strands.

"Come on, let's get this message delivered, then we'll look for a place to rest."

Mark led the way toward the bar, where a formidable bouncer stood. His muscled body blocked Mark's entrance. Adison moved around him and into the bar's dim interior while Mark distracted him. The smell nearly slowed her down, but she pushed through the stale odor of people, beer, and latrines toward the bar.

A sullen bartender paused in wiping a glass.

"I'm looking for Billy Haggart. Do you know when he'll be in?"

"Whose asking?"

"None of your…"

"His cousin." Mark appeared at her side. He shook his hand out. "You got two bottles of Bud? We've been riding since early this morning, and I'm so thirsty I'm almost ready to drink water." Mark tossed a twenty on the top of the counter and turned his attention to Amy. Both gave the impression they believed the bartender would accommodate them.

"What did you do to your hand?"

"Some goon at the door didn't want me to follow you in. You'd think this was a 'girls only' bar."

Adison looked around the room, frowning. "Not likely."

130

Two bottles banged on the bar top.

Mark turned back to the bartender.

"So, what about Billy? And you got a pool table?" Mark asked, picking up his beer.

"It's booked," the bartender told him coldly. "What do you want with Billy?"

"We got a message for him from his family. Do you know when he'll be in?" Mark asked.

"Not today."

"Good. Let's go." Adison moved away from the bar, but Mark grabbed her elbow. "Hold up, Amy. Since we're here, let's have a couple of beers, relax a minute, then we'll get going. I could use a break."

"Does this look like the place you want to take a break in?" she asked disgustedly in a low tone. "In a place like this, even standing above the toilets will probably get you crabs."

"A bar's a bar. My butt's numb, to say nothing of other important items, and I want a break. Come on, Amy. Relax."

"John…" she turned toward her partner irritated.

"We've been in worse."

"One beer. Then let's find a hotel to get some sleep."

"One it is. Hey, bartender? You got darts?"

"No, and we don't have pinball machines, either."

Mark smiled and nodded. "So when is Billy due back at work? We got a lot of miles of travel still ahead of us, and the sooner we get this message delivered, the sooner we can move on."

The bartender glared at them. "I ain't the boss. I don't know his schedule."

Adison eyed him over her beer bottle as she took a gulp. "When aren't you here?"

"That ain't your business," he retorted.

Adison looked at Mark. "It's the beer. Even the bottled stuff tastes like vinegar."

"You don't like this place, the door's right in front of you." The bartender was getting surlier. He suddenly left them to wait on someone at the other end of the bar.

"It's amazing they do any business." Adison pushed the beer away from her.

Suddenly, a basket of darts slid in front of Mark. He looked up surprised.

"Haven't had any new meat for a while." The leather-jacketed man was tall and skinny. His clean-shaven face had a few nicks as if it was his first shave in a while.

"Now that's a nice friendly challenge," Mark drawled.

He chose the blue plastic darts and followed the man to the dartboard. Adison made sure she sighed as she carried both bottles of beer to a table nearby.

"My name's John. You want to go first or draw for it?"

"Draw. Name's Howard. Whose the sourpuss you're with?"

Mark laughed. "It's your beer. Bad tasting beer gets her grumpy, especially after a long ride. Seems like your bartender had some, too, by his attitude."

Howard snorted. "So you're Billy's cousin?"

"Not me, Amy is. Billy's sister asked Amy to deliver a message since we were headed this way."

"What kind of message?"

Mark looked at the guy for a moment, then threw his dart, hitting the center. "I don't know. Family business. You know when he's going to be in so we can deliver it?"

Howard shook his head, then threw a dart that missed the winning mark.

"If you and Mr. Friendly are so interested in what the message is, why not just tell us when he's going to be in? Is Billy on the lam or something?"

"Nope." Another toss and Howard lost the game.

Mark shook his head and nodded to Howard. "Thanks for the game. I think we'll finish our beers and head out."

"Hey, how about another game?" Another roughly dressed biker slapped a twenty on the table.

Mark pushed the twenty he had just won toward the other.

"So that's Amy?" The new player asked as he threw a perfect toss.

"Yes, that's Amy."

"Billy's talked about her," the other offered.

Mark nodded, then took his turn.

"So is she as tough as he says she is?"

Mark eyed his opponent. "Why don't you ask her?"

"Maybe I will." His toss went wide.

Mark laughed. "You know if I didn't know better, I would swear Billy's got himself into some trouble and you guys are covering for him. Listen. We don't care."

"He's on a bike trip. Won't be back for a while. You're pretty good with the darts."

Mark grinned. "I learned a few tricks at a bar in a town called Hudson. Her name's Candy."

The guy nodded. "Maybe I'll visit. What state?"

Mark shrugged his shoulders and laughed. "We've been riding for so long, I didn't keep track. It's not like we're gathering postcards, you know what I mean? We're just driving."

"Must be nice to have the money."

Mark shook his head. "Amy's daddy gave her a credit card. I'm going along to make sure she gets home alive and not too bruised."

He looked over toward the dark-haired woman whose curt replies to one of the larger customers reached them. "I can see you have your job cut out for you."

The drunk sloppily slammed his empty beer mug down in front of the woman. He stared at her, studying the stranger through red-rimmed eyes. She was dressed in tight black leather pants that cupped her buttocks. Her leather bustier revealed a hint of a tattoo that swept over her small breasts. Her boots were well worn, her ear piercings started at the top of both her ears and ran down to her lobes, and the gold ring over her brow hinted that she would be sporting piercings elsewhere. Her boyfriend looked too middle class with his brand new leathers and shiny boots, but he was proving to be a good dart player as he finished up on his second challenger.

Before the biker could say anything, his face was squashed between the woman's hands, surprisingly strong for someone her size. If he had thought being drunk would numb the pain he was feeling, he was wrong.

"Did I invite you?" Her voice was husky and carried, and from what he could see of her dark eyes, she was pissed. Smoke curled out of her mouth from the dark brown cigarette that dangled between her painted lips. He followed her hand as she removed the cigarette from her mouth.

With his large beefy hand, he took a swat at the woman's hand that gripped his face. The next thing he knew, he was looking up at the ceiling of the club and being helped up by the woman's boyfriend.

"You shouldn't be pissing Amy off. She hates it when drunks ruin her vacation," Mark laughed good-naturedly at him.

The large man could not figure out how he landed on his back. One of his friends sitting at his table staggered over to hurt the young man and found himself on his back.

"Hey, we're just passing through. We dropped in to see Billy. He's not here, so we'll just finish our drinks and leave." He was watching the bartender out of the corner of his eye, while the cause of all the trouble was sitting quietly in her seat, sipping beer with a grimace. He had to admit she was good at this.

According to their research, Billy's cousin, Amy, was a hell raiser, which Adison had been itching to play. Mark had a difficult time talking her out of the stiletto heels and riding crop.

"Let me buy you another beer, and if you ask, you can join us," Mark offered, angling his body so the tiny camera in his buttonhole could take a picture of the man.

Adison sniffed indifferently and looked toward the bartender. "Why not bring a pitcher? Why not invite the whole stinking drunken crowd, Johnnie?

You're not going to make a night out of this, are you?" she complained in a low voice.

"Let's mend some fences first, after all, Billy works here and we don't want him to be suffering from lack of tips."

Adison glowered at him and slid farther down into her chair looking sullen.

The two men staggered to their feet and fell into the chairs Mark provided them.

Mark poured a drink in the empty mug that had been plopped down and filled the one the bartender brought with the pitcher, pushing it toward one of the men.

"So you guys have today off or do you work the night shift?" Mark asked, hoping it sounded facetious.

"What the fuck is it your business?" one of them slurred.

"It's called social conversation," Adison muttered sarcastically.

"Who the hell are you?"

"Well, that's a start. Amy Haggart," she nodded, "and you?" She continued with the attitude.

"Hey…" the other leaned over and leered at Adison, leaving a bad odor hanging in front of her. "You related to our bartender, Bad Billy?"

Adison refrained from thought for a moment, hoping it would cut the sarcastic reply that was on the tip of her tongue. Silence brings more information, she reminded herself.

When Adison didn't reply, the man continued, "I'm Monk. This here's Angus. You two aren't from here."

"Nope. Hi, Monk, Angus. I'm John. We're from Coverley, in Nebraska."

"Nebraska?"

"Well, not originally from there," Mark smiled. "We move around a lot."

"So are you related to our bartender?"

Adison looked at the bartender behind the bar and returned her attention to her beer. "Nope."

"That's Boots," Monk informed the two visitors.

"We came by to see Billy, Amy's cousin. She has a message for him," Mark said with a grin.

"Took a bike trip to Alaska," Monk continued. "Going to be gone for…a while." The pause was for a belch.

"Yes. Left about a week ago. Pity you missed him. Maybe you should've called first."

Adison's eyes flickered over to Boots the bartender, who brought another pitcher of beer and with it his sarcasm and suspicion. She gave him a disdainful look.

"So we going to chase him down, Amy?" Mark asked quietly but loud enough for the men to hear.

"I said I would deliver a message here, not up to Alaska." Her voice was cool and indifferent.

"Hey, is she always this way?" Angus asked Mark.

"Yes. It's in her genes," he smirked. "I'm going to use the head." Mark got up after getting a faint nod from his partner that she felt she was safe enough. He moved to the bar to find out which dark hallway led to the restrooms, not wanting to walk into something he was not meant to. No sense in pressing his luck. He wanted more pictures of the bar's interior.

"Them real tattoos?" Angus asked as he stared with bleary eyes at Adison's bare skin above the deep V cut of the leather vest she wore. His height gave him an interesting perspective of the mounds that had a colorful drawing over them.

Adison's attention was distracted from watching Mark move to the bar. "No, I drew them on this morning with a pen."

He stared at her for a moment, then took a gulp of his beer.

"I can draw some real good ones if you want some more somewhere else," he offered, looking hopeful.

Adison refrained from thinking about being touched by Angus. It was for a good cause, she reminded herself. In a few hours, a very elaborate dragon was drawn on her arm with black, green, red, and blue ballpoint pens. In the action of drawing the design, a bonding experience occurred between her and Angus.

Angus was in between jobs. He traveled a lot and knew the California roads like the back of his hand, so Mark dutifully quizzed him on biker-friendly towns for their supposed journey up the coast.

"You mean you don't even do it together?" Monk asked disbelievingly after Mark answered a question about their relationship.

Adison sent Mark an irritated glance before focusing again on Angus, as he chose another color for a line on the nearly finished dragon. The smooth movement of the ballpoints over her skin created an erotic experience. With all the testosterone around her, it was making her twitchy. Angus finally finished with his signature in the fireball the dragon held in a claw.

"Where's the woman's head?"

Monk made a comment that she should be careful in the restroom. A glare from the bartender squashed his speech into an unintelligible mumble.

"Hey, you, I got your cousin Billy on the phone. Want to give him your message?" the bartender's voice oozed with false friendliness.

Adison straightened up and put her hand out to take the phone, making a point of cleaning the receiver with a handkerchief dipped in beer. She was careful not to look at the bartender's expression.

Mark kept his attention focused on his beer and to one of the men who was engaged in the telling of an old war story, while keeping an ear open to what his partner was up to.

Adison said hello and listened for a few moments before she handed the phone back to the bartender. "This ain't Billy. Is this supposed to be a joke?" Turning toward Mark, she told him in a low tone, "I'm going to the head, then let's get out of here."

She was taking a chance in separating from her partner. The hall she had to walk down was dark and smelled of urine. Hopefully, the camera hidden on her person was able to get clear pictures of the people in the dark environment. She easily found the women's room due to the vulgar character drawn on the door. Pushing it open, she found a stall without a door and a sink with two women huddled around it.

Well, at least I found the right place, but I've come at a bad time. Amy wouldn't back out. She would just walk into that stall and do her thing, but I'm not going to sit on the seat.

Finished with her business, Adison stepped forward, which took her out of the stall and in plain view of the two women. While she used her foot to flush the toilet, she pulled up her zipper. She ignored the women as she attempted to leave. The skinny bleached blonde, helping the shorter woman, whose name Adison heard was Cindy, get her arm ready for a fix, planted herself in front of the door.

Adison put her hands on her leathered hips. "This is not my kind of show, so move out of the way."

"Care for a go at it?"

"No. I'm not into that."

"That's too bad. I was thinking with that attitude you're throwing around, you would make a good match with someone I know. He likes your type."

"I guess this is where I'm supposed to ask, 'just what type is that?' but I'm not. Get out of the way or I'll move you."

"Really?" She held the emptied syringe as a weapon.

"And here I had thought this bar was for low-class bikers. Apparently, it's also a place where real stupid bitches play a silly game reminiscent of the male pissing contest. Since I'm one of those people who doesn't play stupid games, I'm going to tell you once more, get out of the way," Adison said in a soft voice, not wanting to draw the attention of anyone on the other side of the door waiting for some sign to come rushing in.

The blonde pushed Cindy to the sink. That gave Adison the opening to grab the wrist with the syringe and bend it painfully back as she kicked the left leg out from under the woman. Either the woman had slow responses or she was all bluff and no fight. Adison kept the other woman in view and stayed out of her range in case she should decide to help her friend.

"Drop the syringe and I'll let go of you."

The syringe dropped and Adison moved it with her boot behind the toilet. She hoped they were not going to use it again.

"You sure you don't like them rough? I know a guy…"

"I don't want to know your friend. Or anyone else who has anything to do with this stink hole."

Adison pulled the door open, pausing long enough to be sure there was no one waiting for her, and as the door was closing behind her, she heard the other woman's voice.

"We can turn her onto Danny. She'd teach him a lesson or two."

"Shut up, Cindy," the other voice hissed.

Adison was gone longer than Mark knew a woman needed to be. He kept an eye on who was heading down the hall until the guy in the tight T-shirt walked in that direction. Mark paused a few moments, giving his partner more time. Adison reappeared looking irritated.

Mark stood up. "What's going on?"

Adison shook her head. "Let's get out of here. The people here are a real pain." She pulled on her coat while walking toward the door. She gave her tattoo artist a wave and mumbled that the bar was too strange for her liking.

Outside in the clean air, Mark and Adison kick started their hogs. A few people doing their drug business outdoors seemed to be impressed with the noise and flames that flashed from the exhaust pipes.

Adison pulled out first, followed by Mark, who then pulled ahead.

Ten minutes later, Mark gestured and banked the cycle around a curve. He gunned it up a small path not really meant for a Harley, and Adison gamely followed. Mark pulled his bike behind a power shed and started to go over the motorcycles with a SureFire light while Adison kept watch. He then added more pipe, giving them bends that would make them quieter. He then Velcroed a cover onto the gas tanks, changing the color of the bikes. While Mark changed the bikes' appearance, Adison pulled out warmer tops to wear under their leather coats.

"Okay. I found one on each."

"They aren't exactly intelligent. A GPS on the tail pipe? That's what an amateur would do. Are you sure that's it?"

"Take a look."

Adison knew he was not insulted for his mantra was two pairs of eyes on a scene were always better than one.

Why are my little alarm bells telling me something's not right?

"What about pixie dust?" She took a shot in the dark.

"Then we're either going to have to find a car wash or a yard hose, and even that isn't going to remove it all. Come on. We have to keep moving."

Back on the road, Mark backtracked, looking for the off-ramp that promised lodging and food. Twenty minutes in the opposite direction, they rolled into a hotel parking lot looking around them for weaknesses and possible places to hide should they need to.

"Wait here, I'll see about a room." Mark left the engine on, walking quickly to the office.

"So…" Mark looked down at his partner stretched out on one of the beds looking tired. Mark cleared his throat to get her attention.

"What clued you the call was a fake or did you know?"

Adison had been nodding off, letting her thoughts wander. She yawned, put two pillows behind her head, and resettled herself on the bed.

"If he's in the wilderness, how is he going to be reached? Cell phones don't work all that well in the mountains, which we all know. Besides, while he was talking, there was an *I Love Lucy* show running in the background. I guess they thought with all the noise in the bar, I wouldn't hear it, or they just never thought to turn the television down."

"Did you notice a few of the folks who walked in?"

"Yes. They all gave me the creeps, especially the guy talking to the bartender most of the time. His cell phone conversations must have been boring, though, because he kept them real short."

"I wonder why they didn't toss us out sooner. The longer we stayed there, the more of a chance the beer would loosen tongues."

"Maybe that's why the bartender wanted us out, until he had a conversation with Mr. T-shirt. Then, did you notice people started to approach us? Trying to find out about us as much as we about them."

"You think what information we were given is reliable?"

"If we look deeper. For example, Monk said he drives a lot. You asked him about biker bars along some roads." She shook her head in disbelief and laughed. "If I hadn't seen that map in your friend's bike shop where we got our bikes, I would have not been able to say yea or nay on his story."

Mark smiled. "Yes. It sounds like he drives a truck. Some of those stops he mentioned I recognized as trucker stops."

She nodded. "Angus is a trucker, too. He referred to gas as diesel a few times." Adison appraised him critically. "You know, Detective Scripts, your disguise is really good. Change of facial bone structure, facial hair, eye coloring…even the FBI would have a problem. I think we can say we did good with our disguises."

"Aren't you being a bit cocky on your disguise?" He leaned over and pulled at the edge of her ear where the piercings ringed the outside of her ear. It came off in his hand.

"Ah, ah. You didn't even know who I was when you first saw me." She wagged a finger at him. "Even my mother wouldn't recognize me, but then again, she didn't recognize me in a prom dress." She pulled off the other fake part of her ear and handed it to him.

138

Mark carefully placed the outer ear cuffs in a plastic bag he had in his pocket.

He leaned back in his chair pleased with the operation so far. "I'd like to see you in a prom dress."

"Not likely," she enunciated each syllable. "I was cured from the urge to dress up after doing two years in tight dresses, perched on stiletto heels."

"Ah, yes. Your rookie years."

"Being a rookie was one year of harassment. The second year was abuse." She changed the topic quickly, realizing she was giving out too much personal information. "There was a drug dealer standing out on the street, did you see the woman with him? Real skinny? Her taste in clothes was better than the rest of the people in the bar. She spent a lot of time talking to the two women who were in the restroom I visited."

"What went on in there that took you so long? If it was a BM or something like that, I don't need to know."

Adison shook her head. "If I had to, it wouldn't have been there. Would you believe it if I told you that I thought I spotted surveillance cameras behind some badly camouflaged decorations in that water closet? One was angled so one's gender could be determined."

"I guess they don't like gender benders. I spotted two in the men's room, one over the trough and one over the toilet stall. You're getting me worried that you might get ink poisoning. Why don't you wash that stuff off your arm?"

Adison looked at her decorated arm with a dragon that went from her shoulder to her wrist. "You don't like my dragon? If it didn't hurt so much to get a tat and if they weren't so permanent, I wouldn't mind one like this. Matt or Emily could do a good job of copying it, huh?"

"Hold on a moment. That gives me an idea. Angus is very good at this. Good enough to maybe have a reputation in the business."

"Right. We can ask Matt and Emily if they know his art."

Mark aimed his buttonhole camera at Adison's arm and took a few pictures.

While Adison scrubbed the ink off, Mark stood outside the door continuing the conversation.

"So about the women in the restroom..."

Adison looked up at her partner. "That room was a closet. It had a stall around the toilet—without a door, where the space was real tight. The sink looked like the toilet bowl and hadn't been cleaned for a long time. I tried not to touch anything that wasn't mine. It was crowded with three of us in there. Two women were leaning over the sink when I came in." Adison paused, rinsing the soap off to see how much more scrubbing was needed.

"They were involved in a very intimate passing of fluids." She glanced at Mark. "Not of the sexual type, unless you're into Freud. It could have either been heroin or insulin. Cindy was the woman getting the injection. About four inches taller than me, not chunky, but not skinny. She wears her brown hair tucked back behind her ears."

Mark nodded that he knew who she was referring to.

"I don't think she's into heroin because she was coherent enough to talk after the injection."

Mark nodded.

"The two could pass for cousins. The one with Cindy was tall and had meat to her, too, wore a leather skirt with her breasts nearly falling out of a skimpy blue top…"

"Did all the talking of the two at the bar with the woman you identified as a drug dealer," Mark added to show he knew who she was referring to.

Adison nodded. "She wouldn't let me out until I knocked her down. I was wondering if maybe they were waiting for someone. She made the comment that she knew I would make a good match with someone she knew because I had a smart mouth. When I was leaving, Cindy mentioned I should meet up with someone by the name of 'Danny' to give him his due or something like that. The other woman told her to shut up."

"Too much information."

"It wasn't free, but I didn't have to work very hard for it," Adison agreed.

"How about in the bar? Did you notice any of the guys Danny meets?"

"Yes. Mr. T-shirt. He was sitting in the darkest part of the bar saying a few words to the bartender. Did you get a look at his tattoo? That's the first time I noticed he wore one."

Mark nodded. "I recognized him too from meetings with Danny near the freeway on-ramp. Well, so far, the only thing that stands out is that we weren't tossed out as fast as the other agents who tried to get in. And we left on our own accord."

"Maybe the pictures we got will help. I don't know about you, but this went too smoothly. It's not over yet," she cautioned. "And I'm not so sure that what we were allowed to see can be believed."

"Ain't that the truth? Let's get some downtime before we go into our next phase. I'll take the first watch. I'll give you an hour." Mark glanced at his watch.

Adison nodded. She rinsed off her arm once more and returned to the bed, falling asleep quickly.

Adison woke an hour later, according to her watch. Mark was not in the room, nor in the bathroom.

Where are you, partner? I know you don't smoke.

In the dark, Adison pulled on her boots. She listened at the door but heard nothing. Carefully, she peered out the draped windows. The parking lot was semi-lit. She could see dark figures moving around the vehicles near the office. They were methodically checking the parked cars, working their way toward their room.

"Oh, joy. I think we shook someone up," she muttered under her breath. "They must've been working real hard trying to locate us since we left the bar."

After checking the room for anything that should not be left behind, she hurried into the bathroom. The washrag was stained with the ink from her arm. She stuffed it in her pocket, grimacing at the dampness.

The bathroom window was small but would do for an emergency exit. She tossed her favorite leather coat out first, then squeezed out, dropping into a crouched position below the window. Carefully, she studied her surroundings for any movement before picking her way in the dark toward where she remembered they hid the bikes. She paused as a familiar figure headed her way.

"If you hadn't crawled out of there then, I was about to make some noise to wake you up," he laughed. "You had me worried for a moment. I thought I was going to have to tie a rope around you and the bike and pull you out," he whispered.

"Funny," she hissed.

"These guys have silencers," Mark warned. "Let's get out of here while they're still on foot."

Once they had rolled the cycles back onto the road, they started their engines and shot off toward San Francisco.

"What's the plan?" she yelled.

"No need to change it. We'll drop the bikes off, change our identities, split up, and meet back in Sunrise on Friday," he yelled back. "I take it you're heading to your cabin?"

"Yes. Get in some rest."

Larry's Bike Shop was closed when they arrived, as was expected. Mark bypassed the alarms and they rolled the bikes in. The owner, who was not Larry, was an old friend of Mark's from his Navy SEAL days.

After returning the bikes and changing their appearance, both split up. Adison headed to her cabin knowing Sam would be waiting for a debriefing.

Adison arrived at her cabin early Wednesday. Sam was waiting with a warm cabin and hot tea. He also had a message from Mel.

Adison sat with her chin cupped in her hand. "I think I'm brain weary," she complained. "Because I don't care. So two more names on the list, Gene Blackmond and George Matthews, and both had an asterisk next to their names. It's the sniper's trainee," she said. Sam nodded. "Got anything planned these next two days?"

Sam shrugged. "I thought I would let you get some rest. You look like you need your two days."

Adison nodded.

"How about lunch, my place tomorrow? I know how you like to do reality checks on your cover work. How about doing it over soup and grilled cheese sandwiches?"

"Right now, anything that is *later* sounds good. I feel more than tired." The offer of food that she didn't nuke in the microwave was always her first choice.

Chapter Fourteen

"Mark, Alex...good morning."

Alex settled in the lumpy seat next to Mark. She dipped her bagel in the hot coffee. Mark was munching on his onion bagel heaped with cream cheese and a slice of onion and tomato on top.

"Any word from any of your contacts, Chief?" Scripts asked.

"No. Were you careful about prints?"

"We kept our fingertips covered, even at Larry's Bike Shop."

"So, Eric, did you get any hits off the names or faces from the bar we supplied you?" Alex asked eagerly.

"Yes." He pulled out pictures with a typed history attached to each photo. "They all have records, except the guy in the corner. I got his name from the FBI files, too, but on another list. He started training as an agent and dropped out two weeks before graduation. No reason given.

"I gave a photo of your tattoo to Matt and Emily, Alex. It was real nice. If you kept it, it would have really batted some eyes in town. I didn't tell them it was on your arm," Eric teased.

"If you did, I would've shot you myself," the chief grumbled.

"Yes. Matt and Emily would have been drooling over Alex every time she came near their office with the prospect of a new canvas," Harriet chuckled, "and I would have to make a new porcelain doll of you with a nice tattoo."

"Oh, gods. Don't do that to me. I'd have to buy them all out," Alex begged.

"Matt and Emily ID'd the artists of both tattoos. They said yours was done by Angus Adams. Been to jail throughout the U.S. many times on transporting stolen stuff. He's a favorite in the prisons for doing tattoos. This guy," Eric tapped the picture of Mr. T-shirt, "his was done by an artist in Alabama called the Alabama Tattoo King. You'll find his designs in a lot of tattoo magazines." Eric pulled out another paper with the design blown up. "This design, however, we are all familiar with. A legionnaire's sword with a flower wrapped around the blade. It's exclusively worn by the White Knights. Emily and Matt didn't recognize the type of tattoo, just the artist and said the tattoo looks new." He pointed to a reddish outline. "It's not from the photo, it's from scarring of a new tattoo."

The chief frowned. "If you were able to pull this information, then someone else could have, too."

Eric nodded. "If anyone accesses his name or fingerprints, it has a flag. But as always, I took the usual precautions in covering my tracks."

"Officer Burns, you are one heck of a hacker," Alex teased.

Eric Burns smiled at her, looking pleased, then his expression turned serious. "That list of names your contact gave you, Chief? I got two hits this morning. And, Alex, it was confirmed that Gene Blackmond, the doctor, committed suicide. He sold a bad batch of heroin to a family member of someone important. Rather than face that person, he OD'd. No chance of anyone else in that room."

"Due to?"

"He had chains on all his doors and his windows were burglar-proofed. They had to use a battering ram to get in. By the coroner's report, he was a hard user. Arms and leg veins were tapped out. He didn't even get the needle out of his neck. About the two hits in another state...George Mathews was killed in a freeway accident outside of Piedmont. He lost control of his vehicle and it flipped over. The second name, Al Brentwith, fell off his balcony drunk."

"Five more to go with the asterisks if you don't count the doctor." Adison looked around the table.

Chief Harper glanced at his watch. "Anyone else have something to add or discuss?" Harper asked, looking at his team. "Then let's get to work."

"It's the most information we've gotten in a long time," Harriet said as they rose to leave.

"Enough for my dreams to keep busy with all night," Eric snorted.

"Don't tell me you're into dream interpretations," Alex asked more serious than her tone implied. She was aghast that another talent in what her one auntie playfully referred to as the "woo-woo" field was on SPD.

"Oh, no," Eric smiled. "That's Connie Lynch and Ray Zodiac at the Golden Eye."

"Alex, you are way too nervous about psychic phenomena. I thought you said your aunties were into stuff like that," Harriet said.

"That's exactly why I'm a skeptic with a healthy respect for not mixing it with police work."

"I know you're not serious about that," Harriet said as they descended the stairs.

Alex didn't answer her, leaving a puzzled Harriet at her desk.

"Mark, she can't be serious. There's a lot of detective work based on hunches, dreams, and other stuff, not just logic," Harriet argued, watching Alex crossing the street in too much of a hurry.

Mark shook his head. "Maybe she's uncomfortable with discussing it. Who knows what she went through as a kid or in her other police jobs."

Mark hurried after his partner, sensing that Alex was upset about something.

"Hey, Alex. Hold up," he called. He was tempted to just let her walk and he would follow her, but that was not what he thought she needed. "Let's go get coffee before the early lunch crowd fills the booths."

Alex glanced back at Mark, whose long strides quickly caught up with her. She was feeling exhausted with knowing more than what her teammates did. Now she understood why Mel kept information from her. Lying was a guilty burden she kept thinking someone would see through easily.

Later that night, Alex wearily climbed the stairs into her apartment disgusted with the day's business. Next week, she would start her two weeks off and she was grateful she only had one boss to make the arrangements with.

She dropped her gun belt on the couch/bed and went into the kitchen to boil water for her Earl Gray decaf tea. While the water heated, she dug out her TD53 transmitter detector and made a sweep around her place. She only located her equipment. She checked her camera to see if anyone tripped the alarm and visited. No uninvited visitors. With her SureFire light, she looked for hidden cameras or mics and found none. Satisfied, she changed into more comfortable clothes, retrieved her cup of tea, and started her next set of business duties.

She flipped on her computer and flopped down in the only chair in the front room. It was comfortable and well used. Struggling to not fall asleep, she wiggled out of the chair and signed on to her PC. She first opened her security program looking for any indication that her PC had been accessed. Her lips curled in a smile. Nope. Over the year, she had been able to spot three unsuccessful attempts to get into her PC from the Internet.

"Okay, let's see. Mia and Gary Oberman. Mia Lu is from Canada, Gary from Ohio. Right, right. He's a chemist...right, same ol' stuff. Met Mia at the family clinic in Canada...Yes, yes...tell me something new or this stuff is a waste of time." She moved onto Mia's bio. Her eyes scanned Mia's credentials and the new information...dates and destinations of when she traveled outside of Sunrise.

Now, why does that ring a bell? Whole Life Expo? Right...three years ago in Seattle. Alan Gibson. We ran a sting operation on contraband with Interpol. He was using conventions as a cover.

Alex tried to remember if she had seen Mia in Seattle. Shaking her head, she frowned. At the time, she had been too focused on her assignment to have noticed what didn't pertain to the bust.

Well, if she recognized me, she hasn't mentioned it. However, I can't leave this loose end. I'm going to feel like I'm sticking my finger in the socket to find out if it's hot.

She moved on to the next profile and the next. By midnight, she had read over ten of the names her SPD fellows had eliminated as not likely to be the boss of the Jaded Amulet, substantiated by SID's group.

Alex sighed and rubbed her neck. She didn't have to CC a copy to Harper since Mel had already done so. Time to move on to the next group of names, but that was going to have to wait for another day. She was more than ready for bed. Mark would be waking her up early for their run.

Noon the next day, she happened to spot Mia leaving the sandwich shop. It helped that Mia had regular hours for taking her midday walk, stopping to pick up her husband's lunch.

"Hi, Mia. Do you want a lift to the clinic?"

Mia looked surprised.

"Are you going to tell me that you can't take the kid's class tonight?" she asked as she drew the seat belt across her tiny frame.

"Oh, no, no. Not at all. Kids are the right skill level for me. Besides, they aren't shy about trying to beat me up. Keeps me on my toes."

"Uh-huh."

Alex cleared her throat and maneuvered the car away from the curb.

"Alex, are you going to talk about the weather...or get to the point of what's bothering you?"

"I'm just giving you a lift, Mia."

"Alex, you're a terrible liar," she said without ill will.

Under normal circumstances, Adison liked Mia's forthrightness and attention to detail, but not now. She was wishing she had thought this out better.

"Last night, I remembered meeting you about two or three years ago."

"We didn't meet, but I do recall seeing you. You were a bit preoccupied with an older man, who by the headlines the next day, wasn't the kind of man one's mother would like her daughter knowing."

"Uh, yes." Alex waited for the light to change, hoping something clever would come to her by the time it turned green. Unfortunately, she was drawing a blank.

"You don't need to explain yourself, Alex. Keeping one's life private in Sunrise is quite an accomplishment. I have no intentions of disclosing it."

Alex pulled into the clinic driveway.

"Thanks, Mia."

"Thank you for the ride."

Alex wondered, as she drove through town with no real destination, what she would have done if Mia said she suspected something and reported it to Mark. Mel's theory to keep a cover near as close to a person's real self had no validity in this case. There was nothing on her résumé that would have put her in Seattle. It was something she needed to let Harper know about.

Alex was about to sit at her desk when Mark came out of Eric's domain. "Alex, got a moment?"

"Sure." She followed him into the chief's room.

The door was open, and the chief looked up as Mark strode in. He put his pen down and motioned for Alex to close the door. He pulled out his small jamming device and waited as Mark handed him a printout and a copy of the same to Alex.

"What's going on?"

"Remember that lost hand? It belongs to a Bo Chasley. His wife in Burling, Alabama, thought to file a missing persons report a few weeks ago. Her excuse is that he travels a lot and they aren't that close." Mark pointed to the photo of a young man dressed in camo gear.

"From what Eric got from the FBI files, the Chasley clan makes up a large percentage of the White Knights. That's an early picture of him when he was in the Army. He was about forty-five. DNA matched. He belongs to an elite group of enforcers in the White Knights. They had their own tattoo on the inside of the wrist, and they have a circle on the inside of their palms. It's part of their initiation into this elite group."

"Is it a payback for the ten dead Salvadorians?" Alex asked.

Harper frowned. "Maybe. Let's see what more Eric comes up with. Doing anything special for your two weeks off, Alex?"

"Yes. I plan on leaving my pager and cell behind. I'll be up at my cabin with a *friend*, so I don't want to be bothered."

"Good." The chief nodded pleased. "Mark and I can handle whatever comes up here. Just like the old times, huh, Mark?"

Alex grinned. "You plan on running with him, too?"

"Not if it's early. Bessie gets grumpy when I get up too early."

"Well, I plan on forgetting all about work for the next two weeks, so resist any calls or visits."

"Just don't forget to come back. I got spoiled with not having to be out more nights than there are days in a week," Mark reminded her.

Alex was not lying about her plans. She was planning on being with Leslie Adams, a friend of Alex's from her rookie days. She was a bartender who could not stay away from the booze and eventually drank herself into the streets. She was six years sober, an electrician, and just broke up with her lover of five years. Both were recovering alcoholics. Leslie was going through some difficult times.

Alex wanted to give her a breather of two weeks in a place she wouldn't be tempted to fall off the wagon. She owed it to the woman who gave her advice that changed her life, though Leslie believed it was just a truism that anyone could have told her. Alex agreed it could have been the atmosphere and timing, but it still changed her life. It made her rookie year more bearable and the men she worked with less powerful to stress out her life.

Leslie was petite but had a black belt in jujitsu and used her martial arts as a means to control her urges to drink. Katas came in handy. Alex paid for her plane tickets, not trusting a bus that would give her too much time on her hands and no one to help her through her rough moments of loneliness. The airport was a small one that private owners with nothing bigger than a company jet landed at.

Alex found Leslie staring pensively out the glass window onto the runway. She had one hand under her arm and the other holding a cup of coffee.

"Hey, Leslie," Alex called softly, so as not to startle her.

Leslie turned to look at her, startled at first, then she smiled broadly. "Good grief, Alex. What have you done with yourself?"

"I cut my hair and cut out the makeup. How are you doing?" They hugged each other, then parted.

"I've had worst days and I've had better. So let's see what this cabin of yours looks like. A jacuzzi in the woods, huh?"

Both women had a good chat on the way to the cabin, catching up on news and getting reacquainted. When Alex left the police in the small town of Leabetter, Leslie was still bartending. No one would hire her for what her family trained her as—building contractor. They kept in touch even when Leslie hit rock bottom and through her first AA meeting. Phone calls were their method of contact.

Alex parked the SUV next to the cabin, watching Leslie's expression.

"Looks a bit rough for the likes of you. Does this have outdoor plumbing or indoor?"

"Not amusing. Do you think I would have a jacuzzi indoors and toilet outside?"

And so began their vacation, and for Alex, the first real one she had for years.

Chapter Fifteen

S o, Alex, what are you doing for the new year?" Mark started their run along the back alley, leading toward the ocean.

"Staying off the road, going to bed early, and not waking up with a hangover."

"That's what you did last year. You starting a tradition?"

"I do that every year, Mark. It's already a tradition. What are you guys planning on doing?"

"Linda and I stay up to watch the ball in Times Square drop and reminisce about the year we went to New York to see it in person. We got engaged there. We were freezing cold and hopping up and down to keep warm. I don't want to do it again. Too crowded and too cold. Now Linda and I snuggle together on the couch, Jon usually crawls in his sleeping bag and Katie last year fell asleep in her bean bag with Angel curled up next to her. Who knows what it'll be this year."

Adison chuckled. She was grateful that this year everyone accepted her desire to not spend her holidays surrounded by crowds. She worked the holidays to give the others that had family a break.

As they started up the hill on their morning run, Angel sprinted to the top, leaving her running companions to huff after her. The two detectives were quiet in their thoughts. Alex thought about her seventeen months on assignment in Sunrise and the last four months of little progress with the Jaded Amulet and the White Knights. The Jaded Amulet members continued to live nearby, but there was a standstill in all their social meetings and business dealings, including meetings with gang members on militia nights. Something happened to make everyone lay low, and it was causing Mike and Amos to be irritable with their compadres to the point that the two men spoke very little to each other. Mike's Internet chatter was silent, as well, and email addresses he once mailed to were changed. Without the chatter, Eric's embedded Trojans could not send him the new addresses and copies of what the sender mailed out.

SID's instructions for her were to sit tight. Mel through Harper was reassured that things were happening. Harper asked if she knew just what Mel had up his sleeves and Alex said no. She wished she did.

Worrying about becoming lax in her vigilance, she was grateful Sam had her working on wilderness survival games.

Does someone in the Jaded Amulet know about the list besides the killer or killers? Maybe one or both of the bosses names are on that list.

Back in her apartment, she glanced at her calendar on the kitchen wall. It was Monday, which meant card night at Claire and Genie's. Though she was no longer asked to play cards, she visited because she felt safe there. While showering, she realized she no longer referred to the women's shelter as a shelter but as Claire and Genie's. Her soapy hands paused when she heard her phone ring.

There was the anticipation again. Something was going to happen. Wrapped in a towel, she grabbed up her phone, not bothering to turn the light on.

"Hello?"

"Adison. Briscolle."

Alex could feel her heartbeat increase and nervously looked around as if expecting trouble to pop up.

"Yes. What's happening?"

"FBI. They're sending in a new team to work on that forest case. Someone wants to know who the sniper is who got away. She's causing ripples of trouble with her steady progress of eliminating names off your list."

"How did they get a copy of the list?"

"Judge Mead. This team will be talking to you. It's an agent you may remember and hopefully he will not remember you. You weren't looking your best when you met."

"Who?"

"Agent Lockwood."

It was seconds before the name registered. Alex's throat became dry, her vision narrowed, and her hearing was as if she were underwater. Briscolle heard the slight intake of breath and let Alex collect herself.

"So, what's the plan?" Alex asked softly.

"You did a profile on him once. You know what you need to do to keep him in line."

"All right." Adison took a few cleansing breaths, focusing on the business at hand to get control. "Anything else going on around here?" she asked, hopeful to get some inside information so she wouldn't feel like... Her thoughts stopped, realizing that if there was nothing more for her to do in Sunrise, she would be leaving.

"We need you to keep a low profile. Word leaked to the White Knights that there's an agent in Sunrise. Right now, the local gang and our target think it's FBI, and the FBI spy thinks it's us or ATF. That's one reason all has become quiet in your area. Don't worry, things will heat up again and get interesting."

150

"That brings me a lot of comfort, Briscolle," she mocked.

"Bye, Adison," she said dryly. "And, Adison, no more surveillance."

"Right."

"Low profile. We don't want to blow your cover," Briscolle reinforced. "Take a needed vacation."

"I got the message," she said grinning.

Leaning back on her pillows, she forced herself to think about Agent Lockwood. She needed to keep flashing on his face so when she did meet with him, if it came to that, she wouldn't go pale and throw up. Or really lose it and pull out a gun and shoot him in the foot.

Chapter Sixteen

It was Friday morning just before daybreak, and Adison was pulling out of the airport parking lot after seeing off her weekend friend when she spotted a familiar car in the lot. As she drove out of the parking structure, she glanced around to see if she could see the owner, but Amos was not in sight. Instead of leaving, she circled around the airport and pulled out her cell phone.

"Morning, Mark. Sounds like I caught you on the run." She grinned at the thought of missing out on three days of running early in the morning.

"Good morning, Alex. What's up?"

"Amos Anders. I'm at the small airport in Dalemont where his car is parked. I'm going to snoop around and see what he's up to. I'll be in late."

"Just be careful. Do you have a camera?"

"Candid camera is my middle name."

"I'll pass it on to the chief."

"Bye."

Alex could hear the excitement in Mark's voice. It was about time something was happening with the Jaded Amulet. She was sure that was his business here at the airport. It was small and planes that flew out of here were shuttles and private. It was still dark, and by the smell in the air, the predicted rain was near.

Adison spotted the SID agent only because she had met her once before on another job. Carla, the nametag read. Carla efficiently and quickly was replenishing the snack machines with cellophane wrapped cookies, sandwiches, and other snacks. Nearby were four thermoses of coffee labeled regular decaf, regular, Starbucks and Hawaiian Hazelnut. Adison normally bypassed the snack area at small airports.

While she thought about what she was going to do about Amos and why SID had an agent here if they were only interested in the White Knights, she spotted Amos walking through the archway leading to the restrooms and telephones. Putting aside those thoughts, Alex slid into a seat facing the window that gave her a reflected view of the entrance to the restrooms. She picked up a discarded newspaper and waited. There were a few people in the lobby, having just arrived, and looking like they had a long night.

Amos came back out quickly. Alex remained where she was and continued to read her paper. She spotted him standing outside the lobby window arguing with someone. It was short and animated. Amos left, running across the street, disappearing into the early morning darkness toward the parking structure. It was just beginning to sprinkle.

The person he argued with remained outside the window. Alex could not see the face due to the umbrella that was in the way. The woman remained until Amos's vehicle pulled out of the parking structure and took off. Alex casually moved over to the coffee kiosk.

"Thanks. Hawaiian Hazelnut. Leave enough room for milk."

Alex sipped her coffee, watching her mark walk unhurriedly onto the runway and into one of the hangers. She set her coffee down and followed.

With a newspaper opened to the classified ads on airplanes for sale, she peered inside the first hanger. She heard voices coming from the center of the building. Her target was speaking to someone who had grease on his clothes and was pointing to something underneath the wing of the Cessna single-engine plane. Adison pointed her sonic ear toward them.

"...two days. Have to order the part. Cash in advance." The mechanic shook his head at whatever the woman told him, which was garbled to Alex. He laughed, so it must be an amiable business deal.

Alex slid out of the building and was headed to the payphone when she heard hurried steps behind her. She continued past the phone and ducked behind the trash bins the first chance she got, pulling up her coat collar to keep the cold drops out. Alex stuck her earpiece in her ear and pointed the sonic ear in the direction of the phone booth.

"Yes, this is Rita...no, the part has to be flown in."

Hot diggity, no voice scrambler. Alex glanced around again, not trusting in luck alone.

"I told you it needed to be replaced," she yelled angrily. "Marco, get your head out of your butt...No! I don't care if you have a date!...Then get one of the others...No!...How's her leg...I know he'll be there. This is one of the biggest comic book conventions. He won't miss this one...Just get it done!"

Alex heard the handset slammed down. She waited, hearing a long string of tapping.

"Magi...this is Rita...voice scrambler? Of course I have..." That's when the conversation ended for Alex's earpiece. "Do you think I'm stupid!" Rita hollered, then lowered her voice.

Alex quickly shut off her devices and looked for a better spot to hide. If Rita suddenly realized she was sloppy, the chances of her making an inspection nearby were slight, but Adison didn't like playing the odds in this type of game. A small gate was within sight, but the space between her and her goal was too open. She played that card already, and it got her shot at.

Another hang-up was followed by expletives that got louder as Rita approached her hiding place. Alex scurried farther back into the trash area.

Alex held her breath as the woman walked by. The perfume was vaguely familiar. Alex's heart was beating faster when she realized the footsteps had stopped in front of the trash bins. It could have been ten minutes before Alex heard someone brush by one of the wet boxes. She was coming to look.

She strained to listen for Rita's movements over her pounding pulse. She moved around one side of the trash bins while Rita was on the other side. Alex found herself in front of the bins, realizing she would have to find a place to run to quick. She chose the payphone to hide in, confident of her disguise she had hastily put together. It would also take her out of the rain. Reaching to lift the receiver, she hesitated to touch what would have a good set of prints she wanted, but she was pushing her luck not to use the phone. Instead she made as if she were looking for something in a nonexistent purse. A shadow suddenly appeared next to her, handing her a pencil and paper. Guiltily, she looked up into Carla's face. She was wearing a bright yellow rain parka.

"I always lose mine," Carla said and waited, using her body to shield any view Rita may have of her. After a few moments of Alex writing a note to SID, she heard the agent give a small sigh.

"You certainly push the 'keep a low profile' envelope. I'll get the prints and pass the info on to HQ. You need to get out of here," she admonished.

Alex's drive back to Sunrise was through heavy rain and eventually snow. By the time she reached town, it was back to a heavy rain. It was nearly lunch time and she had not stopped for anything more than coffee, and that was to check to see if she was being followed. Alex hung up her coat and walked toward the chief's office.

"Chief, can I speak with you?"

He nodded and gestured for her to close the door behind her.

"We were worried when you didn't call in."

Alex nodded. "My cell phone battery needs replacing. It's not charging, and I didn't want to stop anywhere in this weather or leave myself open if I was being followed." She plopped into one of the more comfortable chairs near his office couch, feeling tired. Chief Harper moved to the couch.

"Amos met someone at the airport we don't have any photos on," she began in a low tone. "She's a pilot. That would fit the profile of one of the bosses, no? Before she remembered to turn her voice scrambler on, I got her name, Rita, and two people she spoke with besides Amos—Marco and Magi. She mentioned a comic book convention where I believe a hit is going to be made, and I believe it's by our sniper. It could be a coincidence, but how many snipers do you know who have a leg wound?" She smiled at Harper, who was grinning. "I may be wrong, but I knew someone who had been shot in the leg, and he limped for about two years before everything was healed."

"Mike goes to a comic book convention every year this time in San Diego."

The chief picked up his phone and informed Mark he was going to be taking a trip and where. After he hung up, he turned back to Adison.

"What else?" he asked.

"All the way here, I've been trying to figure out what is familiar about her since I couldn't see her face. It's her mannerisms. She reminded me of these two women I saw on a stakeout I did in Bales over a year ago. Remember the CD I handed to you? They were the two in the bar. Mari and Margo. Unfortunately, they weren't good photos. The man they were with was John."

"You take any pictures?" the chief asked.

"Yes. I'll send them over to your mailbox and burn a copy. Something interesting about those names, Chief. They all begin with an M."

For the entire weekend, Adison was edgy. Sunday night, to take her mind off of what Mark was doing in San Diego, she focused on printing each of the names she had on paper the size of nametags, cutting them and arranging them in various categories starting with gender. She was an hour into her game when her doorbell rang.

"Whose that?" she muttered.

She heard a dog bark from outside her front door.

"Angel?"

Checking her front surveillance camera, she could see Linda, Jon, and Katie with Angel at her door. She left the paper clippings on the floor and ran downstairs.

"Linda! Hi, kids. Angel."

Angel went up the stairwell without being invited in.

"Since you're alone tonight and so are we, the kids thought you would like to have dinner with someone. We brought the food."

"Ah...sure come on in," Alex mumbled.

"Is this a bad time?" Linda asked as they climbed the stairs.

"We didn't call because we knew you wouldn't answer," Katie said seriously.

"Katie, that was our secret," Linda said without blushing.

"What are you doing?" Jon asked, looking at the pieces of paper scattered everywhere. Angel's tail was sending others off into the corner.

"Studying. Detectives are always studying."

Jon and Katie helped her gather her thirty-five pieces of paper, while Linda went into the kitchen to prepare their meal. Finished with gathering paper, the four of them trooped into the kitchen to see what Linda was doing.

"Katie, hon, can you pick out plates for us? Detective Alex will show you where they are."

Alex picked up Katie, who threw her arms around her neck and gave her a hug. Katie found a pink plate with a pink bowl for herself, then she lost interest in helping to set the table. "Do you have a TV?" she inquired with a frown.

"She told you no, remember?" Jon said. He was carefully laying out the two normal-sized forks and the two dessert forks she had, then the only two glasses she had. Linda and she would use coffee mugs and the adult-sized forks.

"How come you don't have a TV? Are you poor?"

Linda didn't answer but merely chuckled. Unfortunately for Alex, Linda and Mark liked to see her squirm when Katie would ask tough questions. Sometimes they would rescue her. This was not going to be the case.

"What has poor got to do with not having a TV? I don't have a TV because I don't have a reason for one," she explained.

"She goes over to aunties Claire and Genie's, honey. They have a big TV there," Linda teased.

"As big as ours?"

"Yes."

"Well then, what can I do here?" she asked in a plaintive voice.

"Eat dinner, have a nice conversation…"

"And play cards." Jon pulled a deck of fish cards from his pocket. "I've come prepared," he announced proudly.

"You have," Alex agreed, and Linda laughed.

"She doesn't have enough chairs," Jon said.

"That's okay we can…"

Linda was shaking her head. "Not a good idea."

"Oh." Alex was going to suggest sitting in the front room, but mothers knew best.

"Jon, you and Katie will sit and eat," Linda directed.

"I have a half step ladder and the folding chair in the front room," Alex remembered.

Dinner was filled with the children recounting what they did for the day. Katie's five-year-old mind wandered on subjects Alex had no idea what she was talking about. In those instances, she let Linda and Jon reply.

When it was time for them to leave, Alex was tired but in a good mood.

"The kids like to set you up because you're the only adult who has no idea what you're being led into," Linda said as they headed out the front door.

Alex smiled. "It took me a while, but I'm not as surprised."

"Mark told us to make sure you ate one dinner this weekend with someone. Genie said you missed your Saturday meal with them," Linda confessed.

"I feel like I belong to this big extended family and…" she didn't finish for lack of an expression.

"And?"

"Well, it takes some getting used to."

"It's been over a year, Alex, as opposed to a lifetime. Habits are difficult to break. You have improved since your first year here. You visit more and actually are more relaxed with the gossip or teasing about your private life."

"Thanks for stopping over, Linda. I really do appreciate the visit. I was feeling down," she admitted, though for selfish reasons. She wanted them to leave without too personal of questions.

Alex stood near the truck as it pulled away from the curb. *This town is growing on me whether I use weed killer or not.* She looked at the stars that were brightening up the night sky, trying not to think how that made her feel. She was too tired to bring out her names again, so she ran them through the shredder and went to bed.

Monday morning Mark was at her back door with Angel.

"Hey! When did you get in? By your looks, I would say you found something of interest."

"Yes. Ever visit a drag show? Very touchy feely crowd, if you know what I mean," he said.

Alex nearly stumbled off the steps as she laughed in the dark. Angel had run ahead, but it was better that she had because an SUV came roaring out from one of side roads with Alex and Mark diving out of the way.

"Jeez!" Alex huffed as she brushed mud and water off her clothing.

"Did you get the license?" Mark scrambled to her side.

"No, I was too busy saving my butt. Did you?" She shook her stinging hands out, picturing them with scrape marks.

"No back lights. Dent on the back fender. I remember that dent from an SUV parked outside of school."

"Do you think the driver just didn't see us?"

"I think the accident was that he or she missed us."

"It looked like an American-made SUV."

"Yes, that's fifty percent of the vehicles around here. Angel! Angel!"

The dog barked and came careening into them and ran off again.

"For a moment there..."

Alex could hear the relief in his voice.

"Did anyone recognize you at the convention?" she asked, changing the subject.

"Are you connecting that with this? No. I don't think so. I had a friend who had a booth, so I dressed as one of the boys. I wore a vendor tag. At night, I went with him to a drag show. He loves old queens. No. I don't think this has anything to do with it," he finished. "Doesn't have that feel to it. You know what I mean?"

"Where did you meet this friend?"

"When I was doing undercover work in another state. He showed me how to change my appearance, just by changing my body language, then the facial features with putty and such. He left the police business when he found out his partner was taking bribes and wanted him to front for him on a drug steal."

"Wow. From cop to comic salesman."

"Yes. Making a whole lot more money, he's safer, and he's his own boss. He started Jon on collecting them, but Jon lost interest because he ran out of room in his bedroom. He won't give up his toy space."

Alex chuckled. She noticed Mark had them circling the plaza and passing the woman's shelter.

"This is a new route. Does this mean we've become too predictable?"

"Yes. I'll have to think of a whole new approach. Like knocking on your front door sometimes."

"You're going to have me nervous."

"Angel will protect you."

Alex laughed and added, "Can you see someone trying to sneak up the back way and barking like Angel for me to come to the door?"

"Angel will not like someone trying to take her cookies," he growled at the dog, who had returned when hearing her name. She barked on cue.

Alex knew not to ask details of his weekend business until they got into work, so on her return to her apartment, she showered, dressed, and was out the door in record time. She even beat Harriet. Since she forgot her office key, she ran to the doughnut shop where she knew Harriet would be purchasing the goodies and filling the thermos for the morning coffee.

"Morning, Harriet. Could you add more jelly ones, Larry? Thanks." She reached over the counter to take the large thermos. Harriet paid for the doughnuts and coffee and the two left.

"Nice of you to help out. Any reason you're so early? Not that I'm complaining. What did you do to your hands?"

Alex was holding the thermos awkwardly, her palms still stinging from sliding on the asphalt. "Mark and I were nearly run over by an unidentified SUV this morning. Sort of took the fun out of the rest of the run."

"How can anyone miss him in his getup?"

"I don't know, but we're happy we both were missed."

Five officers sat at the meeting table with the chief, looking disturbed at Mark's recounting of the incident.

Gary shook his head. "It could very well be you weren't seen, Mark, even with that glow you got about you." He started to laugh, then looked serious and started to laugh again when Harriet giggled. Then everyone joined in. Mark's running attire made him look like a neon pole. It was difficult not to see him in the dark, which was his intention.

"Anything to report, Gary?"

"Not as exciting as Mark and Alex's run. Two alarms went off. Hale's market and a call from the guard at the warehouses. Said some cars were parked too long near one of the buildings."

"That's the second time this week Hale's alarm went off," Mark said as he wrote that down.

"Whose cars?" Alex asked, making a notation in her pad.

"Don't know. They were still there when I got off. Outside of Conklin's warehouse. If they were there tonight, I was going to run a license check on them."

"Okay. Anything else? Then that's a wrap. Sleep well, Gary."

The second meeting started after Gary left.

"Burns, do you have the pictures ready?"

"Yes. Can you get the lights, Mark?"

The first picture was that of a robust man who wore a beard and had a Superman T-shirt on.

"This is Jinks Wilde with a new face and new identity but same old fingerprints and nickname. He was one nervous mark. The comic vendors know him well. I got him out of there, which took some doing. He's not easy to hide."

"Did you get a chance to talk to him?"

"Sort of. He's under the FBI protective witness program. He had witnessed a crime syndicate hit when he was on leave from the military and had attempted to save the person shot. He thinks this sniper is from that time. I got a short life history of him, where he's been throughout his life up to the point he saw the hit. He won't talk any further. I suggested he give up comics because it's going to be the death of him."

He clicked to another picture.

"This picture is someone I thought could be a person in drag…keeping in mind that our sniper likes to dress as a guy as is this one."

The ten other shots were of people who may be the sniper.

"Any pictures of Mike and who he hung around with?" Alex asked.

"Yes." Mark clicked forward a few more, letting them view different shots of other potential snipers. "I saw him around. He hangs out with a guy called Wheeler. Here's the two of them. And where Wheeler was staying. An RV that he carries his collection around in. He also deals over the Internet. His specialty is GI Joe magazines and old Betty Boop flicks. I heard he also sells porn over the Internet. He has people do the videos for him, and if he likes it, he buys and sells them."

"Sounds like the type of guy Mike would like."

"He's also a motorcycle enthusiast and has been to the Watering Hole, that new biker bar in Brisbane, by Mike's invitation. He has his bike on a trailer that he tows with him."

"How did you find that out?" Alex asked, amazed at his fact gathering.

"I saw him with Mike at the Watering Hole two weeks ago. Linda and I met some friends there. It was Pink Ladies Night. We took the Harley. Linda wore her new pink leather outfit, and I wore my black leather pants."

"Did you take pictures?" Alex giggled, then changed her face quickly, clearing her throat. Eric grinned, which made Alex laugh again.

"We took second place in the contest," he bragged. "By then, Mike and his friends were gone. It got too busy for them, I guess."

"Did Mike see you?" the chief asked concerned.

"I kept an eye on him, but he was drunk by the time we got there and too involved with his girlfriend and trying to keep Wheeler's attention. And Wheeler was too involved with the woman he was with. Some blonde from Brisbane. Hangs out with Mike's crowd. Judy something."

"Judy Miller," Alex said. "She and Carrie Lynn went to high school together, and they do just about everything together." Alex's high pitch nasal voice parodied the bleached blonde.

"So that's all he did at the convention, hang out with Wheeler?" Harper asked.

"Nope. He made his rounds. Checked out the tables, made some purchases. That was Saturday. Jinks didn't show until late Saturday. Someone else was holding down Wheeler's table in the morning and afternoon. I hear there was some interesting side sales among the serious collectors in a closed room. Someone said Wheeler was one of them. Bought four comics in very good condition of Spider-Man. Unusual for him since that's not his thing. Sunday I didn't see Mike anywhere. He could have passed out in Wheeler's RV. I heard they had a rocking party all night and into the morning. Wheeler didn't look too hot Sunday, but he was at his booth."

"So we're still not sure about the sniper."

Mark shook his head. "Nope, and I didn't see any Jaded Amulet characters besides Mike. I asked my friend if he heard anything about Reiner seeing how he was into the drag scene. He said he would ask around. Since Reiner's dead, someone may say something if they know of him. I think anyone who was as good as he was would be known on both sides of the Atlantic."

Chief Harper nodded to Eric to switch the laptop off. "Good work. This near run-in this morning, I want you to treat it separate from our other cases. I want you all to take a deep breath. Getting paranoid can be healthy, but it also helps to step back now and then and see if maybe we lumped apples with the oranges just because they can be peeled."

He looked around and the others nodded.

Later that afternoon, Mark identified the vehicle that had nearly run them over. An adolescent from the track team was behind the wheel. He had been late for morning practice and was speeding. Mark gave him a ticket and his parents removed his driving rights when they heard he had nearly run the two detectives over.

Late Tuesday night, Adison parked her Range Rover near the cabin and unpacked her dinner for two days and some miscellaneous supplies. She planned on talking to Sam about the sniper but fell asleep after she had everything stored. It was late and she was not feeling well. When she woke Wednesday afternoon, she felt like she was coming down with a cold and her body felt like she had been in a fight. Sam's knocking woke her. She was still dressed. They had an arrangement that if she had a date, she would pull across red curtains on the kitchen door's window.

"You look terrible," Sam said as he put some water on the stove for tea.

"I feel that way, too," she groaned, wrapping her robe tightly around her. On her feet, she had a thick pair of socks.

"I'll get your tea prepared, then I'll let you sleep it off," he said as he pulled a cup out of her cupboard.

"No, don't leave. I wanted to talk to you about my favorite sniper." She plopped into one of the chairs at the small breakfast table, miserably holding her head in both hands.

"You work too hard. It's no wonder your body is asking for a rest."

"Is that what this is from? A simple cold would do. This feels terrible."

"Mel said he sent a crew out to find Jinks in San Diego. Your sniper was hot on his tail. They lost the sniper and Jinks. He could be anywhere, alive or dead."

"Mike Learner was there. He's buddies with a guy named Wheeler."

Sam sat down, looking thoughtful. "Matthew Warren. Calls himself Wheeler. These days, you can hear him on his CB radio talking trash with the truckers. He deals in GI Joe comics, Betty Boop flicks, and porn. Over thirty years ago, he was arrested and discharged from the Marines for raping a young girl in Okinawa. He paid the family a lot of money for them to drop the charges. You see, this young girl was not the typical poor unknown Okinawan the American military preys on. She had the fortune to have met and befriended a congresswoman's family. The Marines were a bit red faced and gave him his discharge papers. He didn't even spend the night in the brig, and no attempts to investigate were made. The Japanese and American governments have this unwritten agreement, and since there's a standing centuries-old prejudice the Japanese have against the population of Okinawa, it's pretty much a setup."

"What happened to the girl?."

"By now, she's an adult with a new identity."

"What brought his case to your attention?" Adison asked, knowing there had to be more.

"There's always that worry of retribution from the Marine or his buddies. I was a newbie and given the assignment to keep tabs on him so he wouldn't locate her and do something rash. He became involved in a scam deal with a sperm bank when sperm banks were just getting started. It was in a small town trying to stay alive; the college, hospital, and one pharmaceutical company that supported them had a business going. Four characters used the liaison to run a scam, collecting and selling important people's sperm. Went on for about seven years. Jinks Wilde, who was in the FBI witness protection program, Gene Blackmond, and John Meadows were the top guys. Thomas Meadows, brother of John, was found dead and the others and their associates split up and just went into other businesses. No evidence for the prosecution, so no prosecution."

"Whoa, that's something Harper needs to hear." Alex took the cold cloth Sam handed her and put it over her eyes. "What was the school's name?"

"College of Sciences or something like that. It had four name changes before it folded."

"Yikes, this is hot stuff." Alex thought for a while. Her thoughts were moving slower than the painful thuds in her head. "John Meadows," she said slowly, "was one of the bodies we found in the forest. And if Jinks was under FBI protection, how come he got involved in that scam?"

"John Meadows is a common name," he cautioned her to not jump to conclusions. "Jinks witnessed a gangland slaying when he went AWOL from the Marines. He thought since he could finger the hit man, he could use that to get out and get a new life. He was working at the college when a few people he knew showed up. Thus began the con game."

"So just what busted the scam?"

"Dr. Blackmond and his laboratory contact, Joe Carson, who handled the implanting, thought it would be a good idea to add some notable names to their venture as donors. They had drivers, salesmen, and all sorts of people to get the people with names a squirt of their sperm. It was quite a racket."

Click, click. Names are falling into place. So maybe this list is someone who got burned on this deal. But there are other names not connected to this scam. Forget that angle.

"So," Adison took a sip of the lemon tea. She could not smell it, but the heat was nice as it moved down her sore throat. "No Wheeler or Joe Carson was on the hit list, but there is an Ed Carson."

"Brings an interesting twist to this case."

"Twist? It's an endless pretzel," she whined. "One measly case for SID and I have hundreds of other crimes and loose ends. No more jobs that are more than a month," she groaned.

Sam chuckled. "Isn't that what being covert is all about?"

"Then I like the ones that are less complicated and just require information gathering. In and out."

"Uh-huh. You're talking about being recon, and that's a lot more dangerous than what you're doing here. You sound depressed."

"I feel awful. If anyone wants to shoot me, I won't put up a fight."

"You should be careful about tempting the fates, Agent Adison."

Alex groused, "You sound like my aunties. Forgive me, fates. I know not what I say," she mocked. Her voice sounded strained. "This is one of those times that I wish I could drug myself, but I get hives from flu shots."

"Bed and sleep then. I'll be by later. I'll bring some soup, so don't shoot *me*."

"Not the cook, the nurse, and dishwasher" she agreed.

Alex's weekend was spent sleeping and drinking soup. By early Friday, she felt a little better. Sam drove her in her SUV back to Sunrise and made her promise to visit the clinic later. She managed a shower, dressed reasonably warm, and somehow got to work. She promptly spewed her tea in the trash can near her desk and was sent home.

At three in the afternoon, Mark woke her, unasked, to drive her to the clinic. Loaded up with herb capsules, after sleeping through her acupuncture treatment, she was assigned to her bed to sleep some more. By Sunday night, she was feeling a whole lot better and deeply touched by the arrangement friends made to see that she was not overwhelmed by concerned visitors and had plenty of soup when she woke. The numerous get well cards in her mailbox had surprised her, and to her astonishment, she actually read the cards. The side remarks reminded her that these people didn't know that she wasn't a real person. It struck a profound cord within her, and most of her waking hours were spent trying to demystify the feeling of community the townspeople gave her.

Monday morning, Adison walked to work, not feeling energized but not feeling ill. She pushed opened the front door to the office, and Harriet was already settled behind her desk. She looked up surprised, then relieved.

"Well, you sure look a lot better," Harriet said. "Good morning." She put a lot energy into the greeting. Alex suspected her being out put a strain on their personnel coverage.

"Good morning, Harriet. Thanks. I feel a whole lot better."

She climbed the stairs, wondering if by noon her energy would be at a respectable level.

"Good morning, Nurse Scripts," she grinned as she hung up her coat, removed her gloves and took a deep breath.

"You're looking a whole lot better, Alex."

"I'm happy to say I feel better, though I wouldn't want to test myself by running around the block yet," she said just in case Mark might want to resume running Tuesday.

"You're lucky then. It's predicted to snow the next few days."

"Morning, Chief," they said in unison as Chief Harper leaned out his door to let them know he was ready for the meeting.

"Good morning, Alex. Looking a bit pale, but you're up and moving. That's all I need from you today."

Alex's eyebrows lifted. "Yes?"

They all settled around the table.

"Hale's store was robbed while you were out." Chief Harper leaned forward and handed her an evidence envelope.

Adison opened it and slid the contents out. One was a plastic bag with a Mickey Mouse watch, not unlike her own, in it.

"Wow. Mickey is getting around." She looked at her wrist, which was noticeably missing her watch. "I can't remember the last time I had it to tell you the truth."

"I can," Harriet told them all. "I was working your shift on Saturday, Alex, so when Mark came back with the evidence to log in, I could see it was a watch like yours. You had left your watch in the bathroom downstairs Friday, and I brought it upstairs and left it on your desk, only it wasn't there when I checked Saturday. I asked Mark, but he couldn't remember seeing it on the desk."

Alex rubbed her forehead. "I honestly don't remember what I did with it."

"That was Friday morning after you puked at your desk," Eric Burns reminded.

"Thank you, whoever cleaned up after me," Alex mumbled embarrassed. "But who picked up the watch if Harriet left it on my desk?"

"Wouldn't be able to tell you," Harriet said. "I was at the shelter doing a talk on reporting a crime. Mike and Danny may have come in during their breaks, then this weekend was the big Writer's Board and Breakfast seminar. They had a few popular writers who were going to give a little background on their books. People not signed up for the seminar lined up at the bookstore for autographs. You missed a great weekend."

"And to think I slept through it all." Alex shook her head regrettably. "So those alarms Gary reported during his shift for the last few weeks were just testing," she mused.

"Sounds like it," Mark nodded.

"What about the cars parked at the warehouse?"

"Two guys from Bales. They said they thought it was militia night, and when no one showed up, they sat in their cars and got drunker. They called a girlfriend to drive them home."

"Militia night is the first Friday of every month with the dates posted on their Web site," Harriet snorted, "so that means they were either too drunk to know or they think we're stupid."

"How many days were the vehicles there?"

"Four," Mark said, pulling out his notebook. "I also noticed they were moved during that time, by the tire tracks. Unfortunately, I didn't take pictures."

"What was stolen?"

"A fresh shipment of jumbo lobster tails, Canadian sea bass, shrimp, salmon, swordfish, and a delivery of small bills and change from Wells," the chief read from his report. "They were expecting about five thousand in bills also, but the time for shipment was changed to when Sunrise Bank could get the cash to them."

"So it's either a guard for the money delivery company or the driver for the fish. With fish, you have to move it quickly. That means they would have to have a buyer for the stolen merchandise already set up, so my money is on the fish delivery person. They would also have someone on the inside, but not close enough to the owner to know that the bank changed delivery time. Why did the bank change delivery time?"

"Very good, Detective. Looking a bit wan, but you come out swinging. The bank is short staffed with the flu going around, and they want to stick to the dual custody in accessing the vault. We're already looking at those angles."

"When did this happen?" Adison asked.

"In the wee hours of Saturday morning."

"The night I'm usually on call," Alex said. "How fortunate that I was sicker than a dog, but alas, no witnesses that I was home at that time. What time did the crime take place?"

"We're not sure," Mark said. "The alarms didn't go off this time. Gary swung by at one in the morning just to see what was going on because of the previous alarms and found the back delivery doors wide opened."

"And what a stroke of luck for someone to have found a watch like mine to leave at the scene," Alex drawled.

"So, Detective, where were you on Saturday morning between the hours of midnight and three a.m.?" Mark asked.

"Well, Detective, what makes you so sure it was between those hours?" she countered.

"Because the store had the last employee closing up at midnight. That would be the nephew of the owner, Jack Linton. And, yes, we are doing a background check on him, too."

Eric nodded and raised his hand, looking smug. "I've got some information on the nephew. He's out on probation for car theft. His mother sent him up here to live with her brother."

"Jack? No wonder he's so sour about his sister," Harriet said.

"There's more," Eric interrupted, looking uncomfortable. "His father, Duffy Castleton, is in jail for a bank robbery that went bad. He was the driver and the only one who survived."

Alex suddenly felt the world become narrower and her breathing constricted. *What is happening?* Images of Duffy, a slightly overweight man with nothing remarkable about him except his occupation, flooded her mind. He was the getaway driver to a gang of robbers who had been targeting small town banks. It was suspected that someone in the FBI was involved with the heists, so SID was called in to investigate. This was too coincidental. Lockwood—her nightmare—was the investigating officer of that mess.

"Alex. Alex!"

Alex looked up startled. "What? Oh. I was just remembering something," she said faintly. Even to her ears, she didn't sound well.

Eric pushed a sheet of paper she didn't need to see to the center of the table. It was a computer printout of a newspaper picture of her and several others lying with blood all over them before the triage team could get there. Luckily, it was black and white and didn't pick up the grisliness of the shootings, and some may not recognize that she was one of the unconscious faces on the floor. She had been a teller when the group hit the bank.

Alex forced herself to breathe, trying to push the memory away. But there she was. Back in that nightmare. The robbers were all high on something, so talking them down was impossible. The FBI was running the show and was delayed in meeting the demands of the robbers to supply a helicopter. For every five minutes they delayed, another hostage was rolled out the door, shot, though not necessarily dead. Of course, the small town of Wentworth didn't have a helicopter nor did any of the neighboring towns. But the FBI did, and the robbers knew it was there because everyone heard it fly in. It was a no-win situation for the hostages in that farming community. She had to make a snap decision to blow her cover and give her partner a shot at the leader. Her face was already bruised from the blows she received for trying to talk the two accomplices out of doing what they looked like they didn't have the stomach to continue.

She spent a week in the hospital and three months recuperating from a broken collar bone and a bullet wound to her leg and side. Most of the blood on her in the picture was that of her partner who died at the scene before they had a chance to make their move.

Alex felt a warm hand squeeze hers. She didn't notice Harriet had moved closer to her for support. "You do get around," Harriet looked at the picture, then her. "Are you okay? That must have hurt."

"I didn't consider it a good career move," she said weakly. Her stomach was getting queasy. "Thanks," she whispered when a trash can was moved near her leg.

"Anything to add?" Mark asked, watching her pale face become paler.

"I was just a teller, Mark. It was a job between jobs until I could figure out what I wanted to do. I spent some time in the hospital, then went home to my aunties to recuperate and rethink my career plans. I would appreciate if you don't mention this to anyone. Memories like this I don't want to revisit."

The chief nodded. "We'll all respect that. But that ties you in with the nephew, our main suspect."

Alex looked at him with a sinking feeling, "Chief, that's stretching it."

"We don't know if it's your Mickey yet. But someone left a watch that looks like yours at a crime scene," the chief said, "coincidentally, with no fingerprints."

"I don't believe in coincidences myself, however, this may very well be one. Have you talked to the cleaning crew? Maybe one of them picked up the watch. Friday is their cleaning night."

Mark nodded. "You're right." He made a notation. He touched her shoulder, "Glad to see you made it out all right."

Alex didn't look at him or any of the others. "Me too."

"Okay. Mark, you check with Jesus on who was here cleaning Friday and I'll go tackle Spenser Castleton, the nephew. Alex, you…"

"I know. I get the phones."

"Only because I don't want you passing out," the chief said firmly. "You still look gray around the edges. And professionally, it would taint the investigation if you were to work on this case."

"And I get the foot patrol," Harriet said happily. "I'll do some nosing around, too. Spenser likes to hang out at Lee's Music store."

"All right, everyone meet back here at…" he glanced at his watch, "one. That should give us enough time to collect information. Bring your lunches. Burns, when Mark gives you the names of people from Jesus's cleaning service…"

"Run a check. Got it."

Alex settled in front of the phones, refreshing her memory on how to work the touch screen on Harriet's desk.

"Harriet, before you go, how do I call up my stuff so I can do some work on my cases?"

"You can't from my workstation. It's logged on as me, so get your spelling right," she teased. "I guess Eric could add you to the database that has the same stuff as me, but you wouldn't have access to the way I've rearranged things. Why not just get the laptop and hook it up to the phone back there. It's a single line. You can login via SecureID and do your stuff that way. Just remember, this is not a secure place."

Alex snorted. "Our office is not a secure place."

"Well, not from the cleaning crew, but from the public it is. You may not be aware, but when someone enters the office upstairs, a red light goes on in the server room, the chief's room, and down here." She pointed at a row of small lights below her desk. "This light is the ladies room, the second is the office, and the third is our evidence room. And that one there is to the cells."

"But no cameras?" *I didn't see those when she was training me...or did she just forget to mention it?*

"Budget. We had to make a choice between the Sherlock program or cameras. Chief Harper chose Sherlock but got a donation for the cameras in the cells."

"Ooh. And I like Sherlock. Okay, I'll be right back. I'll bring the laptop down and my coffee mug."

"Best stick with the tea for a while. Otherwise you'll be spending more time in my restroom. You still don't look so hot. Alex, I'm really sorry about what happened in that shot. You must have been close to the people killed."

Alex nodded and went upstairs, seeking a brief respite under the guise of retrieving her laptop.

Monday morning was busy. Tourists were calling in about events that were scheduled for weekends in the future, and since the tourist bureau didn't open until ten, she had to check Harriet's listings on happenings. Then there were the stack of complaints taken during the weekend that needed to be typed into the database. Alex hesitated over the information recorded about Gary's call in on the Hale robbery. She read over it and typed in the missing information needed for the program, then sent the update to Mark's queue. For evidence, a Mickey Mouse watch, a button, cigarette butts, one crushed empty box of cigarettes, and three different shoe prints on a freshly mopped floor. How stupid could they be?

Mike and Danny put in an appearance. She was grateful she was on the phone and they didn't make any comments.

Well, at least we know it's not a Jaded Amulet hit. They do not crap in their own backyard. I don't know if that's any consolation to the chief, though.

At one, Mike was given the front desk while the five of them rehuddled to present new evidence.

"One of Jesus's new hires, Carlos, has a brother who makes fish deliveries," Mark said. "Also, Spenser stayed home Friday night, which is unusual for him, according to his aunt. Usually, he's out with his friends right after he closes up shop."

"His friends..." Harriet said. "He's been here only six months, and he's managed to find the wrong type of friends. Mr. Laramie said he and his buddies weren't around Friday night or Saturday, which meant business was better than usual. People stayed around longer and picked up more merchandise in his store."

"He didn't say he was being harassed by them, did he?"

Harriet shook her head. "He wouldn't. His son is a practicing Buddhist monk and shows his respect by not complaining or causing disharmony. You'd think he thought that would put a bad mark on his son's monkship or something."

"Ignore the problem and maybe it'll disappear," Alex muttered. Alex and Mark made a notation to visit his store more often to make sure he was not being harassed.

"His son must look weird in his orange robe if he inherited his father's blond bushy eyebrows," Eric said.

"Adopted. His son is Vietnamese. I think it's a relative of his wife's family," Harriet said.

"Harriet, you are a wealth of information," Alex said. She was worried about what Harriet knew about her. She was going to have to have a chat with Harper or maybe Briscolle to make sure there were no loose ends hanging about the bank heist that went bad. It was bad enough that FBI agent who was involved would be visiting soon.

"I told you, Alex. Just talking to people."

Alex made a face at her.

Harriet laughed and didn't push the subject any further. Chief Harper was writing something down.

"Did anyone check with the local watch sellers to see if anyone bought a Mickey Mouse watch recently?" Harper asked.

Everyone shook his or her head.

"I did." Harper smiled and sat back in his chair until it squeaked. "The Meyer's drug store had a sale on their watches two weeks ago, and Mickey sold out. Seth said he doesn't know who bought what because he wasn't at the cash register. Hazel was and said three of them were to tourists, and that was all they had."

"Great. Tourists pay by check or credit card," Alex said.

He nodded. "Yep, one of the checks was to a nonexistent bank."

Mark groaned. "Two pieces of ID and it's still not enough. Well then, I'm going to hustle over to the fish market and see if I can hook up with the drivers of the delivery truck and take some photos. They were making deliveries and aren't due back until after three. We can then match up my pictures with faces on the tape. If any of that evidence we picked up belongs to them, I thank them for being such amateurs." Mark pushed back his chair, and the rest also rose at the chief's nod.

"Chief, can I talk to you a moment?"

"Sure, Alex. Harriet, you can relieve Mike. And, Harriet, nice information collecting."

Harriet patted Adison's arm and so did Eric.

Jeez, I wish he had not found that picture. They're going to treat me like I'm fragile now.

Chief Harper closed the door and moved back into the conference room.

He studied her for a moment, and Adison knew he was curious about the heist.

"I was working for SID and…"

"You don't have to tell me, Alex," he said softly. "I've witnessed enough hostage situations to know the trauma you must have experienced. The fact that you're still working tells me you've worked it out. I remember the FBI report on it."

Alex nodded, not daring to say anything lest that act of kindness open up something she didn't want to deal with…the death of a partner.

"I need to tell you about it because the FBI agent who handled it is going to be in town soon." She took a few breaths, then began her story, retelling it like she was making a report. From there, she told him about Briscolle's warning that the FBI was setting up a new team to investigate the murder in the forest with the same agent in charge.

The next morning it was white everywhere. The snow had started about nine the previous evening. Adison didn't expect Mark to want to run in the morning, but she was up early anyway. An impatient bark at her back door informed her she was wrong.

"Mark, we can't run in the snow. I have no snowshoes nor the interest," she whined and was ready to go into pleading mode if that didn't work. "And I'm still recuperating from being sick."

"We can work out at the office gym. Come on. I stopped there first and turned on the heaters," he said. "You can pedal slowly."

She grumbled as she went through her closet for the warmest coat she had. His truck's warmed cab helped her mood. While Angel watched them on the bikes, Mark explained why he wanted to speak with her before work.

"I have some bad news for you."

"I'm not going to get three days off next Thanksgiving?"

Mark grunted. "You never told me you wanted it off. No. That's not what this is about. The FBI has sent Chief Harper a note that they want to interrogate you about the bodies found in the forest. They've taken a sudden new interest in them."

"Interrogate? Bodies? Which case is that?"

"Heinrich Reiner."

"We only found one…his."

"I think they finally got their heads out of their assess and looked at Dr. Sherwood's work of fingerprints on the rifle barrel and made the connection to what was found outside of Sacramento and San Francisco."

"Oh. When is the interview?"

"About noon, Monday. But there's another snowstorm heading our way.."

"So, what's the big deal?"

"Well, there are some things we aren't supposed to know. So I thought we should go over it before they get here."

Alex groaned. She knew a lot of things that others were not supposed to know. It was getting complicated.

Adison called Chief Harper when she got home.

"Chief, this is Adison."

"I'm secure. Go ahead."

"I was thinking the way to keep the interview on the up and up is to get Judge Mead in on it. She's their buddy. She can act as referee with you as a witness to keep her clean."

"She called me last night to warn me they were coming to town. A bit late since you already told me. She admitted it had to do with her turning over a list of names you found in the warehouse. I had refused to let her know who my contact is and where I got the list. I think this is her way of retaliating."

"It's going to backfire on her," Alex said. She trusted Mel was monitoring the judge and was hoping the woman was not going to get them killed.

"Let me work on this. The judge is way over her head here. I'll have someone jerk her husband's chain who can then jerk hers."

The interview was postponed until Tuesday. Midmorning, Alex was walking along the stores with Mark, who felt she needed moral support. Alex wanted to just walk in peace and quiet and let normal life soothe her jangled nerves. When her pager went off, both jumped. Alex's hand automatically pulled the pager from its holster.

Mark glanced at the readout over her shoulder. "Looks like your interviewers are here. Now remember, don't volunteer anything," he said.

Like I don't know this.

They spotted the U.S. Ranger SUV headed back up the mountains. The interviewing had started early that morning. Mark stopped at the bottom of the stairs to the office, and Harriet gave her a thumbs-up and a grin. It seemed everyone thought she was going to battle for the SPD. If she was not so worried about being recognized, she would have made light of this meeting. She kept reminding herself that her face was so bruised and battered from her run-in with the robbers that he wouldn't have been able to know what she really looked like. It was also years ago.

Eric closed the chief's office door quietly and made a face at Alex.

"Your turn," he whispered.

"Detective Adison, you ready?" Chief Harper asked

"Ready, Chief."

She was waved to the meeting room where the lumpy chairs were. She noticed neither agent was sitting. Agent Trent Lockwood was leaning against the wall reading a paper when she came in. She took a seat across from Agent Braden who was conducting the interview. Judge Mead was sitting at the head of the table, the one nearest the office door. Chief Harper closed the door and sat next to the judge. The questions started the moment he took his seat.

For what seemed like hours, Agent Braden asked questions about Dr. Sherwood's findings, and each time Alex referred him to Dr. Sherwood. She was beginning to wonder if he was dense or just practicing on how many times he could reword the same question. Judge Mead cleared her throat. Agent Braden glanced toward her.

"I think you can move on," she hinted.

He then started to ask what Ranger Gray Horse did, and she referred him to the ranger. It seemed that Agent Braden had the same distain for local law enforcement as Agent Lockwood or maybe he was just slow to getting around to asking her what she found, saw, or thought of the crime scene.

Alex heard Judge Mead shift in her chair again.

Ah, she's going to make her move soon, Alex thought.

Judge Mead tapped her fingers on the table. "Agent Braden, I've had enough of this. It's been almost two hours, and you keep asking Detective Adison irrelevant questions. You are wasting her time. She has told you she arrived hours after Dr. Sherwood and was not present when the doctor and ranger investigated further into the forest. Dr. Sherwood pointed out to you that your team had picked up the body and whatever evidence Dr. Sherwood had in her possession, as well as all her notes. Did you lose them?"

"Judge Mead, this is our investigation…"

"Not much longer if you don't investigate. What have you so far?"

"That's not your business, Judge Mead. And I'll remind you…"

"I will remind you! I know Commander Argent personally, Agent Braden. He spoke to me about the interviews before you were on your way here. Neither of us want another fiasco where you alienate the local judge to the point that nothing gets done. So my support is what you should be nurturing. Detective, tell us about your findings and what your professional observations are of the crime scene and the two agents will not interrupt, am I clear, agents?"

"You are very clear, Mrs. Mead." Agent Braden responded frostily.

"It's Judge Mead, and if your attitude does not adjust quickly, I'll see to it that your next assignment fits your abilities. We need to focus on working toward a common goal…solving a crime."

Alex nervously pulled out pictures of the scene and went over each one. The air was thick with tension and Harper wisely kept silent. For one hour more, she gave what she knew and threw in the information that the hit man was a transsexual and chances are his associate was also. She was curious what they would do with it. As expected, they made no comments nor asked her any more questions. Following her recital, they asked if she had anything else to add, then leaned over to take her file.

"I'm sorry, but these belong to our department," Chief Harper told the agents. "I sent copies of our work to your office already."

Both men left without imparting any information.

"Keep in touch, agents. I expect an update without having to go through Commander Argent," the judge told their parting backs.

"I somehow don't expect timely updates, Judge," Alex said as she filed the pictures neatly in the folder, then slid the folder to Chief Harper.

"I want to know why you have so much information on a murder that is on federal property," she returned testily.

Alex raised her eyebrows.

"Detective Adison, you may leave," Chief Harper said quietly. "Judge Mead," he began as Alex closed the office door. "You want to grill my officers, you go through me first."

It was the monthly Saturday meeting, and the weather was bleak. Adison looked out the window from Chief Harper's office window. The wind was blowing hail against the windows. The day was so cold she wore thermals, extra thick socks, and her new one size larger uniform so she wouldn't be ripping seams out of the uniform with all the warm underwear. She felt like a stuffed doll, but the good thing was she would be spending her time indoors unless she got a call. During the winter storms, the tourist crowd was nonexistent. She wandered back to her place on the couch. It was warmer in the chief's office than the meeting room and more comfortable. Chief Harper hung up his phone and turned to the four.

"I want to commend all of you on the case you have worked up on the Hale burglary. We have so much evidence it makes one wonder what they learned from watching television. Mark, you're due in front of the district attorney on Wednesday. She'll do a review of the evidence to see if there is enough to charge all of the group. While you're there, see Chief Goodkin about that suicide three months ago. The family is all of a sudden interested in his death. I'm not sure what stirred them up, but make sure you have everything covered.

"The underwear disappearances, let's go ahead and put that case into the dead files. We haven't had any more occurrences since Claire got her team of counselors to work on it. Well done, Detectives.

"Moving to the sniper case...the FBI has nothing to contribute to finding anything worth mentioning to us, but I have a contact in Interpol who confirmed that the surviving sniper is female, about thirty-five. She was spotted..." he leaned over and handed out pages to the others, "talking to Reiner in France about seven weeks before he came over here. They know absolutely nothing of who she is, including her nationality."

"She's dressed as a woman here. I would think if she's a cross-dresser, she would have dressed differently," Alex murmured.

"She's a looker," Eric said.

"They're masters of disguise," Chief Harper reminded the group. "Any disguise. Reiner didn't just use female impersonations."

"So what about the names on the list?" Harriet asked.

"No new deaths reported," Eric said. "My program checks daily."

Alex looked around the table, wondering if all of them felt as weary as she did.

It was the first Friday of the month, so it was militia night. Adison was huddled on the side of the slope in the rain as the militia men practiced pitching tents. They finished early, and when the last of them left, she stretched out her legs. She was wearing a long–brimmed fisherman's hat to cover most of her night vision goggles from the wet weather. Taking one last look around to be sure she was alone, she started up the slippery path grabbing onto rocks and vegetation to keep from falling. The wind was gusting and whistling as it drove sand against her. As she pulled herself to the top of the ledge, she immediately dropped back down, losing her grip and backsliding. She grabbed frantically onto some vegetation and pulled herself off the path, hoping she was not going to roll off the cliff.

I can't believe it! A Jaded Amulet meeting? It's got to be! Who else would be crazy to meet in this weather, besides the militia and they parked on the beach?

Slowly, Alex made her way back up the side of the cliff, hopeful the meeting was still in progress. She crawled under a truck to get some relief from the wind and rain. She pulled out her camera and photographed what licenses she could.

Through her goggles, she located the group, which was hidden under rain gear. Ten to twelve people standing around. Five were in the inner circle. Her eyes squinted at one of the members. It was that hand gesture. It was one of the Ms and she was irritated about something. Even under all the clothing, she could recognize the body language of Rita. Rita was a hot head, she had guessed.

The other four were people Alex didn't know. She had her pictures, and since she was not carrying anything to listen to their conversation, she decided it would be better to leave.

Backing down the cliff was not as easy as climbing it. Alex slipped and rolled, managing to grab a fistful of the ice plant that grew along the cliff face. The camera was not comfortable to land on.

Headlights cut into the darkness above her. She waited until the four vehicles had left. Taking a deep breath, she moved back up, hoping her squashing the vegetation wouldn't be too noticeable in the daylight should someone care to return and check it out. She slowly searched the parking area for more cars. There were still two. She didn't recognize the two men, but they had what Alex thought may be bodyguards standing away from them. Finally, they shook hands and parted.

Not wanting to be sloppy, Alex took another path that wound around the cliff face and came up at another public parking turnout. It took her ten minutes of running through the slanting rain to get to the private driveway where she had parked and a minute more to get her cold fingers to lift the latch and open the gate to drive out. All the while, Alex kept peering into the night for anyone who may be watching.

Saturday morning, she was jubilant when Mark came to pick her up for a workout in the police gym. It was too wet to run.

"So I can see you are just about bursting with news. What happened last night?" Mark asked, turning the truck around and heading toward the office.

Alex leaned back in the truck cab grinning. "I saw Rita last night."

"The woman who talked to Amos and set up a hit on Jinks," Mark recalled.

"That's the one. She was meeting some out of town people last night. The militia boys left early, and when I got to the parking lot, there she was with five guys and their bodyguards standing out of earshot. After she left, two of the visitors remained and talked for a while. Get this, Mark. They shook hands."

"Rita. So maybe another name to one of the gangs, like our locals. Did you get pictures?"

"Yep. Did you hear me? They shook hands. They didn't do any of that gang sign stuff."

"I got you," he said. "But how many gangs does that rule out?"

"California gangs. They all have their special shake." She paused for a long time. "European?"

Mark chuckled. "Makes the world of crime suddenly bigger, doesn't it?"

"Oh, gods," she muttered. "We have an international sniper, we have Jaded Amulet. Do you think Rita is the boss? No. I don't think this big of an organization would want to be run by a woman. Most of the people we've been seeing are men. Mike for one wouldn't work for a woman. Certainly not Danny."

"Looks like you need a mental break," Mark said. He slid out of the truck and unlocked the police department front door.

Alex pedaled furiously to get out her frustration. It was times like these that she wished she was back to working the short operations with SID. This was getting too intense in a lot of ways. Following their workout, they ran upstairs into the office and sat before Alex's PC.

"What's 'Follow the M trail' mean?" Mark asked as a reminder note popped up.

"Oh, that's to remind me to look up Marci, Marcos, and Margie. Rita is the only one not an M in this group, so I thought I would look the names up on the Internet. Seems odd that out of three kids, the mother stopped there. She was on a roll."

"Sounds like fun. So which one in this photo is Rita? In that weather, I can barely see anyone."

Monday, SID sent an ID on Rita Monroe and matched her fingerprints to one of those on the list of names Alex had found in the warehouse over a year ago.

Tuesday, Eric had matches on the men at the meeting. They were gang members from the L.A. area, but all immigrants with valid passports and immigration papers.

Everyone was excited at the Saturday monthly meeting.

"All right everyone, settle down!" the chief ordered. He had a broad smile and was just as enthused at the information. "Rita Monroe served time, passing bad checks. We didn't find her because she was a juvenile, but someone remembered her. She was adopted when she was younger, but the family split up ten years later. We only have a childhood picture of her with her adopted family. Her adopted father was an airline pilot and taught her to fly. She remained close to him until he died of a heart attack six years ago. She has no contact with her adopted mother since she remarried and started another family. Rita has a P.O. box in Orange County. She flies charters all over the United States and sometimes Canada. Works for Holden's Flyers, an Arizona based company."

"So...is she the boss?" Alex pondered aloud. *Orange County? John Wayne Airport is there. Where have I heard that from? Ah. Margaret. Gary's girlfriend. She takes bus trips there, or did. Another M. Darn. I forgot to follow that up.*

"If she is, her job sure gives her the opportunity to be everywhere," Mark muttered. "Don't we have someone else who makes trips to Orange County?"

"Gary's girlfriend. Margaret or Margo something," Alex said. "What a coincidence. Lots of Ms."

"Sure is," Harriet agreed, tapping her pencil eraser on the tabletop as fast as everyone's thoughts were going.

"We didn't find anything interesting on our background check on her. Do another, Eric," the chief directed. "And follow the M trail. This is the best we've done in a long time."

"Not since the bar visit," Eric agreed.

April and May, the militia meetings with gang members visiting on the side resumed. It was getting more difficult to watch the meetings since the members identified from Los Angeles were bringing their own guards. Chief Harper was reluctant to share this information with LAPD. He didn't want to give away how he knew of the meetings.

In April, Adison got a hit on a name search on Gary Krieger. He was adopted, which everyone knew. SID was able to supply extra information about his birth parents. His mother was an unwed teenager who committed suicide a month after the baby's birth. Her death was due to depression, the autopsy report read. The baby's father was never identified; however, the mother's history showed a pattern of abuse from her own father, including sexual abuse. The baby's father and her own could very well have been the same man. It would be difficult to prove without DNA. Alex noticed he died three years before in a hit and run accident.

She opened her small file on Margaret Hamilton and cut and pasted SID's information into her own notes.

So, Margaret was also adopted. Margo Lipton until...twenty-one when she could officially change her name. Wonder why? Nothing on her juvenile record.

She was adopted by a middle-class suburban family with working parents. Her mother worked part time for a liquor store, and her father was a full-time plant worker. He died seven years before from a heart attack. Hmm. Margaret and her mother were away at the time getting her settled in her college dormitory. Has no siblings. Wow! The life insurance is nice. So the mother moved to Orange County. I wonder why she chose Margaret Hamilton. I need a new list.

She had a list of three. Rita Monroe, Gary Krieger, and Margaret Hamilton aka Margo Lipton. The only connection was between Rita and Margo because they both had ties in Orange County. Gary had never been there. He supposedly met Margaret in a bar in Sunrise. Then there was the name Rita, which she found to be a derivative of Margaret. So her list of Ms had also grown. Now she was interested in Gary's Margo and Gary.

Gary has dogs. I think I'll grab some hair samples from his coat...difficult but not impossible.

A couple of days later, Adison arrived late to the morning departmental meeting intentionally. While everyone was waiting for her, she used tape to run over Gary's coat that he draped over a desk chair. She tucked the samples into an envelope to give to Harper to okay her sending it to SID laboratories. Sometimes this process was a pain.

A few weeks later, SID told her the hairs were not to any pit bulls. It was to one dog and two humans.

Gary said they have four dogs between them. So, does that mean he has one and Margaret has three? I think I'll send the ROV over their property. If Mark or I take a run that way, too many curious minds will want to know why. Too far off our beaten path.

The ROV found no dogs. The dogs were in a covered kennel.

Her next idea was to check the town veterinarians, Jane and Sandra, just not directly. She bumped into a lab tech for the animal hospital at lunch. The tech said Margaret was loyal to her original vet in Brisbane, where she had lived before she moved in with Gary.

For further information, she asked Harper to ask SID to check it out.

In June, the store owner to the baby apparel shop died and her son took over the store. If he had not stuck out like a sore thumb, the chief and his team wouldn't have been suspicious. As it was, he looked too macho to run a baby's apparel and supply store. His fingerprints were checked against the FBI database and a hit came back. Another crook.

In July, the meetings with the gangs ceased, but out-of-town customers dressed in gang attire started to frequent the baby apparel shop. By then, L.A. was calling Chief Harper about arms their local gangs had. Someone was saying they were coming from his neck of the woods. L.A. wanted to send a pair of officers to observe. Chief Harper reluctantly agreed with stipulations.

Alex sent off an email through Harper to SID asking what's up with the L.A.'s investigation. Agent Briscolle sent Harper and Alex a profile of the officers. Both were in trouble dealing with a Ramparts scandal and were being shuffled out of town until the heat of the investigation died down.

Tuesday, Adison met Harriet at the doughnut shop to help with the extra doughnuts and coffee they were getting for the officers from the L.A. gang squad. Harriet had met them with Chief Harper late Monday. She had a sinking feeling they were the typical big town cops with an attitude.

Harriet and Alex were silent as they set up the goodies in the coffee room, when a deep male voice greeted them.

"I can see right off we're going to get along just fine." He sniffed the air and added, "I sure hope you didn't just bring that sweet-smelling coffee, otherwise, you're just going to have to trot back and pick me up some real coffee. I like mine black with sugar."

Alex turned around and studied the smirk on the tall, slightly overweight, dark-haired officer. He had that mean-spirited energy around him that she often picked up with dangerous criminals. Alex had worked with this attitude through her first four years as a police officer in a city where women either worked the desk or were used to hustle johns while her so-called partner, if he could get his hands off the other hookers on the street, made the arrests on the johns. She found the male cops were more interested in busting the hookers for favors than busting the johns and cleaning up the streets. This guy, for her, was the epitome of what she felt was a social injustice.

"Well, if you don't like..."

"Whoa, little woman," he spoke over her words.

"...what the office supplies, then you'll have to run down to the doughnut shop and get your own," she finished.

"You got a smart mouth there. You talk that way to your boyfriends?"

"Or," she continued, "when it's your turn to bring in the coffee and doughnuts, you can bring in what you like, provided you're here that long. I'm sure it won't take but a few days for you to collect your information."

"Doesn't take much to wind you up. A pretty thing like you should be home taking care of kids. It'll use up some of that hostile energy you're putting out. Unless you're one those man haters. You one of them?" He again talked over Alex as if she were saying nothing.

"Officer Guido," Mark's voice was cold, but it didn't wipe off the smirk on Guido's face."

"It's detective," Guido said, looking Mark over as if checking out the competition.

"Detective Adison and Lieutenant Sams, would you two mind giving us a moment alone?"

Alex turned back to Guido, knowing if she let Mark step in for her, he would always be harassing her when no one was around. Mike and Danny were bad enough. However, as Claire pointed out in her classes on abusive behaviors, words would be wasted on some people. So for now, she just gave him an even stare that was meant to say only that she was not intimidated by him.

"We don't go in for innuendos, name baiting, leers, or sneers. You got me, Detective Guido?"

Mark's voice was low, but the two women heard him.

"This conversation was between me and the ladies. You butting in was not called for," Guido bluffed.

"This is not a bar. On the PC assigned to you is a file with our department's policy manual. I suggest you read it and practice it or you can go home."

Guido snorted and tried to pass Detective Scripts, but Mark's body was firmly planted in the doorway.

"In case you're not aware, you are here at our discretion. If you can't show respect for the people of this town, especially fellow officers, I will file an official complaint. I'm sure you don't want another complaint in your file, not at this particular time. Got me? I might also point out both of those women outrank you."

"Get out of my way, Scripts."

"Detective Guido," the chief's voice came from behind Mark. "I can see we have a culture clash here. Since our previous meeting didn't seem to make an impression, let's you and I discuss again your status after this morning's meeting."

The meeting was chilly. Detective Tony Guido and his partner who arrived late, Detective Mike "Deets" Dieter, were introduced to everyone and the chief had the two detectives tell what exactly they were going to do. No one bothered to tell Guido and Deets that in Sunrise, their sitting in a surveillance car in front of a store wouldn't fool anyone.

In less than a month's time, there was no working relationship between the visiting officers and Sunrise officers. Mike and Danny were considered beneath the two LAPD detectives, being uniformed cops, so their rudeness to the two cut off any friendliness at the bars their type would visit. The two visitors had a lot of car rental problems, which Alex guessed were compliments of Mike's buddies.

In dealing with the LAPD detectives, it was almost a daily mantra that Alex reminded herself that she was in Sunrise to blend in, monitor, and report, nothing more.

July 31, Alex sent an email to Mel through Harper to see how SID was doing with finding out about Margaret's dogs. Adam, who supplied her with SID vehicles, worked in the car parts yard in Brisbane, and they had dogs. Surely they shared vets, she thought hopefully.

Agent Briscolle sent Sam the information. Sam found that one dog was a registered pit bull but not under Margaret's name. It was under a Marco M. Wollas.

Alex, Harper, and Sam were huddled in a small room going over the information.

"The dots are connecting, but what has the list to do with the JA?" she murmured.

"Unless he's the male head of this operation. Except, he's down there and JA is up here," Harper said.

"I think we're getting closer to something. Agent Briscolle, however, doesn't want us to not take any action. I understand she's your backup when Mel's occupied. Seems that some operation is being planned for our neck of the woods," Sam said. "She said continue keeping a low profile."

Alex looked at Harper. "That means WK is involved. That's his target. JA is just on the periphery, but if he's saying to not take action, then JA will be part of his bust. Hopefully, the JA's boss is one of those he's planning on nabbing."

Harper nodded. "I can't see focusing on the list as interfering with Mel's operation. What we've decided was that the symbols refer to an assassin. If we can figure out who the checkmark represents, we'll know who tried to kill Mike. The astrological sign may be an assassin's aka."

"We don't know if there haven't been any attempts on Amos's life or on Mike's. The ranger is still alive and isn't looking nervous when I occasionally drop in at the station." Alex scratched out names on a new list, then drew lines connecting others.

"Brother and sisters? Margaret is visiting Orange County…maybe she's really visiting her mother, her real one. I think I should stop by and see this Margaret."

"I think you need to keep a low profile. Leaving town for Orange County is not a low profile," Harper said.

Sam nodded. "I trust Mel's warning. Let's see what develops."

"What about Gary's Margaret or Gary for that matter? Doesn't that put some doubt on his name? I mean, this list is for sure the Ms's hit list."

"I know people and I trust Gary. He's in love with Margaret. If anything, he may be duped if Margaret is part of this group. I'll say for sure, these Ms are involved with the JA, and they're important decision makers. The fact that we haven't seen Amos or Mike with any of them means these men aren't that high on the member pole."

"Something or someone is not acting on their mark for a reason. Maybe they need Amos's warehouse still, and if something happens to him, it will alert the other two. Or if another attempt is made on Mike's life, it will cause questions and the person with the list needs them."

"Burns will have to do some more digging. Let's see what he can find on residents of Orange County. Maybe he can locate Margaret's mother."

Chapter Seventeen

A dison was in Sunrise for over two years, and the only results and/or conclusions she was seeing were on the cases she worked for SPD. She had to constantly remind herself that she was here for SID to gather information and not to solve anything. She was comfortably ensconced in the town's life and had only her weekly status reports to Harper to forward to SID to remind her that she was more than a detective for a community.

Monday morning, back from her three-day weekend at her cabin, she followed her ritual of checking her apartment for unwanted entry while she was gone, then powered on her PC. While it booted up, she took a shower to wash her hair and dress for street work. Her pager had been vibrating since she turned it on as she passed the Sunrise town markers, so she was expecting to be out of the office most of the day, taking reports on crimes or doing follow-ups after seven that morning when Mark went off duty.

With her cup of steaming coffee sitting on the small table near her reading chair, Adison watched the logon process to the SecureID server, then logged into the PD server. Absentmindedly, she towel dried her hair as the PD server, more ponderous about remote access, ran through its steps to get her into her files. Her thoughts were on her three days off.

Doggone, Mel. You're right. If I didn't have some place of my own to retreat to, I think I would have had a meltdown by now. This is the last time I take on a long term project.

The thought had her sitting up straighter on the metal folding chair. If she had not been on assignment for this long, she wouldn't have formed the relationships she had now, and frankly, she really liked the people of Sunrise and Sam Bear, too.

Oh, bother. If Mel doesn't tie this one up soon, I'm going to be so embedded in this community I'm going to not want to be unearthed.

A message popped up on her screen, bringing her attention back to the present.

"Speaking of the devil," she muttered.

Alex leaned over and quickly punched in SID's phone number.

"Mel, got your message. What's going on?" she asked. Her heart was beating in anticipation. He was calling her direct and not going through Harper. "No, I haven't yet....He did...you did?" Adison let out a low whistle as Mel informed her that SID's plan had just moved into high gear. It was a little unnerving since that was just what she was thinking about. "So what's the plan?...Baiting? Who's the bait?" she asked suspiciously. "A civilian?"

She detested using civilians in her assignments. Not because she worried about their safety, but because civilians involved with gangs typically were as dirty if not more so than the gang member the Feds were attempting to arrest. Usually, it turned out that the bait was just exchanging prison time for helping out. They were still dirty and therefore unpredictable when things got hot.

"When is she due in?...Today at the shelter?" Her eyebrows lifted in surprise. This would also involve Claire, Genie, and their residents. Too many civilians. "Right...Okay. Did you fill Chief Harper in?...Briscolle? Okay. Soon?" she asked hopefully. "Okay. I'll look forward to meeting her."

That was a bright spot. That meant the locals would be playing an active part in SID's game. However, she wondered how Claire would feel about taking on a hot one among her fragile residents. Alex hung up and sat for a few minutes. Glancing at her PC, she wondered if she would have time to see the bio on the "civ." Shaking her head, she decided it could wait. Sherlock was blinking rapidly on her desktop, letting her know she had cases waiting. Clicking on top priority, she didn't see any critical waiting in her queue. It meant the cases that were blinking were follow-ups to what Mark had been working on. Quickly, she shut her PC down and went through the ritual of securing it. Grinning, she thought of the glimmer of light at the end of a long assignment.

She ran her hand through her short hair and sighed heavily. She personally knew the danger of staying in one place for a long time. Ties, friendships, loved ones, which thank the gods she didn't have that problem, and sometimes forgetting that she was living a lie, which leads to mistakes. Her face reddened for a moment. Chief Harper had offered her the detective job on her two-year anniversary with his department if she should decide to stay. That was probably why she was feeling so out of sorts lately. She was actually thinking about his offer.

Settling down? Nah. She took a deep breath. *Well*...She wearily shook the thought out of her mind. It was a distraction. At this time, so close to the end, she needed to stay focused. This was where mistakes from inattention to detail, sloppiness, and a rush to finish could cause dire problems, especially where a civilian was involved.

Before she knew it, Adison was pushing the PD door open. She waved a greeting to Harriet seated behind the entry desk, laughing at something a caller was telling her. She took the stairs two at a time. She popped her head into the tourist bureau's office and waved at Emily and Matt Sparks. Either they were early or she was late. Her eyes glanced at their clock. It was both.

"Good morning, Alex! We're redesigning the town's Web site," Matt said. "We're thinking of adding pictures of elected officials and SPD to the Sunrise Web site. What do you think?" He looked pleased with the idea.

"Not a good idea about the rank and file. If Mark or I appear up at the campsite as fellow campers to nab someone who's making trouble, what if he or she recognizes us?" *What if someone recognizes me from a previous job?*

"Oh, I didn't think of that. Maybe just the elected officials and the chief."

"I know you're going to clear that with the chief," she hinted. "So, how's Sally? I take it she didn't deliver the goods."

"Another false alarm! Worse than Maxine."

"Please. I hope it's not as bad as Maxine. I have to go, see you later." *I wonder if the baby will come out with tattoos since the grandparents and parents have them all over their bodies.*

"Don't forget to visit Dougie's art table at the street fair!" Emily shouted after her.

As Adison entered the office, she could see the "Out" sign on the chief's door.

Oh, right. He's meeting with the new mayor and board. I knew there was a reason I wasn't in a hurry to get to work today. Darn. Tuesday and Wednesday, he'll be in Bales for meetings with the judge. I guess it'll have to be Thursday when Mark is back. I'll send them an email.

Looking around carefully, she made sure neither of the detectives from L.A. were around. If those two were any representation of the mentality of the rest of the LAPD, Alex wished they all get swallowed up in the next earthquake.

Plopping down in front of her computer, Alex booted it up, typed in her password, and watched her icons load while idly playing with a pencil.

With all the cases we have going now, how on earth did they manage with only Mark and Harper working cases assigned to a detective? No wonder Harper took Mel up on his offer.

She was grateful Harper blended her SID investigation with his own. Otherwise, she wouldn't have lasted this long.

Alex scanned the first report.

Reporter: Ranger Gray Horse
Problem: Missing camper/hiker
Witnesses: None
Suspicions: Abducted
Evidence: Property of missing person found in bushes, tracks showing someone was injured, no verbal message to companion campers that she was leaving.

The campgrounds were a two-hour walk from Adison's cabin, which had mixed blessings. The time the crime was reported was eight that morning while she was walking to work. Touching her pager, she glanced at it to see if it was still on. It had not vibrated after she got back into town. Batteries low. She switched batteries, then headed to the server room to pick up equipment.

"Good morning, Eric. How's it going?"

"All right. Good morning to you. Had a good weekend?"

"Sure did."

"I saw you had a call to the campgrounds a few minutes ago. I have a new camera for you to test out. If it takes good pictures, we'll add it to our equipment."

"Listen, Officer Burns, I just point and shoot. I'm not all that technically savvy to test out this thing." She held the expensive camera away from her, worried that if she dropped it, she would owe someone more than two months of her salary.

"That's why you're the perfect person to test it. And you do take good pictures. Don't let the price tag scare you. But don't drop it or lose it. If a bear chases you, take copious amounts of pictures—but don't lose the camera."

"Right. Don't bears sleep at this time of the year?"

Eric shrugged. "I'm not a wilderness person. Let me know if you find out."

"Good morning, Gray Horse. How are you?"

The ranger rose from his chair to greet her.

"Alex, how are you? If you read your tea leaves this morning, you wouldn't have left your cabin so early," he teased.

"Did you get a chance to check the place out?" she asked, knowing he did. He took Alex's map she held out and opened it on top of his desk.

"Here's where I found the woman's backpack." He tapped a spot. "Here is where the group she was with had set up camp." His finger tapped an area that allowed campfires and had a few outhouses nearby. "This small bridge here," he circled the area, "is washed out, so you'll have to go this way."

"The new fire road," she murmured. "It's not finished yet. I checked it out Saturday with Sam."

He leaned back. "There were four college students. They came up that partial road. Didn't check in with us, so we didn't know they were up here. I sent Ranger Mayhew out to check the rest of the area while I interviewed the students. They only had soft stuff like weed. I don't believe they were out there for anything more than what they said—getting away from the university for a few days."

"What did her camping buddies say about her disappearance?"

"They didn't know her before the trip. Three gay men and a straight woman. They needed four people to split the cost of the trip, and she took her friend's place. She spent her days alone taking pictures. Here are copies of my notes. Here are pictures of the area. And last but not least…her pack. I retrieved it from a bed of thorns."

"A bed of thorns?"

"Uh-huh."

She took the backpack and notes. "Is there anything else I should know?"

"I'll wait until after you look around. We can compare observations."

Alex nodded. "Okay. Did you mark off the areas?"

"Yes. Small yellow flags. I would appreciate it if you would retrieve them when you're finished."

"Will do. Thanks, Gray Horse."

Adison walked slowly around the deserted campsite, then headed to where Gray Horse had left a yellow flag. After ten minutes of meticulously searching the area and taking pictures, she paused to look over the site again. Alex remembered an animal trail near the rock wall. It was barely wide enough for a person to walk. Booted prints, deep in some places were at the edge of the branches that grew against the wall sporadically.

She pulled off her backpack and prepared a mold mixture. While waiting for it to set, she studied the prickly brush. Leaning forward, she strained to see what was not natural in the center of the brush. After about an hour of trial and error, she had a discarded camera case that felt heavy enough to have a camera in it. By the condition of the case, she determined it had not been out in the elements long. Alex bagged the camera and added it to her collection in her backpack. After a few gulps of water, she resumed her search.

She picked up the same boot print leading away from where she found the camera, heading toward the main road. The prints had a deeper indentation, and the heel and toe looked like the person was landing harder and pushing off with more force. He or she was carrying considerably more weight.

Returning to her SUV, she booted up her laptop, linked it to her cell phone, boosted the signal through the SUV's GPS connection, and sent a bbc file to SID and a copy to the SPD in care of Eric, who would download them, clean them up and CC everyone. She attached a note of what the pictures were and why she was sending them. Any woman disappearing in this area she felt was a potential White Knight's hit.

"Nothing like modern technology," she muttered as she watched the last of the zipped file finish its send. She carefully stored the plaster castings she had done, then closed the tailgate.

She still had to check with the McMullens who were vacationing at the south cabins. Maybe they saw something. And then return to chat with Gray Horse.

Adison got back late that night because the McMullens had seen something that disturbed them—Humvees driving along the old fire road the previous day. After going over Gray Horse's evidence, Alex took his suggestion not to investigate alone and stopped by Sam's cabin. He was away. She left him a cryptic note to be careful.

Alex stretched her legs and stared at her computer screen as it finished loading the icons on her desktop. She opened her email to see what Burns had for her and found something from SID. She checked the CC as always to see if Harper received a copy.

Mel sent her information on Linda Brek, the missing woman from the campground, and her three companions. The information on the three men was shallow with not even an arrest record for drugs; however, Linda Brek had a story to her name.

"Linda Brek, an eighteen-year-old photography student witnessed a possible crime in Colorado while visiting a friend," she read softly. *Did she take pictures of something that would threaten someone? Why did she decide to come on this trip? Class project? If that's so, why haven't I found more than a memory card? Maybe she put them in her pockets.*

Alex rubbed her hands over her face tiredly. SID added further instructions to the email. She let out an exasperated sigh. She was to make sure the White Knights and no other agents kidnap Ms. Elizabeth Duke. These directions were in bold print. If they didn't want her kidnapped, why set her up as bait?

What do they mean no other agents? Just how many people are interested in this woman?

Alex focused her tired eyes on her clock. *It's late, but I need to see what Burns found.* Clicking to open up the file, she propped her jaw in her palms and read softly to herself to keep awake.

"She's at Berkeley on a scholarship, holds accolades for her photography, and according to her professor, was on this trip to complete a project."

The next page had her sitting up quickly.

She's running from a Colorado group that deals in drugs and other contraband. What did she see or take pictures of that would cause this group to put a contract out on her? This report doesn't have what she was reported to have seen. Why would a police report omit that unless the FBI was involved? And why is SID not telling me this? Who are the people in the military getup? I'm sure they have this photographer. White Knights? It fits their profile, but what are they doing up here in military drag? What are you up to, Mel?

Burns had an image of the girl on an attachment. Adison opened it and memorized the face. If she saw her anywhere, she would remember her. He had a note attached saying he would work with the pictures in the recovered camera in the morning. Alex had downloaded them without looking at them along with her notes earlier. The woman was using a professional digital camera. Handy for them.

"Darn, the WK is in town," she whispered. "It's getting hot, all right. Jeez, Mel."

Twenty minutes later, Alex was asleep, dreaming of a vacation on a beach.

The next morning, Alex was finishing her first cup of coffee when Mark and Angel knocked on her back door.

"Hi, Angel. Hey, Mark."

Angel wiggled her way through the door for her cookie. She moved from one foot to the other her, eyes glued on Alex, and her long thin tail whipped back and forth.

"So…what's with the missing woman up on the ridge?" Mark asked.

"By this afternoon, I should have an idea of what is on the memory chip in her camera. She's a photography student, so maybe her pictures will be nice and clear." Alex locked her back door and tested it. "I'm also going through her backpack again. If she's a photographer, how come she only had one memory chip? Her backpack only had clothes and food."

"Send me an email with what you find. Today, we run the dunes."

"Why the dunes?" Alex demanded, remembering the last time she not only had to stop several times to empty the sand in her shoes, but her calves ached for days afterward.

"Alex, don't you like the beach scenery?"

"Don't try that tourist stuff on me. You have something in mind," she accused.

"On my fishing excursion yesterday, Ernie was nonstop with complaints about some nasty strangers on the beach without lights scaring him to death this weekend. Then he left a message on my phone late last night that one of them nearly ran him over about midnight."

"What are you looking for?" she asked.

"A boat."

"Well, what do you see?" Adison was impatient as her partner studied two small unfamiliar yachts off the coast through his binoculars. The early morning mist made it difficult to see clearly unaided.

"One guard on each bow smoking. No weapons in sight."

He handed the binoculars to his partner.

"Uh-huh." She adjusted the viewer, swept it over the beach area to see if they had company and finally settled her sights on the yachts. "The first yacht looks like its length is about fifty-six feet, sitting a bit low in the water. How many people do you think it sleeps? Six or eight comfortably?"

"About that, if you're into sharing."

"They're anchored away from the other boats," she said.

"Uh-huh. When the fog lifts and Jenny and Jack head out to do their daily patrol, I'm sure we'll see them lift anchor and leave. They're close enough to shore for Jen to politely ask their business and make some suggestions as to where to dump their bilge."

"Yep. We do have our laws on dumping in the bay."

"You got the names of the yachts?"

"Yes. I'll run a check on them when I get back to the office. You finished here, boss?"

"Let's go for that run now."

Adison made a habit of visiting Genie and Claire on Wednesdays for lunch if it was not her rotated day off, which she spent at her cabin. Wednesdays were Genie's traditional tuna fish sandwiches with her famous potato salad. It was the most idyllic break in her busy life that Alex could ask for, sharing lunch with friends. If the weather permitted, they ate on the backyard patio, enjoying Claire's garden. Standing on the front porch, Alex could hear the doorbell ring echo inside. The locks clicked and the door swung open. She could barely see through the reinforced metal screen door.

"Hi, Claire."

"Hi, Alex. Come on in. Genie's in the kitchen. Go on through. I won't be long on this call." She had her hand covering the mouthpiece on the handset.

Alex nodded. As she walked across the thick hall carpet, she could smell the delicious aroma of something baking. She pushed open the kitchen door and watched Genie as she put the last of the lunch dishes in the dishwasher.

"The worst part of cooking," Alex said.

Genie turned around. "Alex, you startled me. In your case, I would think the worst part would be grocery shopping. Why not take our tray out to the patio and I'll bring the rest. Our new resident is out there. She may be asleep, so try not to scare her."

Well, this will make it easy. I can get a good look at my new assignment and not feel embarrassed at staring... if she's sleeping.

Alex picked up the tray that had three halved sandwiches and a bowl of potato salad. Pushing the door open with one foot and balancing the tray, her eyes sought the table to rest her load. In one smooth move, she slid the tray off her shoulder onto the lunch table.

7. Christie

She spotted a blanketed form on one of the chaise lounges, lying in the weak autumn afternoon sun, protected from the cold ocean breeze by the patio walls. Bright cerulean-colored lanterns unmasked as lids fluttered open, and for that brief moment, each woman studied the other. The opening of the back door caused Alex to break her gaze and turn to greet Claire and Genie.

Genie had dessert and Claire carried plates, plastic ware, and beverages on her tray. Claire followed Alex's eyes that returned to the sleeping woman. She gave Alex an odd look. Alex opened her mouth to ask her what that look was for but changed her mind.

"When did she arrive?" Alex asked instead.

Claire was quiet for a few minutes. Alex glanced at her, picking up on her silence. Claire's brow had frown lines and her lips tightened into a thin line.

"Yesterday afternoon," she finally answered softly, so as not to disturb Ms. Duke's slumber. "She looked awful, so I took her straight to the clinic to have Mai look at her. She's already doing better."

Alex blinked in surprise. SID didn't say anything about the civ being sick. "Who is she?" Alex held her plate for Genie to spoon a generous helping of potato salad for her.

"Elizabeth Duke. She's an author. Her perp is a law officer from Alabama." Claire picked up half a sandwich and bit into it. "This is different, honey. What did you change?"

"Yum, this is different. I never knew a tuna salad sandwich could take on so many flavorful variations. Isn't this your third try for a different taste?" Alex remarked as she hungrily munched her way through her sandwich.

"Uh-huh. For someone who only will admit to making coffee, it's amazing how sensitive your palate is," Genie teased. "I don't want the residents to get bored with my sandwiches."

"Ha," Claire laughed. "Did you get the way she added flavorful variations? She's buttering you up, hon. She knows she won't get a better lunch. It's free."

"I donate!"

"Yes, you do. If you want chocolate cookies, you bring the condiments."

Alex grinned. "I bet you couldn't say that ten times quickly."

A buzz sounded and Claire rose, gesturing Genie to stay. Alex and Genie fell into a comfortable silence as they focused on their meal and Alex on her thoughts.

An author? SID must love using that cover. Wonder if she's got my laptop. Alex nearly snorted at that thought. In the one look they exchanged, Alex was not sure her preconception of Elizabeth Duke was correct. Then her thoughts stilled from the discomfort of the contrasting views of the woman. Unconsciously, her eyes slid over to the blanketed form repeatedly as she munched her meal.

She was intrigued.

When Claire returned, she had Mark in tow. "Genie, Mark brought over a package the post had for us. We'll be right back, you two. We need to check it in. Mark, try one of those sandwiches. Genie's trying a new recipe, and pour yourself a drink and dip into the potato salad."

"Thanks." He pulled out a chair. Mark scrutinized the women on the lounge, then looked at his partner as she sipped her tea.

Alex shifted her glance to the woman, then back to Mark. "Something wrong?" she asked in a low voice.

"No. No."

She took a few chews, trying to decipher the tone he used. "You've taken up delivering packages, and it's not even Christmas," she tried another tack.

"Hmm." He chewed to empty his mouth. "I stopped at the post office to pick up some stamps, and Pat asked if I could drop off a large package for the House." He smiled at her and looked amused. To appease his partner, he added, "Pat said they've been pestering him about its arrival for weeks. He couldn't reach them because their phone was busy." He looked down at his food, hiding a wide smile. "I love her potato salad," he told her without looking up. "I figured since it was so close to lunch, I would get invited."

Alex nodded, still watching her partner closely. *So what is so darn amusing, partner?*

He leaned forward. "By the way, you haven't said anything about Mike's email. I just got to my inbox a while ago." Whatever was amusing him was replaced by a serious face.

She straightened up and switched to her cop mode. "In the excitement of your morning surprise, I forgot to mention it to you. So is that why you're really here?" Though she asked it, she didn't believe it for a minute.

"I want to make sure this place is secure. I don't want another woman to disappear."

Alex nodded. She glanced at Elizabeth Duke and remembered the brightness of the eyes that studied her. The back door opened and Claire and Genie returned.

"Mark, you're a lifesaver. We've been waiting for that delivery for a month," Claire said as she sat down.

"What is it?" Alex asked curious.

"A surprise addition to the gardens. Wait until we get it set up," Genie told her. She shared a smug look with Genie. She bit into her sandwich and nodded to Mark.

"So you like the sandwich?"

"I guess all tuna salad sandwiches taste the same to me. It tastes just like my wife's," he managed with a full mouth.

Genie nodded. "Good. It's her recipe."

Conversation was kept minimal as they enjoyed their lunch. When the potato salad was gone, Alex and Mark took their leave.

Alex slid into Mark's passenger seat and demanded, "All right, Mark, I can see it in your eyes. What are you planning?"

"Planning? Nothing!" He backed up the truck, and while turning onto the street, resisted glancing at his partner. "Where do you want me to drop you off?"

Alex frowned. Obviously, they were not talking about the same thing.

"Oh, you mean about Mike's chatter on the Internet."

To Alex, Mark was acting strange. What else would she be talking about? "Drop me off at the office."

"I called the chief in Bales. I got him at a break in the pretrial rehearsal, and he was already in a bad mood."

"He didn't answer my email."

"He's buried. The case is a toughie. The defense lawyer brought five other lawyers with him," Mark said.

"What did he say about Mike?"

"He's going to check with his contacts at the Fed. Did you get anything on the boats?"

"Yes. They're registered to Roger Hatfield from Newport Beach Harbor. He rents yachts."

"Roger Hatfield..." Mark's voice trailed off in thought.

Alex studied Mark for a moment. "Do you ever relax?"

"Do you?"

"Yes. That's why I take off to my cabin on my days off. No phone, television, fax, or beeper," she grinned. "It prevents me from going crazy."

"That's why you're the grunt and I'm the supervisor," he smiled back.

They parted company at the police station.

That evening, Adison was restless. She had soaked in the tub for five minutes, trying to relax, then made an attempt to concentrate on work.

"I need to take a walk. That should tire me out." She heaved herself out of her reading chair and tossed her book onto the bed. She dressed quickly in warm clothing, adding her gloves to the pocket in the front of her hooded sweatshirt, then clomped down the stairwell, looking like she had a destination in mind. Standing for a moment on the sidewalk, the first thing that assailed her was the cold wind, then a mixture of fragrances from heavy perfumes. Unfortunately, a car's exhaust wiped out the mood the fragrance set. With another breeze came cooking odors from the nearby restaurants, then there was the heavy scent of brine which she loved.

Her eyes adjusted to the darkness where people were still busy shopping and moving along the sidewalks, taking a last look through the shop windows before they closed. Unconsciously, she moved in the direction of Mollie's coffee shop. Various people nodded to her as she walked by. Her walk took her outside of the business area away from the lights and busy walkways through the park. Small lamps a few inches off the ground on both sides of the sidewalk gave her enough light to know where to place her feet.

Anxiety, restlessness, not able to sleep, what does that tell you? Huh, Alex? Too much coffee after five, she scolded.

Alex stopped near the edge of the cliff, leaning into the stiff wind. For long minutes, she breathed in the cold air and relished the chill on her face while the rest of her was warm. She pulled the hood of her sweatshirt over her head and sat on a rock near the edge. She pressed her gloved hands between her legs, more for comfort than warmth. Around her, the sounds of the waves crashing below and the wind whipping through the surrounding brush were indistinguishable and blotted out the rest of the world. Closing her eyes, she let her thoughts wander. Alex flexed her fingers. Sighing, she straightened up, trying to get a kink out. A numbing blow across her back knocked her over the cliff.

Instinctively, Alex grappled for something to stop her tumble. Dirt, sand, and bits of plant life slid down with her, covering her face and causing her to choke. She bounced onto a small overhang where she dug in her toes and fingers. Coughing, her mind put together what happened, then took stock of her pounding heart, labored breathing, and a numbness across her back. Whether she had a wound or it was just a hard blow, she couldn't determine. A heavy thump next to her brought her back to her tenuous placement on a small lip on the cliff. The next thump was closer. It dawned on her that if she had not straightened up, it would have been her head and not her back that would have taken the blow.

The next heavy object hit the back of her leg.

Slowly, so as not to upset her precarious balance, she pulled herself closer to the wall of the cliff. The next rock bounced and hit her in the side. Thankfully, the first bounce in the dirt took most of the force, but it still hurt when it hit her.

Gods! All right already! You knocked me off the cliff! Oh!

She lost her grip and started sliding, then the ground disappeared from under her. Grabbing onto a small protrusion, she dangled, unable to see in the darkness. Her body swayed, loose dirt stinging her face. Tired fingers from her free hand groped for something else to cling to. The next rock bounced and hit her shoulder, dropping her another level down the cliff. For a moment, she was able to hold onto a small shrub with one hand. The shrub came loose and she fell farther down.

"Alex!" a voice whispered urgently near her ear.

She stifled a panicked reaction as she attempted to look up. "I'm blind!" she whispered back horrified.

"It's night. Can you move?" Mark asked anxiously.

She tested her limbs and realized she was hurting. A good sign in some aspects. No broken bones, another good sign. Her back hurt. Hurting meant this was not a dream. She let out a small yelp when she moved her leg. "Yes," she gasped.

"We've got to get off this ledge. It's not going to support our weight. Can you move on your own?"

"My head is spinning. Give me a moment."

"You're lucky I saw you get knocked over the edge. I only wish I had the time to chase after her."

"Her?" She closed her eyes to gather herself.

"Yes. Whoever it was runs like a girl. Maybe it was one of your Ms."

Alex groaned as she moved into a standing position on the sandy shelf. "It's got to be Rita. She's the impulsive and nasty one," she muttered.

"I'll move your hand nearest me if you can't find a secure place. Follow me. We're going to move farther along this cliff face then go up," Mark explained near her ear.

Stinging bits of sand blew into her face. She brushed her face against her long-sleeved sweatshirt for relief, forgetting it was covered in dirt.

Getting to the top seemed to take forever, and Alex found her limbs trembling with exhaustion before she was pulled over the top by her partner. Both lay exhausted on their backs, ignoring the wind blowing around them, staring up at the night sky. Alex finally broke the silence.

"What was that all about?"

"Opportunity."

Alex could imagine Mark Scripts, her partner and mentor shaking his head at her lapse in judgment. He was right. Not only was she distracted with her thoughts, but she had also placed herself in a vulnerable position. How much more stupid could she get than sit on a rock near the edge of a cliff in the dark? She got complacent and didn't allow for either of the groups they were monitoring to get aggressive.

"Thanks for the rescue."

He was quiet for a while, then rolled to his side, propping up his head in his hand. "I'll give you a lift back to your place."

"You think whoever knocked me over the cliff is waiting for me somewhere on my walk back?" she asked disbelieving.

"Nope. Her opportunity has passed. But I think you're going to be hurting. Were those rocks she was dropping over the side?"

"Ow and yes. She got a few good hits. I wonder if she did it because it would be one less cop."

"Maybe."

"Mark, they couldn't have known I was going to take a walk. *I* didn't know I was going to take a walk. Something is coming down. Big. There's too much activity with Mike, with Danny, and this. Do you think it's tied in with those morons from the L.A. gang squad?"

He snorted in disgust. "They have their own problems in Ramparts Division. That's more of why they're here. They lucked out that L.A. wanted to send someone up to check out who from their neighborhood is buying weapons here."

Somehow Mark found his vehicle in the dark. Both were cold and welcomed the heat pouring from the vents, though for Alex, it was only to be a short ride. Mark pulled up in the alley behind her apartment. In silence, they climbed the dark stairs, using Alex's small SureFire key chain light to light their way.

"Darn," she whispered.

Mark nearly ran into her when she suddenly stopped. Someone had intentionally cut the wires to her door alarm and left it plain for her to see.

"Let me go in first," Alex said with a hand pressed on his chest as he attempted to go past her. "I know the layout better."

Once in the apartment, they made a thorough inspection. They came up with one bug her visitor had planted.

"You would think they learned by now," Alex muttered, lying her hand on her computer. "It's warm." She flicked the PC on, and while it booted up, she gave a quick glance around her apartment again, noticing that the area she hid her working hard drive had not been disturbed.

"Okay, let's see what the surveillance film shows," Mark muttered as Alex hit enter on the keyboard.

Alex could be seen leaving by the front door and just as she closed the front door, a man had entered the apartment through the back. He was dressed in black with a sniper veil concealing his face.

"You'd think this was all planned. What would they have done if I didn't go for a walk?"

"Maybe it's better we not know," Mark murmured.

"Look, does that seem like he's talking to someone? I bet he's talking to the creep who tossed me off the cliff."

"You may be on to something, Alex," he mocked her. Alex nudged him with her elbow. "Let's send this file over to our server. We'll see if Burns can do something with it."

Mark moved to her phone. "Yep. Things are starting to happen. Wonder why he planted a bug on top of being obvious about the cut wire out back."

She peered around her room again, looking for anything else that may look out of place. "You know with this change of attitude, we're going to have to change our methods of watching each other's backs."

"I know. And I don't believe it's going to stop with just us." His voice softened at the thought of his family.

Maybe with the pressure from SID, both groups are changing their MO toward the local PD. "I think it's the JA," she ventured.

"You don't think this is WK business?"

"No. They've been using men to do their muscle work," she said, realizing from the White Knight's MO they would be a greater threat to his family. "I must have really pissed someone off."

"*We*," Mark reminded her. "We're all in this together. Alex, not to make you feel too special, it makes sense that you were chosen. You live alone." Mark leaned over the desk to dial the chief's number. After speaking with him for thirty minutes, he hung up.

"The chief has an issue with that email to Mike. It was date stamped weeks before Elizabeth Duke was scheduled to arrive. How did they know she was coming here? I'm going to have Burns look at the House's firewall tomorrow and its logs and ask Claire how far in advance they know who and when their new resident will arrive."

"Tomorrow I'll stop by the House and get more in-depth information on her, like who she's running from and why," Alex said.

"We can't protect her if we don't know her entire story," he agreed. "We usually just have a name and some statistics, not a complete profile, which I'm sure Claire has. Has Claire given us the usual information on her yet?"

"Not yet, but it could be that she wants her to look a little healthier before introducing her to us." *I wonder if SID said anything to Claire. She's no dummy and is very protective of her charges. This woman really looked legitimate. Or is that SID's intention?*

"I'm not going to let them kidnap another woman, Alex."

She looked up at him startled. "The feeling is mutual, partner. Look, my brain is tired, my body is tired, and I'm sure yours is, too, so let's sleep on this. And don't wake me for a run tomorrow. I'm going to have problems moving at a slow walk."

"Are you going to be all right alone? We have a guest room and a jacuzzi."

"I'll be fine. I'll see you tomorrow. And thanks, Mark."

He nodded. "If you don't feel well, don't come in." The glare he received reminded him she hated to be treated like anything less than superwoman. He really needed to talk to her about that.

"Go home, Detective. You have a family who needs you."

As soon as her partner left, Adison made a closer inspection of her apartment, finding nothing to indicate a serious inspection of her place was made. That was disturbing. She ran another virus detect program on her PC, and while that ran, she collapsed on her futon and fell asleep, not getting a call into Mel as she intended.

The next morning, Thursday, she called in late. When she woke up, she was sore and stiff. Maybe she should have taken Mark up on using his jacuzzi. The herbal salve she had for bruises was applied to all that she could see.

While waiting for the salve to heat up, she called SID. "Briscolle, what's going on?"

"How are you doing? I heard from Harper you were knocked over a cliff"

"They were aiming for my head and missed. Lucky me. Does one of our targets know about me?"

"Just that Harper's detectives are getting too nosey. It was a warning."

"I don't buy that. It's too close for something big that's coming down the pipe for them to knock off a local who would cause everyone to go on the alert, including the FBI since Judge Mead is warm and cozy with them."

"Maybe that's their plan. With their own FBI agent in charge, they can slip in and out, leaving the local PD to blame for the FBI loss."

"Briscolle, don't brush me off like this."

"Harper about burned my ears about your attack. Seems to think it has to do with Mel's operation. Well, that it might. I'll be coming down to brief him soon. We're going to need his office's full cooperation to make this work. Can you hold off with any more questions until then?"

"Depends. If the next attempt succeeds, you won't need to ask."

"Now don't get melodramatic. Take care of yourself. You're one of our key players, you know?"

"The last time I was, my partner got killed," she grumped.

"Get your head back into the game, Agent Adison," she ordered. "Just how bad did they get you?"

"Enough to question whether our intelligence is all that great on this group. I'll make a bet it was Rita who pushed me over and the guy was Marcos. Why haven't you been able to get information on that family?"

"Because we have our focus on WK, in case you forgot who you're working for."

"I'm serious, Briscolle. I'm a target for them. I don't want to be a sacrificial lamb. I know how the Homeland Security outfit works. Everyone is expendable but their select group. Civilians running law enforcement is as bad as them running the military."

"They don't run, Mel. We minimize casualties and you know we don't sacrifice our own. What's got into you?"

"I have to get to work," she said and hung up. For a few more minutes, she sat wondering what was wrong with her. Was it because she was singled out? She faced her own death several times and was caught in difficult situations where she needed to be rescued a dozen times. It was the nature of her job. Her thoughts focused on Elizabeth Duke. Would they sacrifice her?

Not if I can help it.

Awkwardly, she rose from her seat and limped to her dresser. She needed an Ace bandage for her leg.

Stepping out her front door, Alex realized she was going to have a long day of pain. Waving at Harriet as she moved up the stairs at the station, she prayed she wouldn't meet anyone who demanded an explanation of why she was moving so stiffly. Mark was in the chief's office, so she tapped on the door and joined them. Stiffly, she sat in a chair that normally would have been comfortable.

Chief Harper let out a low whistle when he saw Alex. He critically studied her face. "You want the day off?"

"I didn't spend any time in front of a mirror this morning," she admitted, sidestepping the question.

The chief dug out a small mirror in his desk and handed it to her.

She had a bruise on her chin and forehead and cuts and scrapes on one side of her face. When she was applying the salve, she was not looking in a mirror.

"This is not going to be easy to hide." She frowned at her reflection.

"This is not the MO of either group where we are concerned. I'm not going to be naïve and say they aren't aware we know about them, but something has changed the atmosphere." He looked directly at Alex, then sipped his coffee, letting his eyes move elsewhere. He thumped his emptied cup down. "I suspect there's a leak in the judge's office, which means we've been compromised. I told the judge she's out of the information loop unless I feel she needs to know something."

The chief looked down at his vibrating pager on his desk. Picking it up, he glanced at the message, then resumed. "Alex, are you going to be okay working or would you like a day or two off?" he pressed.

Alex looked surprised. "Ah…uh."

"You do get days off for hazardous activity," the chief assured her with a small smile.

"No, no. I'd be pacing and driving myself nuts. Something is coming down, and pushing me off a cliff is not going to make me miss the show."

"Okay. When you have lunch with Claire and Genie, see if you can get more information on Ms. Duke. The file they sent on her is the usual stuff, but it's not enough this time." He frowned and added, "Maybe looking like that, you shouldn't go over there."

"Chief, most of the current residents saw me with bruises after I dumped Genie's trail bike in the sand. They've also seen me with bruises after I was dumb enough to challenge Patty to a race on the top of a trash can to the bottom of the driveway in the snow and…"

The chief and Mark laughed.

"Okay. I think the whole town has seen you with bruises after all your disasters. I'll call Claire and let her know you two are on your way over."

As Mark and Adison hit the pavement to walk to the House, the sidewalk tables were already creating pedestrian traffic. The weekend artists were putting up their stands, getting ready for the Saturday crowd. More than a few shook their heads at Alex's bruises. Some reminded her about her attempts at learning roller hockey, something she had forgotten. Though Alex didn't think herself clumsy, she did get bruised and battered from her night work, so she kept up the appearance of being foolhardy and clumsy.

Alex poked Mark on the arm with a finger to get his attention. "Emily said Doug will have a table up. Have you seen some of his work besides his tattoos?"

"Yes. He took a class Linda taught about a year ago on creating art out of broken or discarded jewelry."

They spotted the large tattoo artist laying out his art on a tablecloth.

"Hi, Doug. I heard your wife had a baby boy," Alex greeted, smiling at his open grin.

"Hi, Alex...Mark. She sure did. Tiny little guy. We named him Ulysses Grant Harmon. You wouldn't think he would be so tiny with most of us being so big. Grandma Emily says that's exactly what she said when she had Junior."

"Good grief! He's the largest in the family." Alex stepped back surprised.

"Alex, you been roller skating or something?" he asked seriously.

"I can see tattoos aren't your only talent," she said, politely changing the subject.

"Thanks. If I can get a following here, one of the shops will carry my stuff." He took the hint, glancing at Mark and grinning.

Mark and Eric talked about his art while Alex perused his work. One was an interesting bit of twisted glittery stuff connected to other stuff she was sure didn't start that way. Why it attracted her attention was a real mystery because it all looked like junk to her. The title of the piece "Lost Treasures" told her little.

Leaving the budding artists and their tables behind, Mark lengthened his stride. Alex had to practically trot to keep up with him and it was a pain. Mark easily took the house stairs three at a time. They could hear the chime ring.

"Showoff," Alex muttered when she hoisted herself up the stairs, using the handrails. Mark gave her an apologetic grin. It was five minutes before they heard the sound of locks moving and the door swung open.

"Well, good morning, you two." Genie was not dressed in her usual uniform of stained kitchen apron. She beckoned them in. Her bare knees were covered with dirt and grass, and her shorts had a pair of well-used gloves hanging from one pocket and string from the other. "Is it all right if I ask what happened to you, Alex? You haven't been skating again, have you?"

"It's okay to ask, and no, I have not been roller skating. Why does everyone remember that particular event? I went over the cliff last night," she admitted irritated.

Genie's eyebrows arched. "Maybe you should have taken us up on the dinner invitation. Or was it from one of Mark's practice sessions?" She glanced at Mark.

"I wish," two voices muttered.

"This I've got to hear. Let's go out back. The winds last night blew the tomato trellis over, so we're fixing it. You can also explain just why you want to look at our files." She glanced at Alex and chuckled. "You have to admit, that roller skating incident is an event to remember. Not many people get a chance to see a cop on skates pass through four red lights, knock over Mrs. Edna, scare the dogs and their walkers, and end up flat on her back in the day care center's wading pool."

"It was one red light, Mrs. Edna was already down when I jumped over her, and if the dog walkers and their dogs stayed on the other side of the street, I wouldn't have had to take the turn into the playground."

"It was a fancy piece of skating, Detective," Mark told her solemnly as they walked to through the hallway.

"And I caught the shop thief who knocked down Mrs. Edna. How come no one remembers that?"

Mark and Genie smirked, letting out snorts of laughter.

"You did *run* him down," Mark said.

"Darn right. All the bruises were worth it."

"What did he steal anyway?" Genie asked as they stepped onto the deck.

Mark leaned over to Genie. "A purse. Mrs. Edna's purse. Detective Adison yelled at her cat, Maximilian. Of course, Maximilian should not have sprayed her leg, but everyone knows that if that cat likes you, it's going to let everyone know."

"Oh, yes," Genie grinned in remembrance.

"Gods, what I have to put up with as a public servant," Alex muttered. "And what has that cat got to do with roller skating?"

When the two walked out onto the wooden deck that stepped down to a bricked patio, their hollow footsteps brought the napping residents' heads up.

Alex felt her eyes moving to one of the reclining figures. They locked gazes, and Alex felt her breathing deepen and slow as everything around her dimmed. All she heard was her breath. With noticeable mental effort, she shook off the effect and followed Mark onto the grass where Claire was wrestling with a trellis that was taller than she was, and covered with tomato vines. Mark lent his height and strength, and after considerable muscle power, it was re-anchored.

Claire stood back from the trellis and looked Alex over. Alex had taken a safe position near the porch, leaving plenty of room for maneuvering for those who knew what they were doing.

200

"What happened to you, Alex? You didn't get back up on skates, did you?" Claire brought a gloved hand across her forehead, lifting an errant orange curl off her sweaty brow and leaving another smudge of dirt.

"Cliff diving, she says." Genie smirked at her lover's uplifted brow.

"Ah." Deciding to take care of one issue at a time, she addressed the detectives. "So Chief Harper said you want to check out our firewall and logs. He was cryptic in the why."

Chairs were set out in a circle in the center of the lawn under the warm sunlight. Mark started the tale, and Alex finished up with her cliff incident.

Claire nodded. "Mike, huh? Can't say I'm surprised. I can't think of any of his girlfriends who would risk pushing a cop off a cliff, though, so maybe that incident is separate from his interest in Elizabeth. But they don't stand a chance in nabbing her here. We make it our business to protect our residents from outside harm. And thanks to the Sunrise community's active involvement in our shelter, it's going to be darn difficult to kidnap any of our residents."

"Well, they must think they have a chance, or they wouldn't be targeting her," Alex persisted. *I can't believe she's so calm about this.*

"Then it'll be a good test for us to see just how well our lessons and our own experiences bear out," Claire said with confidence. "Speaking for myself, I'm not an amateur. I've been at it for over fifteen years and had a lot of tough cases. And, Mark, you've been training Genie, Ms. Commando, here," she leaned toward her mate and gave her a peck on the cheek, "in I don't know what, but she feels confident she can take on anything short of an elephant charge. Anyone looking at her would think she was just a chef in Sunrise, not a lethal weapon. And we have Bruno, who was trained by Mark to look after this place and has been invaluable so far."

Claire leaned toward Alex who was looking doubtful. "It has been tried before you got here, Alex." Mark nodded. "We didn't have Bruno then and didn't we do ourselves proud. We not only nabbed the perp, but y'all got to confiscate his vehicle and cache of weapons and whatever else you found in his vehicle because the idiot had a big stash of crack cocaine there."

"He was dealing to pay for his trip across country to kill his ex-wife," Mark explained.

Alex nodded toward the blanketed woman on the chaise lounge, who appeared to be asleep, not at all impressed with Claire's bravado. "How's she doing?"

"On the road to recovery. From what Mai said, someone's been prescribing unnecessary drugs to her. It's probably because she's been on the move for almost a year, trying to get away from her stalker. She's had to visit different doctors in different cities." Claire paused with a frown creasing her brow. "But, she's been in the shelter medical system all this time, and we have a central database that keeps updated medical records on all our women."

"Maybe your database has been compromised. I would like Eric to look into that. Will you give him the authorization?" Mark asked.

"Sure, with the usual paperwork filled out, judge's okay, and the woman's consent, if it involves going into her records."

Would SID allow the White Knights to tamper with her meds? Wait a minute. That would mean her perp knew at all times where she was.

Claire's cell phone buzzed. She rose and walked out of hearing distance to answer it. After a few moments, she returned.

"You got your authorizations to check the firewall. Your chief works fast."

Alex again glanced toward the still figure on the chaise lounge. The sun's light was crawling across her covered legs.

"Is that what her blood test showed?" Alex asked.

"Gary Oberman did her blood work right there. Remember he's a chemist and they have equipment there for some lab work." Claire chuckled. "Of course, Mai didn't need the results. She knew. Elizabeth said she hasn't been keeping solid food down for some time now but give the treatments a few more days. It's no wonder she's a bag of bones and feeling so weak."

"Oh, boy. Easy pickings for her perpetrator," Alex muttered.

Claire shook her head. "She may be weak physically, but she's a fighter. She's already looking much better than when she arrived."

Alex didn't realize her eyes were fixed on Ms. Duke until she moved her gaze back to her partner who was watching her with amusement.

"What?" she asked puzzled.

Claire nodded to Mark as if the two had been in conversation.

Alex replayed the last remembered conversation she had heard. Did she totally miss something? She glanced at Genie. "So are you going to join us for the 'cliff climbing in the dark' drills?"

"So, Alex. How's your love life?" Claire asked suddenly.

Startled Alex looked at Claire. It then dawned on her what the look was about. "Oh, no. Don't be trying *it* on me. I don't even want to hear with who." Alex could feel her face burning.

The smug look on Claire's face only made her more insistent.

"Claire, I'm not in the market for or even interested in a...a...a mate." She had seen their skills at picking out suitable couples many times, but it had been directed at other people more amusing than threatening. When she glanced at Mark, he grinned back at her.

"Give me the CD and I'll work on the files. You all can sit out here and laugh yourselves silly for all I care, but I'm not playing this game." Alex left the three laughing. She could hear someone following her but didn't care.

It was really disgusting to be their pick of the month. Alex shuddered at the thought of what a possible match meant at this time in her life. She slid the disk into the server's drive and typed in commands.

"Don't take it so personal," Genie tried to soothe her. She sat in a chair next to Alex.

"Personal? Just what am I taking personal?" Alex demanded grumpily.

"You in a relationship. That's really stretching her skills or the power of cupid's arrows."

"Doggone it, Genie! I don't want a relationship. I'm doing fine with dating."

"Aren't you even curious about who it is?"

"No," Alex told her firmly.

"Well, I am."

"That's all I need is to be the butt of everyone's joke."

"Alex, you've always been able to handle the teasing with some witty or caustic remark. Especially when those college students were sniffing after you."

"That's not what I wanted to be reminded of. Who is the doctor who oversees your medical records?" she demanded.

"Someone in Atlanta, Georgia. Dr. Severt. Too rigid in his practice. Claire and some of the other managers have found another doctor up in Seattle who's thinking about their offer to take over. Severt doesn't believe that herbs, acupuncture, chiropractic or massages are beneficial. He thinks chemicals are the only answer a reputable doctor should prescribe."

"You would think he works for a drug company."

"He does. He lectures for one of the leading pharmaceutical companies besides overseeing the shelter's medical profiles. It's supposed to give us a discount on drugs for our residents, but in the long run, it doesn't."

After capturing the information Burns' CD was programmed to look for, it automatically sent an encrypted email of the results to Eric. Mark and Alex left, reassuring Claire and Genie that they were in the information loop and would hear what they found within hours. Alex headed back to the office to see how Burns was coming along on the photos from the missing photography student's camera and Mark headed out to do some shopping after telling her to send him a copy. It was supposed to be his day off.

Burns was still working on making the pictures clear, so Adison sat with him rather than walk around town and listen to comments on her bruises.

"These have a lot of possibilities," Alex said as she zoomed in on one. The pictures were close-up shots, though blurred, of tattooed arms, woman's boots held in a muscular armed man's hand who also had a tattoo, Humvees with no license plates, and one picture of a woman's face.

"Looks like trouble, Alex," Eric said.

"Uh-huh. CC everyone, then let's play with these two that have blurry tattoos."

That night, as Adison climbed the stairs to the House, she shut her brain down. She decided to visit the women's shelter rather than her other favorite night stopover, Mollie's coffee shop. Both had bookcases and copious amounts of fresh coffee or tea, which was just what she needed to stop thinking shop, but there would be too many people at the coffee shop with comments about her skating days.

While Claire and Genie played bridge with two other residents, Alex took her usual place in a chair and read. The conversations and joking among the women belied the harsh life the residents had suffered to end up here. Their chatter was so normal, Alex felt she was a voyeur.

She closed her eyes for a moment, letting the words of the book she was reading repeat in her mind, but they still failed to hold. A soft shuffle caught her attention. Elizabeth Duke limped into the room.

The other women glanced up and waved, then returned their attention to the game. Ms. Duke's return wave also included a glance around the room, her eyes resting briefly on Alex. She went to the bookshelves, seeming to know exactly where the book she was looking for would be located. After picking out a thick book, Ms. Duke left the room.

"Goodnight, Genie. Thanks again for the cookies. Night, Claire." Adison waved.

"Good night, Alex. Better take care of that old body of yours. Soak in some Epson salts," Genie suggested.

"Yes." However, before leaving, Alex decided to take a look around the grounds. Without using a light, she limped slowly to the back of the House, listening and smelling for anything out of place. In the pitch darkness, she trusted her other senses to warn her.

Snap!

Alex's heart beat faster, and she slowly pulled her small but powerful SureFire out of her leg pocket, willing her eyes to see in the darkness that was beyond the fence that surrounded the House.

The lights to the property suddenly went on and she could hear a soft curse from around the bend of the fence. Breaking into a hobbled run, Alex flashed her light at the figure running toward the road behind the House. By the fast pace, Alex thought the person was wearing night goggles.

"Halt! Police!" she hollered.

Behind her, she could hear Genie's voice commanding Bruno to "arrest" the trespasser.

"I hope Bruno remembers I'm the good guy," Adison muttered, then her foot stumbled on an uneven part of the ground. Painfully falling on the previous night's bruises, she let the light fly from her hands. It went bouncing crazily, then rolled into the prickly brush along the fence. For a moment, she thought she heard a pop, but she was being overwhelmed with Bruno who caught up with her and was overenthusiastic with finding her. She heard a car start and slide in the sand as the accelerator was floored.

"Bruno, let me up. Good dog. Genie!" she yelled.

"What are you doing?" Genie demanded when she caught up with Bruno. "Bruno. Good dog. Sit!"

"Did you get a make of the car?" Alex stiffly rolled to her feet with Genie giving her a lift up.

Genie picked up her light and handed it to her. "Where's your sidearm?"

Alex looked at her puzzled. Genie had a large red lamp at her side. Alex felt her back and found it was still secure in its holster. "Why?"

"I heard a shot. Sounded like someone had a silencer on and it hit something."

Alex remembered, too. "It's too dark to do a good search without messing up something that may be important." With a sinking feeling, she realized she would be spending the night, making sure no one returned to mess up the crime scene. That meant dressing warm and trying to stay awake in an uncomfortable beach chair.

"Bruno will secure the area until morning. Why don't you get some sleep?"

"How's that?" Alex asked skeptically as she pictured dog prints everywhere.

"Mark trained him. He won't wreck your scene. Hey, Bruno! What's got into him?" Genie muttered as the women went after the dog who was calmly sniffing along the far side of the road with a short leash dragging after him.

Alex groaned as she thought of the leash messing evidence in the sandy ground. Both women took a long curved route to the dog that was sitting with his mouth open and tongue hanging out as if wearing a grin. At his feet was a small packet.

Genie dug her elbow into Alex's arm. "What did I tell ya?" Her grin was as wide as proud Bruno's, who seemed to know he found something important. "Mark trained him good, huh? That shows you a Heinz 57 makes a great crime fighter."

"Yes, it sure does." Alex pulled non-latex gloves out of her pocket and snapped them on. She grunted with pain from bending over and the exertion to stand. "Except he nabbed me and not the visitor," she huffed. "But then again…" She sniffed at the packet she was holding between her fingers, "it's a good thing he hadn't. If that was a gunshot, he may have been hurt." She dropped that in the bag and flashed her light to where something else caught her attention. She cursed whoever dropped it because it meant she was going to have to bend down again and pick it up.

"You're not moving so well, Alex. Do you want me to pick up things?"

"Genie," she warned in a low voice.

"You're being stubborn. I didn't tease you once while you were over tonight, and I haven't told anyone how you got those scrapes and bruises. I'm just trying to help."

"I'd believe you except you're wearing a big grin on your face when you made the offer." She flashed her light toward Genie, verifying that the smile in Genie's voice matched the one on her face. "I'm fine."

"Bruno, guard," Genie ordered. "Okay," she told Alex, then she turned to return to the house. "I'm going to let Claire know you're doing 'just fine' after you did a slide face first." She laughed as she headed back to the house.

"Gods, the abuse I take from this town," Alex muttered as she painfully dropped to her knees and picked up the fuse and secured it in another plastic bag. Bruno looked up her when she squeaked from the effort of rising to her feet.

At six in the morning, after a thirty-minute soak in Epson salts and sleeping for three hours, Adison was at the office picking up equipment to check out the crime scene. She had left the packet and fuse locked up in a file cabinet that few people had a key to.

The sun was barely up when she was out at the back of the House with an almost empty cup of hot coffee from the doughnut shop and a camera. Her crime case was sitting near the trash bin. While she was inspecting the bin with her magnifying glass held in her left hand and coffee cup in the other, she heard a vehicle pull up. Turning slightly, she smiled at Mark who was dressed in his running clothes. She noted that Angel was not in the vehicle. He must have checked his work queue before he started out to pick her up for their morning run. She had input the information the night before, so it would have been available for him to review. She had also taped a note on her back door saying she would be here. He stepped under the tape Genie had helped her twine around the area.

"If shots were fired, how come you didn't call?" His calm voice belied his anger. He was her supervisor and his rule was that she notify him if her life was in danger.

She shook her head. "I wrote that I was not sure about that, and until I find evidence, I still don't know. However…" She pointed at one mark that looked new on the trash bin. "Looks like it went that way," she gestured with her coffee hand.

"Uh-huh. Where's the string?"

She pulled the roll from her jacket pocket. "I'll hold, you can run around since you're dressed for it," she offered.

After two hours of combing the site, cleaning up their tape, packing up their gear and having a word about what constitutes life endangerment, both were ready to eat. There were only old bullet casings and one bent shell gathered.

"Hey! Where you two going?" Genie called out as they were about to drive off.

"To eat!" they yelled back.

"Come on! I've got plenty."

Both sighed, knowing she would want to hear what they found, and it was not much. Keeping them in the loop when it had to do with their residents was not just a courtesy, but also their duty that the chief was firm about. However, the detectives wanted to talk to the chief first.

"You might as well sit down and wait. Chief Harper's on his way over," Genie said when they walked with her to the back gate.

"Well, good morning, you two. Nice day for a friendly breakfast, no?" Claire asked as she sat at the head of the table in the dining room. The residents were respectfully upstairs having their own meal in the sitting room, letting Claire handle their affairs with the police.

"Hmph. Depends how much sleep you had last night," Alex grumbled.

"None," both women told her.

"We've been watching the place to make sure no one came back for what you found. We don't want Bruno to think he's all alone and vulnerable out there."

Mark grinned, "He's a winner, huh?"

"You trained him good, Mark. He saved Alex's life, then found evidence the guy left behind," Genie said proudly.

Alex lifted an eyebrow at the "saved Alex's life" part but wisely said nothing as her cup was refreshed with her favorite flavored coffee, Hawaiian Hazelnut. The remark that "the guy left behind" hit the nail on the head of what was bothering her.

Claire got up when the door rang. By then, Mark and Alex were finished with their omelets and home fries and leaning back for another cup of coffee.

"Well, what do you have?" Claire asked once the chief was seated.

"The C4 plastique Alex...excuse me...Bruno found, was enough to put a gate in your wall."

Genie chuckled amazed. "If someone blew a hole in the wall, it would have all of us up and the whole town, too. What a nightmare. We would've not only killed the stupid fool, but the noise would have brought every militia member out armed and dangerous, hyped up on adrenaline, surrounding the House, looking for something to shoot at. It would have terrified the residents to say nothing of me."

Everyone silently agreed.

Is that the plan? Alex asked herself worriedly.

"Any of the profiles on the perps your women are running from have that type of background?" Harper asked.

"All of them. That's why they had to leave their states and take refuge here. So where does that leave us?" Claire asked.

"Where you always are, Claire. The second to know if anything is going to be a problem," the chief assured her.

"Well, Genie took some castings of a print she found on the side of the house."

"I hope those aren't mine," Alex grimaced. "I was looking around the place after I left when I heard some noise and went to investigate it."

Genie laughed. "This person's foot was two sizes larger than yours, Alex." She got up to return a few minutes later with her dry/wet casting. "It was fun practicing some of the stuff Mark teaches. I think the girls would like to learn it, too. It'll keep us occupied when cards and knitting get too slow."

Mark took the casting and nodded to the others. "Well, I'm heading to the office to log in our evidence and check on where that stuff can be bought around here. You coming, Alex?"

"I want to take another look around."

"Eric should have something by now on what we pulled from your server, Claire. I'll call you when I get in the office," Chief Harper said.

As Mark and Harper took their leave, Alex followed them out.

"What are you looking for, Alex?" Genie asked as she let them out.

"The reason why some idiot would want to blow a hole in your fence, if that was the intention. Where were those footsteps?"

"If you stir any more trouble up, Alex," Harper warned, "just remember you're on call this week and it only adds to your work load."

"Yes, but Mark is my backup, and I may have to take a medical day off," she returned.

"Just remember who sets up the training schedule," Mark smirked.

"And just remember *this* volunteer hasn't signed up for Navy SEAL work," Genie warned Mark for her friend's sake and for hers.

When Mark and Harper left, Alex nudged Genie's elbow. "Thanks. I like his night training sessions and you're a sport to join us, but sometimes, I think he forgets we're not a SEAL unit."

"Yes," she agreed. "I almost told him the other night that I quit when he took away my night vision goggles. I like the toys." She grinned at Alex and gestured to the fence. "It's off this way."

For an hour, Alex paced around the House taking pictures and wondering what the visitor had in mind. It was not blowing a hole in a wall. That was ridiculous. Was the idea instead to scare someone? Locally, everyone knew about Bruno, the alarms set around the House, and how well protected the shelter was. Was someone just testing it like with Hale's fish store? Who were they intending to go after? Her thoughts kept returning to the story of the boy who cried wolf. Why? False alarm? This was a real alarm. Maybe this was a fox tale and not a wolf tale. Someone was making it seem like the place was being tested. Okay, why? To scare someone? Who?

She returned to where the footprint was. Alex knew the layout of the shelter's garden. Directly on the other side of the brick wall was where Bruno's doghouse sat. Bruno never slept in his doghouse, something she only knew from a comment Genie made about a stray cat liking it better. By the deep indention in the toes, it looked like the person tried to jump up. That was dumb, too. The fence was seven feet with decorative wood on the top adding two feet to it, and that was embedded with alarms. Was the person intentionally leaving tracks?

So, they're trying to flush someone out. Alex pursed her lips, making a good guess on who. *Who are you, Ms. Elizabeth Duke, who warrants all this attention?*

Later in the afternoon, Adison was at the east side. She purchased the *New York Times* at the only place that had it, the Cigar Shop where the militia boys liked to spend idle time when not drinking. Mark had commented about an ad that was placed for voodoo work. It was not the ad but the name of the person claiming to be able to hex anything. With coffee and paper, she found a seat at the coffee shop next door at the outside tables. She was scanning the ads and sipping coffee she paid for so that she was not needlessly taking up a table.

"Move aside, ya fat dyke," Joey's voice came from the interior. He was talking to Wanda Rangler, one of the patrons.

Alex sighed. For six months, she worked alongside child services where she learned that physical abuse was reportable but not verbal. Shuddering, she refocused on the newspaper, momentarily off balance and unable to comprehend what she was reading.

Taking a deep breath, she reminded herself if anyone needed her help, they knew where she was. Usually the "boys" didn't go into the coffee shop unless they wanted sandwiches.

"Well, look what we got here…a cop. You should wear a uniform so no one mistakes *you* for a dyke in leather." Joey laughed it up with the other men exchanging smirks. "Oh, that's right, you are one." He dramatically slapped his forehead.

A handful of people came out of the shop, tourists and some red-faced patrons.

"Sounds like you're harassing patrons of this coffee establishment, Joey," Adison said.

Joey made a snorting noise and would have continued on if his companions had not left him and headed to the smoke shop with their sandwich bags. Alex watched him, curious what he would do now that his support group was gone. He muttered, "bitch," and hurried after his friends. Alex turned to the patrons and Marty, the day manager of the shop.

"If you have a complaint, now would be a good time to call the office. You have me as a witness." She went back to her newspaper. She learned in the past when it involved Mike's friends, if she took the initiative and stepped in to stop the harassment, the witnesses and victims wouldn't back her up. Having them call in a report meant it was on the record.

She rose from the table when her pager vibrated. She pulled it out with her radio. "Alex here, come in."

"Detective, a complaint of harassment from some patrons at the coffee shop came in. I understand you're out there."

"Yes, Harriet. I heard some of it."

"Was Joey within ten yards of Wanda Rangler?"

"Yes."

"Bring him in. He broke his probation terms."

"Our cells were painted yesterday and the fumes are still strong."

"I'll check with Bales. Do you need any help?"

Alex thought about it. "Stay on the comm and we'll see how this unfolds." She turned to the faces watching her from the doorway. "Wanda, I didn't know there was a writ for him to stay away from you. If I had known, I would've done something right away."

"Claire got her to fill out the paperwork yesterday," Matthew spoke for her. "We didn't know it would work so fast." He glanced at the cigar shop. "They aren't going to start messing with us, are they?" he asked softly.

"You made it official by calling in a report. We can only do something if you put it in writing." *You ruined your chance at just making a verbal complaint, then backing down when it came time for you to step up to bat.*

Alex mentally prepared herself as she folded her newspaper and tucked it under her arm. She reminded herself what her role was…a bad cop…however, fighting fire with fire meant she would get burned, so she decided to try the nice cop routine.

She stepped into the cigar shop, trying not to breathe too deeply and let her eyes adjust to the interior lights.

"Hey, cop, looking for a bust?" Joey called, making it easy to locate him.

"No, you. Can you step outside with me, please?" she asked in a soft voice that she schooled to be friendly.

"You going to bust me with those little things?" Joey mocked, turning around on his stool, trying to keep his eyes on his audience.

"You broke your probation."

"This is harassment. I got my friends here to testify on that."

"Are you resisting arrest, Joey?" she asked in the same even tone.

"Says you!" he accused her, then looked around at the others in triumph.

Some of the patrons had left by the back door, thus avoiding brushing by Alex to leave, which she was grateful for. The only ones remaining were Mike's two cronies from Brisbane. She kept an eye on them as she watched

Joey get up and dramatically wave his arms about. He was attempting to get her to turn her back to them. Instead, Alex pulled her radio out.

"Control, come in."

"Control here."

"Harriet, did the judge say anything about Joey Thompson resisting arrest? Over?"

"He gets a month in jail. It'll have to be in Brisbane. Our cells are closed and Bales is booked up. You going to have to do a hog?"

The hog was slang for hog tying him and dumping him into the back of the squad car, which would spread around town in no time, particularly in the bars Joey frequented. He didn't want to go out looking like a fool.

"I ain't resisting arrest!" Joey shouted, leaning forward as if to be heard on the radio.

"Then why aren't you in Detective Adison's custody?" Harriet asked reasonably.

"She ain't got no reason to be hauling me off! You pressing that button of yours?" he asked.

Alex was pressing her send/receive button on her radio to allow Harriet to play her partner.

"You have five complaint calls of harassment that says she does. If you don't leave with her in six seconds peacefully, this will be written down as resisting arrest. Judge Mead will not be happy to see you again in her court after you swore you would obey your probationary terms."

As Alex pressed the speak button to say something to Harriet, one of the men spoke up.

"You best get on with the officer of the law, Joey. Don't want to hurt her feelings by denying her her simple pleasures," he mocked.

Alex released the button to put her radio away so she could pull out her equalizer, pepper spray. She could feel the tension in the room rise considerably.

"Harold Granger, if you incite Joey to misbehave, you'll be arrested for interfering with an officer of the law," Harriet's voice boomed over the speaker. "You best go on back to your own neighborhood if you want to start trouble."

Alex reminded herself that this was not a battle of egos. She palmed her pepper spray and listened to the movement around her, keeping everyone in front of her. She waited for Joey to collect his dignity and decide what to do. Alex wondered if Joey was hoping his buddies Mike and Danny would show up. She knew, though, that they were both getting used to being off departmental probation. Which suddenly had Alex wondering just where they were. This was one of the places they liked to patrol. Was this a setup?

"You're ruining business, Joey. Just get on with it!" Earl said grumpily.

Joey was having a difficult time turning himself in, and she knew why. The two remaining men belonged to a special group of hard and brutish men who teased each other cruelly as well as anyone who came to their attention. If he showed weakness to a woman, he wouldn't be a part of their crowd. Harold, she knew by name and number, but not the other. He started appearing at the bar in Bales she monitored and befriended Mike and his friends. He was not part of the Jaded Amulet group or the militia, and she was sure he was not a member of the White Knights. Alex was curious who he was and would love to have a reason to check his driver's license to find out.

More minutes passed and still Joey was wavering. Casually, Alex drew up her left arm to look at her watch. "If we start over now, we can get a dinner plate for you," she said in a conversational tone.

"What are they serving?" he asked suddenly.

"Crow," one of the men laughed sarcastically.

"You ain't taking me in!"

Joey rushed her, but she lifted her arm while deftly sidestepping him, spraying him in the face as he crashed past her. She heard him hit the floor hard, sputtering and crying. She continued walking toward the smirking stranger next to Harold, resisting the impulse to smile. She got what she wanted. The pepper spray was returned to her pocket.

"I am placing you under arrest for interfering with an arrest. You can go quietly or like Joey."

He swung at Alex, but she had seen it coming. It was Harold she was worried about and the person who walked in behind her. Alex quickly pulled her short nightstick out and tapped him in the solar plexus, then behind the knee to get him down. If you knew where to hit to disable someone, it didn't take much, provided they were not on drugs. Without breathing hard, she waited for Harold to make his move.

Harold walked out of the shop, stepping carefully around the two fallen men. Chief Harper stood in the doorway and Judge Mead was standing outside. Alex watched her as she stared Harold down. The woman was taller than her barefoot 5'4'' in heels, though not by much, and her dark suit with a single diamond in the scarf, sparkled as she gestured for Harold to approach her.

"I want to see you in my courtroom on Monday. Ten sharp," she ordered.

Harold started to say something, thought better, and left without a backward glance.

Joey, who was screaming in high-pitched squeals, was dragged to his feet by Harper. Alex placed cuffs on the stranger and dragged him outside to search him. He was limp from the breath knocked out of him, and he was heavy.

Alex pulled his wallet out of his pocket, glanced to see if it had a picture ID, and tossed it to the side, then went through the rest of his clothes, patting him down thoroughly for hidden weapons. She propped his bent form against the wall and looked through his wallet more carefully.

"Well, Mr. Blake J. Headers," she said out loud for the chief's benefit. "By this expired ID, you're from Idaho. In this town, we don't suffer bad behavior nor disrespect of the law well," Alex said conversationally. "Now attacking an officer, that's going to incur jail time and a visit with the judge." Alex was careful not to add anything about punishment. She lifted her radio. "Control, come in."

"Control here. Go ahead, Detective."

"Harriet, I need the police van. I have two to haul over to Brisbane."

"I'll get Max to chauffer them. Over."

"Thanks, Harriet. Over and out." Alex shook her head. Joey was an idiot to be so easily led. Now Blake Headers, he was really dumb.

The judge and Harper were talking to Wanda, who was getting emotional. Judge Mead was uncomfortable with emotional displays unless the person was experiencing physical pain. Odd coming from a woman who spent most of her professional life as a child advocate.

The van arrived, but instead of Max driving, it was Mike.

"Chief," he began gruffly. "Since Max is busy with one of the cars, I volunteered to take the prisoners to Brisbane."

"Alex will. You can continue your beat but not this side. These shops will be off your beat for a week." His hard stare at Mike was meant to convey something, and by Mike's tightening of his lips, he knew if the chief caught him near the coffee shop on his patrol, he would be looking at suspension.

Chief Harper glanced at the judge. "Why don't we get back to our meeting?"

The judge nodded, studying Mike with pursed lips, not a good sign for Mike, then at the others who had gathered.

Without assistance from Mike, Alex moved the two into the back of the van and secured them. She turned the van around and headed to the freeway. She glanced nervously in her rearview mirror often, hoping she was not being tailed.

So is this the *BJ Headers? Holy cow! What a coincidence. How many names on that list are around here now? Maybe it's not a hit list but a party list. Then how come some of them are dying. Go back to the hit list, Alex.*

It took her an hour to reach the parking lot at Brisbane's PD. An officer was waiting for her, waving her in as she backed into their bay where prisoners were unloaded. While fingerprints were being taken, Alex filed her reports.

"Detective Adison, you fill your cells already?" the desk sergeant asked as he took her reports.

"No. We just painted two cells an overnight guest managed to damage by plugging up the toilet. Blew up in his face."

They shared a laugh at the image.

Sergeant Reed scanned her report. "Interfering with an arresting officer and attempting to strike an officer. Not so bright with Judge Mead and Chief Harper to witness it."

Alex nodded and headed to the parking lot. Automatically, she glanced around her as she pulled out her cell phone and called the chief.

"Harper here."

"Chief, I got them bedded nice and comfy at Brisbane."

"Headers, huh? Eric is running his fingerprints against AFIS."

"So what brought you over to the smoke joint?" she asked as she pulled out of the parking lot.

"A cigar. Judge Mead's husband smokes them. Thought a little bonding was in order, so I was taking her to the Cigar Room. After all that, she decided she could wait until she got home. You handled yourself well. How did you know Harold wasn't going to be as much of a problem as the other?"

"Harriet threatened him with jail if he mouthed off again. His eyes got all round. I gather he knows her enough to not get any further on her bad side."

"They have history" was the chief's response. "We're going to use your ROV. Can you deliver it to me?"

"I can drop it off at your place. Tonight, say seven?"

"Good. Come through the back way through the forest so you won't be seen. You can wait by the white mile marker."

"Okay."

"See you then."

Alex met Chief Harper in the forest and turned over everything that had to do with the small recon plane, including the directions, after she had wiped her prints off every surface. Harper was like a kid with a new toy, knowing exactly how to operate it and just where he and Mark planned on using it when not keeping an eye on the House. Hopefully, it meant she got to take some nights off.

"This will mean no more close calls on your night surveillances," he explained. "And it can cover more ground, like follow whoever happens to be visiting from out of town."

"Except, since the baby apparel store has been attracting visitors of the gang type, militia night hasn't had any interesting visitors."

"We don't know for sure. The ROV will give us better detail and coverage. Listen, Alex. You be careful. I think someone knows why you're here and they mean to eliminate you before or during whatever this is leading up to. I don't want to clean up my yard at your expense. There are other options. There are always other options."

Alex nodded and slid back into her SUV. "I don't see my demise in the cards, Chief," she said confidently.

Chapter Eighteen

T wo weeks later, Alex was sitting behind the driver's seat of the parked police cruiser, listening to the activities around her and letting her eyes take in the sights. She had thirty more minutes to sit there. Alex shifted her position yet again. "Ah, now this I could watch all day," she murmured.

Elizabeth Duke, sitting on the bench that overlooked the ocean, was alone again. Mrs. Hutchinson had left, pushing her walker ahead of her. Adison's practical side pointed out that sitting next to Ms. Duke on the bench would cause the gossip now circulating on their match-up by Mark and Claire to escalate. Unobserved, Alex let her feelings for this woman percolate to her consciousness. The feeling in the pit of her stomach was not uncommon when she spotted an attractive woman, but the warmth that accompanied it was. The women in her past never had this effect on her.

A familiar figure in her side mirror brought a grin to her face.

"Hey, Alex," Mark started in a low voice. "Hungry?"

"It's about time you got here. Between boredom and my butt being numb from sitting so long, I was beginning to think I would have to take some sick days to recuperate." She reached to accept her bag of fries, sandwich, and coffee.

Alex took a sip, letting a smile crease her lips.

Hawaiian Hazelnut. "Mmm."

"Nice view," he said, nodding toward Elizabeth Duke. He settled comfortably in the passenger seat and unwrapped his sandwich.

Alex shifted in her seat and picked out a french fry. "Would you stop trying to make us a couple? Mark, she's a civilian. We're supposed to protect her, not find a mate for her."

"This isn't going to last forever," he said in a reasonable voice.

Alex glanced at her partner who was calmly taking another bite of his club sandwich. "Claire reported that Mike and Danny made separate unsolicited calls to the shelter this morning."

Mark looked at Alex, his sandwich forgotten. "What?"

"Mike stopped at the House about eight thirty and claimed he had a complaint about Ms. Duke stealing from one of the stores."

"Did he say what store complained?"

"No. Claire said he was evasive. Danny stopped by about ten and gave some inane explanation that she said made no sense. The times they came over normally are when Genie and Claire leave the House for a few hours to do chores and socialize since the counselors are there. Claire was hanging around because she was waiting for an important fax. Why would they appear in public at the House where there is a camera and none of the residents answer the door?"

They were quiet as they ate their lunch and thought about the information.

"Mike and Danny. What idiots."

"Right."

Mark sighed heavily. "What are they up to?"

"They have nothing to gain unless it's supposed to scare Ms. Duke."

"She takes walks daily in public," he objected. "If they wanted to harass her, they could do it then, or brush by her and knock her over or..." He let out an expletive.

"Uh-huh. They are rattling the cage," Alex said. "I'll bet my next three days off that all of these confrontations with the shelter are to drive Ms. Duke out of its confines."

Both were quiet as they thought.

Alex made a noise in her throat and swallowed her meal. "To change the subject, how are you doing on your research on the Doc and Lily angle as boss suspects?"

Mark sighed. "Not getting much. Doc's high school records are copies of copies, and I still have nothing on Lily. There was a fire at Doc's high school the year he was to graduate, and all student records were destroyed. I haven't done any further digging. I've got more than a full plate. How about you?"

"Ditto. Couldn't find anything solid on either of them. Meanwhile, I thought I would also look at the financial books of businesses here. I wanted to see if there was any tie to organized crime. I thought I would also look at businesses that have silent partners, like using a corporation. I found five businesses here in town, four in Bales, six in Brisbane, and one in Antioch that have a silent partner. I don't know if it's the same person or persons."

"Hmm."

"Hey," she managed to get out with her mouth full, setting her coffee down quickly. Mark sat up straighter, catching sight of unfamiliar vehicles in the side-view mirror approaching their position.

"Partner, looks like the people you were expecting are here," Alex muttered. Setting the remains of her sandwich in a safe place, she wiped her fingers on a wet wipe and pulled the camera from the side of her seat.

"About time," he mumbled as he finished off his fries and cleaned his fingers.

Four brand new cars parked in front of and near the baby apparel store. The cars had no license numbers, just an advertisement of the place where they were purchased.

"Hold on, Mark, and stop twitching."

"The clicking in my ear tickles," he complained.

"That picture better not come out with something hairy in it. The chief's going to wonder just what I was doing when I took it."

"It's all right, Alex, your secret's safe with me."

"Then it wouldn't be a secret, Detective," she muttered. She was using Mark's shoulder as a tripod and shooting between the headrest and top of the seat. She focused on a new face. "Now this one's real interesting. Very young. Looks like he's barely beginning to shave. He's way too cool. Dresses like the others but doesn't have the cocky attitude. Checking everything out like he's had a lot of experience. Maybe this is a new face for us, but he's someone important who's been around." Alex snapped multiple pictures. "This one bears some watching and checking out with the feds. I can't help feeling he looks familiar, but… hmm."

"Maybe you know his sister," he teased. "We're bringing a movie camera next time."

"Uh-huh."

They were not in the store for long. Alex and Mark watched the last car turn the corner before Mark spotted another car approaching from another street.

"L.A.'s finest is right on time to see and hear nothing," he said.

Alex knew exactly who was arriving. Detective Guido from LAPD's gang squad. She would let Mark give him the status. His patronizing attitude was at the point that if he said anything to her, she would deck him. Mark got out of the car and walked to Guido's rental. After a couple of seconds, Mark slid back in the dark brown car and Alex had the vehicle moving.

"What did you tell him?" she asked curiously.

"What just came down. He didn't believe me."

Both were silent for one block. "How on earth did he make detective?" Alex asked dumbfounded.

Mark made a rude noise, then remembered something he meant to talk to her about. "Hey, what happened Thursday? You left a cryptic message, then took off for your three days."

"Darn. I started to email you and I couldn't remember if I finished it before I sent it. I was in a hurry. I found someone had accessed my PC, about one a.m. Thursday, according to the file date. It wasn't Mike or Danny. And the file was on notes I had made on the warehouse investigation from three years back. It's an old case that happened before I got here."

"I remember it. Two fools in the department worked on it, Danny and Mike. That's what got them busted down to patrols only. That is an old case. What were you doing with it?"

"Doing what you told me the day I was assigned to work with you—study old cases and see how, quote, 'we do things,' unquote. I had found some interesting discrepancies and had noted them and put them in a file. I never bothered to delete the note file. However, it's PGP-encrypted like all my notes, so I doubt they would have gotten anything from reading them."

"I wonder why that subject. Did they try any other files?"

"Nope. Either they didn't have time or they decided if I coded one file chances are I did the rest. Or maybe they noticed it left a date stamp in the properties box when they tried to open it. Since I don't like the L.A. group, I naturally picked them as number one suspects, but they don't have keys to the office. That leaves the cleaning crew. They now clean on Wednesday nights, and it won't be the first time someone with the cleaning crew is working for the bad guys."

"Jesus?" Mark asked incredulous.

"Yes. That isn't as farfetched as you think. He's very PC literate. He's been in a few of the classes I've taken from the Burns. He also told me one evening after class that he personally oversees the station cleaning just to make sure nothing is tampered with by his crew." Alex paused as she remembered back. "I thought that was an odd statement from him at the time. It was a few days later that I remembered about the theft of my watch, but it wasn't his company that was cleaning at the time. He was still working for Angelo."

"Who sold the business to Jesus."

"Right. I have to tell you, that night I couldn't sleep very well because I was trying to figure out why he said that to me and most of all, why it was bothering me. I had a dream of him doing a side business of downloading information on hard drives of the businesses he cleans, then selling the copies to each store's rivals. The real nightmare was when all the shops in town had sales battles. And then, horror upon horror, I got in on the buying mania. I was buying loads of knickknacks that need dusting and I could not…"

"Hey, watch where you're going!" Mark put out a hand on the dashboard as if to brace for something.

Alex's voice trailed off and she sat up straighter, pulling the vehicle back in line.

"Jeez, must you have brainstorms while you're driving? I see where this is going. Have you told the chief yet?"

Alex groaned. "Not yet. I've been busy everywhere. With the holidays approaching, and more tourists and more complaints."

"What a coincidence that a certain warehouse owner buys up the surplus of certain wholesalers in the city that stores in this town had planned on buying later for their future sales. And that owner just so happens to be a member of the Jaded Amulet." He sighed. "Well, at least it's not adding another new case to our stack since we've got so many complaints about Anders and his business practices. How are we going to get time to do a sting operation on Jesus selling the information to Amos or to anyone else?"

"To dry out a bad well, you cut off its source," Alex said, gesturing with one hand. "Then when you have the resources and time, clean it up."

As she pulled their car into the police parking structure, the tires squealed on the concrete surface. Alex stopped the car at the mechanics booth to fill out the form attached to the clipboard.

"Hey, don't forget to put in that the timing belt needs to be looked at," Mark reminded her.

"Good thing we don't do car chases around here."

Gathering up their gear, they headed into the office. After dropping off their equipment at their desks, they went to see the chief.

"Okay, we'll set up some cameras in the office. Harriet, you said we have five cameras in supply from our benefactor?"

She nodded.

"Okay. Burns, gather up what we'll need."

"Yes, sir." A dejected Burns left the room. He admitted that Jesus had asked him and Angie some pointed questions about security at one of the classes they taught, but he understood it was for his work PC. He was hoping it was not Jesus.

"All right, Detectives, what have we for our files?"

Mark nodded to Alex to give the report. "A new player visited Reyas's shop today. He's young, but he looks real familiar." She snapped her fingers, "That's it! Remember about a year ago, the bar we wore our leathers to?" she smirked. "There was the skinny woman with the drug dealer?"

Mark thought for a few moments, dredging up images. "Same build and the way they carry themselves," he agreed slowly.

For a moment, Adison pursed her lips as another face attempted to surface. "I'm sure those eyes and chin…" Her voice trailed off as the image refused to surface completely. "There's someone else in town those two remind me of."

"Just keep it on the back burner and it'll come to you," Harriet assured.

The chief moved his mouse to activate his PC screen. He opened a specific file, waiting for the decryption program to run. "Okay. Which one?"

The four gathered around the chief's monitor as the faces from the bar were lined up.

"No, the next one," Mark and Alex said together.

"Yep," all their voices said in unison.

"Okay. Another connection. A federal agent will be out to brief us tomorrow on something they think we need to know." The chief waited a moment before continuing, "It seems Elizabeth Duke, the new resident at the House, is one of theirs, acting as bait."

Harriet's eyes fluttered. "My word. Did she have to starve herself for the part?"

"Her poor health is real," Chief Harper said. "Make no mistake that the hardship she's gone through has not been real."

Mark shifted in his chair. "Where is this person from who we're going to hear from?"

"A covert arm of the feds, operating independently from the Bureau," the chief explained, leaving the others still in the dark.

"Well, this will put Sunrise on the map," Harriet said dryly.

The chief rubbed a hand over his face. "By the way, Alex, the judge okayed your request to see who the corporation is. His or her lawyer will give me a call. I should get a message sometime today on where that'll take us."

The chief picked up a paper on his desk and read from it. "All right, moving along. I got another report this morning, about some loud noises spooking the horses at Jay's ranch. He's concerned it will upset his new stud. Mark, I want you to take a look around. Be real careful. Sam said there are five armed men who have set up camp in a well-hidden and secured area in the forest. It's the lower side of the forest that Gray Horse doesn't patrol. Very convenient. They may be those guys in the photos the missing woman took. We don't want to stumble into something before we hear what this agent has to tell us. For all we know, those people might be part of this organization that's planning on finally talking to us."

He gestured to the outer office. "This matter of Danny and Mike visiting the House under some official guise." He shook his head. "I spoke with them separately and made it clear that is not to happen again." The chief waited a moment. "I'm not really sure why they would show their hand this way instead of approaching her when she takes her walks where she's vulnerable, unless that's too public. This is too soon following that night visit shortly after Ms. Duke's arrival."

"The House is well-protected, Chief. And the residents would be looking out for her, too. They all know her pattern of taking walks and wave to her or stop to talk. Alex thinks maybe they are trying to scare her to run. But why would she leave the House?"

"People on the inside don't always see it the same as people on the outside. Maybe she's a noble person, and knowing she's bait, she'll leave the House to protect the other women," Harriet offered.

"I don't know. It's two big questions we need answered, why and what did they hope to achieve? I'm hoping this agent has more answers than we have questions," the chief said exasperated. "What else do we have, Mark?"

"Eric took a lot more blur out of those picture's from the woman who disappeared in the forest. It looks like she was shooting from the hip, so to speak. Like she didn't want someone knowing she had a camera while she was moving," Mark said.

Alex rubbed her hands together. "Finally. Those pictures were taking up space in my dream time." Alex sat up and took a deep breath, her eyes squinting as if she were trying to look at something clearer.

"What?" Mark asked interested.

"It's the eyes and chin." She gestured at the picture.

"What?"

"The woman from the bar and the new player and our *Mrs. Dodd.* Can you see a resemblance there?"

"Well…" Harriet said, looking as surprised as the others. "You got something there. Fooled us with her being so old and all. Maybe Eric can run that program of his and instead of aging the person make them young again."

The chief nodded and frowned. "Didn't we do a background on her and it came up with no family?"

"Yep. No children or relatives we could find. She listed herself as an orphan. Mr. and Mrs. Dodd settled here when this was primarily open land, not even set out for farming. He had a heart attack and died a year after they got here. When I checked her out, besides her lawyer, the only other person who visited her was that old doctor from Bales. She only has her lawyer listed to notify in case of an emergency. She doesn't receive any mail from outside of Sunrise with the exception of advertisements and bills. All traceable to known sources. She's mum about her family unlike the other folks." *Now that's a thought. She's been here a long time and I wonder just how much money she has. Could she be the private investor in the corporation? I hadn't thought about her.*

"Eric said the introductory Internet class his wife gave at the retirement home caught on. Some individuals bought their own PCs and collectively purchased two for general use in the reading room. He said he was surprised Mrs. Dodd took to it so readily. She wanted to know just how secure and safe it was to carry on business without someone knowing or interfering with it," the chief said thoughtfully. He glanced at his watch. "Now I regret sending Eric over to the mayor's office," he muttered. "So we have three people with the same face structure and eyes. Anything is possible, even long shots, which at this time, I'm all for. Maybe she does have some distant relatives with the White Knights or the Jaded Amulet. You didn't say why she suddenly went into hiding, Alex."

"About a year ago, her doctor, Dr. Moser, went into retirement. Doc volunteered to be her physician. However, she doesn't want to be seen by

Doc under any circumstances. She went so far as to have her lawyer draw up papers that her medical care has been switched to holistic and natural and that she is not to be forced to accept traditional medical attention. So it's Mai or Gary who look over her health care."

"Since when does Doc visit patients?" Harriet asked dubious. "He's been in the administration part for so long."

"So this is why she keeps disappearing?" the chief brought them back to the business at hand.

"Apparently, the Doc doesn't take 'no' very well, according to Mrs. Dodd's lawyer. That was all I could get out of him, so I spoke with Doc. He insisted it was just a misunderstanding and he only wanted to talk to Mrs. Dodd to discuss her fears about him becoming her practitioner. I heard since I spoke to Doc he hasn't tried to see her."

"That's out of character for him." The chief frowned. "Even at the clinic, he seldom steps in, and even then, it's for minor stuff. Like Harriet said, he's been an administrator for so long I'm not sure his skills as a practicing physician are all that sharp. Mai says when he's at the clinic, he just monitors the doctors and nurses he sends over from Bales Hospital who are studying alternative medicine. He likes to see if the program he initiated is working well."

"Makes me interested in just what's going on with him and Mrs. Dodd, even if it's not connected to this other case."

"You and the Doc are friends, Chief?"

He shook his head. "No. My wife and Lily are on a committee together. Sometimes when she comes over, Doc comes with her, and while the women go off and chat, we do our thing and retreat to the television room. We don't really have much to talk about, though, the other night, he was asking questions about the medical records for my staff. He thought everyone should be getting in their physicals about now."

"He would know that?"

He shook his head. "I have no idea how the city health plan runs. But Margaret sent an email from the clinic to remind me, and naturally, I forgot until now."

Alex rubbed her forehead. "Well, Margaret's the business manger of the clinic, but do all of us go to that clinic?" She got nods from the others. "Well, then it stands to reason she would send out reminders. But she's one of the Ms, so that's something to rattle my cage."

The chief sighed. "So, Mark, do you have anything to add?"

"Not right now."

"Alex?"

She shook her head.

"Harriet?"

"Nope. But I think I got some work cut out for me. I'll go over and chat it up with the ladies at the retirement home."

"All right. End of meeting. Remember tomorrow, Mark and Alex, we have a meeting with the agent. Try to be on time, Alex. I know you'll be out late tonight, but drag yourself in by seven."

When Alex returned from the break room with a fresh cup of coffee for her and Mark, he was at his desk studying the pictures. Alex pulled her chair over to his desk.

"Would you call that a tattoo of an animal?" he asked.

"This reminds me of those Rorschach tests shrinks give their patients," Alex said as she squinted to figure out the design.

"Why don't we talk to our tattoo experts?"

"Good idea. Let's go."

Their experts were out of the office. Two disappointed detectives went to find something else to do.

"I'll see ya tomorrow, Alex," Mark said as she shut down her PC with one hand and pulled her coat off the back of her chair with the other. He leaned toward her and whispered, "Stay safe. Listen, I'll run the ROV over the warehouse when I'm doing my sweeps over the House."

Alex nodded. "Got any tiny paratroopers in the cargo bay?" she teased. "I'll see you tomorrow for the 0700 meeting. Save a cup of fresh java for me, strong."

Alex enjoyed the walk to and from work. She varied her route daily to prevent it from being predictable. The night's autumn air was cold and crisp, so she stuck to the main sidewalks where the ocean breezes were stronger.

For sure, she knew the bosses had to be from Sunrise. Chief Harper was leaning to the likely couple being the Ebbens. Where did the Ms fit and how did Mrs. Dodd fit?

Before Alex unlocked her apartment door, she looked down the alley to be sure there was no one waiting for her. Then once more, she looked up and down the block before stepping in. After locking the door behind her, she pulled out her SureFire and studied the steps as she made her way up. At the top of the stairs, she searched her room, looking for something out of place.

For a moment she hesitated, her routine broken by an image of Elizabeth Duke. The picture of her flicking her hair back replayed in her mind. She had given up blaming Mark and Claire for putting strange notions in her head and instead kept busy reminding herself that she had no business being attracted to the woman. She even started chanting a mantra daily to remind her of her duty, which was not preventing her from feeling... Here Alex's brain froze. Nervously, she ran a hand through her hair.

Job.

Concentrate.

Work the problem.

What is the problem?

She looked around her, recentering by the reality of her nearly bare apartment. It reminded her that this was not home. Alex impatiently shook her head. Why was she going through all this mental arguing?

Just focus on the job.

From her pocket, she removed her bug location device. All was clear. She laid the device near her pillow, then checked the small traps she left to let her know if she had an uninvited visitor who managed to get by her alarms.

After a three-hour nap, Alex rolled out of bed. In her dreams, she was chasing elusive clues. She remembered three vaguely, but the more awake she became, the less she remembered. While showering, she avoided using perfumed soap and her deodorant was unscented. The clothes she slipped on were washed in special non-odor soap.

Where is the dog repellant spray? Should I bring the ultrasonic, too? Don't leave home without them. Okay, I need one thermal body to take my place here in case someone is monitoring me. Humming to herself, she rummaged through a box of supplies in the closet tucked away for night skulking. When she felt she had what she needed and was dressed for the night, she stood before her mirror and studied herself. Usually, it took a split second to realize that the figure dressed in black from head to toe was her. She didn't wonder why after all these years it was still a mental chore to identify herself as the person staring back at her.

The sniper veil covered her light hair and the Kevlar gloves her pale hands. She wore a Kevlar vest underneath, giving her more bulk. Her pants button pockets carried a few supplies, and her fanny pack had whatever else she may need. Mentally, she did a quick rundown of her mission, what could go wrong, what she had at her disposal to get herself out of it, and the amount of time required to accomplish it. Satisfied, she exited through the attic, which led to the store beneath her supply room, which led to the door in the alley. She jogged to the SPD parking structure, blending in the shadows. At the vehicle of her choice, she ran a bug detector over it, then shined the small UV light on the inside and around it. Being paranoid was part of her job. Like Sam and Mark would tell her on many occasions, it was better to be overly careful than to get caught for something that could have been prevented because getting caught usually meant death. Since someone was stepping up their pressure against her, she left no room for error.

The moon had not reached its zenith, and the stars were partly obscured behind passing clouds. There was a heavy scent of rain in the air. She wore night vision goggles and kept her headlamps off as she rolled to her destination. She had to pull off the side of the road four times to avoid being spotted by other motorists. Each time, she wrote down the license numbers of the vehicles. She recognized them as belonging to the militia members.

Did I miss the meeting? Using her knees to hold the steering wheel steady, she pulled the face cover off her watch.

Nope. I'm going to be unfashionably early. So what's going on?

Chapter Nineteen

Adison moved away from the car she parked off the side of the road and jogged toward the marsh where she angled back behind the warehouses. She picked up the familiar green fluorescent shapes that loomed before her, the tall structures of the warehouse buildings, the attached sheds, the trash bins, and whatever was left laying next to them too heavy for the evening winds to blow away.

Alex pushed her small fanny pack to another position in annoyance. A sentry dressed in full camo gear, looking every bit of a soldier with some nasty weaponry around his belt and around his left arm had taken her favorite hiding spot. Night vision goggles were on his face. His head moved slowly as he scanned the space between the warehouses. She zoomed in her goggles to study the rifle. A chill ran up her spine.

Glancing around, she spotted more thermal glows where normally a lone cat would be. On the roof, a silhouette of the new camera stood out against a blanket of stars. Her lens zoomed into the camera's movements as she studied the area it covered.

Well, looks like it's not going to be as easy to visit the warehouse as it used to be. The sound of footsteps forced her to scoot back into a small space between the Dumpster and the electric box. Nervously, she pushed farther into the corner, trying to cut off any of her body heat that could be picked up by the men's goggles.

"Roger that, four green, positioned" was murmured from a place so close to her Alex could hear the man breathe.

No cologne. No body odor. And they're dressed in heavy gear as if they were a strike team. No backpacks with food. No water. They aren't U.S. government.

She peeked through a small space between the Dumpster and the boxes to study one of the sentries' rifles.

Jeez. A Barrett M-82A1? That thing would drop an elephant from a mile away. What are they expecting, a wild herd to break up their meeting?

The other soldier moved into view as the two paced nervously. He had an AR15 with a night vision scope attached to a mount and cradled lovingly in the crook of his arm. Both men wore black gloves, their faces were covered by sniper veils, exposed skin darkened, and their tactical vests were covered with the kind of goodies used to take over a Third World nation. Their soft slow speech accented heavily in a Southern drawl confirmed that these boys were from the White Knights. Alex wondered if Mel had put off Agent Briscolle's visit too long.

A bladder break moved both guards to another position, enabling her to escape undetected. Alex found where the vehicles were parked and photographed the license numbers. One truck caught her attention. It could easily be used to transport a large group of people. The image of the tall dark-haired woman came to mind. Nervously, she looked around. How was she going to help anyone if she herself was caught?

You're spooking yourself. Get in control, Agent Adison.

After locating the guard, she moved to the back of the truck to make a copy of the lock. She placed an electronic keying device over the lock and waited. The small vibration against her palm told her the lock was disengaged. Checking around her again, she opened the door. Empty. However, from the odor inside, it had been used recently.

The flutter in the pit of her stomach persisted. Taking a steadying breath, she returned her attention to the situation at hand. Different perfume scents, sweat, and the unpleasant smell of excrement wafted by her. Closing the door and keying it back into a locked position, she paused.

Pixie dust. I got some of that on me.

Rather than spend time arguing with her left brain that this may not be a good idea, she pulled out the small jar of UV dust from her fanny pack and brushed the dust over the inside of the handles, then moved to the cab. She powered the door handle and steering wheel. Finished, she moved out of sight to observe the parking area.

So the word is right. They're planning on a big delivery somewhere around here, and by the armaments they're packing, they don't want anyone messing with their plans. The women they're stashing must be nearby for so many big guns to be here. What would cause so much customer presence? Is Elizabeth Duke that important?

She craned her head and raised the volume of her listening device.

Panting. Dog. That's my cue to get out of here.

Alex nearly tripped when she anxiously looked back over her shoulder to see if the dog was near. A bark gave her his location. It was getting closer. Stopping for a moment, she pulled her can of skunk out. It was supposed to stop a dog dead in its tracks. She was hoping it was not meant literally. She continued her run over familiar terrain, knowing it was uneven enough to slow the dog handler down. She was grateful that handlers seldom released their dogs to run their prey down. Panting, she reached her car and pulled out her scanner. Looking up, she could see lights headed her way. She continued her scan.

When the lights got to a certain point, she heaved herself up a nearby tree, hoping they wouldn't check as high up as she scampered.

"Yep, it's still here."

"Well, tag it and let's move on."

She planned to leave a flat tire as decoy when she left. The next day, she could pick it up. She was also grateful she put dummy plates on. Attention to detail paid off in crunches like this. She waited twenty minutes after the men left, keeping her binoculars scanning the area.

Low profile. Don't want them to even suspect someone is watching them. She kept that mantra up to curb her impatience to just shimmy down the tree and get out of there.

After reparking the car near a tall tree close to the road leading to the state highway, she waited. She wanted to see where the large truck was going. Lightly dozing, she woke with the sounds of tires on asphalt. Five vehicles, with two Humvees headed toward the freeway on-ramp. No truck.

All right, the only place they can hide that truck is in Amos's warehouse.

Alex returned to the warehouse and found only members of the Jaded Amulet, two of whom were her fellow officers, standing in the parking lot. Interestingly enough, Amos was not there, and even more interesting, their voices were not carrying in the night. Maybe they didn't want the monitoring equipment Amos set up in his warehouse to record their discussion.

Cautiously, she moved closer. She aimed her small voice amplifier at the group. The voice she heard was Danny's angry growl. They were not using scramblers.

This is sloppy. I wonder if this is intentional and how many ears are listening.

"I don't like them moving in on *our* operation. We're doing just fine without them." His voice was not raised, but there was a lot of fury in his tone. "Is the boss going to let them take over?"

"Whatever deal the boss made with them will be told to us in due time. And you're not involved in any of this," Mike reminded him, with a pointed finger.

"The last time you didn't listen to me, they took you. This crap that they were just testing to see how far the boss would trust them is just that. They haven't changed. Why are they bringing in all this heavy firepower?"

"You were right about the money, and you were right about the guy who knifed me. But it doesn't give you or any of us the right to question the boss's plans. So shut up and just do what you've been told...nothing," Mike spoke in a low, firm voice.

"You trust them too much," Danny continued. "They wouldn't be carrying those big guns unless there was something else going down. They're going to leave us holding the stink bag."

"Well, what do you think they're up to, Danny?" Mike demanded impatiently. "You think they're going to take over this town or our operations? Jesus H. Christ, Danny." Mike looked up at the sky. "Let's call it a night."

"When am I going to meet the boss?" Danny asked. "I feel like a slave working for a nameless face."

Mike ignored the question as he slid into his bright blue Chevy truck. He pulled out quickly and sped off while Danny cursed and sidestepped the small rocks the oversized tires kicked up.

Chapter Twenty

A lex!" The chief gestured for her to come into his office, giving her the sign to bring her partner.

Tiredly, she moved around the desk chair she was about to collapse in. She grabbed the cup of coffee Mark had in his hand as he came out of the coffee room.

"Thief," he growled grumpily. "There oughta be a wanted poster out on people like you." He returned to the coffee room.

The chief smiled when the door closed behind her. "Stealing coffee is high on the 'don't and dos' in partner etiquette. You may get a reprimand if he files a complaint. Especially if that's his favorite cup."

"He promised me he would have a nice cup of java waiting for me this morning," she grumped. "Morning, Chief. I like the placement of the new cameras. That potted plant, though, that's too obvious."

"That's the intention. Right now we have too much going on to be worried about another illegal game to bust."

Turning slightly, Alex spotted the slim form of a tall brunette dressed in a silk business suit leaning against the file cabinet, studying her intently. Adison returned the stare. *So, this is Agent Amanda Briscolle. Always nice to see the face behind the voice.*

Agent Briscolle wore her hair down, reaching her shoulders, with a slight curl at the ends. Her gray eyes looked directly into Adison's with no wariness or aloofness. It was the appraising look one law enforcement officer gave to another, with the exception of a wink given so fast the chief didn't see it.

To fill in time, Adison mentally gauged the brunette's exact height as shorter than the tall, dark, and thin Elizabeth Duke.

Adison, behave yourself.

A soft rap on the door was followed by Mark sliding into the room, balancing his newly procured coffee. He sat in the chair next to Alex, his eyes scanning everyone in the office.

"This is Agent Amanda Briscolle from D.C." The chief waved to the agent, then to the two detectives. "Agent Briscolle, Detectives Alex Adison and Mark Scripts." At that point, the chief rose from his chair and assumed his favorite position when delivering important information, sitting on the corner of his desk. He lowered his voice, "Agent Briscolle is with a special units division called SID. Sensitive Issues Department," the chief said at Mark's raised eyebrows. "They are investigating two groups we just happen to be interested in."

"Detectives," the agent greeted. Not wasting time, she began, "A gang called the White Knights, who *we* are primarily interested in, are based in Kingstown, Alabama. Membership is family only. One of their business partners on the West Coast is called the Jaded Amulet, who has a local chapter in your neighborhood. For about six years, these two gangs have had a fairly good working relationship.

"However, the White Knights are going through an internal power struggle with friction between various factions rising as the time nears for the present leadership to step down. The friction concerns the 'family curse.' Whoever has this curse is prone to obsessive and violent relationships. Depending on the person, it can be managed with medication and behavior modification strategies." The agent paused as she mentally arranged her thoughts.

"Why are the White Knights so important?" she asked rhetorically. "They are international profiteers, slave traders, illegal arms merchants, and have a finger in politics on three continents, yet there are few college graduates amongst them and they take pride in only speaking American English. They are on the brink of losing their influence with a lot of their international customers who are dangerous terrorists. Naturally, this is what we want to see happen, putting them out of business permanently.

"Their international partners have been looking elsewhere to conduct their business and have not hidden that fact. So the White Knights have procured something one of their influential partner's want. It's a prayer book believed to have belonged to a religious figure in the Muslim world. A female member of his household escaped with it after his death into Canada, and there, she and it disappeared.

"Where we are now is that within the month, a make-or-break meeting will take place somewhere around here. This meeting will bring three very important people together. Two are top members in a Libyan terrorist group, and the other is Bobby Miles." The agent paused and let her audience soak that much in.

"Why is Ms. Duke so important?" Mark asked.

"Bobby Miles. He's slated to be the next leader of the White Knights. About a year ago, Miles was given an assignment to kidnap Duke and add her to their slave trade goods. However, Bobby became obsessed with Duke, stalking her, vandalizing her apartment, and terrorizing her adopted son. This went on until someone in the family took it upon themselves to stop this infatuation by running her over with a truck. Ms. Duke survived, but her son didn't. While she was recovering from her injuries, Miles kidnapped her from the hospital. Our informant alerted us, and we were able to rescue her under the guise of an organization that shelters abused women. We offered her an opportunity to help us get the people responsible for her son's death and for her injuries. She agreed."

"Why not just arrange a hit on Miles?" Mark asked.

"Someone else will take over. They're on their last leg in the international business, but we want them closed down, now, and while we're at it, we can take down two others more deadly than the White Knights."

"If they know Miles has this obsession for Elizabeth Duke, why do you think any of them will let her presence deter Miles from the family business?"

"Family pride, arrogance, and bitterness. All the makings of a soap opera, but more deadly."

"What's the danger to Ms. Duke?" Chief Harper asked concerned.

"He won't be taking her back with him, and we believe he won't hand her over to the slavers."

"So he'll kill her. Is that what you're saying, Agent Briscolle?" Alex asked, feeling the heat hit her face.

"What has Ms. Duke being here, have to do with Miles meeting up with this group? Isn't he coming anyway?"

"The meeting could have taken place in a hotel room in some big city with a lot of civilians around and no Miles making an appearance. He would have sent a representative of his, fearing for his life. We sent Ms. Duke *here*, where there is plenty of open land, access to the ocean and only a small town police department to contend with. He won't be able to resist grabbing her and finding a place nearby to further torment her. That's his foreplay, and he loves it. That gives us time to surround him, capture him, and rescue her."

"Is Ms. Duke aware of all this?" Alex asked.

"She knows her part and what she needs to do, among them is to stay alive," the agent said crisply. "We're not worried about Ms. Duke as much as we're worried about your team's participation. We know our roles, and because of that, we know there will not be a screw-up on our part. It's whether or not your team can follow orders and let our team take over when the time comes."

"This guy must be a real obsessive nut to walk in what smells like a trap and nab the bait," Mark said.

"He is," Agent Briscolle said. "He's been following her progress at each women's shelter, and within weeks or days, he has found a way to get to her. Once we knew he was that obsessed, we knew we could bring down the group and some of their partners at the right time and place, with the right bait for all of them."

"So when does all this take place?" Harper asked.

"There's a Libyan oil tanker that will sail by here within the month that belongs to one of the White Knights' customers. The Coast Guard spotted an oil leak from their hull and has ordered them to repair it before they go anywhere. That has caught everyone off-guard and put the delivery back by two weeks or so, depending how fast they get out of the yard."

"We had a missing student just recently, do you think she's been kidnapped by these White Knights?" Alex asked.

"I heard. She probably stumbled onto something and was added to their booty. They deliver a dozen women each run, a large cache of weapons, and whatever else their customer buys. They like to start picking up the women close to delivery time to reduce the time they're drugged."

"So if this leak didn't set them back, they would be picking up their goods now," Alex surmised.

The agent nodded.

"That means they've had to hide a group of captive women longer than intended. They could have been in those yachts you two spotted in the bay," Harper told his detectives. Chief Harper looked at Alex, "What did you find out last night?"

"The monthly boys' meeting had some Southern relatives drop in at Amos's warehouse, looking every bit like the White Knights. They were dressed to take out a village. Left behind a very large truck that was used recently. I dusted the handles at the back of the vehicle, the driver's door handle, and the steering wheel with UV powder, just in case we have to trail them."

"Or maybe you've tipped our hand. If they realize that, they will take extra measures to prevent us from using the same method again," Briscolle said.

"Maybe." Alex put that thought aside and continued. "After the out-of-town boys left, the homeboys were whining. I'm not sure what came down, but from the conversation I heard, the armed team is running the show."

"That's understandable," Briscolle murmured. "However, I'm not sure why this local group wants to continue business with the White Knights. They are just one of many customers, and this customer is responsible for them having to move most of their operations south after the last FBI witness kidnap."

"Revenge?" Alex suggested. "After all, Danny set Mike up."

The agent smiled. "We haven't been able to confirm that Danny was behind it. The person who attempted to kill Mike Learner has disappeared."

"What about the White Knight hand we recovered in the field?" Chief Harper asked.

She shook her head. "I can only guess it's a retribution, but for what, we don't know. The White Knights have some very volatile members who can pull some stunts that you or I may think would be crazy for business, but with them, it happens and they move on. Remember, they've been exposed to this type of behavior all their lives. This gang was at the top of its business ten years ago and has been slowly sliding down. It needs to cement a relationship with someone high up in the Libyan cartel to keep its other foreign contacts steady," she assured them. "If you don't have any further questions…"

"Agent Briscolle, what's your cover?" Alex asked.

"Auditor from the Women's Shelter Association. Checking out their financial statements, record keeping, that sort of stuff." She flashed a brief smile. "I'm also going to check out one of the women. We think she's a plant from the White Knights. She's been harassing Ms. Duke when no one's watching. Getting into her stuff, bumping her, things like that."

"Sounds like she's trying to drive her out of the shelter. With all the other recent happenings around there, maybe we should do as they want and move your bait to where there's fewer civilians," Alex suggested. It was just a thought that she still had not really worked out. The part of where to put her kept her from going further.

Agent Briscolle was quiet for a moment, deciphering the underlying message her partner was conveying. "Do you have a place in mind that wouldn't be obvious to our group that we're making it easy?"

"There's a house for rent along the cliffs that's wired for sight and sound. If we can get her to rent it and set up Alex as her roommate, that should keep her somewhat protected until it's time for her to jump into the fire," Mark said quickly.

Hey! Alex glared at Mark, who was beaming at his idea.

The chief nodded. "The fewer civilians involved, the better."

"It's a plan I can agree to," the agent okayed.

"Where will you be staying, Agent Briscolle?"

"The Garden Cottage."

"Nice place for privacy," the chief nodded.

"Right." She turned to Alex and Mark. "Nice to meet you, Detectives."

The door closed behind her, and both detectives exchanged solemn glances.

"All right, we need to get Ms. Duke and you moved into Doc's place. Even if Doc is suspect, his place is ideal. Do you think you three can work out a plan within a few days?" the chief asked.

"Three?"

"You two and Ms. Duke. The agent just said she would clear the way for us to make contact. You know small towns. Everyone knows Alex has been thinking of moving out of her small room. The rumor is that Ms. Duke wants to settle here. The Doc just recently put one of his houses up for rent. Should be easy to make the Doc and others think it's all part of the greater scheme of things." He left off the part that everyone also knew that the matchmakers had Alex and Ms. Duke as their pick of the month. Inwardly, he cringed at the timing.

Mark looked at Alex. "Alex, you visit the House enough for it to not be unusual for you to make contact with her."

7. Christie

Mark, you've got me not only moving in with her, but also being her personal bodyguard. If that ain't a shotgun wedding, then it sure is close.

Alex started to walk to the shelter rather than drive, delaying the inevitable. She didn't even think about a plausible reason why she would strike up a conversation with Elizabeth Duke, much less offer to be her roommate.

Ah, she sighed with relief. Ms. Duke was sitting on the park bench staring out to sea. Unprepared for broaching a difficult subject in such a public setting, Alex decided to make store rounds. After close to two hours of schmoozing with the business owners and clerks, she felt good about doing great PR service for the SPD. Glittering merchandise hanging at the shops tempted Alex to stop, look, and sometimes touch, but she resisted the impulse to buy, grateful she had limited space in her rented room.

Her grumbling stomach reminded her she missed breakfast. As she stepped out of the ornament shop with half her attention on food, Alex turned in time to catch the stumbling figure of Elizabeth Duke. Her cane had gotten caught in an uneven part of the brick walkway.

Speak of the devil and who should appear...the devil's quarry.

"Hey, I got you." Her sturdy smaller frame gave the taller, thin one a firm place to catch her balance. Alex took note of how tall the woman was compared to her and how thin she felt as her hand rested on the small of her back. The grimace on the gaunt shadowed face told her she was going to need to sit down.

"Agnes? We need a chair here," she called into the shop she had just left. She pulled a radio from her belt. "Scripts, come in. Got wheels?"

"Ten four, little buddy," Mark replied.

"Little buddy?" she muttered to herself.

"Lunch time. You paying?" he asked.

She pulled her radio back out, shifting her weight into the tall woman to allow her more support when her hand left her. "Pick me up in front of Agnes' Gifts and Wrappings."

Agnes came bustling out with a chair.

Elizabeth Duke sunk into it gratefully.

"Mai's next door, getting something to eat. Do you want her to check you out?" Agnes asked the tall woman.

Elizabeth nodded gratefully. "Please."

The long fingers that gripped Alex's shoulder were surprisingly strong. She could feel tingles where Elizabeth Duke was touching her.

Get a grip, Detective!

As the woman settled in the chair, her hand moved off Alex's shoulder.

"You all right?" Alex asked softly. Bright blue eyes tilted to look into hers. Alex's breath stopped for a moment, and a nice hum ran through her body, causing her lids to flutter. Alex took a slow deep breath to refocus. Maybe she just needed a real vacation, somewhere far from Sunrise.

"Yes," the voice broke her reverie.

When Mai arrived, Alex stepped aside.

"Elizabeth, is it your knee?" Her small-boned hands gently and knowingly probed the leg underneath the panted leg.

The police car pulled up beside the walkway, and Mark was next to Alex quickly.

"Need a lift?" Alex offered. It was obvious the woman was not going to be able to walk.

Mai nodded. "Yes, thank you, Alex. Agnes, can you give the clinic a call and tell them Elizabeth will need to have a room ASAP and tell them she'll need x-rays?"

Agnes nodded. "Sure will, Mai."

"Thank you, Agnes," four voices chimed.

As the car rolled to the front of the clinic, Gary came out with one of the students. Between Gary and Lonnie, they had the tall woman in a wheelchair and rolling.

Once the two women were dropped off, Alex and Mark headed back to the sandwich shop for lunch.

It was easy to find a parking place on the busy street with a police car. They simply parked in the red. They purchased their lunch and found a table next to the sidewalk near their car.

Alex let out a moan as she chewed her turkey sandwich slowly, savoring the flavors. "This guy has this sandwich down perfect."

Mark hummed his agreement. For a few moments, both concentrated on their lunch.

"So," Mark mumbled around a full mouth of meat and cheese, "what do you think after seeing her close up?"

"Not my type." Alex ignored his snort of disbelief and continued, "Too skinny, for one. Listen, you heard the agent. This is business." If only she could stop replaying Ms. Duke's fingers gripping her shoulder and how nice it felt, she wouldn't feel like such a fraud.

"It won't be forever." His voice was calm and reasonable as if he were asking if she could baby sit Angel for a week. "As long as you don't cook, she can fatten up. Why are you fighting this? So far, everyone Claire and I predicted as couple material are happy together. No failures."

"Mark, if she survives this crazy scheme, do you really think she'll want to have any social relations with a cop? I think not." *Oh, shit. Did I just admit to being interested?* "Look. Did I say I wanted to be in a relationship?" she asked, exasperated. She tried to ignore her trembling hands. *What is happening to me?* Alex picked up her empty tray, needing to do something physical, and dumped it on the others.

"Detective Scripts or Adison, come in."

Alex clicked her radio on. Her heart skipped a beat at the official tone Harriet took. "This is Adison, go ahead."

"Call from the Mills's place. Sounds like a real bad one. This is the third call this month, Alex, and I want you to know, I could hear a shotgun going off...more than three times before the line went dead. Over."

"Ten-four, Harriet. We'll be careful. Alert the clinic we'll need an ambulance as soon as we secure the area if you haven't already."

"I told her to hide in the bathtub and that you'll be there right quick. Ten four, Alex."

Family dispute. Domestic calls were always rough.

"Ten four, we're rolling," Alex answered.

Mark slid into the driver's seat, and Alex clamped the light on top of the car roof.

Chapter Twenty-One

Adison felt emotionally drained after writing up her report on the Mills call and having downloaded the pictures she took at the scene. She would have just headed for her apartment and bed if she didn't have another priority to take care of.

She needed to introduce herself to Elizabeth Duke and arrange to be her roommate, all before she went to bed that night so the following day she could begin the next phase of protecting Elizabeth Duke. Her weary brain was not coming up with any plausible scenarios on how to broach the idea. She had not even figured out how to meet the woman.

This should be easy, she mocked herself. *According to the Sunrise telegraph, Ms. Duke looked at the Ebbens house earlier today. Now I just have to do my part. Piece of cake. Right. Just go up to a near perfect stranger and say...and say...Darn.* "I better think of something to say fast because there's the House van," she muttered to herself.

The van was moving toward her with Genie and Elizabeth Duke in it. Vehicle traffic was slow on tourist days. Quickly, Alex moved into a parking place that just opened up. Hopping out and locking her door, she moved through the evening crowd. She was next to Elizabeth Duke when her cane got entangled with the roots of the tree as she got out of the van.

It's the only available place to unload a passenger, Alex, so don't get your gander up and get irritable at Genie's choice of parking. "Hi, Genie, how's the cooking?" Alex greeted, her hand steadying Ms. Duke.

"Hasn't changed. You haven't been over this week," Genie accused.

"Eh, yes," Alex drawled awkwardly, blushing to her added embarrassment. "I've had a lot of work lately. Not much time left for our usual get-togethers." *Please, Genie, don't embarrass me with comments on my love life.*

"So where you headed, Ms. Duke?" She took her hand back from resting on Ms. Duke and looked at her.

"Don't you take her on one of your evening hikes, Alex," Genie interjected. "You attract too much trouble. Why don't you join us for some coffee at Mollie's? Not much trouble there."

Alex threw her dirty look, though relieved she mentioned only that. "Okay," Alex said slowly. Suddenly, it dawned on her just what she was implying. "And I don't attract trouble, Genie. It's my job to look for it." Was she attracting too much trouble? Maybe it's not a good idea to have Elizabeth and her in the same building.

"We'll meet you there," she said distractedly. Suddenly remembering Elizabeth Duke, Adison turned to her. "That is, if you don't mind some company." Again her faced reddened.

Elizabeth Duke gave her a funny look but returned, "Not at all."

"I'll see you two in a bit then." Genie maneuvered the van back into traffic.

Alex took a deep breath, realizing she was just where she was trying to be, alone with Elizabeth Duke, though she would like to know just what Ms. Duke was thinking. "We haven't really introduced ourselves. I'm Alex Adison."

"Hi. I'm Elizabeth."

Elizabeth. "So what did you want to look at?" Alex asked, feeling at a loss on how to move to the next important task.

"Nothing specific," Elizabeth returned.

Her tone didn't offer the opening Alex was looking for. They were still strangers having nothing in common to start a relationship beyond polite hellos.

"Oh. Well, with all the pre-holiday decorations, there's plenty to see," Alex offered, looking around for the mentioned decorations. Shopkeepers were just starting to bring in some of their outside samples and the street vendors had already packed up.

Elizabeth moved slowly as the more agile and faster pedestrians weaved around her and Alex. When Elizabeth stopped in front of the toy store and stared at the train set that ran through a detailed replica of Sunrise, Alex wondered if she was impressed with the work that went into its creation.

"Nice reproduction of Sunrise, huh? The only thing not real about that setup is the train," Alex said. It was her attempt at breaking the ice. She was feeling self-conscious with people's stares and probable misreading of their relationship. It did occur to her that SID and her SPD partners used the gossip to mislead those who intended on doing harm to Ms. Duke.

Startled out of her thoughts, Elizabeth turned her head to look at the detective. It took Alex a few moments to register that she was being stared at and had said nothing.

"Something wrong?" Alex asked, wondering what disturbing thoughts she interrupted her from.

"No." It was a brusque answer and Alex was going to apologize for intruding when Elizabeth added in a different tone, "The house, there on the cliff, I was given a tour of it today."

An opening? "I heard Doc and Lily put it up for rent. It has an alarm system that would make any techie envious." *Step right up to the batter's box, Alex. Don't be shy.*

240

"Yeah?" a doubtful voice asked.

Alex glanced up at her, catching a brief glimpse of blue eyes when the store lights shined around them. "Uh-huh. Old fashion, but highly efficient." *I thought she said she was taken on a tour. Surely, she checked out the security.*

"What's that?"

"Geese." Alex smiled at the surprised look from Elizabeth. "Huge, I might add." That got a smile from Elizabeth, much to Alex's delight. *When she smiles, she really looks different.*

"I didn't see any geese. I did see a lot of monitoring equipment. Hardly something a techie would be envious of."

"Yep. Geese. They've probably been moved to the south pen until the place is rented." *Yep. When she smiles, it changes her a lot.*

"Oh."

Okay, look sharp now. Time to move to the next step. She needs someone out there with her, and you've been assigned the job. Ask. She didn't say she was interested in the house, but that's where they want to move her...us. Unconsciously, Alex cleared her throat. "If you do decide to take it and need a roommate, I'd be interested." Alex felt she sounded casual and normal enough. Of course, in reality, she may have sounded like a jerk.

"That...sounds...fitting."

"So...?" *She's not taking this well. I thought Briscolle told her. She's not making this easy at all.*

"A roommate sounds...I...we've only just met..." She let out a sigh. "It's certainly big enough for two people to avoid clashing with different time schedules."

She sounds reluctant to have a roommate. Surely, she wasn't expecting to be out there alone! Or is it me? Darn. I'll bet it's the rumors. Alex turned to look at Elizabeth as she stopped to let some people by. Her stomach rumbled, startling her and putting a grin on Elizabeth's face.

"Hungry?" Elizabeth asked, her voice noticeably friendlier.

"Mollie's?" Alex offered. She could feel her lips curving into a smile, matching Elizabeth's. *Hey, she's warming up to me. We'll get along just fine.* She gave a little sigh, realizing that Elizabeth may just be seeing the reality of the job.

"Do you mind if I stop in here?" Elizabeth asked.

"No. Not at all."

They walked into Gilroy's Natural Herb and Food Store. Alex watched as Elizabeth was shown to a row of vitamins by Sandra.

Gods, I hate shopping. As Alex tried to stay out of the way of customers and too-helpful clerks, she found a section where she could just wander and be left alone. *Ooh. What's this?* Grinning, she snagged the article that caught

241

7. Christie

her attention, and after locating Elizabeth at the other end of the store, paid for her purchase and stood outside waiting for her.

Elizabeth glanced at her brown bag but said nothing as Alex led them to Mollie's. Genie was seated at an inside table waving at them. Tables were full of people having coffee and reading or just chatting with friends. Genie was talking softly on her cell phone. "Okay, bye, honey. Hi, you two. Sit down. Get comfy."

The two women sat side-by-side on the bench seat since Genie was sitting in the middle of other seat. Elizabeth hesitated at being waved to slide in first, but Alex insisted with a nod and gesture. The wall was against part of the kitchen storage, so she was protected from one side should anyone get desperate and attack Elizabeth in the open. Alex tried to give her enough elbow space, but she was sure she could feel Elizabeth's body heat along her right side. It was amazing how much heat a thin body could put out.

"Mollie's going to use us as guinea pigs. A new pie. If it's good, I've got something to surprise Claire with. She loves culinary surprises in the sweet category."

A waitress came by and took their drink orders.

"So, Elizabeth, did you give any more thought to renting Doc's place?" Genie asked. "If you decide to take it, maybe you might want to think about a roommate."

Alex felt Elizabeth start next to her. Alex stared hard at Genie, suspicious of why she had brought that up but not wanting to kill the goose that just laid a golden egg in front of her. "She decided to take it and lucky me, she does think it's big enough for a roommate, so I'll be renting it with her," Alex said.

"Oh, good. Good idea," Genie said. "See, Elizabeth. Put out the energy and presto. It happens."

Jeez. I feel like I've been tricked into asking a girl out on a first date.

The arrival of dessert interrupted any further discussion.

"Wow!" Alex leaned back in her seat as a generous helping of Mollie's newest art was placed before her. The pie was composed of different colored layers of chocolate with a soft light brown topping.

"Claire is going to be so happy. You tell Mollie I want four of these pies in tomorrow's delivery and one to take home to my honey tonight."

"I already got one in a take-out bag and only four pies you said, for tomorrow?" A robust woman came alongside of the waitress, wearing what used to be a white apron.

"Mollie! Mollie, Elizabeth, Elizabeth, Mollie. The only woman outside of Claire who is worth her sweet tooth," Genie told Elizabeth with a grin. "If I order more than four, they'll all be finished in one sitting. Women, stress, and chocolate." She spooned the first taste in her watering mouth. "Mmm," Genie moaned in delight.

242

"Good, good. That's the sound I like to hear. Well, I've got to get back to my kitchen. I have something cooking on the burners. Nice meeting you, Elizabeth. You need to be visiting more. Genie's not fattening you up right. I have a lot more variety in my lunches and dinners than Genie has receipts." She escaped with that last sentence said over her shoulder.

"Hey! That's hitting below the belt!" Genie objected. Her mouth had been full of pie to have caught her earlier.

The three women were silent as they ate, save for the moans of pleasure. Alex easily focused on dessert, letting the closeness of Elizabeth fade out.

Genie pushed her empty plate aside. "Well, the good thing about you moving out is that at least you won't have to worry about Karla."

"Karla? That new girl?" Alex demanded. Alex had taken an instant dislike to her and her dramatics at being a woman on the run from a jealous husband. Claire was flabbergasted that the woman was recommended for shelter assistance and had asked Mark and her to come out and give her a second opinion. They all suspected she had a rap sheet and were determined to find out who Karla Johnson was by her fingerprints.

"I certainly won't miss her," Elizabeth said wryly.

Alex, not daring to stare at her since she was so close, nodded with her eyes focused on her hands wrapped around her mug of tea.

"I need to get back with Claire's dessert. You two take your time. I'll call the House from the van and let her know you're with Alex." Genie smiled at the two women and slid off the bench, moving toward the cash register before the two had a chance to finish their good nights.

Alex watched Elizabeth play with her glass of water.

"Want to take a walk or would you like a lift back to the House?"

"Well, neither." Elizabeth smiled nervously. "I don't want to return to the four walls at the shelter right now, and my knee is sore from the walk."

"Then how about a ride over to Doc's house?" she offered hopefully.

"At night?"

"Best time to see if the security system works."

"You mean the geese?"

"Uh-huh. Let me get the bill, if you don't mind," Alex offered.

Fingertips grazed as Elizabeth passed the bill. While Alex thought about that pleasant sensation, Elizabeth went to wait at the door.

"Alex, Genie beat you to the bill again. What's the score?" Leah laughed at Alex's expression.

"I think she's got this game fixed," Alex said, then grinned. "But the punishment isn't so bad." Alex waved goodbye and joined Elizabeth. "Looks like Genie got to the bill before us."

They walked slowly along the now nearly deserted sidewalk. Alex motioned Elizabeth to her SUV.

"A Range Rover? The terrain is that rough, huh?"

Alex could hear the smile in her voice. The SUV alarm chirped. Alex smiled back at her, feeling that whatever mood Elizabeth had been in earlier had passed.

"It can get that way. When it rains or snows here, the roads get too messy for our patrol cars. I also take weekend trips to my cabin in the mountains where it really comes in handy." Alex flinched at the personal information she rattled off. She flicked on her SureFire and made a quick inspection around the vehicle, looking for marks that indicated someone crawled under her vehicle. With the way things were heating up, she could not be too careful.

The drive was quiet and uneventful as both women settled into a comfortable silence. The gate to the property swung open, and the SUV headlights picked up gray shapes huddled around what Alex knew was the pond. There was movement from the birds as the lights flashed across them. The SUV stopped in front of the brick walkway to the porch. The security light came on, lighting up the driveway and entranceway to the front door. Alex pushed her door open and hopped down, walking toward the porch. Not hearing Elizabeth behind her, she turned around. Elizabeth remained in the SUV staring at the birds that were rising to their feet and flapping their wings in agitation. Honks and other noises of unhappiness filled the night air.

"They're still locked out of this area. They don't usually get over that temporary utility fence. Watch your step, though. The experience of slipping on duck droppings is as bad as finding dog poop in the dark."

"Geese poop. That's a first," Elizabeth muttered under her breath as she cautiously slid out of the SUV.

Alex chuckled, remembering her own reaction when Mark told her that and he promptly slid in the muck. "The Macs rent their geese out to keep unwanted visitors off vacant property. I want to turn on the indoor alarm system." By Elizabeth's expression, Alex knew geese were not her first choice as a security system and probably not her second. Her eyes swept over the walkway, noting the bricks that had been lopsided or missing were reset since her last inspection of the place. *Doc spent quite a bit of money to fix the place up. Wonder what else he's done to make it enticing. This puts more pluses under his name as a possible Jaded Amulet boss.*

"You have a key?" Alex asked as she reached for the doorknob.

"Uh," Elizabeth hesitated a moment.

"Hang on to it." Alex jiggled the doorknob, then pushed opened the door. She returned her lock pick to a small pouch in her palm. "Too easy," she said. She stuck her head into the foyer to look around, then turned the lights on.

The two of them inspected the rooms, each with new eyes. Alex picked out what room she wanted and mentioned the center room separating their sleeping areas as ideal for a study. The fourth room on the other side of the kitchen with one wall against the front room, faced the front yard with bookshelves lining two walls. It obviously was meant to be the study, but it was too closed in for both women. Alex was thinking a guest could use it.

"In the morning, Detective Scripts and Officer Burns will stop over and set up additional security," she said as she glanced into a shared bathroom.

"Then I can tell Dr. Ebbens we'll rent this place?"

Alex nodded. "Give me a few days, and this place will be secured," she told her softly. "Will you trust me in that?"

"It's a bit too late to be asking that, don't you think?"

"You can always back out, Ms. Duke...Elizabeth. Don't feel you're trapped into being the bait without any say."

Elizabeth gave her a puzzled look. "I made my decision to be part of this operation with my eyes wide open." She added in a softer voice, "There is no victim here, Detective Adison. I know my part and the consequences."

Alex studied Elizabeth, not knowing what it was she really wanted to convey. She took a deep breath, then let it out to settle a disquieting feeling in the pit of her stomach. What was going to happen when they moved in together? Internally, she groaned. She knew what she wanted to happen.

Alex stopped at the cabinet with the monitors and opened it, turning the cameras on to see if the equipment was working. The night cameras picked up red spots from six different angles around the house.

"What are those?"

"Animals. They're small." She jiggled the cable behind one of the monitors to get an image. "We'll need to check this one out. The LED light on the monitor is on, but nothing is showing," she muttered. Closing the cabinet, she took another look around the front room.

"Want to look at anything else?" she asked.

"Nope."

Alex shut the foyer light off before she opened the front door, took a long look around before stepping out, then waved Elizabeth to the SUV when she felt everything was as safe as it could be.

The ride back to the shelter was just as quiet as the ride over.

"I'll see you tomorrow," Alex said as she parked at the House.

"Okay. My appointment at the clinic tomorrow is at ten. If you want to go shop for..." she stopped suddenly.

"What's wrong?" .

"I forgot that you probably have your own furniture. I need to go shopping for a bed, for one."

"How about lunch at one and we'll inventory what we need? Mollie's?"

"Okay."

Alex waited until Elizabeth disappeared into the shelter before driving off. "What are *we* getting into here?"

Chapter Twenty-Two

Adison stepped into the clinic, looking around for Elizabeth. She was conscious of six pair of eyes that studied her as she closed the door. Word was already around the coffee shops that they were roommates. She spotted Elizabeth at the admittance desk signing papers. Alex went to join her, nodding at the smiles and greetings she received.

"Hi," she said loud enough for the others to hear. But when Elizabeth's cerulean eyes turned to her, she forgot they had an audience. "I have a break," Alex smiled, reflecting the smile on Elizabeth's face.

"That works out well," Elizabeth returned. "I was just thinking of checking out furniture…namely a bed."

"I got that covered."

Margaret handed another set of keys to Elizabeth and a large manila envelope that had information on the house and its security system. Alex recognized it and her handwriting on the envelope. About six months before, Doc had a burglary and vandalism. After the place was cleaned up, he took the chief's advice and had the geese moved in. The house keys and security system directions were kept in the envelope.

Alex held the door open for Elizabeth to pass through, conscious of how close they were. Her heart was pounding, and unless she shook off this feeling, they were going to be in trouble. Alex gestured toward her vehicle, unable to trust her voice. Elizabeth climbed into the passenger seat, strapping herself in.

Take a deep breath and get your head out of the bag, Agent Adison. What is wrong with you?

Alex pulled herself up into her driver's seat, feeling more in control of herself.

"I…umm…gave a bottle of my hair conditioner and shampoo to Gary to check." Elizabeth exchanged glances with Alex. "He said you normally give them things to check for chemicals?"

"Yes," she drawled, her eyes slitting from her thoughts of suspicion. "Did Karla mess with your stuff?" Her voice came out harder than she intended.

"If anyone, it would be her, but I don't know yet. Maybe it's just paranoia. They didn't have their usual smell."

"In your case, Elizabeth, it's a healthy condition called caution. I take a dose of it every morning." Before shifting gears, she added, "There are only two people in Sunrise who know I work for SID, besides yourself. Chief Harper and Agent Briscolle. I would like to keep it that way for as long as possible."

Elizabeth nodded, "Okay."

On the drive to the shelter, they spoke on practical matters of setting up their new residence. At the House, Elizabeth signed out and arranged for Claire to pay Doc, as well as any other bills that may come up until her own money was transferred to her new checking account. Both women cleared Elizabeth's room quickly. There was not much to pack.

"This yours?" Alex asked, holding up a capsule she found in the carpet.

Elizabeth looked at what Alex was referring to, then her eyes moved to the gloves Alex had donned when she spotted the wayward pill.

"It's habit," Alex explained.

"Umm. It looks like one of the pills from the bottle I returned to the clinic. They gave me a new one."

"Why?"

"I don't know for sure. But since they've switched bottles, my knee has been feeling a lot better—as odd as it sounds."

"Hmm." Alex checked her pockets and found a small plastic bag she used for evidence collecting. She slipped the pill in, then resumed checking the room, more focused in her role as a law enforcement officer.

She heard Elizabeth zip up her laptop in a case that had wheels. Alex noted she was more concerned with those possessions than her other few belongings. Alex straightened and picked up the small clothes bag sitting on the stripped-down bed. Elizabeth had stuffed the bedding in the green netted bag. Each residents' room had a different color, making it easy for everyone to identify whose clothes were in the washing machine or dryer.

"Is that your personal laundry?" Genie asked as they stopped at the office before leaving.

"Yes."

"Until you get your washer and dryer hooked up, why not just toss it by the washer here?" She walked over to the utility room and came out with a green basket. "I'll bring them by tomorrow or when you're ready for visitors."

"Okay." Elizabeth laid her four articles of clothing in the basket.

"Take care of yourselves," Claire said, sounding more serious than was her nature.

Alex nodded to her.

Elizabeth hugged both women and whispered something to each, then climbed into the SUV. She looked straight ahead, appearing to be relaxed, however, her hands were white knuckled over the paper bag Genie had handed her with a thermos of food, bread, and a note to call if she should need anything.

"Claire offered to sell a washer, dryer, refrigerator, stove, and if we need it, some furniture real cheap," Adison smiled at her new roommate, who was also her assignment to protect, she firmly reminded herself. "I told her we could use everything but the furniture. Mai and Gary have some furniture I wanted to buy from them only I didn't want to lug it up to my cabin. Do you mind me moving it in?"

"No. Any furniture right now would be nice. Does there happen to be a bed in that collection?"

"Yes, a big one," her face broke into a wide grin. "I'm sure you're going to like it." She glanced Elizabeth's way, her excitement evident. "I'll let you see it before I say anything more about it. So we have utilities being delivered tomorrow and the furniture later today. The electricity is already on. The water is on. The gas is on. Oh, and Claire is throwing in a rug for the front room, and I have a few from my old place." Alex hesitated for a moment. "I noticed you don't have much in the way of winter clothes. It's going to start getting real cold, especially along the cliff. How about tomorrow when we shop for groceries, we stop by one of the shops and pick you up a warmer coat, heavier shoes, pants, and stuff?"

"All right."

Alex glanced at Elizabeth. It was difficult to keep her eyes off her silent passenger. "You know, you're leaving yourself vulnerable out there." *Duh, Alex.*

"Yes, that's part of the plan," Elizabeth drew out slowly. "Are you nervous? Afraid?" she added, watching the knuckles whiten on the steering wheel.

"For you," Alex responded.

"When he hears the rumors in the coffee shop, the ones about you being involved with me, you're very likely to get hurt. Surely, you've taken time to read his MO?" Elizabeth paused. "Why are *you* doing this?"

Alex pursed her lips before replying. "Ah, warning me before the action starts? Do the rumors bother you?"

"Won't sully my reputation. You're avoiding the question," she said.

"It's my job." *Gods, that sounds so patronizing.*

Elizabeth was silent, as if waiting for something else.

Alex breathed a sigh of relief, grateful that Elizabeth expected more. It gave her a second chance to say something more significant. And then her mind got stuck. Just what was she trying to say?

"It may come as a surprise to you, but when this is all over, I'd like to…" It was at that moment that she realized what she was saying and nearly bit off her tongue in the effort to stop before she humiliated herself. "…be able to have dinner with you without having to look over both our shoulders." Mentally, she replayed the comment to see if she had stepped over the line. She could feel her face heating up.

While she waited for the automatic gate to their new home to swing open, Adison surprised herself by putting her finger in the proverbial socket.

"So is the rumor true that you intend on staying after all this?" Alex held her breath, thinking that maybe she needed to rethink how to release her nervousness.

"Funny how a casual conversation spoken between two people in a coffee shop is suddenly the talk of town." Elizabeth opened her door and slid out.

You didn't answer the question. Or did you?

"Whose truck?" Elizabeth asked when she appeared next to her.

"It belongs to Detective Mark Scripts, my partner." Alex stopped Elizabeth with a hand on her arm. "Agent Briscolle just briefed the local PD on who is after you and why. SPD's been given the task of making sure you're not grabbed by anyone but Bobby, and only when the freighter is off the coast so your delivery is within hours and not days. Hey, Angel." She caught the dog's muzzle as it poked her hand, looking for a pat on the head or maybe the cookie Alex usually had for her.

Angel moved to Elizabeth and stuck her cold nose into the palm she had open. As Angel inspected her for a few moments, her long curved tail moved slowly. Elizabeth waited for the dog to finish her examination.

"Friend, Angel," Mark's voice commanded from the porch. The dog's tail moved back and forth faster.

"Elizabeth, this is Mark Scripts, my partner. Mark, Elizabeth Duke."

"Hello, Elizabeth. Nice to finally meet you."

Mark looked at his partner who had moved to study his work on the outside of the door. "It's a handy alarm," he said.

"But is it user friendly?"

"You mean do you have to key in a secret code or click your heels? Nah. It's not as nice as ours at the station, but it'll do. Place your palm here, and it recognizes you. It's an upgraded version of what was here. Let's set up your profiles now. Just to be on the safe side, I put in a new hard drive and Eric programmed it. He's the town's computer geek and works for SPD," he told Elizabeth.

He moved to the side and demonstrated with his handprint first. "Okay, let me file and save, and now it's your turn, Elizabeth."

Finishing with the copies of each handprint, he straightened up.

"The builder of this house installed plenty of security. Eric and I have already done a sweep through the house to remove any monitoring equipment that we could not use."

Both women nodded.

"SID was kind enough to supply us with what we requested for additional protection." Elizabeth nodded for him to go on. "We've added four movement sensors in the attic, two in the driveway, two more around the duck shelter, and around the house. I've also switched ducks, Alex. The Macs gave us young geese, so this is their first night out." He smiled. "I wanted to be sure no one's been over here befriending the feathered guards before you took up residence."

Mark took the two through the house, pointing out shortcomings and advantages. The last place he showed them was in the kitchen where three bags of groceries and supplies sat on the counter.

"Thought you could use some quick stuff," Mark said. He pointed to the kitchen closet before Alex could get out an embarrassed thanks. "It's a floor exit that leads to a cavern and from there out to the beach. The chief remembers a while back that Doc told him before the house was set here, the contractor discovered an old stairway leading to the beach concealed with a concrete cover. It was found when they were preparing the foundation. Doc decided it would be fun to put the entrance below the house where the cellar entrance is. The stairs were rebuilt, and they have their own private way to the beach. I was waiting for Alex to get here before exploring it." His eyes glinted with excitement. "I would invite you down, too Elizabeth, but I don't think your knee is up to it. Do you mind if we leave you up here with Angel?"

Elizabeth shook her head.

"How many people know about this?" Alex asked.

"Probably the majority of the town. The chief said Doc and Lily liked to use these stairs when they went for walks along the beach or for sailing. It's not something I recall, but I haven't hit the ten-year resident mark yet. They used to have a dinghy tied up on the beach."

Alex pushed a section of the floor, and the panel opened up. The smell from the passageway was damp, stale, and cold on her bare arms.

The entrance on the beach must have a fence or something blocking it.

"Shall we go and see what's there?" Mark handed Alex a flashlight. "Angel, stay here and *watch*."

"We won't be long. Just want to be sure no one can come up this way without us knowing," Alex explained as she removed her shoes and socks, "and see if there is any monitoring equipment down there."

Alex shined her light slightly ahead of Mark so he could see where he was going. "Brr," she muttered. Stepping off the ladder, her feet felt firm on the sand.

They both played their lights along the opposite walls, silently agreeing to cut the job in half by each taking a side.

"There aren't any wires on this side," Alex said when they joined up again just inside of the tunnel that looked out onto the ocean. The beach was short with rocks and boulders scattered about.

"There's an alarm system." Mark shinned his light along a crack on his side, "but the wire needs to be replaced. I'll get a roll of cable."

As he glanced around the tunnel entrance, his smile turned to a frown. "This place is not easily secured from the ocean." He kicked at the aluminum boat that looked like it had been chained to its mooring for a long time. "I wouldn't mind taking it out. How about you?"

"I get seasick in tiny buckets," she said. "So *is* some type of security workable?"

"What do you think?" Mark countered to see what his partner knew.

"We can start here with motion detectors. We'll have to program it to change its coverage with the tide level. We can use the water marks on the wall as guides. I'm sure Eric knows of a program that can do the math work for us. There's underwater security if we can get it. Why haven't the local kids invaded this place? If I were a kid and knew about a tunnel to an abandoned house, I would have been among the first to check it out."

Mark nodded. "I don't know. I would have been the first to explore it, then fixed it so no one else could get in just so I had my own private hideaway. It's possible to set up that type of system but costly." They looked at each other and grinned at what they could buy and charge to SID.

They clambered back into the kitchen where Angel and Elizabeth were waiting.

"Well, it goes out to the ocean," Alex said. "When the tide comes in, it comes up to about four feet. We found a dinghy attached to the wall near the exit." Alex's eyes noticed the bags were gone. "I didn't mean for you to get stuck with putting the groceries away."

"No problem. Gave me something to do."

"We need to get back to work," Mark said, giving a tug on Alex's elbow. "Linda, my wife, thought you might need some supplies right away and Alex without a list is not the greatest at shopping for food unless it's take-out. The casserole you can microwave right away, but since you have no refrigerator, better finish it up quick." He glanced at his partner. "But if you have any leftovers for this evening, Alex here will take care of that."

"Hey, it beats having to cook." Alex tapped him on the elbow with hers.

"Thank you. And thank Linda for me. That was thoughtful of her and you," Elizabeth nodded to Mark.

Alex smiled. "That was. Do you want to be dropped in town?" She asked Elizabeth. *And we still have Genie's thermos of yummy soup.*

"No, I'd rather get used to this place. Walk around and see what's what."

Alex looked around and decided maybe Elizabeth just liked being alone because she could not see anything interesting to investigate for a civilian.

"Stay and protect, Angel," Mark said.

Angel closed her mouth with an audible click and a short whine as if replying.

"I'll pick her up when I drop Alex off after our shift. Come on, partner."

Alex nodded and looked at Elizabeth. "Are you going to be all right being all alone here?"

"I won't be alone. I've got a flock of geese in the yard, a big Irish Wolfhound at my side, and a long stick," she held up the cane, "to beat anyone up if they happen to get by my bodyguards." Elizabeth lifted an eyebrow as if to ask what more could she ask for.

"Here are my SUV keys, just in case you need to get out of here."

Alex's stomach rumbled, interrupting anything else she might have to say.

"Let's stop at the coffee shop, Alex, and grab a sandwich." Mark pulled his partner's sleeve and started down the walkway to his vehicle. "Oh, and…" he turned to face Elizabeth as she stood in the doorway, "if you get any visitors from SPD other than your roommate here, myself, or the chief, call us and don't let them in. You have a cell phone?"

"Agent Briscolle gave me one with all its attachments to keep it charged and working."

"Good, good. You have someone to call on a regular basis?"

Elizabeth sighed. "Yes. Claire. She's not comfortable with me being so far out here, but she doesn't want to stop me from setting myself up. She obviously doesn't know about the geese, the dog, and my own common sense."

Detective Scripts stepped back to stand in front of her. "Ms. Duke…" he started in a low voice, "Elizabeth," he amended hesitantly, "I know this is what you signed up for, but it would make me feel a lot better if…"

"You were running the show?" she guessed.

He looked uncomfortable. "That's not the issue here." He paused. "I don't like the feel of this, and by Alex's twitchy behavior of late, I don't think she does, either."

"I see. Does SID know you feel this way?"

"I work for the Sunrise PD, and I take my job seriously. I just don't want to see you get hurt if it's preventable."

Elizabeth held up her hand to stop any more of what he had to say.

"Detective Scripts, you have set yourself up with quite a task because the damage has already been done. I want this to stop. If it means that I have to play with a psycho for a little longer, then I'll do it. You may not feel confident with SID, but I do. And I would appreciate it if you don't undermine my confidence in them. If you have an issue or an alternative plan, by all means talk with SID, but don't give me the message that the 'vibes' aren't right and leave it at that. Okay?" She took a deep breath to regain her composure. "Have a nice day." Elizabeth turned and walked back into the house, quietly closing the door behind her.

"That went well, partner," Alex said as they both got into the car.

"Do you think so? I think it was a bit patronizing myself. It's no wonder she blew me off," Mark said embarrassed.

"I've been finding myself saying some really stupid things along that same line, so don't feel bad. I think she's right. We need to step back and stop putting our misgivings about this on her." Alex rubbed her chin ruefully.

"Is it full moon or something?" Mark asked solemnly. "I've never been that sorry in front of a civilian since I asked Linda to marry me."

Alex looked at him alarmed. "Are you feeling something for her?" she asked.

"Just worried about her safety, Alex. I'm not horning in on…"

"Ouch. Let's not go there. Okay? Let's just agree that this job has us both acting shamelessly sentimental when we need brevity and more common sense."

"Sentimental?" Mark looked at his partner startled. "The last time someone accused me of that was when Linda was pregnant. Oh, boy." He pulled out his cell phone and made a call.

Chapter Twenty-Three

A t three in the afternoon, Mark and the movers had the furniture and appliances packed in a large truck and headed to the house on the cliff. Adison drove the police cruiser, and Mark sat in the passenger seat, his preferred place when he wanted to watch something closely. Alex glanced at him now and then. Behind his dark glasses, she was sure he was studying the terrain around them. Though he knew the area well due to their exercises for polishing her night commando skills, as Genie termed their games, she wouldn't be surprised if he was seeing new places where a sniper could pick off someone from the Ebbens' house.

The gate swung open as they approached, sweeping a few geese before it. Alex parked under the carport with the truck parking just inside the gate. Two pairs of eyes searched the area for anything out of place as the men hopped out of the truck and pulled out the planks to roll the heavy items down. Alex herded the geese that were not sitting around the pond back in the small fenced in area. Mark had moved to help the men carry the furniture. Alex unlocked the front door, leaving it open.

Where is Elizabeth? Not sensing anything amiss, Alex checked the front room first, glancing at the security monitors. Her eyes caught Angel's head, her golden eyes peering at her through the sliding glass door. Elizabeth was lying on the back patio on one of the chaise recliners, the only furniture in the house.

Smiling, Alex walked across the wooden floor, hearing her footsteps as they echoed in the empty room. Her eyes were drawn to a few bits of splintered wood on the floor. *What is that?* Unconsciously, her eyes were drawn back to the reclining figure. Alex slid the glass door open, careful to make enough noise to wake her. Elizabeth's breath changed, her chest rising slowly as a deep waking breath was taken. Angel sat up and pushed her nose under Elizabeth hand.

"Have a nice nap?" Alex asked softly. She knelt next to her so Elizabeth wouldn't feel obligated to rise quickly.

A smile curved on Elizabeth's face and her eyes fluttered open. "Uh-huh. Couldn't resist the sun and a chaise lounge." Elizabeth's voice was just as soft as Alex's as the two women studied each other at close range.

Elizabeth rolled to her side and looked for her cane. She held up its remains.

Oh, that's what the pieces of wood were about. Alex felt a pang of guilt at not being concerned with something that *was* out of place in their residence. She had something else on her mind. "Doggie chews are a must," Alex said solemnly, while silently promising herself to be more vigilant.

They heard a shout from the front door. It sounded like someone's finger was squished in the door.

"That's the guys moving in our furniture. I hope you like it."

Elizabeth moved to get up.

"Here let me help you." Alex gently guided Elizabeth up.

Their walk to the door was a studied moment of intimacy in Alex's mind. Elizabeth held onto Alex's shoulder for support, and Alex lent a supporting arm around her waist. It was only when they reached the front door where the three men were angling a large screen around the corner that Alex dropped her arm. It was no longer needed, and she reminded herself that she was on duty.

"That's the screen that goes around the bed frame," Alex explained.

"Ah, yes. The opium bed. It's not too close to the ground, is it?" Elizabeth looked at Alex.

Eyes met and both women were caught in timeless space, deciphering what the other was feeling and pleased it was similar. Another shout woke Alex. She shook her head to keep the haze that threatened to envelop her away.

"No." She moved her eyes back to the men who were now moving down the hall and into Elizabeth's bedroom. She took a slow deep breath. *This is going to be a hard one. Why do I have to be attracted to her? Gods! What did I just admit?*

"Angel! What did you do here?" Mark's voice rang out from the hall. Angel moved to stand behind the two women, with only her nose protruding between them.

Mark caught sight of the rest of the cane in Elizabeth's hand. "Jeez, Louise. I'm real sorry about that, Elizabeth. It was a nice one, too."

"It's replaceable. I'll pick one up on my next visit to the shops and some toys for slow times."

"She's working. She doesn't need toys when she's working." Mark looked at Angel sternly. The dog replied by making little noises in her throat and pressing her face against the back of Alex's leg.

"Doesn't she get coffee breaks? Lunch breaks? A break?" Alex pleaded the dog's case. "Elizabeth's right. All work and no play. If you can carry that puzzle in your pocket for when you're bored, your protégé should be able to carry her own toy for when she's bored. Don't you worry, Angel, honey. I'll bat for you."

255

Elizabeth looked down at the long thin hairy face that looked from Alex to her beseechingly. Elizabeth crossed an arm around her waist and the other covered her mouth in anguish.

"Hey, uh..." Alex was caught off-guard by the sudden display of distress from Elizabeth. She glanced at Mark. His lips tightened and gave a slight nod to her, then disappeared back outside. Before she could think of what to say, Elizabeth turned away and limped back into the dining room, stopping in front of the sliding door. Alex watched her for a few moments, feeling helpless. She felt too much of a stranger to barge into her space when it was obvious she wanted to be alone.

Trusting Angel's presence to be more comforting than hers, Alex went into her room to unpack and put her feelings into order. The earlier connection she had felt with Elizabeth had come to such an abrupt disconnect that it left her out of sorts. With studied care, Alex arranged her underwear drawer, then her T-shirts, and was about to refold her socks when the rumble of a truck reminded her she was not alone.

"Alex, we're leaving," Mark called.

Alex slid the drawer closed, surprised she was relieved at that. She joined Mark at the front door. The furniture truck was already gone. Angel was leaning against Mark, gazing with rapt attention out at the pond where the geese were.

"See you at work, Mark. Thanks," she added in a low voice.

Mark nodded. "I know of a nice cane in our attic she can use." He looked down at Angel and affectionately tapped her nose. "Darling, you embarrassed me. Take care of her, Alex. She looks like she needs a friend right now."

Alex nodded. *Why do I feel so lost here? As a rookie, I had plenty of experience in consoling a family member of a murder victim or survivors of a gang hit.*

When the gate closed behind Mark, Alex let the geese out. Walking back to the house, her eyes swept the area. A cry from a gull had her lifting her eyes, spotting a few birds gliding along the currents in a darkening sky. Nothing appeared out of place. She closed and locked the front door.

Stopping in her bedroom, she picked up the stuffed purple and green dragon she had purchased the previous day in the herb shop. Staring at it for a few moments, she pressed it to her chest and went looking for Elizabeth. Alex tapped on the doorframe of the master bedroom, announcing her presence. Elizabeth glanced at her. The only piece of furniture in the room was the elaborate bed. If she had any clothes or belongings, Alex guessed they were put away in the closet.

Alex gestured to the screen around the bed. "Beautiful, isn't it?"

"Yes." Elizabeth smiled, seeing the dragon Alex was holding. "Who's your friend?"

"Whoever you want it to be." Alex felt her face flush. "I got her as a housewarming gift for you."

"She's lovely. She's going to have to sit on the bed until I get a dresser."

"How about if we make your bed? I have some fitted sheets you can borrow until we get to the linen store, but I did stop and pick up two new pillows for you and I have extra blankets."

"Thanks. I appreciate it."

Alex came back into the room, her arms full of bedding. When the bed was made, Elizabeth sat down, looking around her. She nodded, pleased at the atmosphere it created.

"Opium bed, huh? I would've thought it was made this way to drape mosquito nets over the sleeping occupants. Did you make your bed yet?"

"Yep." Her eyes didn't leave Elizabeth, enjoying this livelier side of her. *Like she's being friendlier? Duh, Alex. Of course she's friendlier. You're roommates now.*

"Well then, how about dinner? Are you hungry?"

"Yes." She turned to follow Elizabeth. "Listen, I've arranged for the phone company to stop by tomorrow to check the outside box and look at the wire from the house to the post. I'll be here when he arrives. Don't open the gate or door until I'm here. Okay?" Elizabeth turned to look at her. Before she could speak, Alex hurried to explain. "It's for Angel's sake. Can you image having a big dog like that staring at you like you were its next meal? I'll pen the geese, too, so they don't attack him."

In the kitchen, Alex opened a box that had her coffeemaker and assortment of coffees. Elizabeth opened the other box and pulled out one of the hundreds of mugs she was gifted.

"Now that's a puzzler. What is with people who feel they have to give a mug for every conceivable occasion?" Alex asked.

Elizabeth glanced at her but said nothing.

"What's terrible is that I can't dump them in the secondhand store because then everyone will know and I'll make everyone's black list. I hate it," she finished.

Elizabeth continued to study each one she put away in the cabinet. "They are cute and one of a kind," she said.

"One of a kind. Just one, would have been fine."

"You don't like to keep much, huh?" Elizabeth asked casually.

"I don't like to accumulate things. Then I have to clean and or repair them." *And pack them when it's time to move on to the next job or more than likely, let SID clean up.* Opening up another box, she began to move her utensils that were still in their plastic separator into a drawer.

"Wouldn't those work better in that drawer?"

"Uh, sure."

9. Christie

Adison was lying awake. For the thousandth time, she played with the idea of taking Chief Harper up on his offer of a permanent job. No one had to know of the change in employers.

I'm not doing this because of Elizabeth, she told herself. *I'm just at that stage in life where I'm getting tired of living as someone else.*

Is Elizabeth really going to settle down here after all this? Maybe I'm reading her wrong. She sighed. *Jeez. This is scaring me. Is it just lust? So what if it is? She feels it, too. I know she does.* She turned to her other side. *Well, after all this is finished, we'll just have to see where it goes.*

She glanced at the clock. It was past midnight and she was wide awake. She sat up and listened. It sounded like her roommate was restless, too. An image of what Elizabeth's night apparel would be flashed across her mind.

All right, Agent Adison. Can it.

Disgusted, she flung herself back under the covers, counting to keep her thoughts elsewhere. After tossing and turning for another thirty minutes, Alex got up. She pulled her robe on and wrapped the belt loosely around her waist. She looked up the hall and saw the door to Elizabeth's room wide open and a soft glow coming from the front room. Softly padding into the kitchen, she looked in and saw Elizabeth's head bent over her laptop, busily typing away.

Long bare legs were stretched under the coffee table.

Wanting to see more of her, Alex pulled two mugs out of the cupboard, poured water in both, and heated them in the microwave. Finding her tray, she balanced the heated mugs of water with a box of crackers and a selection of teas and went out to the front room. Elizabeth's eyes drifted to hers.

"Thought I heard you playing with the microwave," she said by way of greeting. She stopped her typing and shifted position on the pillow.

"I would hate it to be some ghost haunting this place. Something hot but without caffeine?"

Alex found there was no vacant space on the coffee table. Papers were neatly placed over every available space.

"Am I disturbing you?" Alex asked, watching a slim hand reach over a T-shirt-covered shoulder and twitch dark hair back. It was a struggle to keep her eyes from seeing if nipples showed through the cotton cloth. *That is so not nice,* she warned herself.

"I could use a small break about now. It's rather uncomfortable sitting on the floor."

Alex's heart thudded against her chest as she realized the print on the T-shirt covered any evidence of her seeing more than round mounds under them. After Elizabeth selected her tea and a mug, Alex laid the tray on the breakfast counter, then settled on the opposite couch, balancing her tea on her knee as it steeped. Her eyes watched as Elizabeth pushed the table away and rose to sit on the couch behind her.

258

"So this is when you write?" Alex asked, settling into the corner of the couch and curling her feet under her legs. She forced herself to stay focused on Elizabeth's face.

"It seems to be the best time. It's quiet and usually people don't call trying to sell something."

"Makes sense."

"What do you know about me?" Elizabeth asked abruptly.

Alex's gaze moved to the long fingers that closed around the mug, then lifted it to waiting lips. She swallowed as Elizabeth's top lip curled over the rim. Taking a deep breath, her eyes traveled back up to the almost violet eyes that were studying her intently. Alex cleared her throat as she focused on the question. "Well, I know you were a single mom. You and your child were involved in a hit and run, and you were the only survivor. You have a contract out on you by the White Knights for their slave market. You're a writer, and…I guess that's all." *No personal information like what you like to eat, watch on television, or where you like to vacation. I don't even know what your hobbies are or if you have any.*

Alex fiddled with her drink. "If I'm not being too nosy, how did you get mixed up in this? You don't seem the type to play with fire for revenge."

Alex felt captured by Elizabeth's eyes as they studied her for a long moment in silence. She was grateful when Elizabeth finally broke the gaze and took a few sips of her tea.

"It's a long and complicated story, but in a nutshell," she began softly, "I had moved to Alabama by court order so that my adopted son could be close to his biological grandmother." She sighed, looking down at her hands. "Noel," she paused, "Rusty, our dog, and I had been out most of the day at the retirement home visiting with Grandma Chasley. She's a disagreeable old woman and not at all the type of person I would have chosen for Noel to associate with." She paused for a few moments. "However, they were court-ordered visits. A taxi picked us up. Though she wasn't partial to Rusty, the other folks at the home loved him." A tear slipped down her face unnoticed by her. She took a steadying breath before continuing. "We had a burglary with vandalism our first week there, and I called the police. Just as the officers were leaving our apartment, Bobby shows up, laughing it up with the other officers and none of them taking the incident seriously."

Alex could hear the anger in her voice.

"The moment he walked in the door, I knew there was going to be trouble," she answered Alex's silent question. "He didn't waste time hitting on me, making comments about me, and other inappropriate remarks that a stranger does not make." Though Elizabeth's voice was low, it was shaking with fury. "After that day, no matter where I turned, he was there. I finally made a complaint to his station chief, then things got really bad. I had to check my car before getting in it to make sure I had air in the tires or parts from the engine were not missing. Once, the steering wheel was actually removed. My brake line had been cut twice." She shook her head. "It escalated toward the end, where he started to break things inside the apartment. In my bedroom, he would paint vulgar remarks about my sexual orientation on the walls in bright orange paint and leave dead animals on my bed. The carcasses ranged from rats and cats to a neighbor's small dog. Two days before…before we left, he took a knife to my mattress and sliced it so it was unusable. The only room he left alone was Noel's. On top of all that, we were getting pressure from the landlord to move out. You'd think I had sense enough to leave when the first sign of trouble started."

Elizabeth paused a moment as tears flowed down her cheeks.

"Hold on a moment." Alex rose and returned with a roll of toilet paper.

Elizabeth accepted it silently, taking time to get back in control.

"What did he write on your walls?"

"The usual banal comments. Queer, lesbian, cunt eater, and so on. Toward the end…" she took a deep breath, "…it got worse. I tried to keep Noel from my room, but kids are curious. For each incident, I had the police there because I wanted it documented. But they didn't take notes or pictures, so I did. When I asked them for a case number, they told me they hadn't gotten around to it yet. The time I mailed my notes and pictures to my lawyer, they were returned to me the next day…cut up with a dead rat in the box. I tried to leave town, but Grandmother Chasley wouldn't have any of it. Called me spineless, said she would handle it.

"After three weeks, I decided I had enough of it. I made the mistake of packing our things to move out like normal people do. No one would rent me a van, trailer, or even a handcart. That's the first time the brakes to the car were tampered with." Elizabeth laughed bitterly. "But, I'll tell ya, when the weekend came, there was a taxi cab waiting for us to take us to the rest home. The only time I could get a taxi.

"There was a bus station about an hour's walk from our apartment we went to. Not only did the attendant refuse me any tickets, but he flat out told me dogs were not allowed on the bus. Noel didn't want to leave Rusty behind and neither did I. I didn't trust what Bobby would do to him. I made arrangements with someone in the rest home to meet us at the edge of town, then drop us off at the train station in the neighboring town. My only contact with the outside world," she said dryly. She wiped a tear from her cheek. "But…Rusty…he…

Suddenly, a deep painful sob came out followed by others. Elizabeth curled in pain.

"Rusty, Rusty, I'm so sorry," she finally got out so softly Alex could barely make out the words. "I should've left sooner. Oh, gods, I should've left sooner. Then Noel. I should have just left. We could have just walked until we got out of that town."

Alex moved to sit next to Elizabeth, rubbing her back in slow circles, letting the woman cry out her pain.

"He poisoned Rusty." Her words were mixed with sobs, making them difficult to understand. "Noel was so terrified. Oh, Noel. He blamed himself for it. I...I shouldn't have let him see his grandmother alone that last day. When he gets angry, he just blurts things out, and she loved to get him angry for that reason."

Elizabeth continued to sob out her personal retributions.

"I think he told her that he hated her for making us stay in that town," she finally got out. "He told me he believed she was mean enough to have someone do all those things to me. When he gets an idea, he holds onto it, and the only thing to do is to let him run it out of his system. Oh, gods." Elizabeth looked up at Alex. "She wouldn't order her only grandson's death, would she?"

A dark anger burned in the pit of Alex's stomach, the very anger that brought her to work for SID. "I don't know, Elizabeth. I've never met her."

Chapter Twenty-Four

Far away somewhere, Adison could hear her alarm go off. She wanted to roll over and go back to sleep, but there was a heavy weight lying across her. She opened one eye and looked down at shadowed face of her roommate. A tingling started through her body as she rolled the word roommate in her mind and felt the warmth and weight of her. The long body shifted, and a mumble Alex could not make out came from her body warmer, pleasantly vibrating against her collarbone. A leg that was comfortably resting between hers moved to a less intimate position.

"Good morning," Alex said softly, struggling to keep her voice even but not able to stop her hand from stroking Elizabeth's warm back.

"Aren't you going to shut that alarm off?" Elizabeth mumbled. Her warm breath ticked Alex's neck.

Alex could feel her chuckle vibrate in her chest. "I would, but I'm pinned down here."

Elizabeth groaned and lifted herself. "This couch is not made to sleep on."

Alex's body objected to the parting of her sleeping partner.

"A long time ago, I used to have a waterbed. More comfortable." Elizabeth gave Alex an apologetic grin. "Not to say your body was too lumpy or uncomfortable. You were very comforting. Thank you, Alex."

Alex nearly gulped as she watched Elizabeth's eyes look over her reclining form before handing her her robe. "No problem." Alex heard her voice respond.

The alarm kept up its racket.

"The alarm," Alex mumbled. She wrapped her fingers around the extended arm and was pulled to her feet. It occurred to her she needed a cold shower and not just to wake up. But Alex kept to warm water, chickening out on the cold. When she realized the water heater had a lot more hot water capacity than her small apartment had, she stood for a long time under the water. Finished with her dressing, she leaned out of the bathroom, listening for any movements. There were no sounds from inside the house, not even of the house settling. She slipped her bathrobe on and went looking for Elizabeth. Peering through the carved bed panel, she spotted the sleeping form curled up under blankets.

A beep from the alarm alerted her that something larger than a rabbit was within ten yards of the property. She laid her cup of coffee down on the kitchen counter and went to open the door to Angel, who came pushing her wiggling thin frame with her rope toy clutched between her jaws. Alex laughed and looked up at Mark who had a long cane draped over his arm and a small bag in the other hand.

"Good morning, Alex.

"Good morning, Mark. Good thing it's you or I would've bashed the unannounced visitor over the head with my coffee cup. Is that the cane that has a knife or something sharp attached?"

"Sure does. I had to hide it because of the kids."

Alex leaned out of the door and looked at the clouds of fog that were rolling in. "We're going to need radar to find our way back to town."

"No running today. I don't want to challenge the fates on getting hit by a car or running off a cliff. We'll work out in the gym."

"Sounds okay to me. Come on in while I get my bag together. Elizabeth just went to bed. She works at night."

"Writing?"

"Yes. Did you know we have four of her books at Mollie's? I read them. Not bad. She has seven pen names and now and then writes romance novels. Her specialty is adventure like spies and such." She peeked inside the bag he handed her. "Ooh. Doggie toys."

Mark looked embarrassed. "Yes. Well, it's a good thing I brought them if she's going to be sleeping in. By the way, I didn't hear the geese."

"The monitor shows them around their pond. I guess they don't want to wander off the cliff when the fog's so thick. Smart birds. Where's Angel? Usually, she doesn't leave my side until I give her a cookie."

"She's working," Mark said.

"I feel hurt."

"I won't be surprised if our fellow officers are a bit snippy. They had to get off their duffs and take four complaint calls yesterday while we were unloading stuff here."

"Yeah?" Alex looped her gun belt around her waist and tossed her fanny pack into her workout bag. "How many complaint calls did they generate about their attitude? The chief always gives time off for moving. They know that. How many times has Danny moved in one year, milking that?"

"Uh-huh," he agreed. They stopped at the coffeepot where Mark held two travel mugs. Alex filled both cups and turned the pot off, following Mark out to the police vehicle.

"So what's on our schedule for today?" Alex shivered and pulled her collar up to keep the dampness out.

"After we work out and the chief has his meeting, chances are we're going to be foot patrolling until the fog lifts. Maybe spend some time in the coffee shops, picking up on the latest gossip."

"Ah, my kind of duty." Alex settled behind the wheel while Mark balanced the two coffee cups and kept an eye out for anything coming their way.

"As much as I trust Claire and Genie's talents to protect their residents, if the White Knights chose to invade the shelter, it would traumatize the other women. Moving Elizabeth out was smart," Mark said.

"It's going to be a pain dealing with the gossip." Alex didn't dare take her eyes of the road, but she wanted to give him a glare, even if it was going to be halfhearted. *Gods, Alex, you are so in trouble here. You love rooming with her, and if he hadn't thought of this, you would've been thinking of all sorts of ways to bump into her.*

"So what do we have to worry about at the house since Doc and Lily are suspects in this operation?" Alex didn't have to look at Mark to know he was frowning in thought. "If we had blueprints, we could see what other surprises the original owner had going," Alex suggested.

"Yes. The contractor moved to Oregon. Too many odd things about that house. Like, why is there is only one entrance to the master bedroom, especially with the way the other bedrooms are set up? Have you thought of which room the original owner's brother stayed in? He was paranoid enough to set up the protection to this house, so where did he sleep?"

Alex shook her head, curious also.

Mark's cell buzzed. He pulled it out of its holster and flipped it open. He listened, saying little. When the conversation was finished, he closed it and slid it back into its holster. "That was the chief. Briscolle called him this morning to let him know that the Libyan freighter is still stalled with the harbor master."

"Any new orders?"

"Nope."

Alex squinted out the window at the swirling clouds of fog. Using the windshield wipers to clear the moisture off the windshield was pointless. She cleared her throat. "We talked last night."

Both were quiet for a while.

"From what I gather, the whole town wouldn't help her when Bobby Miles was harassing her, even the local police, whom he worked for. She had mailed evidence of the harassment to her lawyer, but it was returned to her the next day cut up along with a dead rodent."

"Didn't she have any friends outside of that town who could've come to pick them up?"

"She was effectively isolated. She had no cell phone. Her calls and mail were blocked and her car immobilized. Their dog was poisoned, and when she and Noel tried to escape on foot, they were run down." The same dark cloud from the previous night engulfed her as she imagined the guilt Elizabeth must be feeling.

"Piddle heads," he muttered.

Alex turned her head toward Mark startled. "What did you say?"

He continued to stare out the window. "Piddle heads. It's a 'safe' curse to say in front of the kids. You know, piddling?"

"Piddling?" she repeated blankly. "As is in, oh. Hey, that's clever. Piddle heads. I can't wait to use it."

"Slow down even more, there's a side road…right…make a right here," Mark directed.

"Just where are we going?" The tires slid slowly on the wet sandy road before gripping and making a good turn.

"Near the shelter. The fog doesn't hang so thick on this road. See, it's clearing."

An hour into their workout, Adison and Mark were joined by Harriet who liked to pedal on the bike an hour before starting work. She played bluegrass music. The three of them hummed, and Alex tapped her feet between reps. She gave a shoe shuffle jig she learned at the dance hall on Country and Western nights as a finale before heading to the shower. Under the hot water, she reminded herself to get a copy of Harriet's CD for those days she needed a lift.

Showered and changed, the trio met in the coffee room and chatted about the weather, waiting for their meeting to begin. The chief was in his office on the phone. It was hours later when his door opened. Harriet, Eric, Mark, and Alex took their seats around the table in the meeting room. Because the meeting was so late, Mike and Danny were there also and snagged the seats closest to the door.

"Good morning, troops. The duty roster for today." His voice was clipped. "One of the women at the shelter is missing. Alex and Mark, that's your beat. Mike and Danny, you two are assigned to the outer rim until next week. You both have been charged with harassment, and until next week when the provo from Bales gets here to take your statements, you are not to engage in any contact with a tourist. Am I clear?"

"How are we going to know who is stealing from the shops if we don't check out suspicious customers?" Danny demanded angrily.

"Ah. So you know what this is about." The chief's eyes became intense as he shifted his weight to focus on the two problem officers. "Frisking customers without cause. That is harassment in legal terms, and you both know it. What David's customers purchase in his shop is not your business unless he says someone stole something or you have proof he is selling something illegal. This is the fifth time you've been reminded to stay away from his customers. We are here to serve and protect, not to humiliate or harass anyone. Nor are you to allow it to happen in your presence." The chief paused as if to collect himself. "This is official, so I'm saying it for everyone at this table, so hear me good," he continued in a calmer voice. "This suit against Sunrise covers verbal and physical harassment. The town is being sued for a lot of money, and I don't think the committee will be swayed to keep either of you. Use this time to update your résumés and to huddle with your lawyer."

"What about my rights, free speech?"

"Your rights? At this moment, you have the right to take a personal day off, which will be without pay, or park where your only communion is with nature until next week when the board reviews the case to see if you will still have a job with SPD. In case you've forgotten, you have used up all your paid sick time, personal time, vacation time, and floaters. If you'd like to quit, that's also an option. The victims are taking this to court, and they have plenty of witnesses. And may I remind you, you are not to interfere with any of the witnesses or potential witnesses. If any of them pulls out of this case with a change of tune, it will be investigated as if evidence was tampered with and you will be arrested immediately. Do I make myself clear?"

Danny wrapped his arms around his chest, appearing to puff out in defense, while Mike sat back in his chair, his hands folded on the top of the table looking unconcerned.

"Dis...missed!"

The chief looked at Alex as they passed. "I want to see you two in my office before you take off to the House."

When the others had trickled out, the chief gestured to the chairs, then pulled one out for himself. "Sit down, sit down." His voice was still brusque from the meeting.

The slim form of Agent Briscolle entered the office.

"I had Agent Briscolle wait in the computer room until those two left." The chief rubbed his chin as his irritation subsided.

"Last night, we believed everything was put on hold due to the Libyan freighter tied up at the harbor, but our contact says Bobby Miles has boarded a private plane with his guard. If he leaves his state, a bounty hunter will have a fair shot at collecting a fee for bringing him back. If he shows up here, any law enforcement officer can arrest him on charges related to his stalking Elizabeth Duke across state lines. He'll be breaking the court limits set for his release until his case of kidnapping is brought to trial."

"So you're saying anyone can make an arrest on Miles? Won't that be defeating the purpose if some bounty hunter gets it in his head to collect?"

"No one knows where he's headed, and no one knows where Elizabeth Duke is."

"Besides the Jaded Amulet and White Knights. Seems that right there leaves too many people in the know."

"There are no perfect plans and no guarantees that our side will win. We do our best with the highest goal possible—no one but the bad guys get hurt—and strive to make it happen," Briscolle said. She turned to look at Alex.

"So are you comfortable with the security at the house Elizabeth Duke is staying at?"

"Officer Burns and I removed all the old monitoring equipment we found and put in our own," Mark assured her. He held up a small device. "And as you know, I'll get a signal if anything disrupts them that is bigger than a rabbit." He glanced at Alex who regarded him with surprise.

"I have no intention of letting Miles have her longer than what is needed to catch him and the others," Briscolle explained to Alex, who looked irritated that she had been left out of something that involved the safety of her assignment. "Perhaps you can give Ms. Duke an update as soon as possible. I like her to be kept abreast of what's happening."

"Okay. She's sleeping right now. Angel and the geese are guarding the place for now. The phone company is sending a man out to check the switch box about noon, so I'll be out there before then. We also have some more furniture and appliances that will be delivered and hopefully, installed today. That will give me a legitimate reason for being out there most of the day."

"Okay. Miles will have the house checked out. He won't grab her just yet. Remember, harassment is foreplay to him," Briscolle cautioned.

"How does he know that we aren't setting him up?"

"Not *we*—*you*—her roommate. I've heard the gossip in the coffee shop that says the two of you are romantically involved and you moved out there to protect her from her ex-boyfriend." The agent shrugged at Alex's uplifted brows. "I just changed what was originally going around a bit. Not by much, but enough to give any of Miles's group an idea that you'll be acting as a bodyguard for romantic reasons."

"What's keeping the other factions from not going after Elizabeth Duke now, with this fog giving them cover?" Alex asked.

"They haven't done a reconnaissance of the place yet. From what I've seen of the area on my walk last night with Detective Scripts, the terrain is pretty rough going with a lot of chances of twisting an ankle or running into a trap. She has a dog, geese, and a cell phone. She need only press one button for it to call me. The only way to take her in that situation would be to use heavy artillery, and they don't want that type of attention. They do things under the public radar. If they didn't, they wouldn't be able to use their plant in the FBI.

"They'll send in someone to look over the place and if possible, do whatever they can to make sure she's out of the picture in a quiet way." The agent smiled faintly. "So far, they haven't hired an outside hit on her, so we know it's going to be one of their own."

"Oh, great," Alex muttered. "It doesn't take much to block a cell's transmission."

"Not with Angel there," Mark disagreed. "She won't let anyone near enough to Elizabeth without letting out a howl. And when she does howl, believe me, the town will know it. Besides, it'll set off all the other dogs around town."

Agent Briscolle nodded. "Good training. The cell phone gives off regular signals. If the signal is disrupted, that alone will set off an alarm. Claire and Genie also are monitoring the signal."

"Are they part of SID?" Mark asked curious.

"No, they're part of the organization assisting us to set up this scenario. They have a leak in their system, and by helping us, they're finding the source of the hole."

The chief stood. "Let's get moving then. The mist should be lifting soon and Mike and Danny will be heading to their assignment."

"Where are they now?" Agent Briscolle asked.

"The Cigar Room," three voices chimed.

The meeting broke up.

Alex looked at Mark curiously as she tried to keep up with his long strides while they walked to the House. At the pace he set, it would take them about twenty minutes to get there. "You never mentioned you were going to be salting the land around the house. Anything else you've been doing that would interest me?"

Mark shrugged. "I was thinking about it, and Agent Briscolle just happened to be able to get access to some nice wireless alarms. It slipped my mind in telling you, just like your password change, huh?"

Alex nodded. "Wireless are easy to detect, Mark. But geese and a dog, uh-huh. I sure would like to ask Doc why he has all the cameras around in the house, just to see how he handles the question."

"I'm not sure it was his idea. They were all new. Interesting that the cable to the cameras in the cavern aren't working."

"Like how new?"

"I found wire casings tossed into the grass outside. There wasn't any traces of duck poop on them, and you know they poop everywhere they go, so it had to be recent."

They quietly nodded at storekeepers and weaved around the stands that the stores were setting out.

"So we're back to Doc," Alex said softly. "I was leaning heavily toward my list of Ms."

"Don't give up on them yet. They and the Ebbens have too many things going for them. There's no family connection, so maybe it's something else or maybe just separate interests."

"Oh, that reminds me." Alex pulled out her cell phone and pressed a few buttons. "Hi, Margaret, is Gary in? Yes, I would like to talk to him...Hi,

Gary. What did you find in the pills Elizabeth brought you?...Okay. What about the pill I gave you?...Thank you. And, Gary, don't mention this to anyone else...Oh, I have one more question. Who is your silent partner? Honest, it's not for public consumption...Emily Chasley? Who...you mean our Mrs. Dodd?" There was a long pause as Alex listened, her eyebrows rising to her hairline. "No, I didn't know. Thanks, Gary." Mark and Alex exchanged looks. "Gary, I want you to...Yes, yes. I'm sorry, Gary. Just you two be very careful. Okay?"

Alex hit the off button.

"Mrs. Dodd is the silent partner, but it's under her maiden name. Did you know that Lily Ebbens is a third cousin of hers? They had a falling out when they were teens and haven't spoken to each other since. Mrs. Dodd told Mai the story when she was explaining to her why she refused to be treated by Doc Ebbens. So..." She smiled to herself more than to her partner, "there is the connection between Doc and Mrs. Dodd and the White Knights, but not why she fears him. Cousins. It sure must have been a doozie of a spat between them if it still stands between Lily and her."

"Those two we think are from the White Knights have a resemblance to Mrs. Dodd. So Lily Ebbens is related to the White Knights but just how close? You said Mrs. Dodd and Lily are from Florida. The White Knights are based in Kingstown, Alabama. Maybe they belong to the list of family members that have been booted out."

"Noel's grandmother is a Chasley. It sure is a small world."

"Yes," Mark scowled. "Now that we know more about the family history, I'm really curious why we can't find Doc's pictures when he was young. You know so far, his fingerprints match up to who he says he is, but what if we get DNA?"

"How and match it up to who? Those pills Gary tested that Elizabeth had brought in at their request, Gary said he found nothing wrong with them; however, I gave him a pill I retrieved from Elizabeth's floor in the bathroom at the shelter. He tested that and got back some interesting results. Gary said the pill had carbonate of lime in it. That would take someone with the knowledge of chemicals to pull that switch. He said it causes the joints to swell, especially with exertion and cold moist air. The bottles of shampoo and conditioner that she brought in the next day were easy. They had the garden variety of poison in them. Literally. Bug poison for plants. That would be Karla. She probably got it from the House garage where Claire keeps her garden supplies."

Mark let out a puff of air.

"I can't help but feel Karla's job was to drive Elizabeth out of the protection of the House. However, if Elizabeth had gotten any of the poison in her eyes, she would have been taken to the hospital in Bales..."

"…where the Jaded Amulet has one of their members working but where she would've been vulnerable to anyone who wanted to finish her off or kidnap her," Mark interjected.

"But then, she would be damaged goods. That is not the MO of Miles, who likes to do the torturing himself, and it's not the MO of the Jaded Amulet. They don't get involved with this stuff. It's got to be another brain-warped member of the White Knights, only not on Miles's team."

"Right. Unless Karla did more than what she was instructed to do," Mark added.

"Could very well be. So who is she related to or should I say which faction is she representing?" Alex pursed her lips in thought.

"Was Doc in the day she picked up her pills?"

"No. That's the twist in this. He was in Bales, and Lily was nowhere in the clinic. She doesn't visit the clinic. But our M person works there."

Mark was silent for a while. "Well, I'd like to pursue this connection with Mrs. Dodd. Maybe we can get another big clue from her, such as Lily's maiden name. Did you notice Lily doesn't have a middle name? In all my research on her, she has never listed her maiden name or given a middle name."

"I noticed. She also has Doc as her nearest relative. It's on my list of 'so what's with this?'"

The two climbed the stairs to the House and rang the bell.

While Alex confirmed the delivery of the utilities with Claire, Mark looked around the sitting room.

"Mark, what are you looking for with that thing?" Claire asked as she and Alex walked into the room.

"UV devices, listening devices, or anything suspicious."

"If my residents didn't find anything, you can be sure you won't. Why do you think anything would be here?"

"Karla," Alex said.

"You won't find anything. Last night, we had a class on planting listening devices. The women found seven, and seven was how many I hid. Karla wouldn't have left anything since she knows about the classes."

"Do you tell the women how many you plant?"

"No, I give them an hour." Claire paused a moment as if a thought had occurred to her. "Well, you know, the last room Karla was in was the upstairs sitting room. I haven't planted anything up there for about a week. Maybe we'll have another egg hunt before lunch."

On the way back to the station, they walked by the Cigar Room. By the laughter, they figured Danny and Mike were still inside with their buddies.

"Let's go look at some furniture. Elizabeth needs a desk to work at," Alex suggested.

Mark resisted teasing her. He was not sure if she was aware that she was taking a permanent attitude toward Elizabeth. Somehow out of this chaos, he felt, they would all survive—battered and bruised perhaps, but alive.

It took them thirty minutes of fast walking to get to the side of town Alex was interested in. She was huffing and slightly out of breath when she stopped next to Mark as he peered into a darkened store.

"How about that desk? If Elizabeth likes the style, that would really be nice." Mark quickly rapped on the window of the used furniture store, Antiques for the Discriminating. Walter's thin face was seen behind the closed sign.

Waving his wrist in a foppish manner, the thin man opened the door enthusiastically. Walter had a crush on Detective Mark Scripts.

"That desk over there, mind if I check it out?" Mark asked, trying to put more space between him and Walter.

Alex rescued him by pulling on Walter's sleeve. "Walter. Tone it down. Remember our talk?" she reminded him before moving to join Mark. Walter was a nice person but was not politically correct and didn't care if he shocked others with his exaggerated posturing and effeminate displays. Walter often declared that at his age he earned the right to be however he felt and if he felt more "girlish" one day and less another, so what?

Mark was regarding the table with a critical eye. "This would be great for her. Jeez, Alex. It must kill her to sit on the floor and work."

"I'm sure she'll appreciate your consideration."

Walter frowned. "Just who is this for?"

"My roommate. So what's the price?" Alex asked.

The desk and chair were a deep cherry red, almost black, with bronze handles on the desk drawers, and simple deep lines around the table.

Walter stood staring at the desk. It was the look he gave when he was preparing a long-winded story.

"Walter," Alex called impatiently. "I haven't all day. Can we do some business here?"

Walter looked indignant. "Well, I'm not sure. I'll have to look and see what the price is."

Alex warned herself not to roll her eyes, instead she looked at her watch. "Got to get back to the house. Let me talk to Elizabeth and see if she wants to come over and see it."

"Okay," Mark and Walter responded.

"How about if we meet you at the Palace Gardens for lunch at two?" she asked Mark, "after the lunch rush. The telephone guy should be finished by then. Okay?"

"You sure you have enough help with unloading the other stuff?"

"Yes. You have enough on your plate right now."

271

"If you're sure. Give me a call to keep me posted." Mark girded his belt and got ready to do some serious negotiating with Walter before he checked out Mike and Danny. For Elizabeth and Alex, he could do this.

"Walter, you and I know you can sell it for anything you like," Mark told him after Alex was out the door. "I don't expect you to take a loss here, just give a fair price for our friend."

"Well, for a small favor, I can let it go for, say...a lesser price."

"Walter, I'm married and I'm not gay, nor have any desire..."

Walter looked shocked. "That's not what I was going to suggest," he said indignantly, drawing himself up as tall as he could. "I was thinking maybe lunch one day."

"Today would be fine. At two. With two conditions..."

Walter nodded frantically, listening to the conditions. He then gave an extremely low price for the table and chair. Mark refrained from looking surprised.

Walter settled in Sunrise after his longtime lover died in a car accident. An old crony of his had moved here. Both men had more money than they could spend in Sunrise. They entertained themselves and the town with the weird and oftentimes outrageous bets they made on occasion. One bet was that Detective Mark Scripts wouldn't be caught dead in a public place with an old queen like Walter.

This was going to be the best meal ever, he thought, rubbing his hands together as the automatic phone dialer beeped as it worked.

"Alfred, honey?" His voice oozed with sweetness as the familiar voice answered the rings. "Is business too busy to have lunch at say two today? Detective Mark Scripts and I will be..."

Assignment Sunrise

Chapter Twenty-Five

Adison felt a little disappointed at not seeing Elizabeth at the front door waiting for her. The alarms had to have let her know the gate was being opened.

Get over it, Adison. You're acting like you're a couple. Ruefully, she shook her head and parked her vehicle under the awning. The image of Desi Arnaz opening the door and calling, "Honey, I'm home," mocked her. *This is ridiculous! But darn it, at least Angel could bark a hello.*

A sudden thought that something might be wrong with Elizabeth had her pulling out her semiautomatic and sliding out of her SUV, carefully closing the vehicle door but not latching it. Leaning against the body of the vehicle, she listened for anything out of the ordinary and snorted to herself. There was nothing ordinary about this house.

All right, first of all, I have to get these geese penned. I know no one is around because they're nice and calm...sort of. She moved to one side as three of them glared at her with their beady red eyes. She moved to their enclosure and dropped grain into their feeder to entice them back into the smaller area. Honking and flapping of wings covered any other noise. Impatiently, she waited for the last one to waddle into the pond area so she could swing their fence closed. It was something the Ebbens put in when they hired geese to protect their empty house.

Into the house she moved, closing the door firmly behind her to shut out outside noises. She cocked her head to one side, not quite understanding what she was hearing. She found Elizabeth and Angel by the sounds of crying.

Elizabeth had her arms wrapped around a pillow sobbing, and Angel was standing near whining.

"Elizabeth," Alex whispered. She sheathed her weapon and sat next to her. She would have taken her into her arms, but Elizabeth had a firm grip on her pillow. Instead she wrapped one arm around her and gave her as much comfort as she could. Angel gazed at them and whined forlornly, then the dog's demeanor changed. With a growl, she whipped around to point her nose at the ocean window.

Alex felt her heart pound out adrenaline as she pulled her weapon and held it before her, gripping it between two steady hands. She was aware that Elizabeth struggled to her feet behind her. Looking toward the window where Angel was growling, she saw nothing.

"I disengaged the alarms so they wouldn't go off with the telephone guy walking around. Wait here until I see what's going on. Angel, good girl, *protect.*"

Alex moved into the hallway and listened for any sounds. Not hearing anything, not even Angel, she moved cautiously into the dining room, then to the front door. Pulling the door open, a telephone truck was sitting in their driveway. A young man standing on the side was holding some wires and doing nothing else.

Maybe he's the lookout.

He nodded to Alex, looking relieved at seeing someone.

"You have an ID?" Alex asked, stepping off the porch and glancing around them. He appeared nervous. "Anyone else here with you?" She handed him back his ID.

"Two. Just two others. We wanted to check the outside and inside boxes to make sure everything's okay," he began in a rush. "Since no one's been in this house for a while."

"Uh-huh. Where's the other two?"

"Checking the phone box on the side of the house," he repeated nervously.

"Names."

What he stammered out was not translatable. "What?" she asked impatiently. *Is he doing this purposely to keep me occupied?*

Not waiting for a third try at deciphering what he was mumbling, she left him at the truck, pointing a finger at him to stay where he was. She knew where the phone box was, and there was nothing wrong with it. The wire was frayed and needed to be replaced from the pole to the house. She tapped out a distress code over her radio.

She found a husky guy dressed in a telephone jumpsuit uniform that looked like he was wearing someone else's clothes. He nodded at her and resumed his work of stripping wires.

"Hey! Even I know you don't strip wires that way! Stop right there and pack up your gear," she ordered. Her eyes moved to the sliding glass door at the back of the house and found it was opened. "Did your partner enter my house?"

He shrugged, giving her an expression that he thought she was crazy. "Get back to the truck. I'm going to have a talk with your supervisor." She watched him gather up his things slowly. Impatiently, she moved to the sliding glass door and entered the dining room. The guy had been wearing military boots instead of the usual shoes lineman wore.

Alex's heart was pounding as she moved into the house with her gun extended. Looking over the front room and giving the laundry room a quick glance, she moved silently through the hallway into Elizabeth's room. A tall blond guy was walking out of the bathroom. He didn't even bother with the customary repair uniform. A quick glance told her there was no Elizabeth or Angel.

"Hey, there, ma'am," he said in a slow Southern drawl. He put his hands up in a playful gesture. "I'm just the telephone installer."

"How did you get in here?" *Never mind the fact that you were checking out the bathroom.*

"Back way. The door was opened. No one answered my knock."

"I didn't order any phones to be installed. Just the outside wire to be replaced."

"Well, ma'am, my mistake." He moved toward the door as the woman with the gun pointed at his forehead moved into the center of the room to let him by.

She did a scan of the room and glanced into the bathroom, not lowering her weapon. "Stop right there. Go out the same way you came in." She had no intention of giving him any more views of the house. She followed the guy out and around the house to the front yard where the young guy was still fiddling with some cables, not looking like he was doing anything.

"Where's the other guy?" she asked suspiciously.

"Ah. Working, ma'am."

"Call him," she ordered, nodding to the walkie talkie on his waist.

"He ain't carrying one, ma'am. Hey, Jake! Yo!" he yelled.

Five minutes could have passed, though it seemed longer before she heard the light tread behind her and knew that most telephone workers didn't walk quietly. Not with all the gear hanging from their belts.

She moved so she had all of them in sight, her weapon sitting in her holster.

"Let me see your IDs," she ordered.

The two men flashed their IDs, not giving her a good view. They all could hear a vehicle approaching. It gave a few honks as it rushed into view in a cloud of smoke. Alex was hoping it was the good guys, her cavalry.

So is it worth pushing the ID business? They look real enough.

Amanda Briscolle and Genie were in the van. Both took in the three men and Alex.

"Alex, we thought you could use some help with the furniture. It's just behind us," Agent Briscolle announced, jumping out of the van.

The guy fixing the wire let out an expletive in an exasperated tone. "I need another type of cable. This isn't the right type. We have to go and…"

"We'll be back to finish the job," the tall blond told her before he climbed up into the telephone truck's cab.

"Right," Alex said, ignoring the chill he gave her. "I catch you here again, buddy, and I'm going to hurt you," she muttered just loud enough for him to hear.

His leer told her he heard and didn't take it seriously. The truck rolled out with the dust from the side of the road, churning up as they moved over for the furniture truck.

Alex looked at the two women. "Was that who I think it was?"

The agent nodded. "That's one of the cousins. Did you see any tattoos on the back of his wrist? We won't know his affiliation then. You have cameras in the house, don't you?"

Alex nodded.

"Well, then, we can get a closer look at him. Someone now knows what the place looks like and most probably its weaknesses. Genie said some of the women spotted a person out on the dunes earlier in the day as the mist was lifting. Detective Scripts sent us over. Said he got an SOS from you. He's keeping an eye on Mike and Danny to see what they're up to."

"Well, if Miles is out there watching and this guy is with the other side, I sure hope he gets pissed and takes those three out, so we won't have to worry about them."

"You couldn't have arrested them?" Genie demanded angrily.

"For what? I don't have cause!" Alex responded just as upset. "Their IDs looked legitimate. For all I know, one of them may file a complaint against me for drawing a weapon on him. Elizabeth!"

Alex ran back into the house, not daring to call for her just in case the place was bugged. She put a shushing finger to her lips and the others nodded as they fanned out. She found two listening devices in the carvings. She turned to look at Agent Briscolle who nodded. They were going to have to run a sweep through the whole house. Rather than go through this again, she decided that Mark, a man of many talents, was going to have to help her tie in the phone lines.

She slid the closet door open and whispered Angel's name. There was no one there. She heard a faint whine and scratching. A door swung open. A very happy Angel came out, followed by a frightened Elizabeth.

"That was one of them," she said softly. Her hand on Alex's arm was shaking and cold.

"Yes. Which side, though?" Alex took a deep breath. "According to Briscolle, there's two or three factions in this organization and each with its own agenda."

"How did he get in?" Genie asked.

"The sliding door. I shut the alarms off, so the telephone repair guy wouldn't set anything off."

A honking from the front and a yell sent Genie heading for the door. "Oh, I forgot to tell them it's okay to bring the stuff in. I'll see to it."

Elizabeth limped to the edge of the bed and sat down. Her hands were shaking in her lap.

"Are you going to be able to go through with this?" Briscolle asked. "It's just as complicated as it was in the beginning."

"I've gone this far. I'll be fine. I was just surprised."

Alex rested a hand on her trembling shoulder.

"I'll call Detective Scripts and give him a report," Briscolle said. She walked out of the room with her cell phone out and ready to use.

Alex gave her a grateful smile. Kneeling in front of Elizabeth, she wrapped her warm hands around Elizabeth's fingers. Nothing was said as the golden brown-eyed bodyguard looked from one face to another, then rested her shaggy head on Elizabeth's thigh with a soft sigh.

"Once we get the utilities hooked up, how about we go into town for lunch? I found a nice desk for you. I'd like you to see it. We can also pick up some cheap rugs. These floors are cold at night." Alex knew she was rattling on, but it seemed to relax Elizabeth, and it was helping to thaw out the cold knot in her stomach.

Elizabeth nodded and took a few deep breaths. "Bookcases and a desk are a necessity for a study," Elizabeth rasped, "and chairs to sit and read in. A lamp or two."

Alex nodded, gently squeezing Elizabeth's hands. "Do you want to shower and change? There's a lot of us here, so you'll be safe."

"Do you have some shampoo? I haven't had a chance to replace mine."

"Sure. I'll go get it."

When Alex returned, Elizabeth was already in the shower. She dropped the bag of cleaned laundry Genie brought over onto the bed and headed into the bathroom. The shower stall showed the outline of a tall form. She managed to calmly rap on the door and wait for a dripping hand to take the bottles. As Alex left, she gave Angel, sprawled out on the cool tiled bathroom floor with her chew toy, a doleful look. *This is going to be a rough one.*

Alex followed the sounds of the grunting, as two big guys, Kinney and Alan, maneuvered the double-door refrigerator into its space.

"Good grief! At my apartment, I had one that came up to my knees and kept a few things in it."

"What did you use it for? You never ate at home. I don't even think you had leftovers," Genie teased.

"With friends like you and a great place like Mollie's, there's no incentive to learn to cook," Alex returned.

Next was the oven. It matched the refrigerator, a light tan. It didn't take the men long to connect it. Elizabeth arrived, dressed and cleaned up and ready for Genie's instructions on how to use the electric stove and opened the refrigerator to impress the two women.

"Is that a hint to stock it full of food?" Elizabeth teased her. "And by the way, thanks for the clean clothes."

Genie nodded chuckling. "You're welcome. Speaking of food, anyone hungry?"

"I told Mark I would meet him at the Palace Gardens at two."

They all looked at their watches.

"Well, let's get going, we'll be just a tad late, but he knows why. Maybe after lunch, you all can look around the stores for some more stuff for this place. You need carpets on these cold floors. Oh," Genie paused and gave a thick envelope to Elizabeth, "cash of yours we still had in the vault and your lawyer said he transferred money into your new bank account. Here's your account information. It arrived today in the mail. Took them long enough."

Lunch was pleasant with Walter being entertaining and witty and his unfortunate gambling buddy, who gave a brave front by adding his quips to the happy atmosphere. They didn't stay long after lunch was finished. Adison was sure they had a lot to discuss and argue about. After the two men left, the conversation turned to gardening. Elizabeth, Linda Scripts, Genie to a small degree, and Agent Briscolle shared tips while Alex and Mark were content to sit back and enjoy the sun. Angel was sprawled out under the table, covering Linda and Mark's feet.

After lunch, Agent Briscolle parted company and the others, including Linda with her arm wrapped around her husband's waist, went to Walter's store to look over the desk Alex described to Elizabeth.

"It's perfect. Very nice," Elizabeth praised. Walter was standing by with a serene smile. Alex chuckled to herself, thinking he must have made a killing on his bet in more ways than one. Turning to see what Elizabeth's attention was drawn to, Walter was nodding and gesturing to one of his workers.

"Add this bookcase to the table delivery," Walter looked at the young muscular man for a few moments. "And see that you don't add any nicks to it."

Mike winked at the group and gave an extra wiggle of his hips when he went into the back to get the furniture dolly.

"If he weren't so naughty, I wouldn't put up with him," Walter said. "He has more sick days than a woman her..." He stopped suddenly, realizing who his audience was. There was a time when Walter wouldn't have cared, which to Alex meant even old dogs could learn new tricks.

"He holds down two part-time jobs and goes to school. He works for you as a favor, Walter. Don't be ruining his reputation. Elizabeth may want to hire him." Alex glanced at Walter irritably.

"You ruin the whole effect when you take things literally," Walter said.

"Hey, we can use some lamps," Alex said, joining Elizabeth, Genie, and the Scripts where they were all testing out a reading chair.

"Walter, I'll take this, too." Elizabeth turned to Alex. "I picked out two already. One for my room and for my desk. Do you want another for the front or dining room?"

From the furniture store, the group parted company. Mark received a call and said he would meet them later. Linda left the three women to prepare for her late afternoon class while Genie dragged the two women into a linen store.

"Hey, Mark," Genie greeted. She set the last bag of groceries next to Elizabeth's new clothing purchases she was talked into.

Mark peeked in the van. It had bags of groceries and other items. He spotted new throw pillows sitting atop one collection of bags. "Hi. So are you ready to head back?" he asked the three women with a grin.

"Yep. You going to come along and help fix the telephone lines for me?" Adison asked, hoping for the best.

"Uh-huh. I just happen to have all that we need in the patrol car."

Alex went to the car trunk and helped Mark transfer cable and equipment to the van. He hopped in the van, sitting next to a wiggling and dancing Angel. "Let's go."

"I've ordered three services for the house," Alex explained. "They should already be set up once we get the wire repaired."

"Three?" Elizabeth asked surprised.

"Yes. I thought you would like one for yourself, and I usually have one for the computer and one for my phone. The house was previously set up for three separate lines, so it wasn't that difficult to reactivate them."

Mark and she exchanged looks, passing the unspoken message that there was another point in favor of Doc and Lily Ebbens being the boss of the Jaded Amulet. What didn't fit were the Ms, and they had to fit somewhere.

Back at the house, the van was quickly unpacked. Alex paused to study a dust cloud heading their way. "That must be the furniture truck," Alex said.

"While the guys unpack the furniture, Genie and I will work on the wires."

Elizabeth and Alex directed the movers as to where to place the furniture and carpets. Then Alex spent time in her bedroom unpacking. She could hear Elizabeth laugh as the two men teased her about her elaborate bed. Alex grinned. The idea that the bed was hers and Elizabeth was sleeping in it gave her pleasant shivers. Symbolically, she realized she was placing ownership on Elizabeth, and right now, it was comforting to her. Shaking her head she thought she had better go help Mark, something that was not related to setting up house.

She found Mark up the pole.

"Hey," she called up. "Need help?"

"Yes. Can you feed me some more line?"

Alex pulled cable from the box and fed it to Mark as he needed.

"Where's Genie?" she asked.

"Replacing the outside box. They trashed it."

Alex snorted. She could have told him that. She frowned as she replayed the scene again. She could not remember unlocking the sliding door, so how did he get in?

"Hey," Mark called to her. "Pay attention, Gumby!"

Alex looked up. "Oh, sorry."

Finished, the two went to look for Genie.

When Genie had enlisted in the Army, they assigned her to communications where she climbed many a pole and wired many a station. Somewhere in there, her CO found out she not only liked to cook, but she was good at it, so he had encouraged her to take lessons when she was posted in Germany. That changed her career track, and she was moved to working in the officers' mess.

From there, her life went downhill. In the Army, a good chef was an important asset for a CO to have. Important dinners with important people discussing important subjects, on the record and off, meant someone had to keep tight control of all those serving at those dinners. The control went over to all levels of her life to the point of marrying into an abusive relationship. Her only way of escaping was to divorce both Army and husband. If it was up to her, she would still be in the Army singing cadence and standing proudly in her uniform.

By the time it grew dark, the house was beginning to take on the aspect of a home. While watching the gate close behind the van with Genie, Mark and Angel, Alex breathed in a sense of contentment. Even if it was pretend, the idea of settling down gave her a nice feeling. *I'm getting too complacent. First a cabin and now a roommate and...*

Shaking her head, she closed and locked the door and went to join Elizabeth in the kitchen. She had to remember this part was not real, even though she wanted it to be.

Elizabeth was fixing dinner.

Having nothing better to say, she announced, "Phones work."

Elizabeth glanced at her and smiled. "So I heard. If I hear another test ring, I'll toss it in the clothes basket." She paused a moment. "We don't have one. Maybe in the cellar."

Alex grinned. "You and Angel must've been going nuts. I was thinking of exploring this place closer tonight."

They now had tall stools for the kitchen counter, and Alex climbed up on one as Elizabeth prepared their dinner. Plates were already set out. She looked at her arms resting on the counter. "I think I need to clean up before I eat. Be right back."

Alex scrubbed her skin with the washcloth that was saturated with the new herbal-scented soap Elizabeth purchased for her as a housewarming gift. Whatever it was smelled nice, filling the steamed room with its fragrance.

She turned the shower off and stepped out, mentally reprimanding herself to keep focused on her assignment. Alex plopped down on her bed and promptly leaped up, letting out a screech she didn't recognize coming from her. Her heart was pounding as she stared at the offending article that she sat on. It was Angel's soggy chew toy.

Ewwww! Oh, my god. Ewww. Disgustedly, she picked up the object with as little of her skin touching it as possible and turned to the bedroom door that flew open.

At first, Elizabeth had a comical look on her face, then she doubled over with laugher. Alex tossed the horrid toy at Elizabeth's feet.

"You wouldn't be laughing so hard if you sat your naked self on it," Alex told her irritably. She grabbed up her towel, wrapping it around her, and with as much dignity as she could muster, headed back into the shower. At the bathroom door, Alex turned to say something more, but Elizabeth was laughing too hard to hear.

Elizabeth finally straightened up. "You sat on it?" She held onto the doorframe for some more laughing, then surprised Alex by limping over to her and wrapping her arms around her. Reflexively, Alex returned the hug.

"I hope you're not expecting me to repeat something like this," she said.

"No, I don't think my heart will take too many of those squeals."

"Squeals?" Alex pushed away from Elizabeth affronted. She would much rather stay in complete body contact with Elizabeth's, but something very important needed to be understood here. "I don't squeal. I shout. I have on occasion screamed, but I don't squeal," Alex said firmly. It was rather difficult to maintain an offended expression when Elizabeth's face looked pinched from her struggle not to laugh.

Finally, with a great deal of aplomb, Elizabeth gave her a sweet smile and suggested, "Well, while you're taking another shower, you can think of a description for that sound I heard. It was not a scream and it was not a yell." Elizabeth turned to where she had tossed the wooden sheath to her sword.

"Oh, here let me." Alex moved to pick it up.

A little flushed, Elizabeth took the reassembled cane and limped back to the kitchen.

Alex went back into the shower grinning. *Some towels are just not made for bending over in.*

When she reappeared, she was dressed in a T-shirt and sweats. Elizabeth looked up from the pan she was cleaning.

Alex's eyes took in two place settings waiting for dinner to be served. "You didn't have to wait for me," Alex said, "but thank you for doing so."

She could feel a slight flush at the thoughtful gesture. Elizabeth's back was to her as she turned to the oven to bring out their warm meal.

"Since we're exploring tonight, would you mind if we checked out the space in my room first?" Elizabeth asked.

Alex nodded. "That sounds like a good idea."

Armed with SureFire lights that left no corner unseen and a first aid kit just in case, Adison led the way to explore their home. Pushing the back wall, the door popped open, and Alex flashed her light around, then descended the stairs. Elizabeth laid a hand on her shoulder to steady herself.

Focus on what you're doing, Alex. It's just a hand.

Ten steps down, they hit a flat spot…a cement floor.

"It appears to extend beyond the foundation of the house." Alex flashed her light above them to show the ceiling where she thought the floor above them ended. "This is under the back deck."

Elizabeth flashed her light to the side of Alex's to give a larger view. Someone had used it at one time. There were pipes that came from the house down the wall but were capped about two feet from the floor.

"In your writer's imagination, what would this be?" Alex asked as she turned around, studying the walls for any mark. There were no other exits. It was just a small concrete room. No electrical outlets, no attachments for a light. So what was the advantage of having this hidden space?

"Well, no iron hooks or holes in the walls or wax drippings on the floor, so dungeon is out. A hideaway, perhaps. Those are water pipes not gas. Maybe some water for whoever used this place. A dark place like this could be used for someone interested in photography, but the trapped fumes would kill the photographer in no time. No ventilation. Come to think of it, water drainage needs ventilation. Maybe a wine cellar. Let's get out of here. It's giving me goose bumps."

Elizabeth continued up the steps and waited in the closet for Alex to come up. They moved out of the bedroom into the kitchen for their next adventure. Alex pulled up the floor in the kitchen closet. Shining her light down the stairs, she looked for anything that might jump out at them. When she was sure there were no strange apparitions to threaten them, she started down.

Elizabeth followed closely. The dampness was all around them. The thick smell of wet sand and the booming sound of the pounding waves echoed around them. Alex read her watch. It was ten at night. Where had all the time gone?

"What time do you normally break off your writing?"

"Three, maybe four in the morning."

They didn't have far to descend before finding water covering the lower steps. They shined their lights along the walls and as far as it could go in the cavern, looking for anything that may be out of place.

"We'll check out the rest in daylight. I want to know when the tide covers the ground and when it starts to go out. When the camera's fixed, we'll have better coverage. I was hoping for more, but we'll have to make due."

"Well, I think I'll get to my writing since the exploration is over for tonight. Right?"

"Yes. That was enough excitement for one day. Want some tea?" Alex offered.

"Yes. Thank you."

As Alex prepared their drinks, she remembered Mai's instructions for Elizabeth to exercise her knee and wondered just what that involved. Her imagination got the best of her and took off on an erotic binge.

Snapping out of the daze, Alex looked around to see if she was caught in the act. *How did that happen?* Clearing her throat, she decided to do something. With nowhere else to go, Alex walked into their new study. Elizabeth's back was to her, and by the shaking of her shoulders, something was wrong.

"Elizabeth? What is it?"

Elizabeth turned a stricken face to her. She handed her a note. "It was left on my laptop," she explained faintly.

"We did a search after they left, how did we miss this?" It was a scanned picture of a young boy and a dog. "I take it this is Noel and Rusty."

"Yes. It was inside the case."

Elizabeth looked at the picture and touched the face of the smiling boy gently. Tears streaked her face. The microwave bell dung, and both women jumped.

"Why not give it a rest tonight?" Alex suggested. "One night of interrupting a ritual shouldn't hurt."

Elizabeth looked at her with sadness and Alex stepped forward, sliding her arms around the woman and pulling her close. They held each other for a while, letting their combined warmth wrap around them. Alex reluctantly broke the contact.

Elizabeth looked down at the laptop. Frowning, she tapped the floppy button. "I don't leave floppies in my drive. I'm too paranoid," she said as she ejected the suspicious disk.

Alex took it from her and stuck a small reminder note on it.

"Maybe you should check yours," Elizabeth suggested uneasily.

"Will you look at that? I know I didn't have a floppy in the drive. I checked it before I moved my stuff here, and I haven't booted it up yet."

"I think they are quite angry with me. Karla made a copy of my files from the dummy hard drive I leave in the laptop for this very reason. It had a Trojan virus on it."

"You created a virus?"

Elizabeth smiled wanly. "No. Agent Amanda Briscolle, your other partner, thought I would like something to fight back with in case they got that close. It sends a copy of the address book of each person it reaches to SID, a bug to each person on the address book, then starts eating away at the operating system of the computer it infected."

"Oh, joy." She caught Elizabeth's uplifted brow. "Mark and I monitor those sites since its part of our case. Darn. I wonder why she didn't say anything to me about it. They know I monitor those sites. Ah. I get an updated version of their virus detect on a regular basis. That will protect me but not my partner."

"Then you should warn him."

"Uh-huh." While her PC booted up, she watched Elizabeth in the reflection from her monitor.

"You're not going to call him?"

"No, I can send him an encrypted message along with the most recent virus update. We share a PGP file. Darn ex-SEAL is sneaky about his codes. And I thought I was real paranoid. He has his family to worry about, so he has all these tricky ways to make sure they're safe while he does his cop thing." Alex listened to the dialer log on to her browser. "Mark believes that all these precautions will one day pay off for that one nut case who will try to hurt him or his family."

"From my own personal experience, I see nothing paranoid about taking precautions." Elizabeth pulled the chair from her desk and rolled it over to Alex. "Here. Sit down. This is far more comfortable than that fold-out you've been sitting on."

"It won't take long." Alex smiled up at her, but she got up anyway and exchanged chairs, realizing how nice the change was as soon as she sat. "Whoops. I need to change my phone number here. Oh, and post a note to go DSL tomorrow. This is way too slow."

Alex finished her typing and stretched while she waited for her computer to shut down, then headed to her room to get ready for bed. As she was pulling the covers back, she had the urge to check on Elizabeth just to make sure she was all right. She grabbed her robe from the back of the door. Peering down the hallway, she could see through the open door a soft, fluttering glow.

A candle.

Curious, she padded quietly over the cold wooden floors. From the doorway, Alex could see Elizabeth's feet flex slowly, then relax. Alex moved in farther, past the ornately carved bed frame, letting her eyes follow Elizabeth's bare feet up to her ankles, past the bare calves, resting momentarily on her scarred knee, then up to the bare thighs. Here her eyes lingered while her fingers flexed involuntarily, wanting to run her hands along them and everywhere else on Elizabeth's tall body. Swallowing, her eyes continued their journey, up past her apex, barely hidden under a long T-shirt to a stomach where one hand rested, rising and falling slowly. From the hand, Alex's eyes moved to the soft mounds that the T-shirt covered. Elizabeth's nipples projected from the smooth surface of the shirt.

Alex found her mouth watering at the thought of using her tongue to bring these nipples to a hard, erect condition. Breathing in slowly and deeply to adjust to the pounding of her heart, Alex backed out of the room. Trembling, she hurried to her own room, frightened at what she wanted to do—cross that line of professionalism and unprofessional conduct.

Gods, its time like these that I wished I belonged to a gym that is twenty-four hours.

The next morning, Alex was up early. She left a note on the kitchen counter for Elizabeth that she was going for a run. Her run was down a path to the beach and back up. It was steep enough for her to feel she got a good workout. When she returned, the study door was closed, Elizabeth's bedroom door was wide open, coffee was freshly made, and the house smelled of shampoo. Alex gathered Elizabeth was closed up in the study writing.

After her shower, she returned to the kitchen to fix herself breakfast and plan her day off. A beep warned her someone was on the property. Alex slid off the chair and peered at the security monitors in the front room. Mark and Angel were visiting.

What's going on? She waited at the opened door as they pulled up. "Hey, what are you doing off?"

"Not off. Two of the cars have mechanical problems, so while Max is fixing them, I'm driving my truck. I thought you could do with a visit from Angel. Linda called to tell me the dog was driving her crazy. I can't get her to take a day off. Do you mind?"

"Just like her daddy," she remarked dryly.

Angel was happy to get out of her taxi and pushed past Alex, briefly pressing her nose against her open palm. Alex shook her head with a big smile. "I think it's her chew rope she's wanting. I had the unfortunate discomfort of discovering it last night."

"How about lunch at one?"

"Great. Get any information yet?"

Mark smiled. "Check your mail. And thanks for the warning last night. Oh, and here. This is the cable for the cave monitor."

Mark opened the truck door and Alex pulled out the black cable rolled in a box.

"Talk to you at lunch." He waved and backed out his truck, disappearing in a cloud of dust.

Alex took a long glance around the yard. The geese were going about their business with an occasional squawk, the breeze bending the trees was not the same that blew along the carport, and the sky was clear. She looked for shiny reflections outside the gate in the open land or cars passing on an otherwise quiet road. Not believing for one moment they were unwatched, she turned back into the house. In the front room where she dropped the cable, she studied the row of monitors. The geese were ranging along the north fence content from their morning feed. All the working monitors showed the usual scenes except the one monitor for the cave. It was black. Hopefully, she could get it working with the new cable.

In the kitchen, Elizabeth was making coffee. Angel's rope toy was at her feet.

"Now she finds it. I'll be in the study."

Alex booted up her computer after making sure there was no disk in the floppy drive. She needed to get in the habit of checking for the small things. After opening up the Internet connection, she pushed the mail button at the top of the keyboard.

Elizabeth had quietly entered with two cups of coffee and a not-so-quiet Angel who immediately plopped down near the two women. Elizabeth sat in the folding chair next to her.

"You certainly have a lot of fans out there," Elizabeth said.

"Making it with chatty friends over the Internet," Alex muttered as she scanned for a particular address. She was hoping Elizabeth would leave it at that.

"Your pen pals have some real strange names," Elizabeth said with a writer's curiosity.

"They're strange people. Some of them are rapists and/or murderers locked up in a prison who think they're setting up some plain Jane for when they get out or to send them money or goodies while they're in the can. Here's the one." She opened it.

"It's on this house." Elizabeth recognized the layout that appeared on the screen. "Why do you write to them if you know they're dangerous?"

"They picked my name out in a chat room, pretending to be something they're not. I guessed who and what they were about and for practice, traced them back to their den. I don't answer them. They just keep writing." Alex looked up at Elizabeth's frown.

"Before you go into a chat room, you have an opportunity to create a profile on yourself, so, no, I didn't say anything that was really truthful about me. I mean, no one tells the truth and everyone knows it's made up." She sighed. She was going to have to engage the spam blocker and put these characters on a bounce list. At first, they were entertaining, but now they were bothersome.

Alex pointed at the floor plan to change the subject. "It's from the original owner's son. He works for NASA like his uncle. By the looks of it, this place was originally set up with a few hidden places. Doc would have had the contractor set up the foundation for them so he knows about them. It seems our stairs to the ocean were once to a wine cellar. Nothing like adapting to a situation." She looked up at the blue eyes that were next to her. For a moment, both said nothing. "Maybe the space in your room is the new wine cellar." Alex broke the spell.

"Could be. Do wine cellars have hot and cold water pipes?"

"I don't know. I've never seen one. Mark left off cable for me to rewire the security camera in the sea cave. I'll do that after breakfast."

"Breakfast. Let me go check on it before it becomes charcoal."

After breakfast, Alex began the dirty job of replacing the cable while Elizabeth cleaned the dishes.

"Alex, the screen is working," Elizabeth's voice echoed through the cavern.

"Good," she muttered, as she drove another pin into the rock wall to hold the cable out of sight. She slipped the hammer into her leather pouch and carefully clambered down the rough wall. Standing back, she looked over her work, trying to see it with a casual eye.

"Well, it'll do. It works, that's the important thing."

Sloshing back to the stairs, she grabbed her tool bucket and carried the rope attached to the handle with her up into the kitchen. From there, she hoisted up the bucket. She then swung it up and dropped it against the panty wall where she left her sandy shoes and wet socks. Padding back to the living room, she studied the monitors.

"That's good. Four views of the cave."

Elizabeth and Angel joined her in front of the monitors.

"So do you want to check out our own passageway to the sea? I don't advocate going out onto the beach at this time, maybe later, but for now, we can see the view."

"I'd like that," Elizabeth nodded.

Equipped with SureFire flashlights, they descended the stairs, letting Angel go first. The dog was dancing in the wet sand anxious to get moving by the time the two women joined her.

The first part of the cave was dark, but once they rounded a corner, sunlight from the entrance gave them plenty of light.

"Nice and cozy until it opens up pretty big here. Looks like someone's been working on the natural cavern." Elizabeth studied the walls moving her light on the walls and ceiling.

"Uh-huh." Alex added her light to Elizabeth's. There was a faint line that ran down the rock wall, then her cable, which blended in with the cuts of the rocks. *Not too bad a job. Can't see them unless you know they're there.*

When they rounded a corner, the daylight nearly blinded them. The entrance from the beach to the cave was well protected by large boulders.

Near the opening, a dinghy was chained to the rock wall. Since the tide was out, it rested in the sand.

"I guess Doc and Lily don't use it anymore."

Alex watched Elizabeth as she looked longingly out of the cave and beyond the beach, then at the dingy, touching it wistfully. "I guess not," she replied automatically. "Do you sail?" Elizabeth asked.

Alex's eyes opened wide. "Sail? Once. I got sea sick," she admitted, looking a bit ill just remembering the experience she had no intention of replaying. That mental image had Alex's face turning red. She managed to get out, "Do you?"

"Yes. Took some lessons. It would be nice to hone them. Want to go out sometime?" Thankfully, Elizabeth was not looking at Alex.

Alex smiled weakly. "No. If it were a date and I went, you would never ask me out again."

Elizabeth looked up at her, and her smile of amusement diminished the wariness in her eyes. Alex mirrored the smile, feeling for a moment a reprieve from the weight of this assignment. They continued to grin, forgetting Angel until she pushed at Alex's hand with something. Alex automatically opened her hand to receive what Angel was handing her.

"Angel!" Alex dropped the offending article and jumped back, bumping into a laughing Elizabeth. "Eew, what's this?"

"It's the remains of a tennis ball," Elizabeth explained between laughs.

"Yuck. I'm not touching it, Angel, so you can just drop it."

"Well, unless you have anything else to look at over here, I think I've had enough temptation," Elizabeth said.

Mark was already at Mollie's, sipping his first cup of coffee when he spotted Alex's SUV pull into a parking spot where only SPD could get away with parking. Unconsciously, a smile curved on his face as he watched a laughing Alex tell Elizabeth Duke something that had both of them smiling. It made his heart feel full when he watched them together. It was not his police side that was rejoicing in the connection he could see between them, but the side that was the antithesis of his military and police training. It was not with any pleasure that he would have to bring them back to the stark reality that they were dealing with a psychopath.

He sat in a booth close enough to the back to have some privacy.

"Hi, Mark," the two greeted.

Elizabeth slid in first and Mark noted that she didn't like sitting on the inside. After they received their coffee, Mark started with his update.

"The FBI is in town, so to speak," he said. "They sent one of their agents to the coroner's office accompanied with three bodies recovered in the forest. They wanted an immediate autopsy. According to Dr. Fishbach, the three bodies, Caucasian males, were involved in a car accident up the mountain. They went over a cliff."

"FBI," Alex muttered. "I take it they didn't part with the information."

"No. Dr. Fishbach thought it was rather interesting that two of them had driver's licenses from Alabama also had IDs from the telephone company in Bales. He had his secretary give Harper a heads up."

"Wow," Alex said softly. *I shouldn't feel guilty about wishing for this and it came true. If those three are the same three at the house, they deserve to get knocked off. So what if it was done by...*"Did he happen to mention how they ended up dead over a cliff?" she asked.

"One had a bullet in his head," Mark hinted.

"Someone didn't like those guys," Alex said. "What a coincidence," she remarked, more to herself than her friends. No one said anything for a while, then Alex said, "That is so not FBI."

"No," Mark agreed but didn't add anything as if waiting for Alex to say something else.

"So, the FBI has landed." Alex turned to Elizabeth to see if she understood the implications. It was a little unnerving to see Elizabeth calmly stirring her coffee as if she had heard nothing of what Mark said.

"It's heating up the game," Mark mentioned, watching the two women.

Alex turned back to Mark and nodded. She felt closed off from Elizabeth. Part of her understood because Mark and her had not been putting on a confident face lately, and Elizabeth probably felt she had to rely on herself. That observation gave Alex a heartfelt pang. Mark's pursed lips gave her the impression he was also feeling sheepish at not being a solid wall of support to Elizabeth; however, Alex didn't feel SID was without its own motives, which would take priority over Elizabeth and her safety, and that left her to protect Elizabeth from being collateral damage.

Later in the afternoon while Elizabeth loaded new clothes in the washer, Alex stood staring out at the ocean from the dining room window, feeling the pressure of being a bodyguard and being isolated. Occasionally, she glanced at Elizabeth, whose composure was disturbing. Her stomach was in knots. It was not the waiting that was difficult, but the allowing someone to be attacked.

"I'm going to check out the beach entrance," she announced, wanting to lift her mood and trusting the change of atmosphere would do it.

"Okay." Elizabeth was preoccupied with cutting the tags off her new purchases before adding them to the washer.

Spinning on her heels, Alex headed to the kitchen. She plucked one of the flashlights off the shelf, lifted the floor, and clanged down the metal steps, all on automatic pilot. Thinking was depressing at the moment. At the bottom, she pulled her shoes and socks off, so she could feel the sand under her feet.

9. Christie

This is nice. She stared at her feet, watching them sink in the soft sand. She shook her head at the image of her sinking as a metaphor for this assignment.

Shining her light ahead, Alex moved it along the sides of the cave and along the sandy floor.

Her mood was not lifting.

Miserably, Alex sat in the dingy with her face cupped in her hands and her elbows resting on her knees.

What is going on with me? I'll tell you since you asked. This case stinks. Too many people involved and everyone with his or her own agenda.

There was something about this whole thing that was unsettling. And what that elusive point was, was scaring her. She had never been a weak link. She was always dependable. There were just too many unseen players, and Elizabeth's life hung on someone getting to her before she was killed.

Looking out at the bright disk, dropping behind the rocks, she was unaware of the tears rolling down her face. Taking a deep but shaky breath, Alex let the myriad emotions wash through her. She had been putting off dealing with her fears, but now she needed to identify each to get back to using her instinct that served her so well in the past.

Unconsciously, she wiped a tear from her chin where others soon followed. She closed her eyes and tried to get a grip on what she feared the most. Alex took another painful breath and noisily expelled the air. "Crap," she mumbled as the tears continued to fall. Alex buried her face in her hands.

A tug on Alex's sleeve brought her tear-filled eyes up to look into Elizabeth's eyes.

"I'm so sorry," Alex whispered.

Elizabeth lifted her hand to Alex's face and wiped a tear away with her thumb. "This has always been a flexible operation with no guarantees. I know what I'm doing. If this doesn't work..." she shrugged.

"Elizabeth," Alex cupped her face tenderly, "not working is failure, and failure is death."

Elizabeth laughed in disbelief. "Do you know that to be an absolute?" she demanded in a soft but strong voice. "We determine our destiny, and I have no intention of letting Bobby Miles and his friends win. Not this time," she assured her with vehemence.

"How can you be sure? So many things can go wrong."

"Because I'm focused. SID has the entire operation to worry about. I just have my role to worry about. Don't lose concentration to where I have to worry about you, too, Alex. We'll survive."

It was Elizabeth who gave Alex a firm hug.

"Come on. I have a nice warm jacuzzi waiting to be shared. Since I don't have a bathing suit, I'm declaring it to be clothing optional." Elizabeth looked at the detective. "Is that all right with you?"

Alex nodded. "I don't have a bathing suit anyway." She sighed heavily, feeling slightly better. "A jacuzzi really sounds good."

In companionable silence, holding hands for comfort, they walked back to the stairs in silence.

"Where's Angel?" Alex suddenly thought to ask.

"Mark came by and picked her up. Her shift is over."

It was dark as they walked farther into the cave, but Alex didn't need to see Elizabeth's face to know she was smiling.

In the kitchen, the two parted company for a moment. Alex went to take a quick shower in her own room and Elizabeth to her room where she would meet her.

Alex was in the shower when she heard the loud buzz and bang then sudden darkness. Her reaction was a trained response, moving out of the shower by feel and finding her weapon and moving toward Elizabeth's room, knowing full well that she needed to be extra careful on not shooting the wrong person.

"Elizabeth," she whispered urgently from her bedroom doorway.

"I'm all right."

By the sound of her voice, she was not. Alex flicked on her flashlight and shined it around the room. Her beam caught a scared and naked Elizabeth clutching a towel in comfort.

"It came from the jacuzzi. I turned the switch on, and..." she gulped noisily. "And an arch of electricity went from the wall switch to the tub."

"Are you all right?"

"I was wearing rubber-soled slippers. Thank you." Elizabeth added. The slippers were a gift from Alex on their last shopping visit.

In her light, Alex found a thin wire leading from the switch to the water. Using Elizabeth's cane, she wound it around the stick and pulled it from the switch. After making sure there were no more surprises, Alex went to the electric box on the side of the house and flipped the switches back on.

An hour later, both women were dressed in jeans and T-shirts, sitting at the counter with Chief Harper, Mark Scripts, and Genie, who was the first to arrive.

Genie had been standing on the back balcony taking a breather from a card game when she saw the house suddenly go dark, then heard the sound of a bang travel her way. While Claire called Mark, Genie headed to the house with a gun and her infrared goggles. Elizabeth and Alex heard Genie's anxious voice calling them from outside the closed gate. Mark came dressed in pajama bottoms, unlaced tennis shoes, Kevlar vest pulled over a T-shirt, and a very exited Angel. The chief was last.

"So the question is who did it and when?" The chief sipped his decaf coffee and placed it back in the saucer with careful movement. Everyone was upset.

"The only time they could have done it was when the phone crew was here," Alex insisted. "The alarm logs would have shown a disruption of service if it happened while we were gone."

"Except if they came from the ocean. We don't have a lock on the floor panel," Elizabeth reminded the others.

"Yes, but I put a noodle on top of it before I leave so it would have been moved if someone used it," Alex explained.

"Oh." Elizabeth's eyebrows rose. "So that's with the noodles I keep finding on the floor. I'll try not to sweep it or let Angel gobble it up," she said to lighten the mood.

"So that's where the noodle keeps going," Alex muttered, giving Elizabeth a smile at her effort to cut the tension.

"Enough with the noodle," Genie said, looking upset. "We need a real lock on that entrance."

"I've got something heavy to move over it," Alex told her.

"We only saw three of them. Could there have been more?" Genie asked.

"I don't think so, but it's not like I had them in my sights during their entire stay."

"This was professional," Mark mentioned the obvious.

"It was," Alex admitted, angry with herself that she was not covering all possibilities.

The chief looked at his detectives. "Let's not waste time with spilled milk. We learn from our mistakes. What else can you remember?"

"One of them left a disk in both Elizabeth's and my PC."

"Disks?"

"Yes. Burns will have to go over both of them and see what nasty social disease is on them." She got up and returned shortly with the two disks in their plastic bags, handing them to Chief Harper.

"Well, there's nothing else we can do tonight," Harper said.

Mark and Chief Harper rose to leave with Genie. When the house was quiet again, Alex took Elizabeth's hand and pulled her to follow her. She was determined to keep Elizabeth in sight.

They curled up on Alex's bed, and though they thought they wouldn't fall asleep easily, they did.

Chapter Twenty-Six

S o what are you doing there?" Alex pulled one of the tall chairs out and accepted the coffee Elizabeth slid toward her.

"Making a stuffing for the turkey I bought. I thought I would practice my Thanksgiving baking skills before the last minute."

"I'm not all that knowledgeable about baking, but isn't that a big turkey?"

"It was the only size they had, and I didn't want to wait for the next shipment. What are your plans?" Elizabeth asked. She slid the stuffed turkey in the oven and set the timer.

"I want to take a look at the hidden area in the den."

"Mind if I tag along?"

"No. Let me get lights and the map." Alex slid off the chair, feeling happy.

Elizabeth did a quick clean of the counter and washed her hands.

Alex was in her bedroom pulling out two SureFire lights and the map of the house. She hurried to join Elizabeth, who was waiting in the den.

"This diagram shows that the entrance should be right there."

They both searched the empty bookshelf for anything to show a doorway to another secret space, but they found nothing.

"It should be right there." Alex gave a frustrated jab in the air.

Elizabeth moved back to the center of the room and was now leaning on her cane regarding the room with a critical eye. "What if this one being so close to the front of the house leads outside? And..." she held up a finger at Alex to silence her, knowing the expression on her face meant she was at the whining stage of frustration. Elizabeth could barely handle children whining so adults were beyond her patience. "And it needs something more than a push button or switch. Say, because it is so important only those with a secret code can pass?" she teased, hoping it would set Alex's imagination off in another direction to solving the door problem. Sometimes getting sidetracked helped.

Alex looked at her as if she had lost it, then her face brightened. "Like a gate opener." Alex ran out of the room.

"Ha," Elizabeth laughed in disbelief. She was not expecting such a dramatic reaction.

Alex came back with the gate opener. She pointed it at the bookcase and moved it along it, pressing it. "Nothing."

She was about to toss it when Elizabeth grabbed it and held it up out of Alex's reach, so she wouldn't damage it. Both were startled when the wall cracked open.

Looking up at the ceiling, Alex snorted. "Well, of all the places to put the sensor. That's a very good place to put it," Alex marveled. "It won't open by accident."

"Well, let's go see if there's a bucket of bright shiny jewels tucked away in there," Elizabeth said.

Alex led the way after stopping on the other side to make sure they could get back in the same way.

"You know this place has so many underground spaces and entrances, I'm surprised this house hasn't collapsed its foundation by now," Elizabeth said in a soft tone.

"It makes me feel real safe," Alex muttered.

Alex and Elizabeth came to a stop at a set of stairs leading upward. Alex tried the cover but could not open it.

"Something has to be resting on top of it. Listen, you go outside and I'll tap on this until you hear me."

Elizabeth made her way back out the tunnel into the den. Just before she released the lever, she remembered to check to see if the room was still empty. Pressing her ear against the back of the wooden shelves, she strained to hear anything unusual.

A noise gave her pause. A soft voice was droning, then stopped.

She nearly dropped her flashlight from a bark. She pressed the lever and peered out cautiously. Angel, feeling terribly smart at having found her, gave her a cute rendition of a dog's version of an operatic aria.

Mark gasped holding his chest in mock shock. "You could have given me a heart attack."

"I doubt it. Your partner there," she gestured at Angel who was staring into the dark entrance waiting to be allowed to find the other missing playmate, "I'll bet gave the place away."

Mark laughed. "Alex had sent me a copy of the house plans. When you two didn't answer my call and there's a turkey in the oven, I sent Angel to find you. She led me to this room and the rest was up to me. So how did you get the bookcase to open?"

Elizabeth pointed to the ceiling. "The gate opener aimed at that spot on the ceiling."

He nodded with a smile on his face. "Neat. So, where's Alex?"

"We found the exit, but she can't open it. We think something heavy is on it."

"I'm parked over a manhole cover."

Both went back outside. Mark backed his vehicle off the cover while Angel waited patiently with Elizabeth. Sliding out of his truck, he pulled out a metal pipe and rapped on the cover his truck tire had pinned down, and it moved a few inches. Mark got a grip and pulled it up.

Alex nearly fainted when Angel was the first to greet her. She was not expecting a hairy muzzle stuck in her face.

"She wants a cookie as a reward for finding you two," Mark said, laughing along with Elizabeth.

"She'll get it, just get her out of my face. Ewww, Angel I love you, too, but let's find another way to express it."

"I'll get her a cookie while I check on the turkey," Elizabeth offered.

"Angel, 'protect' Elizabeth," Mark instructed.

"This is a good place for an exit. It's in the carport away from any casual observers, and if anyone did park here, just by not pulling all the way in, you can still use it."

"This place is fun. And I would adore it if Elizabeth's life didn't depend on there not being so many slick places to hide a monster."

Mark pulled out his copy of the house plans and unfolded it. "Okay, we have this one identified, and this one in Elizabeth's room, how about these two?"

"Haven't looked for them yet. They don't look like they can be accessed from the outside."

"Okay, but check them out to be sure. I came over to tell you the chief and Agent Briscolle are huddled with Claire over what Burns found from his search of the log files on the House server. Meanwhile, I'm off to Bales to deliver a stack of documents on our fellow police officers that the provo wants to review."

"Are you going to take Angel or leave her here?"

"If you don't mind. I'm taking Linda with me. It worked out that the kids are at a sleepover for the weekend, and we weren't asked to chaperone so we thought we could work in a night alone."

"Ah. I hear the Hilton's Estates have masseuses, mud baths, and jacuzzis and, woo. I get the picture," Alex teased. "We don't mind having Angel over for the night."

"I was hoping you would say that. I left her dish and food in the kitchen and don't forget to take her for a walk or run two times a day, if you can."

"Great."

Mark gave Elizabeth a quick goodbye and a pat on Angel's head with instructions that only the dog and her owner could hear.

Angel moved to her favorite corner in the kitchen, happily playing with her rope toy, keeping her eye on Elizabeth.

"How's the turkey coming along?" Alex asked as she slid onto the stool.

"Good. So I gather by her food and bowl she's here for the night?"

7. Christie

"Mark and Linda are spending some time alone at a hotel in Bales and their kids are on a sleepover. Do you mind that I said we would watch her?"

"No."

"What's that?"

Elizabeth looked at what Alex pointed at.

"It's a squeaker toy for Angel. Do you want to play with it or do you want your own?"

"Does it make a lot of noise?"

"I don't know. Any more rooms to explore? The turkey has an hour more to bake."

"Not really." Picking up on Elizabeth's lack of interest to explore more, she easily agreed. Since she had no television and Elizabeth didn't have one, Alex was thinking of reading more of the novel she had been trying to finish for the last two weeks.

"I'm going to write for a while."

Alex was seated in the reading chair, Elizabeth worked on her project, and Angel curled up near her, sleeping. Occasionally, both women would watch Angel as she moved her feet as if running in her dreams. Smiles were exchanged and they went back to their business.

Alex had thought it was going to be a boring evening, but she found it was very pleasant in a domesticated sort of way, and that was a novelty.

Chapter Twenty-Seven

Adison worriedly stared out at the gray blanket before her. She had let Angel out that morning, directing her to check the grounds. That seemed to make the dog very happy, but she was taking a long time. Alex wondered just what Angel was finding so interesting on the south side. She was surprised the geese put up with the dog and even more surprised Angel put up with the geese. Tiredly, she bowed her head and sighed.

"Once it becomes personal, you're in over your head," a familiar voice spoke.

Alex started at the voice and would have spun around demanding an explanation for that remark, but she became conscious that her arms were wrapped tightly around her and her shoulders were slumped. Standing straighter and dropping her hands to her side, she only nodded.

Alex turned to look into Elizabeth's eyes. She felt a little disconcerted from the tilting of her world by staring into Elizabeth's eyes. Consciously, she breathed in and out to let her inner balance reassert itself.

"I'm all right," Alex murmured.

Elizabeth gave a faint smile, shaking her head. Alex shifted uncomfortably as she worked on a list of objections.

A whine gave Alex an out.

"Where've you been girl? The dog danced playfully around her. "Didn't you run off your frisky energy?"

"She has something in her mouth."

"Oh, probably a ball. Mark said she finds them everywhere. Come on, Angel, give it up. Hey." The dog danced away from her and tossed her nose in the air as if to pantomime the toss of a ball, but her jaws remained closed.

"Angel, give," Alex told the dog in a firm voice. "Oh, please don't make it something icky," she pleaded to the amusement of Elizabeth.

"Here, Angel. Sit. Give." Elizabeth took over the situation, deepening her voice and using hand gestures to get the dog's attention. Alex obviously had not the experience of sharing a part of her life in the company of a dog.

Willingly, Angel dropped it onto the floor and backed up, sat down, and waited.

"What is that?" Alex studied the gooey object, not wanting to touch it.

7. Christie

Elizabeth picked it up and took it into the kitchen to wash it off. Sand was encrusted around it, but it fell away with water.

"It's some kind of medallion or…" Alex straightened up startled. Two unrelated events attached to a third. "I'll be right back!" *After two years and I remember this. Let's see where would…* She stopped in front of her closet and cast her mind back to the night she visited Amos Anders's warehouse for a payoff meeting. She imagined herself placing something in…

Pocket…

"What are you looking for?" Elizabeth came to see what set Alex off.

On the floor, Alex had pulled out a box of clothes she no longer wore. The vest with the many pockets was under her Kevlar. It was the upper left pocket she would have dropped it in because she had filled the others. Alex unwrapped a plastic bag and scooped up the earring that fell out of the turned-out pocket. "Something I found about two years back. I forgot I had it."

Elizabeth held up the metal Angel found. "Do you have any silver cleaner? We can see what this is about. No?"

"Hold on, I know who does." Alex slid her cell phone out of her pocket. "Hi, Genie."

"Hi, Alex. We were just talking about you. How are you two doing?"

"Great. How are things going there?"

"Quiet, aside from what Eric and Angie found on our server logs. Not good for whoever has the service contract for the shelter's systems. But that's another story."

"Angel found something on her morning walk. Elizabeth got some of it cleaned, but it's made of silver and neither of us have any cleaner. Do you have any?"

"Yes. You two busy for lunch?"

"No. Do you want to come over here or do you want us to visit you?"

Elizabeth shook her head. "We've tons of food with the leftover turkey and stuffing. Tell Genie I want her opinion of how it tastes and maybe Connie and Ellie want to come visit."

Alex relayed the message.

Genie laughed. "Boy, are you lucky that Elizabeth cooks, Alex. What time do you want us over? The gang has been asking how she's doing and we can bring the new gal over and introduce her to you."

"Sounds like a plan. How many residents do you have now?"

"Ah, yes. I forgot you have a limited supply of dishes and such. We'll bring our own dishes, eating utensils…and. I'll bring dessert. See you in an hour?"

"An hour…?" Alex looked at Elizabeth who nodded. "That's fine."

Elizabeth looked over the front room. "At least we don't have to clean much."

"Where are we going to seat everyone?" Alex asked.

"Let Claire and Genie worry about that," Elizabeth said. "Can you help me get lunch ready? You do microwave, right?"

Angel picked up on the excitement and was pacing around the two women by the time the van from the shelter arrived. Behind that was Mark's 4-runner.

"Just how much of that turkey did you say you have?" Alex asked as they watched the vehicles park.

Scripts's two kids hopped out of the truck with Angel finally getting a nod from Alex to rush over to them. Somehow, she had found time to retrieve her ball and was dropping it in front of the kids who seemed to know to pick it up and toss it.

"Hi, Detective Alex! Ms. Duke!" the young boy greeted enthusiastically as he pounded the wiggling dog on her ribs.

"Hi, and you are...?"

"I'm Jon Scripts, and this here's my sister, Katharine...but...she likes Katie," he confided in a lower tone.

"Hi, Katie."

The five-year-old beamed. From experience, Elizabeth knew the silence would be short lived. Usually, the ones who were quiet at an introduction were information gatherers. Once they had everything in place, they became all questions and conversationalist nearly non-stop.

"Hi, Linda, nice to see you again. Mark," she greeted the couple as they strolled up behind their kids with arms around each other.

Claire and Genie were supervising the women who were unloading the van of more food and furniture.

"Would you all like to stay for lunch?"

"That's a tempting offer. We were going for a walk along the beach before we headed to the pizza place."

"A walk after lunch on the beach would be wonderful," Elizabeth exclaimed.

Alex was startled and for a moment panicked until she realized no one would try to snatch her if so many people surrounded her.

"That sounds nice," Alex agreed. She glanced at Mark who smiled and nodded.

While Linda and Elizabeth, under Genie's direction, prepared the varied collection of foodstuff, the others readied the table on the deck.

Muriel, the new resident, though given to nervous looks over her shoulder now and then, kept everyone amused with her wit. Elizabeth was quiet through most of the meal, but not disengaged. Alex glanced her way often, looking for some sign of nervousness or tension but not seeing any.

Alex excused herself. Dessert was finished with everyone enjoying the view and conversation about the geese. She sought bladder relief in her bathroom. She took a moment to glance out the window at the front yard, her eyes scanning for any movement on the dunes across the street. *I know you're out there.*

Voices from the kids as they fought over who would go first was stopped by Linda who directed each to a separate toilet. Reluctantly, Alex went back into the dining room to join the others on the patio. For a moment, she watched through the sliding door as Elizabeth spoke with a serious expression to one of the women from the shelter.

"Sharing a similar background has a very powerful bonding effect," Claire said.

Alex turned in surprise. She had not heard Claire come up behind her. For a moment, she replayed where she had lost track of Claire's presence.

"Do you think Elizabeth is all right?"

Claire studied Alex's face. "She's not at that stage yet, Alex," she said gently. "She's still in survival mode." She smiled and added, "She's looking a sight better. So what are you going to do with that medal we saved from oblivion?"

"It's unusual, no?" *Do I tell her it's in the shape of one of the tattoos on the back of the wrist of a White Knight? And similar to another one we found?*

"Do you know where Angel found it?" Claire asked.

"No."

"That particular design is rather interesting. I would like to check it out if you don't mind."

Alex eyed her. "What's with the design?"

"I saw someone with a design just like that."

"Who?" A little ball of anticipation burned in the pit of her stomach.

"Patience, Ms. Detective. It's nothing to get worked up about."

"Claire."

"Alex," she responded calmly, "I would never put anyone in danger. Believe me when I say this is not going to hurt anyone by keeping this to myself for now. So how about looking at the games we brought over. Elizabeth has a great talent for Trivial Pursuit."

"After the walk. I really would like her to get a chance at walking on the beach."

Claire nodded. "How about using that secret door under the kitchen? You know, since you guys moved here, everyone is remembering about Doc and Lily's door to the ocean."

"Good idea. Let's see if the others are ready for a walk."

Everyone was excited about the invitation and quickly lined up in the kitchen for their turn down the stairs into the dark tunnel. It was a misnomer to call it secret and dark with all the flashlights that suddenly appeared. Alex suspected that was what really brought the ladies from the shelter over. A bit of old-fashion exploring.

At the bottom of the stairs, they all removed their shoes to feel the sand. Excited voices were added with the pounding of the waves that echoed through the cavern.

The sun was warm, but the breeze was chilly while sitting out on the rocks away from the cliff wall. Alex joined Elizabeth on her private rock island where the encroaching tide was moving higher up. She was not budging.

Elizabeth glanced at Alex, raising a hand to catch her streaming hair. Her eyes were covered with dark glasses, but her cheeks were bright red from the chill. The residents were on the beach collecting seashells, Claire and Genie found their own rock, Mark and Linda were sitting on the beach, and the children were playing with Angel.

"I remember seeing a medallion similar to that one," Elizabeth said. "Grandma Chasley wore one. Noel liked the fiery sword design in the center of the field of flowers. She told him the women usually wore the medal, though some got a tattoo if they married important men."

"That's the second medallion I found in Sunrise."

Both stared out at the ocean, breathing in the salty air and feeling the beat of the waves pounding against their rock.

"This is so nice," Elizabeth whispered, wiggling her toes when a wave splashed over them.

Alex looked behind them, then studied the cliff for anyone watching them. "It is. Once a week of this is better than an apple a day."

Elizabeth laughed a deep throaty laugh. "I can get addicted to this."

"Addicted to what?"

Elizabeth and Alex turned to Claire and Genie who had picked their way to them.

"All of this," Elizabeth gestured to the surroundings.

"We should make this a ritual. Maybe once a month get the ladies to have a picnic out here," Genie suggested.

Angel balanced on the rocks to get a soggy ball that rolled near them with a wave.

"Just keep that slobbery ball away from me," Alex told Angel as she lifted her dripping face.

"You are so uncool, Detective Alex," Jon laughed at her, taking the ball without any qualms from his pet's mouth and tossing it back onto the beach.

By the looks of it, everyone was getting ready to leave. The tide was coming in. Alex stood and gave a hand to assist Elizabeth.

"I thought cops were used to gory stuff and…" Jon continued.

"You don't need to elaborate on the gory stuff, Jon," Linda told him as she and Mark approached the group, holding hands.

301

All of them slowly made their way back into the cavern, taking a moment to watch the sun sit on the tip of the large boulder outside the entrance.

"Well, we now know there are no warning signs out here that this is private property," Mark said as they were leaving.

"This was a wonderful day," Alex told Elizabeth. She was nestled in her reading chair with a recently purchased book and had suddenly realized that she was happy.

Elizabeth was arranging her papers before sitting down to work. Her laptop was booting up. "It was," a distracted Elizabeth agreed.

"We should have more of them. When this is all over..." Alex stopped, realizing what she was saying.

"What?" Elizabeth asked, looking up at her with an unreadable expression on her face.

For a few moments, Alex studied her face partially shadowed by the tilt of the desk lamp. "I was thinking, maybe we can..." Her mind cast about frantically looking for something to say that was not too revealing. Alex's face blushed when she realized what she was avoiding. "I'd like to know you under different circumstances."

"Different as in what?"

"Doggone it, Elizabeth," she exclaimed exasperated. "I want to date you." *Gods. It's not this hard snagging dates over the Internet. Why does this have to be so hard with someone I see every day?*

"Ah." Elizabeth leaned against her desk, studying Alex, who now was clutching the book.

Don't say anything more. You'll make a fool of yourself. Wait her out, Alex firmly told herself.

"Well, the feelings are mutual," Elizabeth said matter-of-factly and turned back to her laptop to work.

Alex let out a slow breath. "Okay," she said softly. *Well, I guess there's nothing much else we can say at this point.*

Alex's phone in her room buzzed. She dropped her book in the chair and went to answer it. She dared a glance at Elizabeth. She was engrossed in her work and didn't appear to notice. *Well, that's a comfort. I don't feel any walls go up, and she didn't ask me to leave her alone. I guess I'll really know if I come back and she's closed the door.*

"Hello?" Alex clutched the phone receiver tighter. "Okay...I'll let her know." Alex hung her head for a few moments to gather her strength. The next level of engagement had begun. She walked back into the study and could see that Elizabeth was not even aware of her.

"Elizabeth..." The dark head jerked up. "The freighter is going to be here by tomorrow."

"Is that what the phone call was about?"

"Yes. With the ATF and SID watching over you, they don't stand a chance."

"And that's why you shouldn't worry about me," Elizabeth cautioned, getting to the heart of Alex's fear. "He'll see you as competition and will make sure you know of his displeasure." Elizabeth shook her head regrettably. "I don't know why you put yourself in needless danger. There's nothing to gain from it."

Alex looked surprised at the emotion that statement had behind it. "Well, it's not like I planned it to happen. It was an ideal opportunity to protect you, and it's a good thing, too."

"Good thing? How's that? You're going to get yourself killed and I'll still be kidnapped."

"If I hadn't been here, you would have been dead by now with those fake telephone repair men." Alex could feel her face flushed with hurt and confusion. "If anything, Miles will toss me in with the rest of the women and sell me."

"If you believe that, you're tragically mistaken. It doesn't take much to break someone, Alex. And you're too dangerous for them alive."

Alex's throat worked down the lump. "I'm not going to lose... "

Elizabeth put a finger over her lips. "Don't say any more, Alex."

Alex's eyes opened to a light-filled room. Stretching and feeling her back pop, she rolled out of bed. She did her morning visit to the toilet, brushed her teeth, and took a quick shower before looking for Elizabeth. She was nowhere, but the smell of hazelnut coffee permeated the air.

From the kitchen, she could hear some murmuring. Alex followed the sounds to the opened front door. From her vantage point, she could see Elizabeth talking to Angel and a very irate and very big gander.

Alex remained still, not wanting to add her presence to the tense situation. Angel backed up toward the front porch and Elizabeth followed, joining her at the door.

"Those two had a disagreement over the ownership of that ball," Elizabeth explained.

Alex looked out. It was a faded red plastic ball.

"Does she think it's an egg?"

"No. I think it's in her territory and Angel didn't ask for it politely. Good morning."

"Good morning. The coffee smells nice. I can fix breakfast if it's getting the cereal box out of the cabinet and setting out the dishes."

"The coffee is for you. I'm going to bed. I was the one who stayed up all night."

"Oh, right," Alex let out a puff of air. They had argued, though not with much heat, on who would take the first shift of watching over the monitors.

Elizabeth was not tired and she was. From years of making due with few resources at her immediate disposal, Alex gave in and slept.

"Well, sleep well." Alex wondered if she would have nightmares, then shook her head at the thought. Elizabeth had been under this pressure for years and like her would have adjusted by now just to survive.

Angel followed Elizabeth into her bedroom, and Alex went to grab a cup of coffee and call into SPD to see if there were any messages for her.

Alex was finishing her coffee, staring out at the ocean by the back patio when a disturbance with the geese distracted her. Her thoughts were on nothing. It was the quiet zone some agents were able to get into before jumping into the fire. Stepping onto the patio cautiously, she looked around, then studied the two geese that were pecking at something.

What the heck is that? She stepped off the patio to investigate and was aware for a moment of a sound that didn't register.

Chapter Twenty-Eight

Bobby Miles stood in front of the makeshift table, a fallen log damp from the recent rains. His command mask appeared calm and interested as each soldier reported. Vapor puffs of air blurred the mouth of the speaker as the news he was waiting for was delivered. He forced himself to breathe, not wanting to give away how important this news was to him. The deep male voices droned on as all external sounds receded after he heard that Elizabeth Duke was captured. His hands were clasped behind his back. A method he found that enabled him to keep a calm exterior.

Faces turned to him. The briefing was over. He nodded to acknowledge the reports, not having heard what had been said for the last fifteen minutes. The plans had already been made. There was no reason to deviate from them and no reason he had to hear them repeated.

"Proceed as planned," Bobby told the group quietly.

As the others left to rejoin their teams, Bobby turned to Bo, his second in command and personal bodyguard.

Taking a careful breath, the cold air cleared the images of Elizabeth Duke from his mind. "Ah don't trust those two dimwits, it was too easy. Ah want cha to handle this matter, Bo. Make sure that woman is dead and buried at sea where only the fish see her."

"But, Bobby..." Bo started.

He turned away, ignoring the objection. Glancing at his other bodyguard, "John, let's go see what's happenin' at the other end."

The two men trooped down the wet forest trail to where they had left their vehicles. The door handle was cold to Bobby's touch, as was the driver's seat he slid into. It reflected the coldness of his thoughts.

As he headed the car to the waiting helicopter, his mental voice was crooning Elizabeth's name. Slow motion images of bright red blood trickling down white skin as he drew a sharp blade across it nearly had him groaning out loud. Abruptly, he stopped the images, not wanting to lose control—yet. He still had to distract John and pick up Elizabeth Duke. Edward had his instruction to hold her separate from the others. Edward listened without asking questions. His thoughts went to the undercover cop, her *roommate*.

Bobby's lips curled up in a snarl at the thought of her touching Elizabeth. Rumors had said they were lovers.

He turned onto a dirt road, then the clearing opened up before them. Both men quickly got out of the car and headed to the helicopter. Before they got too close where yelling would be necessary to be heard, Bobby gave John his instructions.

"John, Ah want ya to make sure Al is at the rendezvous point on time. He doesn't have eyes in the back of his head, and Ah don't trust our kissing cousins. It's been too smooth up ta now."

John nodded. He understood completely as he was part of the small elite group that knew Bobby was not going to be on the beach where he could easily be picked off with a sniper shot. Carney was to take his place. They had the same build and in the dark could be mistaken for each other. John knew Carney was not aware he was being sacrificed, and since the guy was suspected of agreeing with another faction in the family, it worked out well.

Bobby smiled as the helicopter lifted with John.

"'Lizabeth, my lovely 'Lizabeth," he crooned. "We shall be reunited real soon. Can you feel me nearing?" He pulled out his cell phone as he maneuvered the car around a sharp curve down the mountain.

"Andy, this here is Wolf. Have ya got Little Red Ridin' Hood?"

"Yes. Hurry up. We're almost there."

Ten minutes later, Bobby had Elizabeth's limp body tossed into the back of his rental car. Bobby tried to hide the fire that was running in his veins and lighting up his dark eyes. His father had once told him he knew when he was in one of his dark moods because his skin would become flushed and his eyes would have an eerie look to them. He had taken the warning seriously and schooled himself to cover his feelings, exchanging the heat for cold—until he was alone.

When Bobby was out of sight of the Humvee, he threw back his head and howled his madness until he was almost hoarse. It had taken enormous amounts of energy to keep the feelings of absolute joy contained while in front of his men. If they knew how obsessed he was with Elizabeth, Bo would have done more than object to his being alone with her. But right now he didn't care. He had her and now there was no one who could take her away from him. He had two hours to do what he wished with her, and the place to do it—an abandoned farmhouse outside of Sunrise. He had stayed in it with his troops the first day of their arrival. Neighbors were too far away to hear or see anything.

"'Fore Ah say goodbye, 'Lizabeth, ma abominable whore, Ah'm gonna mark ya as mine. Ah see you've dyed yer hair. How appropriate. In some countries, my love, they use a knife blade to tattoo their women's bodies to show ownership. That's what Ah'm gonna do to ya. There's going to be some blood loss, but ya women are used to that." He giggled, then abruptly stopped. His eyes moved quickly to the rearview mirror that reflected the unconscious form on the back seat.

Impatiently, he increased his speed but had to quickly lift his foot off the gas pedal when he came too close to the edge of the cliff. He laughed madly at the thought that after all his careful and brilliant planning that it should end with him driving over a cliff. He had no intention of dying. He had never felt this alive.

7. Christie

Chapter Twenty-Nine

Adison felt like she was having a bad dream. She was suffocating and the noise around her was too confusing for her thoughts to distinguish. Then her body shifted, or more like slid and bumped into something hard. So why did it not hurt? Maybe because she was too busy trying to breathe.

Bright lights suddenly burned her eyes, and she could feel herself dragged, then tossed. Alex struggled to breathe as fear paralyzed her. It seemed like a long time before she hit something solid, then everything went black.

Alex woke to her own coughing, then violent retching of salt water. Thoughts focused on breathing and pushing out the pain that was in every part of her body.

How can anyone hurt this bad and still be alive? It was a long time until she was able to think of anything else.

Realizing she was on her stomach, Alex tried to move her limbs to roll over. Nothing moved. *Stop!* she screamed to the panicked voices in her head.

All right. Finger, move. Damn. Is it moving? She moved her eyes to see if there was any movement. There it was. Two fingers. So why was that not registering with her brain?

What is the last thing you remember? Oh, god. Elizabeth! They have Elizabeth! Move! Damn it, body! Move!

It was past noon by the time Alex could get her body to drag itself farther up the beach. She used a trash can to pull herself into a sitting position, then stand. It gave her reassurance that whatever she had been shot with was not permanent.

Where am I? I don't recognize this beach. Looking up the side of the cliff, she realized the trash can was something someone had tossed from above. There was no road or parking indicating there was public access.

So, right or left? Jeez, what difference does it matter? You're lost! Just shut up and move.

Keeping her balance was a difficulty. Determined, she managed to roll onto all fours. This she could manage. Occasionally, she would rock back on her knees and take stock of where she was.

I think I know this place. She was on the south side of the Ebbens' private beach. "Those SOBs threw me over the cliff!" she fumed. "I could've been killed!"

Alex cocked her head to the right, trying to pick up a faint noise. *A boat?* The sound of an engine grew stronger. "Friend or foe. Great because I don't trust anyone at this point I need to hide behind something."

The tide was coming in and where Alex lay was where she knew her body wouldn't be swept ashore. She hoped it looked like her foot was caught between rocks and that she was dead.

"Over here," a Southern voice called to another.

"I told you, you should have added weights!"

"If you did it my way, a shark would have eaten her by now and weights wouldn't be an issue," the other argued back.

"Just grab her. I'll go get a bag."

Alex felt herself being hoisted by the collar and crotch. For a moment, she thought she was going to be tossed on the beach, but she was carried through the swirling waters.

"You should've had the bag on the raft!" her capturer hollered at his partner. "Jackass," he muttered and tossed Alex's body onto the sand. He sat next to her. After a few moments, she felt herself being patted down. "Wonder if they left anything," the voice muttered.

Alex dared to open her eyes a crease. A heavyset man with muscles was facing away from her, more interested in seeing if anything was in her wet pants pocket. In a quick glance, she could see his sidearm holstered and secured. She tensed her arm muscles to see if they would respond should she need them suddenly. She imaged just what she wanted her arm and hands to do so she would be ready if the opportunity presented itself. But whatever drug they used on her was not completely out of her system and her reflexes were sluggish.

The puttering of the returning boat had her bodyguard stop patting her down. Once more, she was lifted and this time, dropped into a body bag. The bottom of the raft was not as hard as the sand. Alex clutched the knife she had stolen from her would-be killer. In her present situation, she realized choice of weapon made a big difference. Being tossed somewhere in the deep ocean with a knife sounded better than a magnum; however, she had no intention of being dumped again. If she were the one getting rid of a body in the ocean, she wouldn't leave the body in the bag but rather a weighted net so various body parts wouldn't float off while the fish picked the bones clean.

The raft bumped against a hull and started to rock.

Oh, shit. I'm going to puke. However, that was better to think about than being zipped up in a bag.

"Grab the other side of the bag," one directed.

"No. Just leave it. We've got to get beyond the breaker. If we're boarded before we get to the dumping point, we'll get caught with the bag. If we see someone approaching, put a hole in the raft and let it sink with the evidence."

"Good idea," the partner agreed. "We need something heavy then. I hope it doesn't come to that. We'll have to pay for its replacement."

The other snorted. "Better that than jail. It's heavy enough."

The raft rocked against the hull of the yacht as they climbed out of it.

So there's only two of them.

As the boat picked up speed, Alex, who was already cutting her way through the side of the bag, began to get tossed around dangerously.

Oh, jeez. I'm going to puncture the raft at this rate.

Suddenly, she felt airborne and felt the cold water around her. The bag began its decent with Alex frantically sawing her way out of her cocoon. The water was cold, but fear was a colder knot in her stomach, giving her strength to pull through the hole she cut. Frantically, she swam to the surface, then slowed down when she neared it. When her head broke the surface, sounds were rumbles mixed with her pounding heart so she nearly was run over with the returning motor yacht. It was not like the ones she and Mark had spotted sitting in their bay. The wash from the boat nearly was drowning her as the two men frantically searched for any debris. They were arguing over whose fault it was this time for losing her body. Alex grabbed the dangling tie line that was hanging from the side of the boat with one hand, not daring to let go of the knife. After the two spent an hour motoring back and forth, not finding a floating body bag they pushed the motorboat to return to their harbor. Alex wrapped the rope around her wrist and held onto the stairs just above her. If she thought she could, she would be climbing aboard.

The two argued on what story to give to their unit leader. Alex worried below them that she would be spotted as they got closer to the docks.

"Stop here. This is where we're supposed to leave it. Don't mess this up."

"This is not the place! He said near the buoy with the yellow mark. That's green, moron."

"You're stupider by the minute. It's that buoy I'm looking at. If you want to go someplace else and get caught in this stolen boat, fine with me. I'm taking the raft and getting off here."

"You're not taking the raft if this is not the place. That isn't green or yellow. It's blue and orange."

The two started to take insulting each other to another low level, but by then, Alex was swimming underwater to the raft that was still tied behind the motorcraft and slit the underside with her stolen knife. Happy, she swam back to the side of the boat not facing the beach and tried to get her bearings and make plans. It was almost dark and Elizabeth was somewhere with a psycho.

"It's sinking!" a horrified shout informed her.

"That's just great, moron. Now how do we get to shore? I don't swim and neither do you."

"There's a dock over to the south. No one was there. If we have to, we'll blast our way out of there. Damn! If we stuck to the original plan, we wouldn't be in this trouble."

"If we stuck to the original plan, I wouldn't be with a moron like you, and I sure as hell wouldn't be on some boat dumping a local cop's body in the ocean."

"She's not a cop. She's a spy."

"She's a fed, and that means more trouble. This detail was doomed from the start," he mourned. "There's our car! Jeez. We're going to have to walk a long ways to get back to it."

"If you had pulled the raft up on deck instead of taking the lazy way out, we would have the raft and a body to get rid of," the other accused.

"Shut up. You're not too bright for tossing her over the cliff without asking."

"He said get rid of her. I got rid of her."

Alex checked to see if the knife was still secured in her waistband. The men's arguing gave her a idea that maybe she could swim to their vehicle and wait for them. She needed to find Elizabeth.

The men cut the life raft from the motor yacht since it was partially underwater. To Alex, it meant something buoyant was keeping it afloat that maybe she could use. She swam underwater to the raft and hid behind part of it as she opened a side pocket. One of the emergency floatation buoys had been activated. Alex gratefully pulled it out and inflated the other side. Wrapping it around her chest, she began her swim to shore.

Eventually, the waves pushed her to the beach and onto the shore. Her hands were numb with cold as were her legs and feet. Knowing time was moving on she forced her legs into a stumbling walk toward the only vehicle in the side parking lot. As she neared the car, she could make out a rental advertisement on the license frame. That meant no car alarms.

One thing about being in the business of collecting information was knowing how to break into a car without being messy and with just a knife. She planned on hiding in the trunk until she saw what was there. It was filled with their gear, including weapons, a walkie talkie and duffle bags. Glancing around, she strained to hear if anyone was approaching. She pulled one of the duffle bags open and rifled through it. She pulled out what she didn't need and stuffed it with useful gear, including a Kevlar vest. She slammed the trunk closed and moved to the car's engine. She loosened three of the four spark plug cables. Looking around again, she could see two figures walking through the more populated parking area closer to the boats where there were street lamps. It was her two would-be assassins, and it looked like they were still arguing. Alex grabbed her stolen bag and headed to the public restroom.

Dressed for serious business in clothing meant for a larger person, Alex peered out the restroom door. It was dark, but she had night vision goggles on. The rental was still parked and the two men were unhappily waiting for someone to pick them up. They were silent. A Humvee came barreling toward them and skidded to a halt.

"You two idiots. Did you at least dump the body?" an angry voice barked.

"Yes, we did and we're not mechanics, and we didn't pick this car out. What are you so all fired mad about?"

"Bobby's gone, and he's taken the dyke chick with him."

Alex gulped.

"He's not gone," one of the men said sarcastically. "Just having some fun with her. You knew he wasn't going to be at the pickup. He's too paranoid of a sniper. Probably took her to that vacant house that was all shot up."

"Yep. Plenty of atmosphere for carving up that bit of trash," her other abductor snorted.

"Well, that's just the point!" the driver minced. "He's not supposed to be…" but the rest of the words were cut off when the door slammed shut.

When the Humvee took off, Alex ran to the car she disabled and secured the cables. "They are idiots," she muttered. One of them left the keys in the car, which she was sure was done intentionally as a statement to the rental car agency of their displeasure for not being able to get the vehicle running.

Alex pulled out of the lot and at the road floored the rental to its highest speed, fishtailing for a moment, then straightening out. During her drive back to Sunrise, she kept to the side roads and focused on a plan. Psychos were not people you could always reason with since their agendas were their own. She left the rental in one of the pullouts along the dirt road. She disabled the vehicle and left it unlocked.

Armed with two automatic handguns and enough ammunition to reload a half-dozen times, she ran to the house and stopped in front of the car. She rested her hand on the hood. It was still warm. She lifted the hood and pulled out a fistful of cables. She then turned her attention to the house. A flashlight wavered and stilled in the front room. Alex knew the inside of the house intimately from the domestic dispute call.

I wonder how they knew of this house. No matter. I know the back door was broken and the place trashed by local kids.

To avoid losing time going through the back and finding a way to the front without tripping on trash, Alex stepped onto the porch and peeked in through the broken window. She had never seen Bobby Miles before, only heard his voice. A man in fatigues was arranging furniture. Elizabeth, still in her shorts and T-shirt she wore when she went to bed, was leaning at a crazy angle on the remains of a couch. Alex's heart leaped at the knowledge that she was still alive. She guessed Miles drugged her.

Bobby was speaking in a conversational voice as he went about setting the scene. Alex could not hear what he was saying, but his attention was focused on Elizabeth.

A Colt 1911 was lying on the broken coffee table where he was placing candles carefully on its scarred surface. The table leaned from the added weight. Bobby picked up his Colt and went to the side where there was piled debris and used what he could to stick under the table for more stability.

Alex tried to remember if the front door made any noise when it was opened. Holding one of the automatics in her hand with the safety off and her finger on the trigger, she opened the door quickly and closed it, moving silently into the room and to a darker area. The goggles gave her an advantage. Bobby was too focused on watching Elizabeth to catch her moving into the room.

Talk about rituals. That's what saved her life. The psycho has to have a set for the atmosphere.

The floor had been brushed of debris around the couch and coffee table. The couch seats had been turned over so the gaping bullet holes were not as apparent.

Bobby suddenly stopped his conversation, grabbed up his Colt, and glanced at the front door. Alex stopped her movement. Her nostrils flared as she realized he may have smelled her. Though she was wearing someone else's clean clothes, her body odor which now even she could smell, might have drifted to him.

He moved to the front door and locked it, then stared out the broken window for a long moment. He went back to a pack and selected binoculars from his gear. Standing to the side, he studied the outside, then moved cautiously to the other side of the window and studied another view.

"Well now, 'Lizbeth, you just might have someone out there looking to rescue you," he muttered under his breath. "But they're just gonna have to miss the show." He dropped the glasses from his eyes and glanced at his captive. "Ah am about ready."

Alex looked for a way to get to Elizabeth, realizing that she was not exactly at top strength herself. She didn't know if Elizabeth was faking her condition or if she was really that much out of it.

While Bobby focused on lighting the candles, Alex crawled over to the couch and tapped it, hoping Elizabeth felt the vibration and knew she was not alone.

"What Ah am doing here, my sinful ho, is heating the tip of my knife, so when I cut you, it will leave a scar no plastic surgeon can remove. Of course, you won't be alive that long, but it's also something I like to do with my property."

Alex wanted to shudder at the last part of that revelation for his voice took on a tone that frightened her. But she tapped the back of the couch again.

Alex looked to her left and found Bobby with his knife coming for her. Her reflexes were still slow, and the gun was kicked out of her hand with heavy military boots. The next move was expected, and Alex was willing her body to prepare for the stomp on a body part next. However, a lit candle hit Bobby in the eye, causing him to miss his intended target. He crashed onto the various pieces of broken furniture and trash. Alex was on her feet, not bothering with looking for the gun. She heard it rolling somewhere, and she needed to get Elizabeth and her out of the house.

The two women found each other and with the Bobby's curses and threats, they ran out the front door and into the arms of ATF agents.

"Get out of here! The place is on fire!" a goggled voice ordered.

"Bobby's in there. He has a Colt 1911 and a Buck tactical knife, and I dropped a magnum under the couch!"

The voice passed the information through his radio. The two women were directed to wait farther away from the building. People came to guide Elizabeth and her to what looked like a triage area. Alex was handed something to drink and asked questions she answered automatically without being cognizant of what it was about. She was too hyped up to talk and too unnerved by all that was happening to be able to focus on the winding down of a two-year hitch.

Alex took to pacing as the drama unfolded. The ATF team surrounded the building and went in as far as they could while the flames from the candles spread. Alex glanced anxiously at Elizabeth who was receiving first aid. Her head was bowed and she was answering questions. Glancing back at the house, she spotted someone running through the fields and toward the road.

"Damn!" she tried to shout. But whatever was in the liquid she had been given didn't help her dry throat and only a croak came out. Without waiting for backup, she was sprinting toward the road where she had parked the rental, guessing he would see it and head there.

Alex was panting before she reached the road and was not aware of Angel's unsteady pace a few steps behind her. If she had looked, she would have seen the dog was not herself.

Alex pulled the other magnum out from the pocket of her borrowed coat, nearly losing her balance in pulling it free. Gritting her teeth, she pushed on, nearly there. Her goggles picked out someone in the car. Her energy gave out, and her legs stopped pumping fast enough to sustain her momentum and she began to fall. Determined not to lose her weapon this time, she moved her finger off the trigger and tucked to roll instead of slide.

Bobby figured out she had pulled a wire lose from the ignition and was gunning the car toward her. She lifted her weapon and aimed in the direction of the gas tank, not feeling confident enough to hit him, however a cadence of booms behind her peppered the car as it continued to speed toward her. Someone grabbed her arm and dragged her across the water ditch and onto the embankment as the car came crashing where she had been. Uniformed ATF agents surrounded the car and pulled a still alive Bobby Miles from it.

"Where were you? Are you okay?" voices demanded of her.

Much to Alex's embarrassment, she fainted.

Chapter Thirty

Adison's waking mind quickly processed her surroundings. A hospital. With more strength than she last remembered she had, she lifted a hand to assure herself she was not attached to any machines.

"This is the best I've seen you waking up in a hospital," a quiet voice said.

"Mel," she croaked. She opened her eyes a crack and then further. A straw was before her. Her eyes lifted to Briscolle's face.

"Hey, team. How did the job come down?"

"A success. No one on our side was killed. What injuries were suffered are repairable. Good job. Now may I ask what happened to you?" Mel's voice was concerned.

"The last I remembered, I was on the patio. Then next time I woke up, I was being washed ashore. I couldn't get myself together. Arms, legs, they felt paralyzed."

"They used the same thing on Elizabeth and the dog," Briscolle interjected.

"From what I overheard from my two would-be assassins, while I was drugged, one of them tossed me over the cliff. I don't know which one or how I survived, but I did."

"Good thing you did. He gave us the slip in the mountains. He found her transponder and put it on one of his soldiers and sent him up to the woods. Your cabin as a matter of fact."

Alex groaned. "They didn't burn it down, did they?"

"No. Sam caught him making mischief and had him neutralized. It was Chief Harper who suggested the abandoned ranch house."

"We lucked out," Alex said softly. "He was so obsessed with setting the stage for his ritual, it gave me time to get into the room."

"How did you know to go there?"

"The two stooges that were supposed to dump me in the ocean for fish bait were talking about it. Gods. I never want to see another body bag that close up and personal."

"Well, we're going to check up on Elizabeth. She's at the shelter. I'm sure she'll be happy to hear you're awake and doing fine."

"Wait a minute. Why can't I come? I'm awake. Why am I here anyway? Did I get hurt?" Alex started to pat herself down.

"You're still on drugs," Briscolle objected.

"Then I won't drive. I don't need to spend time here," she insisted.

"You're right and, Amanda, stop teasing her. You'll give her a heart attack," Mel said mildly.

"Well, there is the clothes thing," Briscolle reminded her.

"Can I get out of here or not?" Alex demanded.

"The doctor said if you can walk out on your own, you're free."

"Listen, Mel...I need to talk to you," Alex started.

Briscolle excused herself.

"You want out of the org?" Mel guessed.

Alex gave him a rueful smile. "I'm kind of attached to these people, and it's not just because of that," she added in a rush. She took a deep breath and let it out noisily. "I just want to find out if I can settle down with someone, and I can't do that working for SID."

Mel nodded. "How about taking a while off, maybe a year, and see if this is what you really want? You're a good operative in what you've been doing and I hate to just cut ties completely."

"I'll take that." She grinned at him. "It was a long assignment."

"You were not intended to be our sleeper, but as it happened, you were at the right place at the right time."

"How's Elizabeth?"

"Needs time to decompress. Tough lady. She intends on staying in Sunrise. They have a fine program at the shelter there, and it'll help her settle into a normal way of life."

"Thanks, Mel. It was a great experience working for you."

Mel took her hand in his and gave her a squeeze. "See you around," he said knowingly.

When he left, Alex snorted at his parting comment. "Not. I'm too old now, buddy."

Alex reached over to the phone near her bed.

"Harper? Alex. If you spring me from this hospital, I'm yours, that is, if you still want me." Alex grinned at his remark.

It was less then five minutes when Harper and Mark came into her room.

"Hey, you two. Where were you?" she asked happily.

"Out in the parking lot. We just got here. Where's your clothes?" Harper demanded.

"Can we steal some garb that isn't a hospital gown?"

"I'll see what I can do," Mark said.

"Thanks." When he left, Alex looked at Harper. "I appreciate what you're doing for me."

Harper laughed. "Do you realize what you're doing for Sunrise by staying? I talked to Mel about briefing the rest of the force on your dual role. We decided until we get this business of who is the head of the Jaded Amulet out of Sunrise, it's best to keep your cover."

"You mean, we're still feeding information to SID," she interpreted.

Harper nodded, grinning. "They occasionally give us nice toys to use."

Alex laughed, then asked. "How's Elizabeth?"

Harper shook his head, looking worried. "Now that Bobby's in custody, she's doing a slow meltdown. Claire and her group are proving their weight in gold and giving her what support she needs. She's asked about you. I told her you were in the hospital for overnight observation and rest."

"I'd like to see her," Alex's voice trembled, and tears escaped down her face.

Harper leaned over and pulled a tissue for her. Mark returned with hospital clothing.

"Blue for surgeon," he told her smiling.

Alex suddenly burst out crying. For a moment, both men were caught off-guard, then Mark gave her a hug. After a good cry, Alex dabbed her eyes and blew her nose.

"Wow. That makes me feel so much better. I'll be right back." She held the scrubs close to her and stumbled into the bathroom.

Chapter Thirty-One

I just don't think you should be dropping in on Elizabeth dressed like that," Mark explained.

"You might upset her," Chief Harper agreed.

"Well, you should've thought of bringing me some real clothes then," Adison said irritably.

It took an hour to sign Alex out of the hospital, and that was only half of it. She was hungry and refused to say anything because it would mean they would stop and take more time from her seeing how Elizabeth was.

No one expected Elizabeth's kidnapping to take place in the daytime. Alex realized how lucky they all were. Angel had been darted and recovered faster than her. Since she had not been found, it was thought she was kidnapped, too.

While Angel was rushed to the animal hospital by Harriet, Mark had called for a bloodhound to find Alex. Her scent ended near the south cliff where it was just rocks and water. How she survived it was anyone's guess. Logically, she had to have been tossed farther along the cliff to have missed the rocks. Meaning the men got lazy and instead of dumping her on the motor yacht because she was too heavy, they tossed her when they were partially down the path.

Showered and dressed in blue hospital garb, Alex rushed Mark and Harper to the shelter. They would drop her off and leave. She told them firmly she could get home fine on her own.

Alex stood in front of the shelter door, waiting impatiently as the locks were pulled back.

"Alex!" Claire flung open the door and pulled her into a hug. "Gods, we didn't know what happened to you!"

Alex was aware of women gathering around her and patting her back. She was overcome with emotion that so many people were worried about her, but her eyes and heart only sought Elizabeth.

"She's in her room. I'll let her know you're here," Claire said.

"Come on and wait in the kitchen. We were baking cookies. Your favorite," Genie encouraged her.

9. Christie

The women pulled Alex into the kitchen through sheer energy. Grateful for the diversion while she waited for Elizabeth, she allowed herself to be swept along.

"She likes anything sweet," Carol told the new residents.

"Not entirely," Genie corrected. "She doesn't like sugar cookies people bake for Christmas."

The chatter and friendly banter that was intentionally schooled to be non-depreciative was not heard by Alex as she worried about Elizabeth.

"Alex?"

Alex turned to Claire.

"She'll see you now. Same room she had when she was here."

"Thanks. Is she all right?"

Claire nodded.

Alex took the stairs two at a time, regretting it when at the top she had to stop and catch her breath.

Why do they keep telling me she's all right if she's not here baking cookies or won't come downstairs?

The door was open and Alex rushed in. "Elizabeth?" she asked concerned.

Elizabeth was bending over something and turned to see Alex.

Alex opened up her arms, and both women gave each other a hug.

"Gods, I almost didn't make it back," Alex whispered. "I'm so sorry I didn't get there sooner."

"Almost doesn't count. You got there. Thank you."

They held on for a while more, then Elizabeth parted. "Shall we go now?"

"Go?"

"Home. I don't want to spend another night here. Besides," she pulled at the blue hospital clothes, "you're going to be cold in those."

Alex gave her a big smile. "We can call a taxi or maybe Claire won't mind driving us." Alex stepped back.

Elizabeth zipped up her overnight bag and led the way out the door.

"So you're not going to feel uncomfortable in that house?"

"It's home right now, and that's where I want to be. Are you okay?"

"Yes. Chief Harper gave me a few days off, and Mark said if I need more, he'll cover for me, but it's too much work for me to take unscheduled time off."

"You ready?" Claire held up the van keys.

Chapter Thirty-Two

O kay, this is how it works," Elizabeth told Alex, who sat on the other couch. "We both are interested in each other, we both are past dating since we're already sleeping in the same house, so we begin with the rules of engagement."

"Engagement? Errr, as in…"

"Commitment. We won't be seeing much of each other. We have two different work schedules," she explained, "so our relationship won't be developing like others. We don't know much about each other, so we'll talk about ourselves." She chuckled at the grimace on Alex's face, then became serious, "and I don't want any secrets between us about your job. If your life is in danger because of some nutcase, I want to know."

Alex cleared her throat. *Is that all there is to a commitment?* "That's every crook who's out there, Elizabeth. Why is that so important?" She saw the light blue eyes nearly turn to black on the last comment and wanted to know why.

"My last committed relationship…"she paused for a moment, looking pained. "Was with an FBI agent. Helen Fortier."

Alex drew in a breath. She heard about it. SID was asked to investigate. Since she was not involved, she didn't know the details.

"She was executed while on a stakeout," Alex recalled.

"By one of her team," Elizabeth told her.

No wonder SID was asked to look into it.

"Did they catch the SOBs?"

"I don't know. I was only her significant other. Not a wife in their eyes and not a family member. It probably bothered the crap out of them that I was the sole inheritor of her estate, including her memoirs."

"Memoirs? Did it say who could have been behind it?"

Elizabeth shook her head. "I gave the papers to my lawyer. The point is, she was being stalked and harassed by members of her own team," Elizabeth's voice had deepened into anger. "I didn't know. I only knew she was stressed out when she would come home." Elizabeth looked straight at Alex. "I could have done something about it."

Alex was going to tell her the truth of harassment in military structures, but Elizabeth's eyes were hard with anger, and suddenly, it dawned on Alex that maybe she knew someone.

"It won't happen with me. If Mark even got wind of something like that, it would be the end of that person. But I'll tell you," she hurriedly added. "Honest." Alex laughed. "Elizabeth, if someone dares to harass me, I give back and good."

Elizabeth's eyes teared. She shook her head slightly. "Helen thought the same way. Whoever it was walked right up to her while she was sitting in her car and shot her in the face point blank. Her partner claims he was getting them coffee. Helen didn't have to work. She did it because she was smart, courageous, and really good at her job. But she was cocky and too self-reliant." Elizabeth took a deep breath and wiped the tears from her face.

"I'll tell you if someone looks at me mean, but that's going to be a lot of people during the tourist season. I give out traffic tickets, too." Alex got up from her seat and went over to hug Elizabeth. As she held her, she asked, "Is there a specific time when I can kiss you or...?"

She could feel Elizabeth laugh against her.

"Now is a good time."

Alex looked into Elizabeth's face and wiped the tears away with her thumb, then gently pressed her lips against hers.

Butterflies and heat mixed with breathless heart-banging thuds flooded her senses until she broke the kiss for a moment and kissed her again to see what else there was.

Later, sitting in front of the fireplace with the couch as their back support, the two sipped soup while they listened to the popping of the fire and the wind blowing against the house.

"Do you want to go up and see my cabin?"

"Yes, definitely. That comes under the heading of 'no secrets' and subfolder 'extracurricular activities.'"

"What has Genie been telling you?" Alex pushed off the couch and glared at Elizabeth. "Don't forget this town is rumor crazy. They have us already married and raising puppies and kittens."

"Is there something wrong with that?" she teased.

"It wasn't happening. We were just friends."

"So about the cabin."

"It's just a cabin, Elizabeth." She then grinned, thinking about introducing her to Sam. "One of the homesteaders there is Sam. I'll introduce you to him. His hobby is tormenting Mark and me with his mountain survival drills."

"When did you ever rest?"

Alex let out a breath of air. "It seemed like never." She kissed Elizabeth's hand, then started some serious nibbling.

Alex paused when Elizabeth put a restraining hand on her shoulder.

"I know this is one of those bad times to bring it up, but I started my period last night, and I'd rather have our first time together without the cramps and other inconveniences."

Alex groaned and dropped her head on Elizabeth's neck. "I start mine next week. And I'm seldom off. Gods, but I'm not a good person to be around during that time."

Elizabeth chuckled. "Well, in two weeks, we should have perfected our kissing techniques and how to walk around each other when in PMS mode."

Alex hugged Elizabeth tight and whispered, "Thanks for staying."

"Thank *you* for staying, Alex."

Alex released her, and they stared at each other for a while, then both started to say something.

"No, you go ahead," Elizabeth offered.

"I was going to ask if you would like to share a shower. Saves water and takes care of the messy aspect of bleeding."

"My very thought."

J. Christie

ABOUT THE AUTHOR

I. Christie was born and raised in Southern California.

She started writing when she was in grade school. From short stories, she moved to poems, with some of them taking up pages. It didn't quite dawn on her that writing stories would be a lot easier than trying to rhyme every other line of a poem that was taking on epic proportions.

During her mid-life crisis, she decided to return to college and earn a degree in what interested her—there were a lot of interests but one stuck out—psychology. It was while writing a dissertation that she realized how much writing meant to her, and since then, she has been pounding the keys.

Before writing became her daily passion, woodcarving, oil painting, embroidery, and bead art took up much of her spare time.

As a teenager of the '60s, she had gone the route of camping and hiking and taking classes in piano, guitar, flute, pottery, yoga, Tai Chi, Chi Gung, Korean karate, and acupressure.

Christie shares her home with a cat, a dog, birds, and fish. Her hobbies, when not writing, are still dabbling in art, running with Sara, her dog, reading, and watching the birds, fish, cats, and dog play.

Other Intaglio Publications Titles

Accidental Love
by B. L. Miller
ISBN: 1-933113-11-1, Price: $18.15

Assignment Sunrise
by I Christie
ISBN: 978-1-933113-40-1, Price: $16.95

Code Blue
by KatLyn
ISBN: 1-933113-09-X, Price: $16.95

Counterfeit World
by Judith K. Parker
ISBN: 1-933113-32-4, Price: $15.25

Crystal's Heart
by B. L. Miller & Verda Foster
ISBN: 1-933113-24-3, Price: $18.50

Define Destiny
by J. M. Dragon
ISBN: 1-933113-56-1, Price: $16.95

Gloria's Inn
by Robin Alexander
ISBN: 1-933113-01-4, Price: $14.95

Graceful Waters
by B. L. Miller & Verda Foster
ISBN: 1-933113-08-1, Price: $17.25

Halls Of Temptation
by Katie P. Moore
ISBN: 978-1-933113-42-5, Price: $15.50

Incommunicado
by N. M. Hill & J. P. Mercer
ISBN: 1-933113-10-3, Price: $15.25

Journey's Of Discoveries
by Ellis Paris Ramsay
ISBN: 978-1-933113-43-2, Price: $16.95

Josie & Rebecca: The Western Chronicles
by Vada Foster & BL Miller
ISBN: 1-933113-38-3, Price: $18.99

Misplaced People
by C. G. Devize
ISBN: 1-933113-30-8, Price: $17.99

Murky Waters
by Robin Alexander
ISBN: 1-933113-33-2, Price: $15.25

None So Blind
by LJ Maas
ISBN: 978-1-933113-44-9, Price: $16.50

Picking Up The Pace
by Kimberly LaFontaine
ISBN: 1-933113-41-3, Price: $15.50

Private Dancer
by T. J. Vertigo
ISBN: 978-1-933113-58-6, Price: $16.95

She Waits
By Kate Sweeney
ISBN: 978-1-933113-40-1

Southern Hearts
by Katie P Moore
ISBN: 1-933113-28-6, Price: $16.95

Storm Surge
by KatLyn
ISBN: 1-933113-06-5, Price: $16.95

These Dreams
by Verda Foster
ISBN: 1-933113-12-X, Price: $15.75

The Chosen
by Verda H Foster
ISBN: 978-1-933113-25-8, Price: 15.25

The Cost Of Commitment
by Lynn Ames
ISBN: 1-933113-02-2, Price: $16.95

The Flip Side of Desire
By Lynn Ames
ISBN: 978-1-933113-60-9

The Gift
by Verda Foster
ISBN: 1-933113-03-0, Price: $15.35

The Illusionist
by Fran Heckrotte
ISBN: 978-1-933113-31-9, Price: $16.95

The Last Train Home
by Blayne Cooper
ISBN: 1-933113-26-X, Price: $17.75

The Price of Fame
by Lynn Ames
ISBN: 1-933113-04-9, Price: $16.75

The Taking of Eden
by Robin Alexander
ISBN: 978-1-933113-53-1, Price: $15.95

The Value of Valor
by Lynn Ames
ISBN: 1-933113-04-9, Price: $16.75

The War between The Hearts
by Nann Dunne
ISBN: 1-933113-27-8, Price: $16.95

With Every Breath
by Alex Alexander
ISBN: 1-933113-39-1, Price: $15.25

Intaglio Publications' Forthcoming Releases

A Nice Clean Murder
By Kate Sweeney

Bloodlust
By Fran Heckrotte

Contents Under Pressure
By Alison Nichol

Meridio's Daughter
By LJ Maas

New Beginnings
By Erin O'Reilly & JM Dragon

Prairie Fire
By LJ Maas

Preying on Generosity
By Kimberly LaFontaine

Revelations
By Erin O'Reilly

The Path Taken
By Koda Graystone

The Scent of Spring
By Katie Moore

Traffic Stop
By Tara Wentz

Tumbleweed Fever
By LJ Maas

You can purchase other Intaglio Publications books online at StarCrossed Productions, Inc. www.scp-inc.biz or at your local bookstore.

Published by
Intaglio Publications
Melbourne, Florida

Visit us on the web: **www.intagliopub.com**